Echoes Through the Mist

Echoes Through the Mist

A Paranormal Mystery Romance

K. Francis Ryan

Penman House Publishing

Published by Penman House Publishing

Cover designed by: Alexandre Rito ~ rito@designproject.pt

Typesetting services by BOOKOW.COM

Acknowledgements

Life's adventure reveals more of itself daily. It is an adventure that allows me to do that thing I love best, but I am ever mindful of the many people who have made this life possible.

Thank you to my fellow authors and friends Christopher Clarke and Aaron Aalborg for their helpful critiques and insightful comments and for supplying me with the Echoes.

Thanks also go to the many friends who have helped in their own unique ways to put the Vida in Pura Vida. I would say they put the Pura in that phrase, but being my friends they are all evil, wicked, nasty, sinful creatures, so purity isn't high on their to-do list. And that's why I love them all.

A very special tribute is owed to Roxann who brought this book to life. She believed when many around her had given up. And she believes in me still, especially when I don't.

KFR

Contents

Chapter One

"Should we kill 'im now?"

A tall, thin man with a pale complexion and cold eyes thought a moment before he smiled. "This, Mr. Lynch, my large and bloodthirsty friend, this is the Republic of Ireland. So one of your men went to a pub, got drunk and decided to flap his gob and endanger my plans and me, what of it?"

The large man became uneasy with his employer's tone. "Should we kill him? Certainly not." The Pale Man continued as his smile evaporated. "You're the one I should kill for allowing this to happen." The man's tone was casual as though he was discussing the weather, but the air in the room became electric with malice.

The Pale Man looked down at the pulped and bloody body of a small, older man tied to a chair and smiled again. "This is the twenty-first century. We aren't barbarians. No, my little friend, no one is going to put a bullet behind your ear and leave you by the side of the road tonight. Go home to your family and let's have no more of this."

The old man struggled against the rope that bound him to the chair. Gratitude glistened in his eyes.

The Pale Man pointed to the door and said to Lynch. "Have your men throw him out, but I don't think they should stand too close."

Two men emerged from the shadows in the room, untied the prisoner and led him away.

A clock in the deep recesses of the cold, nearly empty manor house sounded the hour. The large man and his employer faced each other and, again, the Pale Man smiled his twisted smile, closed his eyes and drew a long breath. When he opened his eyes, a protracted terror-laden scream sliced through the night and then was gone.

Heavy boots echoed down the hall. The study door was thrown open. "Mr. Lynch, sor, sweet Jeasas, but isn't Donny Pearce altogether dead. His feekin' head exploded like a melon!"

Big Tom Lynch nodded slowly toward his employer. "We'll leave what's left on the side of the road." He looked at the Pale Man and wondered whether what he saw was a look of self-satisfaction or perhaps, madness. What he knew for sure was that he was looking at the face of evil.

***

Julian Blessing couldn't help but grin, a thing one does not often do in New York City. An older gentleman, short and rumpled in a brown tweed suit had crashed onto the park bench next to Julian in a cascade of papers and books.

Julian helped his companion pick up his books and scribbled notes and deposit them in the man's battle-scarred valise.

In a huff, he told Julian, "Tell constables and magistrates alike, Professor Reginald Bragonier, recently arrived here to your fair New York City from Dublin, Ireland, was witched unto death by his esteemed wife, Bridget Bragonier! Bloody hell!" The man's voice was raspy, precise and British.

"I will tell you something friend," the professor said. "One day my bleached bones will be found alongside some footpath. Yes, all because I was rushing along trying to make one impossible rendezvous or another with my wife. She is the very devil when it comes to punctuality. I tell you, should I not survive this trip, I want you to be my witness."

"Witched unto death? That's very good," Julian said with a chuckle as he regained his place on the bench.

"Not my words, old boy, but that doesn't keep them from being true. It was from a play produced in 1620 – or was it 1621? No matter, it was a long time ago. I am so sorry. Here we have been chatting like good companions and I've not introduced myself. I can only blame it on my having been among the Irish for so long. I tell you I endure a veritable shower of savages daily. It is my cross in life."

Julian smiled and said, "Professor Reginald Bragonier of Dublin, Ireland, yes, you said. I am Julian Blessing. I take it you are meeting your wife here and that she is some sort of witch – in the figurative sense of course. I had one of those once – in a terrifyingly real sense, I assure you."

The professor answered thoughtfully, "Indeed, however there is nothing figurative about the lovely Bridget – would that it were so simple.

"Perhaps not a witch in the technical sense," he continued, "but she does have the Sight, what in Gaelic is called An Da Shealladh. Don't try to pronounce it. It will only drive you mad and in the end, you'll have probably got it wrong. No three Irishmen agree on the correct pronunciation of anything in their language. They do that just to irritate the rest of us.

"Anyway, the Sight is quite frightening really, but I've learned to live with it over time. She is replete with bushel baskets of other surprises too, each one more disconcerting than the last. Can't say all of it didn't scare the hell out of me when we first met.

"The woman simply knows things – things she has no way of knowing. That, and she appears where she has no business being. Let us hope she does not know I arrived a smidgen late, what?"

"Surely, you're joking," Julian said. "She's clairvoyant. You honestly believe that?"

"Believe it? I live by it. She glimpses pieces of the future." The professor turned serious and continued. "She perceives things the rest of us cannot see and there is much we cannot see.

"My friend, one does not live among the Irish without developing a robust respect for what we today write off as magic or superstition. I tell you, there was a time when those were considered science." In a distracted undertone the professor added, "In Ireland they still are, but that's another story.

"Oh, yes, I see your sly smile," the professor said. "Well, let us hope my bride does not..."

A tall, slim woman shimmered into view behind the professor. "Reginald," she said, "Are you imparting your silly notions to this good man? Oh, I nearly forgot – you were late again, darling. Twenty minutes late in case you want to add that to your memoirs." The woman's voice was cultured and unhurried with a poetic Irish inflection.

Julian had the immediate impression that this woman would deal with life on her terms and life had better sit tight and wait its turn if it knew what was good for it. Although she had been speaking to the professor, her eyes never left Julian's face and the slight smile never left her lips.

The professor jumped to his feet and with evident delight embraced this graceful woman. Although her smile seemed to Julian to be mischievous and her blue-gray eyes kind, her glance was penetrating. She regarded Julian critically and openly, so he returned the favor.

He saw her as a woman attractive, but not beautiful. This woman he thought of as having a spirit that was at once fascinating, radiant, and ultimately compassionate. To Julian, she was the exemplar of a vanished age. She was the personification of warmth without pretense and grace without effort.

The woman's face was a road map of fine lines and wrinkles giving evidence of a lifetime of full measures of pain and joy, sorrow and laughter. Lustrous silver hair fringed her face and framed perfectly her prominent nose and sensuous lips.

She was of a certain age. That age, in her, bespoke compassion and a pragmatic tough-mindedness. This was not a person whom one underestimated with impunity. Julian knew it and he knew the professor's wife knew it too.

"Darling, Bridget, allow me to introduce my very good friend – even though we met only minutes ago, ah... Mr., hmmm, I knew it a moment ago..."

At forty-two with the graying hair to prove it, Julian was privileged, educated and over the years had assembled a considerable personal portfolio.

He was a modern day alchemist – a high-powered stockbroker with a knack for turning money into a lot more money. Clients wanted him as their broker because he was Julian Blessing. He was somebody in the investment world. Unfortunately, he had only a murky idea of who Julian Blessing really was.

There were things he did know. The economy had imploded. His workplace was toxic and likely to land him in jail. His ex-wife wanted to see him dead and he had been keeping a secret for a very long time. He was a man searching for new possibilities in a world that seemed to be closing off his options by the minute.

Julian stood, hesitated a moment to clear his thoughts and then introduced himself. "I am Julian Blessing, and the professor has been good enough to tell me some remarkable things regarding Irish fables and folk lore." Julian smiled and took Mrs. Bragonier's hand.

At the touch, he experienced a mild and swift disorientation. A moderate electrical impulse left his hand tingling. For a long moment, Mrs. Bragonier looked into Julian's face with open curiosity.

Her hand felt warm and soft and Julian noticed his own trembled slightly in hers. Her eyes narrowed and slowly she smiled broadly, knowingly and released Julian's hand.

"Has he now?" she said and an eyebrow shot up. With a smile playing at the corners of her mouth, she continued addressing Julian. "He is a dear, sweet man and no woman could ask for a better partner in life." She reached out and touched the professor's hand and he beamed with pleasure, "but he suffers from a monumental ignorance as regards the Irish." She leaned close to Julian and with a New Yorker's instincts he drew away. In a stage whisper she said, "The poor professor sadly suffers from the curse of his profession."

Her smile activated the fine network of lines at the corners of her eyes. For his part, Professor Reginald Bragonier reveled in her mischief and basked in the warm glow of her affection and attention.

"You see, my husband is a professor of history at one of our universities. His presence is an oddity to be sure. An Englishman teaching history to the Irish – you need not look far for the irony there. He has dedicated his life to fabricated facts. He will beguile you with his knowledge of history and other outright lies. The man is a humbug you see.

"Darling," she smiled and said to her husband, "You were interested in finding a copy of the Irish Times. There is a book shop just over there," she said indicating a spot at the far end of the park. "They will have your newspaper."

"Was I? Well, yes I suppose I was, but I don't remember. Book shop you say. Right then, off I go then. I'll be back in a wink." The professor gave a jovial wave over his shoulder as he walked away, battle weary valise in hand.

"That will be the longest wink in history," she said with an easy laugh. "I will give him a few moments but soon it would be best if I tag along with him or he will get into no end of trouble. Professors and books are a bad combination to be sure."

Mrs. Bragonier sat down on the bench and inclined her head indicating Julian should join her. "The professor believes you are clairvoyant." Julian smiled.

"And I take it, you do not put much stock in such things. That does not surprise me too much. Still, on this occasion my husband's remarks do surprise me," his companion said. "That is not the sort of thing he would confide to just anyone.

"In most regards, Reginald is cautious with people, although he does not appear so. You may number yourself among the very special," the woman paused, smiled more broadly and continued, "in many more ways than you know." She passed Julian a thoughtful look and they sat for a moment in silence.

"To be sure," Bridget Bragonier said at last. "It is a lovely park you have here Mr. Blessing, but what do you suppose brought you here today and not another day?"

"It is an island in a sea of madness, I suppose. Today is just slightly more mad than most. It helps to get out of my office and breathe what passes for fresh air in Manhattan. Nothing more than that, Mrs. Bragonier," Julian said and turned with a smile to face his companion.

"Is that what you think?" Her smile was eloquent. "If you will indulge an eccentric old woman – albeit, I should point out, a charming one – let me tell you what I know." Julian nodded and waited to see what kind of scam this woman was running.

Bridget Bragonier said, "You see, Mr. Blessing, you are unique. You are a man struggling with a number of mysteries. What I know, and you do not, is that you are here so that I may help you release the truth you have locked away, to say the words you have kept hidden and in so doing, to help you find your footing in the life that awaits you."

The remark caught Julian off guard and he dropped his smile. He was a man with prepared responses for everything. He had no snappy comeback now.

"Something you cannot explain has happened in your life," the woman continued. "That is, without including mental illness as part of your reasoning." Her mood and manner were light, as though she was discussing a lunch menu instead of dissecting a man's soul.

The woman with the silver hair and the deep eyes drew closer to Julian. His thoughts were suspended when Mrs. Bragonier lightly touched his sleeve. He looked at her and any denial he was about to make died in his throat.

It was impossible, he knew, but somehow her eyes had changed. There was a luminescent quality coming not from the mischievous, playful eyes of the professor's wife, but from eyes ancient in depth and rich in meaning.

She reached out and placed her left hand slowly, gently over his heart. He felt himself unable to stop her. Although every instinct screamed at him to run, he was unable to draw back from her. At the touch, Julian felt another low voltage jolt, stronger this time, that left him breathing rapidly and riveted to his spot on the bench.

She was inside his defenses and there was nothing he could do about it. She knew his secret, a secret there was no way she or anyone could know. The woman's hand never left his shirt front, the smile never left her lips and her eyes held his relentlessly.

"The secret you keep regards the echoes you hear, which you have been hearing for some time," the woman said. "You can of course make out the words, but are afraid to acknowledge them, let alone try to understand or accept them. Is this not true?" Julian's silence answered for him.

"You realize the words you are trying so desperately to reject are a key to your future. Therein lies the difficulty. You long to find a life worth living, a life far different from the one you have known. You hold the key to that life in your hand, but are afraid to use it. And that is with good reason.

"You have an important task ahead of you. It is, in fact, the most critical endeavor of your life and the lives of many others. For this reason, I am here to help you focus on what is important and disregard that which is not.

"There is a place you need to be and that place is not here," she said. What you do not yet see clearly is that you must find your place quickly because you have tasks to see to and a life's work to discover."

She removed her hand. The connection was broken. Julian sagged visibly, feeling as though she had been supporting him, keeping him from toppling over.

"What are the words, Mr. Blessing? Tell me what echoes you hear."

"You seem so well informed, why do you need me?" His voice was brittle.

"For now at least the need, sir, is not mine, but yours." Her smile disappeared and her expression turned serious and intense. "Say the words, Mr. Blessing. Not for me, but for yourself. Please, you need to do this. Oblige me quickly before your telephone rings and you are called away."

Julian looked at the ground. For months, he had heard the words whispered over and over. His mind cascaded over the previous months and a sea of emotion welled up inside of him. Anger, frustration, bitterness, confusion and an aching sadness were all in attendance. He looked up, then closed his eyes and said in a strangled whisper, "I don't know what you are talking about."

He opened his eyes and found sympathy and sadness etched on Bridget Bragonier's face. She smiled her encouragement and said, "I will leave you so you may take your call in private." She took a pen and small notepad from her purse.

"Before you are called back to your office, let me give you the telephone number for our hotel. It is very near where the professor is lecturing. We will be in New York only for the week, but do call when you need my help.

"The answers you seek, the direction you need to follow, will be made plain to you shortly. This much I understand. I do not know your answers, but you will know them soon. There are signposts ahead. Look for them.

"Do not become distracted by the life you are currently leading, Mr. Blessing. The price of that distraction is far higher than you know."

The iPhone in Julian's pocket went off. As he reached for it in confusion, Bridget Bragonier smile indulgently, turned and walked away.

"Julian, this is Olivia. You have to get back here right away," said the familiar voice of his assistant. "No one is supposed to know. I heard about it by accident. There is something very wrong and you're not going to be happy about it."

"What did you say?" His mind was racing in entirely too many directions. "Yes, sorry Olivia. I'll be there in five minutes."

Julian pocketed his phone and looked up. Bridget Bragonier stopped fifty feet away. She turned to look at Julian and her face became serious and her eyes piercing. Her lips did not move, but her voice touched his mind. Julian felt every thought of hers, every nuance. He was frightened, but the words began to calm him in a way he could not explain.

"Hush and calm your thoughts. Feel my words and believe me when I tell you, you have much to do and not a great deal of time left in which to do it."

She continued, "*Remember, you will not be able to ignore the life that awaits you for much longer. Soon you will have to acknowledge the meaning of the echoes you hear. Allowing them to resonate within you will be the first step toward embracing your new life, the life you deserve and which has always been yours. Believe me, Mr. Blessing, it will be a life worth living, a life worthy of you.*

"I have troubled you enough. For the present, I will say only go and be well, Julian Blessing. We will talk again."

The lady with the searching gray eyes smiled slightly, turned, and walked off toward the bookstore.

***

Julian walked the few blocks back to his office with labored, unsure steps. He began to tremble with the effort to keep his secret buried in silence. He stopped as a tide of humanity flowed around him on the sidewalk. Eddies of people moved within inches, but he and they never touched, never jostled each other, never knew the other existed.

He looked straight ahead and whispered aloud the words he had kept hidden - the words that haunted his life. They were the words he had feared, the words of an esoteric chant he did not understand. He murmured them, "Go now."

* * *

A few blocks away, in a corner bookstore by the park, Bridget Bragonier looked up suddenly. She closed her eyes for a moment and smiled broadly. The woman said only one word. It summed up her relief, her satisfaction and her outlook for the future. "Good."

Her husband approached with several books tucked under his arm and a sales receipt in his hand. He was always pleased to see his wife happy. "Find something interesting, my love?" he asked.

"I find everything interesting, darling" she answered, a smile on her lips and in her voice. She seemed lost in her thoughts and feelings for a moment and then continued, "especially you." She winked at him and he grinned.

Chapter Two

Julian walked slowly toward his assistant's desk and said, "Olivia, let's take a stroll and you can tell me your secrets. This is turning out to be a day for secrets and bizarre events." He looked tired, but his smile was relaxed.

The Irishwoman in the park had been right. Saying the words he had denied utterance had been more freeing than he could have imagined. He had no idea what the message was or why he was visited with it, but he felt deeply the change repeating the words had made.

He was unhurried and unconcerned which worried his assistant. Few on Wall Street were anything other than stressed and tense. No one in New York City was ever truly relaxed. It was not a place that tolerated it. Olivia felt sure there was probably a city ordinance forbidding it.

After working with Julian for ten years, she knew he was an anomaly. Although lately Julian had been showing the strain, he was always composed, he always had a plan and he had the unusual ability to stay several steps ahead of everyone else. For her part, she was a brilliant broker's assistant and a broker in her own right. She and Julian made a team that was one of the most formidable on Wall Street.

Olivia began. "I wouldn't have called you if it weren't important. I got wind of something, so I examined your personal brokerage account. You own 50,000 shares of Burton Chemical stock at $15½ - shares you didn't own yesterday."

"Do you suppose someone is trying to hide that stock so the SEC auditors don't find it?" Julian asked and smiled.

"Got it in one, boss. More specifically, our firm's chairman, Hal Heward has a stake in the auditors not finding that stock in our inventory. Your personal account is another matter.

"Hal's son-in-law is the president of Burton Chemical and we are busy propping up the stock and issuing doctored buy recommendations. Why are you smiling? Are you feeling alright?"

"Olivia, I can't really explain it. It's complicated, but I feel oddly good. I do appreciate your concern though." Julian smiled and his eyes were alight as a plan began to roll out with each new piece of information his assistant presented.

"Stashing that stock in your account is a perfect solution," Olivia continued. "The firm makes it look like a normal transaction, and once the auditors are gone, the stock magically disappears from your account and is back in inventory.

"You get your money back and all is right with the world. What makes it really perfect though is if the auditors do find all that stock in your account, the firm will claim you've been the one manipulating it all along and they, the poor firm, knew nothing about it."

"Olivia, what do you think of Burton?"

"It is a dog," she said. "The firm, and now you, bought it at $15½ and it is selling at $8. It isn't worth $5. There is a bad smell coming from that stock and everybody on the Street has gotten a whiff."

"What is it that Burton does again? It's not a stock I watch even though I now appear to own quite a lot of it, so you'll understand my curiosity," Julian said.

"As far as anyone has been able to figure, they don't do much of anything aside from paying too much for companies. They buy mostly import-export firms that are on the ropes. Burton is very well capitalized, it is cash heavy in fact and it has no debt," she said.

"So, I'm down $375,000 on what is probably a money-laundering scheme. Seems a bit shady even by brokerage firm standards, don't you think?"

"Looks like a duck and quacks like a duck, boss," Olivia responded.

"Good, that's settled. I don't like ducks. I'm going to sell my little flock to whoever will buy it. Do you suppose anyone would mind?" Julian asked and grinned.

Olivia stopped and looked with horror into the calm, gray eyes of her boss. "You're joking? Of course you are. You would have to be insane to sell it. No, honestly, Julian, please don't look like that.

"The chairman would be homicidal, the SEC will eat your ass off for dumping shit stock in the street and I'm sure there are others who would be more than a bit pissed off. Messing around with this kind of thing is dangerous.

"I say we sit tight and let the firm take the stock back later. Please, tell me you're joking. Oh my God! You're not joking."

"Olivia, not to worry. I am going to sell Burton Chemical to Burton Chemical. I am going to recoup my loss and make a few dollars and I'm going to do it in a very short amount of time.

"The last thing Burton wants is blocks of outside investors asking awkward questions. I'll sell and they'll buy. Trust me."

"Julian, listen, you're scaring the hell out of me," Olivia said. "Screw Heward and Burton. They're nobodies, but there are wise guys or worse involved here. You will be messing with the wrong kind of people. You've got to know this is all very bad business – I mean dead-in-a-ditch bad business."

"Well then, I'll have to be extra careful won't I," Julian said with a smile.

He knew this was a dangerous game. If it worked, he filled a pothole on Wall Street. A worthless stock would be unavailable for casual investors to fall into – at least for a while.

At risk was his life. Julian wasn't feeling invincible. What he felt was far more powerful than that. He knew Olivia was right. He was mucking about with the wrong kind of people. He did not care and that made him powerful and dangerous and very possibly dead.

Olivia had seen Julian pull rabbits out of hats many times before. This time it was a very large rabbit and a very small hat.

By ten o'clock, it was being whispered on the Street that someone had accumulated a large position in Burton Chemical and was looking for more.

By eleven o'clock, the information was common currency.

By one fifteen, the stock was actively trading at $15.50 and Julian watched the computer in his office record his trades.

By the closing bell Burton had run as high as $21 then fallen back to close at $19. Olivia knocked lightly and entered his office crossing the expanse of thick carpet to his desk. "Julian, I've been watching, you're out of Burton. I hear Hal Heward is looking for you. There is going to be hell to pay, boss. Now what?"

"Olivia, here is a list of three brokerage firms who are desperate to talk with you. Go interview them and see which one you like best. You'll be taking all of my clients with you so you'll have plenty of negotiating power behind you.

"It would be safe to say, I am not going to be the flavor of the day around here. It would be best if you made yourself scarce. Besides, you're too good of a broker to work here.

"Where are you going, boss?"

"Olivia," Julian sighed. "I really have not the slightest idea."

***

In his office along the darkened skyline in lower Manhattan, Julian Blessing wondered why no one had yet come to throw him out of the window. He would have given it more thought, but he had recently taken up a nightly ritual of self-castigation and so he began to practice it again.

Julian switched on a lamp and removed three items from his large mahogany desk. He began with an envelope hand addressed by his ex-wife and marked personal and confidential, although it was neither.

He and she had lived semi-detached lives for some time before she filed for divorce. With a house in Connecticut and the apartment in the City, Julian had trouble remembering which was home. Recently he hadn't invested enough of himself in either place for it to be otherwise.

He lived his life as a perennial stranger, a man never touching or being touched. He saw himself as a constant foreigner, an outsider observing life but never living it.

His wife had sent him a private letter and some personal belongings with the divorce papers. The divorce was a civil formality. The real marriage had been dissolved long ago when he discovered her numerous affairs and her pilfering of their joint bank accounts.

The letter, however, was meant to wound him and it succeeded, but not in the ways she intended. He knew her words were conceived in hatred and awash in resentment. But, it was with a different type of bitterness that Julian re-read the letter.

He found himself obsessed with thoughts of a life half lived. He thought if he read the letter enough times, punished himself enough, it would burn away the results of living his life of half measures. Until then, he wanted his emotions kept raw and painful. Julian was not looking for an easy way out.

Julian,

I wonder if you expected me to leave you. If you didn't, you are a bigger fool than I thought possible. Still, I know what a nuisance this must be for you. You will be civilized about this divorce business, won't you? Of course, you will. You are renowned for being civilized. Anyway, back to business – I wouldn't want to waste your precious time.

I am writing to you to tell you a few things about yourself from my point of view. I do have a point of view, darling, even though I doubt you ever noticed.

Julian, even though you are able to make a lot of money – and you are rather good at that – you really are quite a failure on all other areas of life. I just thought you should know that little tidbit.

You are a soulless, plodding coward and a fool and I'm far from alone in that opinion. Most people laugh at you behind your back and no one respects you because you are not worthy of respect. In short, you are a social nightmare. Sadly, it doesn't end there though. Although I did not always think so, you have become the most unattractive man I've ever known. The years have not been kind to you and that isn't going to change, Julian.

Your lack of social talent and physical distastefulness is only surpassed by your complete lack of talent in bed. You've never satisfied me – not that you would have noticed. Is it that you don't notice such things because they aren't important to you or is it because you are so very dim? No matter, you were always too wrapped up in yourself and it is because of your selfishness that you will never satisfy any woman. As men go, you are really a rather poor example.

There is no warmth or tenderness about you Julian – and face it, a romantic you are not. You are not the kind of man any woman would want but if you find one that tells you otherwise darling, trust me, she will be lying. It would be better if you used the services of prostitutes because they are expected to lie to their clients. In that way, they are much like stockbrokers, no? Birds of a feather, as they say, no?

That was catty of me, wasn't it? No matter. That pretty much covers it, don't you think? Although you probably suspect I want to destroy you financially, that isn't the case at all. I would very much prefer to see you dead. See what you can do to accommodate my wishes, won't you?

Good-bye, Julian.

Elspeth

***

Chances lost, loves lost, joys lost, all of them staking their claims for payment in full. For the first time in his life, Julian Blessing had not accrued sufficient assets to pay those bills. The successes in his life were too few and even when squeezed dry, they rendered only drops of satisfaction. "Not enough. It wasn't nearly enough," he thought.

A symphony of sadness welled up within him. Agonizing regret pulled at his soul. He had loved her once, but when love is moved to the back burner, it always goes cold. He wondered if she ever loved him. He listened in silent sadness to the singular notes of life in a minor key.

Julian cocked his head and walked to his office window. He found himself looking into the distance as if trying to see the possible futures open to him. What he saw was his own distorted reflection and darkness beyond.

It was back, a murmur, an undertone, a whisper in the night. "*Go now.*"

For as long as Julian could remember, he had found it impossible to enjoy life. His existence had always seemed like something that needed to be endured. He found it impossible to fully live his life. Instead, he was an active observer rather than a willing participant.

Each of life's mysteries dissolved beneath his cynical gaze leaving him unsatisfied. To him the grace and depth of life were legends – frequently talked about by others, but never witnessed, at least never as far as he could tell. But he was beginning to learn how important mystery, grace and depth were to a life.

Still, the whispered words plagued him. They had murmured their presence at first. The distant whispering had been ignored. Julian successfully pushed the phrase aside for a while, but time was up and he knew it.

Now the whisper had become a growl. It was definitive, insistent and vaguely menacing. There was no ignoring it this time. Bridget Bragonier had been right about that even if he didn't know how or why.

He mouthed the words. "Go now."

***

Julian walked back to his desk as the telephone came alive. He closed his eyes when he saw the caller ID.

"Mr. Blessing, this is Bridget Bragonier. I am sorry I was out when you called. How may I help you?"

"Mrs. Bragonier, I'm running out of time and so I'll come right to the point. I find myself with a life full of questions without answers not the least of which is why I would call you. You said you could help. How?" Julian asked.

"I can help you immediately by insisting you call me Bridget and I shall call you Julian." Julian heard Bridget Bragonier's refined, lyrical voice on the telephone. He heard her smile. She sounded relaxed and welcoming and Julian felt comforted by her confidence. In it, he found a kind of refuge.

Bridget continued. "You are correct, you are nearly out of time. The life you are living is broken, Julian. There is nothing for it, but for you to find another life and to do it soon. I realize this makes little sense to you now. I think it best if you and I could sit and talk for a while.

"You're wrong, Bridget. It isn't that all of this makes little sense; it makes no sense at all. Still, in another way you are right – I'll bet you get that a lot, I mean being right all the time." Julian heard her softly chuckle. "I suppose I should hear you out in person. I can meet you somewhere tomorrow. Is eight o'clock too early?"

"I do not know if we have that much time. But for now, let us say eight o'clock at Café Bravo. I saw it the other day and it looked decidedly decadent," Bridget said. Julian could hear her smile.

***

He dropped the phone back into its cradle then picked up a battered leather bound journal, the second of the things he had laid on his desk. It seemed to be the only thing of interest left in his life, and even there, he found only questions without answers.

A cheerless smile tinged his lips as he touched the embossed volume. He closed his eyes and felt the Celtic knot-work pattern driven into the grain of the kid leather cover. He let his fingers follow the graceful curve of the intertwining knots.

The powerful interlocking of pattern and plane were distinctive even though they had been worn and weathered and locked away for a very long time. Over the next hours, he read and reread his old journal.

After college, he had taken a walking tour of Ireland. The journal was the log of his journey. Next to the journal and his ex-wife's letter sat an old Ordinance Survey map. It completed the triumvirate – the three magistrates that sat in judgment of his life.

As he read his journal, Julian traced the progress of his tour on the map, but an unaccountable mark seemed to mock his memory.

In the north of County Meath, seemingly in the middle of nowhere, a circle had been drawn on Julian's map. He couldn't remember drawing it and knew he had never visited the spot. His tour had ended in Dublin and he had never preceded any farther north along the Irish coast.

The circle seemed to lie in a hilly area and appeared to hold a small valley that led to the Irish Sea.

His journal made no mention of the spot or how it came to be marked on the map, but it did serve to remind him of the lovely verdant island. It caused him to remember some of the people he had met on this travels: a fellow student in Galway, a doctor in James Joyce's county of Maam, a landlord in Limerick who had let him sleep in the pub after closing time.

He recalled a lovely red haired girl in County Cork named Cara who had loved him with a startling candor, so open and loving in fact that he had run away to Killarney at the first opportunity. He had loved her in his own way, but knew his way would not be nearly enough for either of them.

The journal brought to mind a country priest who had walked with him from Tralee to Kerry Head. Shop owners, farmers, barristers, beggars, tinkers, policemen and weavers flooded back to his memory. The feelings they left were warm and good and he clung to the journal as a shipwrecked sailor might to any piece of floating wreckage.

"Warm and good – the last time you felt either of those was nearly twenty years ago. Blessing, you idiot, what have you done to yourself?" he asked.

***

Julian looked up as his office door swung open. Two powerfully built men stood facing him. They wore expensive business suits that did nothing to hide the fact that these men were in the violence business.

They entered his office, securing the door behind them.

At the moment of the first Burton Chemical stock trade Julian knew his life was in danger. He knew revenge would be demanded. Julian now wondered if he subconsciously didn't desire this outcome.

He had protected his assistant; he had made sure of that. Julian knew he would be alone and that this moment would arrive. He had a mechanism in place that would avenge but not protect him. "Sorry, Bridget, time's up," he murmured to himself.

The larger of the two men faced Julian and said with painful slowness, "We have been told by Heward you lose us money. You have made mistake. We will kill you." The voice was deep and matter of fact and the accent issued from the former Soviet Union. "You must suffer first, but we make quick."

Julian didn't know much about suffering and dying, but he knew these men understood all parts of those subjects and not in an academic way. Their eyes were cold, eyes that had seen too much, far too much. Eyes that had witnessed the administration of agony and death. Dead eyes that regarded Julian with little interest. He was an item on a to-do list and nothing more.

"I suppose bribery and begging are off the table, eh? Tell my former boss I tried. It'll make him feel better when he's in prison playing drop-the-soap," Julian said. Both men looked at him and derision tinged their lips.

Julian looked past his executioners and was horrified to see another player in the game. The Russians followed his gaze.

The men considered the slight woman at Julian's office door. He could nearly hear the cogs move in their heads as they recalculated the commission on two dead bodies instead of one.

The door had been locked. This the Russians knew. It was impossible, but they had not heard the door being opened. This they could not grasp. A mistake had been made. In the world of these two men, mistakes like this weren't career ending they were death-dealing. And this they understood all too well.

"Julian darling, we have an appointment." Bridget Bragonier stood with her back to the door. She was dressed conservatively with a simplicity that belied the richness of the fabrics she wore. She angled to see beyond the dangerous men in Julian's office as though they were potted palms.

"My dear, if you look at your appointment book you will clearly see my name, although how you could forget me is more than I could ever possibly know." The woman's voice was relaxed. Her lightly accented Irish English was silvery in its smoothness and seemed to lack any concern for what was happening around her.

"Really, this is intolerable." Her voice sounded pouty but light and carried its cultured Irish melody easily. "You are becoming as ill mannered as Reginald. Forgetting appointments will doubtless be followed by your not listening when I speak to you."

"I'm sorry, I had nearly forgotten," Julian began as his thoughts started to unwind from the concept of his own sudden, painful death and consider his inability to protect Bridget from what was about to happen.

Bridget Bragonier swept into the room and stood before the large men blocking her path. Her eyes narrowed and hardened. In the next moment, they softened and the lines around her gray eyes became alive.

"I am willing to wager both of you have lovely smiles." Her voice was airy and her own smile radiant. "You will, of course excuse me," she said and pushed her way easily between the men to stand next to Julian behind his desk.

"Julian, my dear, you look tired. Do you feel well?" She reached up slowly and touched his cheek then stared into his eyes. He felt an electrical tingle at her touch and felt rather than heard her words clearly.

"Do nothing. Say nothing."

She turned to the Russians. "You will understand gentlemen," the woman began. "Julian and I have a prior appointment. We would happily include you, but our business is of a private nature – finances and investing you know.

"It is all very tedious, but he assures me it is necessary." She looked saddened by the thought but resigned.

"We will not delay you further," she said. The men shifted uneasily. Bridget was composed and her voice had become saccharine. "Do let yourselves out and be kind enough to close the door behind you. We do not wish to be disturbed." She said these words and looked at length into the face of each of the men. They recognized the distinctively cultured Muscovite accented "Goodbye." It was not a wish, but a dismissal.

Again, they shifted. They were prepared, ready and more than capable of dispensing violence to any and all. But everything about this woman set off alarm bells. She was wrong at every conceivable level.

Bridget's eyes narrowed even as her smile broadened and took on a sinister edge. These men, these hard, dangerous men, looked into the face of a slender, old woman, well bred, cultured and gently raised. They looked into her eyes and began to lean away from her slightly.

They recognized something in those eyes, something kindred, something dangerous. They saw eyes alive with unadulterated malice and a terrible iron-willed intent. At a fundamental level, they knew she was every bit as ready, willing and lethally able as they. On a visceral level, they recognized this woman was what she should not have been – eager.

She had gotten into the office behind them and that was one very serious mistake. Compounding it with another could not be allowed to happen. The men turned slowly. The smaller man said to Julian, "We see you again and then you die, not quickly." Neither man looked at the woman, yet she smiled pleasantly.

The Russians reached the office door and found it locked. They exchanged glances and left, closing the door behind them.

"Julian, you have the most peculiar taste in friends." Bridget touched his cheek again, smiled and moved easily to his office seating area to find a comfortable place to sit.

***

Julian walked to his office window, crossed his arms and openly regarded the Irish apparition seated in front of him.

"Don't you understand, they would have killed you too? What are you doing here! We agreed on tomorrow, but here you are. Right, I might add, where you should not be. Forget I said that. I don't even want to get into all of that lunacy." Julian's voice was tight and nervous and he continued to look toward his office door every few moments.

Bridget Bragonier's eyes were warm, and inviting. They inspired trust even in those, like Julian, who had given up trusting long ago. "Julian, there is no reason to keep looking at the door. Your friends will not be back until tomorrow evening, although I believe they will be more than a little cross with you. Even so, we have little time for preamble, so let us begin, shall we?"

Julian looked down at the old journal in his hands. He traced again the Celtic knot cut into the cover and shook his head slowly. Worry and frustration etched his face. He looked drawn, pale and worn out. "How can you help me, Bridget?" Julian asked and looked into his companion's face.

He turned to the window and Bridget Bragonier materialized at his elbow. "I said when first we met, there was a life waiting for you and that you would not be able to ignore it much longer. Now, the time has come. You know this of course. Your life here is over."

Everything Bridget had said was true. Each of the things that buttressed his life had been knocked away one after another. Now he stood in his darkened office with his career in tatters, his emotional life a shambles, a lot of people who wanted him dead and the pervasive feeling this couldn't be all there was to life.

Looking out the window, Julian whispered after a long silence, "Bridget, I am afraid. The trouble is I don't know if I am more afraid of the past or the future. I know my life here is over, but I don't know what's next."

"I know you are afraid, you dear man. Your fear is legitimate, but please, do not deceive yourself as to its source. The past and the future are not your enemies. Your past holds no terrors for you except that you may repeat its errors. The future is entirely unknown to you. This may cause you concern but does not rise to the level of fear.

"You are afraid to trust yourself. That is the root of your trouble and offers the germ of your salvation. You have heard the words. You hold a signpost in your hands. Trust yourself. Trust everything that is right and true and real about you. Trust yourself to say the words, the words you hear. Step off the edge, Julian. The life that awaits you will not so easily let you fall."

Julian drew a breath. He was locked in a battle between what he knew and what he wanted. He exhaled, breaking the stalemate. "Go now," he whispered.

Bridget smiled warmly, closed her eyes and exhaled deeply. "Julian, you know where you must go even if you do not know why or what you are to do.

"Before I came here tonight, I wrote down our information. The professor and I look forward to seeing you in Dublin. Go and be well, but my dear, go now." She handed Julian an off-white sheet of notepaper and with that, the woman with ancient eyes turned and walked away.

As she reached the door her eyes darkened and the slight smile left her lips. Without turning, she thought and Julian heard her thoughts clearly, *"You have a letter. Destroy it for your own good and that of others. It is poisonous and it will keep you from what you want most. Do not fall into the trap the letter sets for you. You must believe what is best about you. That will lead you, in turn, to what is best for you.*

"I tell you this for your own good. That letter is the past and as long as you keep it and believe it, you will be anchored to your past with all its mistakes and heartaches."

Bridget opened the door and was gone leaving Julian at the window alone with his thoughts.

Chapter Three

The flights from New York to London and London to Dublin had been uneventful. To Julian that meant the airplanes shot off the runway on one end and underwent a successful controlled crash onto the runway at the other and everyone survived more or less intact.

It was early morning of his first day in Ireland.

***

In a cold manor house near the Irish coast, the Pale Man sat in his study with his eyes closed. His face was a mask of malicious satisfaction. The steady tick of a clock was the only sound, his only companion. The sun rose, but was held at bay by thick heavy draperies. His work required neither light nor warmth.

Miles away a sharp featured old woman fell to her knees and cried out in agony and terror. Clutching her abdomen as the spasms that racked her body subsided, she gasped for breath.

The Pale Man opened his eyes and smiled.

***

Julian didn't plan on sightseeing. He had prepared for this trip as he had for his college adventure. Galaxy Army Navy Surplus on West 30th Street in New York satisfied all of his travel needs. He had everything he needed from a vintage leather bomber jacket to hiking boots. He had been extravagant and spent an extra three dollars for an upgraded duffle bag,

With a wistful smile and a sad shake of her head Julian's assistant, Olivia, had given him a stunningly complex Swiss Army knife. He was delighted beyond words even though he had no idea what he was going to do with it, but any instrument that came with a fish scaler (hook disgorger included) and ruler had value that was at once practical, intrinsic and aesthetic. Besides that, it was unreasonably cool.

Julian smiled as he waited at the baggage carousel. Olivia was one of the few who had known he was leaving the country and even she did not know why or where he was going. Julian found it was easy to keep the why of his reasons a secret from her. He had only a fuzzy notion of the motives behind any of his recent actions.

As he stood at the baggage carousel, Julian reached into his shirt pocket and removed a note. It was worn and creased from the number of times he had studied it. In a very neat hand it read,

Dear Julian,

Below you will find our address and telephone number. Please send us your flight information and the professor and I will collect you from the airport in Dublin.

You are not alone now. Please, remember that. You will find there are those of us who are anxious to support and nurture you. Just now, you are a man sorely in need of the comfort of a safe harbor. We can provide that if you will only allow it.

The professor and I look forward to seeing you soon. It will be necessary to give Reginald a few of the particulars of your trip. Please trust I will give him as few as possible in order to protect your privacy. I know it does not seem so at first, but the professor is discretion itself. Still, I will tell him what I must and you are then free to tell him what you like.

Affectionately,

Bridget

Julian folded the note and put it back in his pocket as he stood facing the baggage carousel. He collected his duffle bag, cleared customs and proceeded through the low compact structure that was Dublin International Airport.

***

"Friend Blessing!" the professor shouted as he scuttled through the airport terminal. His arms were spread wide and his face beamed its owner's pleasure.

At seeing the professor, Julian's smile became a wide grin and he quickened his pace. The rumpled little man wasn't just happy, he was a carrier of happiness, a regular pandemic of delight.

"Ireland welcomes you. Now come with me. My lady wife awaits in the car and she does not wait well so we must make haste," the professor announced.

Julian laughed in a way that he immediately saw was new to him. His laughter was unrestrained, unselfconscious. It was the natural response to a joke enjoyed rather than the obligatory noise heard so often in New York. There, it was laughter devoid of humor because the humor was vicious and always at the expense of those who were absent.

The professor began to lead the way to an exit, but Julian stopped and redirected their path. "I don't know why I think so, but a short time ago Bridget moved the car. She should be right through this door. It's odd how things come to you like that, eh? Why are you staring at me like that?"

The professor had stopped and was rooted to a spot in the center of the concourse. "What? No! Good God. Not you too. Please, please, Blessing, tell me you aren't one of them. You were my last hope, but now I find you are a mountebank! I tell you this is entirely too much." Julian laughed and pulled the professor along. They exited the terminal together and at the curb sat Bridget behind the wheel of the Bragoniers' automobile.

The car rattled through the countryside, deep into Dublin's central neighborhoods. They parked in front of a handsome Georgian townhouse across from St. Stephen's Green. Moss and ivy encased the brick façade, softened the hard edges and framed the large white painted sash windows.

White marble columns flanked a large entryway with a stained glass transom above the heavy black front door where an elaborate brass doorknocker occupied center stage.

Once inside, Julian found a light, open front room with an upholstered couch and comfortable club chairs bordering a large painted brick fireplace. As he was led through the house on a tour conducted by the professor, Julian found each room to be inviting and bright without being contrived or fussy.

Busy Kildare Street hummed on the other side of the front door, but the street noise was imperceptible inside. The feel of the home was one of a tranquil sanctuary removed from time and space. It was a world of its own.

"Breakfast, gentlemen, is this way," Bridget said and led Julian and her husband into the dining room. Breakfast was simple, filling and Julian savored it with the easy conversation and the frequent laughter of his friends. He felt if he never left this house, he would count himself lucky beyond measure. This was the first time he could remember feeling deeply, truly happy.

***

Dinner was as relaxed as breakfast had been. The conversation centered on the professor and his duties at Trinity College. Bridget looked on and her face glowed with pleasure.

Julian sat captivated by the professor's descriptions of his studies, his students, the investigation of ancient history and the stories of college life.

Bridget was enormously proud of her husband but not nearly as proud of him as she was in love with him. After more than thirty years together, there were no stories she had not heard.

She knew every pause, every gesture, every inflection. She heard the music in his voice when he was excited about a discovery or found a willing audience for his stories. His eyes would light up when he knew he had his listeners on the edge of their seats. He was good at what he did and she was good at loving him for it.

***

With the table cleared and the dishes washed and put away, Bridget and Julian walked into the garden while the professor went to his study to concoct another grueling test for his students.

Bridget put her arm through Julian's and they walked around the garden at a leisurely pace.

"Julian, you are a gifted man and there are others like me who will understand you and help you understand your talents. You see, when someone like you comes along, it is our responsibility to help. In time, you will want to do the same."

"Bridget, I don't get any of this. Gifts, talents, tasks – are you seriously saying this is magic or the supernatural or paranormal or… or… or whatever. I don't believe it. I can't believe it. And that 'being one of us,' business, although sweet in another context, it's kind of creepy if you don't mind my saying so.

"Listen, I like you a great deal, but you must know this." Julian became vehement. "I have not heard any clarion calls. I am not going on any sort of silly-assed quest. I do not have a destiny to fulfill.

"There are not going to be any witches, wizards or dragons in my future. There is no ultimate good or absolute evil waiting for me around the corner. Forget the God damned magical animals and talking trees too. Not interested."

His mouth was hard and tight. Unconsciously he flexed the fingers of his hand trying to dissipate his frustration.

Bridget Bragonier covered her mouth with her hand. She hoped that looking serious and thoughtful might mask her laughter.

"I am in possession of lots of very unpleasant documents, some from my ex-wife and more from her attorneys." Julian had left Bridget's side and began to pace as he spoke. "So you'll understand if I tell you, damsels in distress would be best advised to look elsewhere for a quick rescue. I'm out of that business. I'm retired and plan on staying away from all maidens, distressed or otherwise, for a very long time.

"I don't believe in magic, either good or bad. I don't need any miracles or spells. Do you guys deal in vampires or zombies? Well, until recently, I worked with a whole crew of bloodsuckers and a couple of Russian undead guys paid me a visit as you recall. Trust me, I've reached my lifetime allotment.

"Oh, by the way, you can keep the damn unicorns to yourself or give 'em to the leprechauns – your call." He had become more exercised than he intended, but felt he had said what needed saying.

Julian felt tired. He hung his head, "You said there was a life waiting for me. All I want, Bridget, is a quiet spot where I can rebuild myself without people bothering me and without all the rest of this fantasyland of yours!"

Bridget began to chuckle and it rolled easily into a hearty laugh. "Ah my dear boy, it does my old heart good to listen to you. Are you sure you are not even a bit Irish? Such lush and evocative, not to forget colorful and occasionally salty speech is rare anymore. Such mastery. I am, well, frankly stunned that someone like you would have such a, what shall we call it, singular command of the English language?" Her voice dripped condescension and it only made Julian more tired.

"In order to save you from further embarrassing yourself, I will put it to you like this. You have only a meager notion of what you want, however, you have no idea at all of what you need. You have cataloged an exhaustive list of what you do not believe, but Julian, you have not the slightest idea what you do believe." She took his arm and they continued their walk.

"Please understand this," she continued. "You will notice I said there was a life waiting for you. You will note I did not promise you a vacation. You, Julian, have work to do and it will be the hardest work you have ever done.

"Now, to the business at hand. I cannot answer many of your questions or address all of your concerns and discussing what you do not believe is, well, silly and rather pointless. So instead, let us talk of something important, shall we?" Julian bridled, but Bridget continued unfazed.

"The world you are familiar with long ago accepted a lie. Because this deception was at the heart of so many things, much of what you know to be true is false. There are those who are able to recognize the deceit in its various forms and act accordingly.

"I can see by your face you are trying to make this fit with what you know. That, Julian, is a grave mistake. Almost none of what you know about reality is true. Yet, you propose to use the untruth to find the truth. Tell me, what is your truth worth when you find it is irredeemably flawed?"

Julian was frustrated, confused and it showed clearly on his face. "Bridget," he rubbed his forehead. "You make my head hurt, but let's back up. You said you have a responsibility to act accordingly. Accordingly to what exactly?"

"Now, that is one of your very best questions to date. Simply put, we shine a light into the darkness. We dispel shadows. If we do it correctly, we are able to make the impossible happen." She smiled.

"Do you understand that only makes my head hurt worse? These answers that aren't answers at all are not helping."

"Oh Julian," Bridget began, "petulance so becomes you. When you become cranky, you are absolutely adorable." Her laughter was light and unrestrained.

"I hate it when you do that," Julian said.

"Oh yes I know. I would not do it otherwise."

Bridget continued. "Julian, you are an exceptional man with a truly original mind. The power of your presence, your spirit, your thought if you will, is integral to who and what you will become. To deny this would be like denying the color of your eyes – do it all you like but when you are done, they will still be that lovely sterling gray.

"You are capable of being focused and methodical, but you know how and when to take risks. Julian, you are a man who will come to possess unbelievable talents and you will bring an unimaginable intensity to their application. I have lived a long time and I have seen and learned much. Believe me when I say I know what I am talking about in this regard.

"You are also alarmingly short-tempered, madly impetuous and painfully shortsighted. To be sure, those attributes will change as you gain experience. You may trust me, when you gain that experience, you and I will look back in the years to come and laugh and laugh and laugh."

"One laugh would have been sufficient," Julian said.

Bridget smiled, walked beside Julian a few more steps, then became serious. "Not everyone will suffer you as I do. Some will treat you far more harshly. Trust me, they will treasure you as I do, but they will not allow you to take the easy road. In fact, if given the choice, they will probably send you up the harder one to teach you not to be so cheeky or peevish.

"Keep this in mind also." Bridget's voice turned more serious still and Julian took notice. "This is not a game. There are those who will try to stop you from being what you are meant to be. I must leave that for others to explain. But know it is real and true and deadly. There are those with a vested interest in maintaining the illusion of darkness."

Julian began to realize he had become quite fond of this not-so-crazy, not-so-old woman. "Where am I going?" Julian asked. "I don't mean tomorrow. I know that one, but, you know…"

Bridget stood and looked for a long time searching Julian's face. "As long as where you are going is better than where you have been, does it matter?" She answered, turned and walked toward the house.

Chapter Four

The next morning was clear and crisp. Sunrise was over an hour away, but there was already pink on the eastern horizon.

Bridget confiscated Julian's map and pored over it as the car worked its way through the maze of Dublin's streets that would take them to the N1 highway. The professor relaxed in the back seat and looked out the front window as if for the first time.

Julian drove slowly at first adjusting to the car's right hand drive but picked up speed as his confidence increased. Before they reached the road leading up the rugged Irish coast, the professor was snoring peacefully.

"Bridget, I know you grew up in this, what would you call it, vocation? No doubt, you come from a long line of people who do whatever it is that you do, but this is new to me. You talked last night of skills or gifts or talents or whatever. I have no idea what the correct words are to form questions so I apologize in advance.

"Has navigating whatever reality it is you see that I don't, has this been easy for you? I mean did you learn quickly? God, that sounds stupid."

"The language is difficult at first, but it comes in time. You have, however made a blunder." She looked pleased with herself.

"I've not even said much. This is depressing."

"Normally I would let you finish with your questions before I pointed out your error, however, your error is a perfect place to begin.

"You, Julian, made an assumption, namely that I – to use your words – grew up in this vocation. I did not – no one I have ever met did. This is not a family business. As to whether it has been easy; I would have to say it has been decidedly difficult.

"My family had old money, a thing that is rare in Ireland. As a result, I lived in a privileged world of ideas and debate with large doses of esoteric discussion. The Sight ran in the family, but that was never mentioned for reasons I only discovered much later.

"Ultimately, I was sent away to private school and then finishing school." Bridget smiled and gave Julian a sidelong glance. "So now you know how I came to be so terribly well educated and perfectly charming." Julian smirked.

"Like you, like all of us actually, I was introduced to this calling, by another. He was older, but I was just twenty. At twenty, thirty seemed ancient.

"He was a family acquaintance and was often introduced as a professor, although no one ever discussed what he taught exactly. There were whispers, however and I found that thrilling. Still, he was always treated with great respect. Again, years later I would understand why.

"He saw something in me. I do not know what it could have been. I was headstrong and willful, pretty and popular, ignorant and arrogant. If ever there was a more lethal cocktail I do not know what it might have been.

"Oddly, my mentor tolerated me and introduced me to the broad metaphysical concepts and I was passed on to a teacher. The family was not pleased by this turn of events. After hushed and often heated discussions with my mentor, my parents became resigned.

"My teacher saw me for what I was and he took a rather stern line with me, though not always stern enough.

"I went at my studies blithely with all the diligence of one learning a few parlor tricks. I did not understand the power, the responsibility, or the consequences of what I was doing. It was all just a lovely game of make-believe.

"Like you, I was told there were those who wished to stop my progress. I thought this wildly romantic and exciting. Because those thoughts filled my head, I had not the time or the capacity to pay attention.

"I think of my mentor and my teacher often. They were both loving and giving men, well schooled in the ways of the real world." Bridget closed her eyes for a long moment.

"But," Julian interjected, "it worked out. You learned what you needed to learn and here you are today. Doubtless, you have helped many people."

She drew a long breath and let it out slowly. "Everything you say is true. It did work out in the end. I did learn what I needed to learn and, as you say, here I am many, many years later having helped a great many people.

Bridget continued. "There is no need to spare me, my dear. You have a good idea where this story leads. You need not know the details. It is enough to say others paid the price for my callow stupidity.

"I was badly injured and my mentor and my teacher, those two remarkable and generous men, are no more because of me. The shame I felt was made far worse knowing they died willingly so that I might not suffer more.

"So when you lightly make mention of this being a fantasy, and you have mentioned it frequently, go easily there. People die in this fairytale and I am sensitive to that." Her voice was not unkind, but tipped with melancholy. A single tear rolled down her cheek and she did nothing to check its progress. Julian felt ashamed and stupid, awkward and incredibly thoughtless. Julian looked straight ahead and drove.

Bridget took up her story again. "Well, as you say, it worked out. I was not given up on or abandoned. I received a new mentor and in course a new teacher. They did not need to be hard on me. I was harshness personified when it came to dealing with my failings both real and perceived.

"I studied longer than most. You see, I was steeped in anger and bitterness and for that reason, much of what I learned, I had to relearn again and again.

"In time I forgave myself and once I did, my path became easier. I met and married the professor. He is the perfect partner. He saw all my scars, inside and out, but he never asked questions.

"There were many times I wanted to talk with him, to tell him, but he would not have it. He told me my intention in speaking about my past was not to inform him but to punish myself. At some level, he knew, you see. He always does. He can intuitively feel when and what I need and also when I must be reminded of who I am.

"He calls me a wonder, but he is the wonder. We have made a brilliantly happy life together and we are both content and very much in love. I am very lucky, Julian. Love of this kind does not happen often. Remember that. It is something you will have need of in time."

Many miles later, after the sun had risen over the Irish Sea, Bridget turned to Julian awaiting his question.

"Bridget, I'm afraid. I don't know why I'm here. Everything I am doing goes counter to what I know. You say things that are nice to hear late at night but which are difficult to believe when the sun comes up. How do I understand any of what is happening? I'm really not cut out for this sort of thing."

"I would be worried if you did not have these thoughts," his companion said. "It would tell me you were not taking this business seriously enough," she said.

Julian asked, "You say I will find a teacher or he will find me. How will I know him?"

"I can only imagine how much you are going to hate this answer. He or she will arrive and you will know. You will have no doubts."

"Oh, of course," Julian said with exasperation slithering through his voice. "Why would I think there was going to be a proper answer to that question – to any question? Silly. I am sorry."

"Do not be cross. It makes me laugh," Bridget said but then her mood darkened.

"I realize you do not understand much of what I am saying. Please, do not let your lack of immediate understanding cause you to veer dangerously off course. Believe me, I would like to give you a text-book, but none exists or ever will. You must believe this – the truth of what I say will soon be explained. Do you understand?" she asked and looked earnestly at her companion.

"I would like to say I do, but I can't. I understand the words well enough, but it is as though some sentences lack verbs while others have no subject and none of them have any punctuation. I can feel something, but it makes little sense."

He stared into the distance as the car's engine raced nearly as fast as his thoughts. He was afraid to look at the woman beside him. Afraid he would see her angry or discouraged or sad. Then he heard her chuckle softly.

"Dear Julian, I do wish you could see what I see. You are a man faced with an impossible set of circumstances and what is your response? You tell me the truth and worry that you have disappointed me. How marvelous you are." She reached out and touched his hand as it rested on the steering wheel. The energy that coursed through her to him was mild and this time comforting.

***

A short time later Bridget indicated a side road ahead and asked Julian to turn off. The professor was still sleeping but she got out and asked Julian to stay with the car.

With a near regal carriage, the tall, slight, elegant and wise woman walked slowly into an adjoining field and stood looking into a distant pasture.

Julian watched his companion and realized how attached he had become to her.

For reasons he only dimly understood, his eyes brimmed with tears as he grieved for a life only half lived, a life that was now part of his past. He knew Bridget would not return until he was ready to take the first doubt-filled steps toward his future.

***

He got out of the car and stood looking up the road and away from his friend. His duffle bag lay at his feet. A sea breeze had snaked over a set of low hills and long since dried the tears on his cheeks. Julian did not turn to look. He had neither heard nor seen her, but he knew Bridget was standing just behind him.

"This is where you leave me," he said softly.

"In a way, yes." He heard a slight catch in her voice and she continued. "It is very hard, but yes. Not to sound melodramatic, but this is where your road begins, Julian. And for you to start, I must leave you. If it comforts you, know that you and I are connected. In that way I will always be with you."

"Will I see you again?"

"Yes." She said it with sincerity and a surety he found comforting. "Reginald will miss your driving and will insist." Julian smiled.

"Julian, there is something you need to know." Her voice was a whisper. "I can see none of it clearly, which in itself is worrying. There is something amiss here. I cannot explain it more precisely. What I do know with some precision is that you and your teacher desperately need one another. You can imagine that is not the usual case, but there is something different here. I can only say your teacher needs you."

They stood awhile together lost in their respective thoughts. Bridget Bragonier drew a breath, let it out slowly and said, "It is time,

Julian." She took his hand in hers and closed her eyes. The current that passed through her burned and affirmed and calmed him.

"You know," Julian said with a tightness in his throat. "I don't believe any of this. I'm just looking for a nice quiet place, someplace where people won't bother me and I can gather myself."

Bridget smiled and shook her head. "Yes, the improbable is always possible if that makes you feel better."

Julian picked up his duffle bag and took his first steps. His world had changed, had shifted. He did not look back at his friend, could not look back – at anything ever again.

Chapter Five

He walked for several miles, but the sun and the bite of the sea breeze made the walking easy. At the crest of a high hill, Julian saw a small village in the distance. Heather and laurel grew in abundance along the road leading down to it and the countryside's countless shades of green were shocking. Each pasture had its own version and vied in unruly competition with its neighbors.

The rich odor of wet grass, leaves and heavy black soil was oddly comforting. He moved along at a steady pace, hurrying neither his arrival nor his departure.

He entered the village well before noon. A squat building that looked newly minted rose up on his right flanked by a small pond. The sign above the front door marked it as the police station with the Gaelic words Garda Síochána. A short distance beyond, Julian noticed that the main portion of the town began.

The central dirt road became broader and was lined with clapboard storefronts. It was a place unencumbered by city planning or urban development specialists. The buildings were of strangely similar construction, but style was another matter altogether.

A stark white building rose up on Julian's right. No name or number marked the building, but there was no mistaking what it was. A large golden caduceus was painted on the front window. Julian was familiar with the medical symbol, but the intertwined snakes on this one seemed somehow more aggressive than the benign versions he had seen before.

Across the dusty road, opposite the doctor's office, was O'Gavagan's Pub. Julian tried the door. Locked. Next to the pub was Flynn's General Store, also shuttered and locked. On the other side of the street, next to a repair shop, was an institution painted all in black called Mulherin's Pub. Again, locked.

Julian noted movement in a shop marked Apothecary next to Flynn's Store. He opened the door, walked in and the tinkle of a small bell announced his arrival. He heard hushed voices from the back of the store and two women of identical appearance made their way through a curtained doorway behind the counter.

Both women were dressed in long black skirts and short black jackets, over dazzling white blouses. Each wore her hair in an identical bun arrangement and each had a small silver watch pinned to the left breast of her jacket. They were as old as you would expect people dressed in such a way to be. They looked at Julian and smiled without warmth, but with a great deal of interest.

Julian trotted out his most winning smile and asked, "I was wondering if there was a boarding house or inn here in town or if you ladies would know of anyone who might rent me a room."

"Oi'm sure we wouldn't know of such things," one of the twins sniffed.

"Oi suppose you could ask the Lord Mayor," the other added. "Although finding him and finding him sober may be two different things Oi'm sure," the first one noted curtly.

Julian smiled his thanks and backed out the door. Next to the apothecary was another pub bringing the total to three, two of which were called O'Gavagan's. A livestock feed store rounded out the commercial section of town.

The rest of the village was a jumble of houses with brightly painted doors, thatched roofs and much that needed repair. A shutter on this property hung at an acute angle, a fence on that one had grown tired and lay down in the street. The owners of these houses seemed to believe that, as with anything in life, something should always be just a bit out of place. Nothing had a right to be perfect.

Children playing in their respective yards and the main road stopped and stood in stunned silence at the sight of Julian.

Children had never been his strong suit. He always felt benign disregard was the best policy when dealing with them. For their part, the village children could not help but scrutinize his every move as Julian worked his way up the street.

He navigated the main thoroughfare and then followed some of the small lanes. A curtain would move in the breeze, a door would squeal on its hinges. All the while the children continued to follow this new specimen at a safe distance. At the far end of the village stood a Catholic church and standing adjacent was a rectory, another small attractive home and the village school.

The church seemed slight in size but sturdy in construction. The native stone of the structure rose from the ground and launched a stately spire ending in a heavy belfry. The building was laid out in the cruciform shape prescribed for Catholic churches of the era.

Heather surrounded the lower portion of the building and drifted away to a lush lawn sculpted and maintained with care. St. Michael's – Mass Daily a sign proclaimed. Julian smiled thinking in a village of this size anyone who did not know the name of the church or that mass was a daily event would, in all likelihood, be going to hell anyway. Julian had been a Catholic at one time. He understood these things.

He tried the front door to the church and found that it moved on well-oiled hinges. He knew the children would not follow and he wanted to sit and collect his thoughts. The door closed behind him and he was enveloped by the darkness of the vestibule. The rich smell of incense and old wood filled the air.

Out of habit, he dipped his finger tips into the holy water font, crossed himself and made his way to the far end of the back pew, genuflected and took a seat. Old habits die hard and some never really die at all, but simply sleep.

The air was still and cool. A candle burned in the sanctuary. Dozens of votive candles burned in front of two plaster saints, one on either side of the transept behind the altar rail. In one niche stood a rather martial looking St. Michael Archangel, patron saint of the church; in the other stood the statue of the Virgin Mary looking kind, thoughtful and a bit sad as always.

The sights, the smells, the pervasive silence all seemed familiar to him even though he hadn't been in a church for over twenty years. He smiled as he looked at the altar steps and remembered his days as an altar boy. Fragments of Latin returned to him.

Mea culpa, mea culpa, mea maxima culpa. Through my fault, through my fault, through my most grievous fault…

He had heard nothing, seen nothing. He had no reason to feel he was anything but alone, but Julian felt a presence nearby. Consternation twisted his features as he tried to stop himself from saying, "Reading minds, Father?" Julian said it softly. This church inspired a soft tone. He turned and found an old, wizened priest looking at him with a knowing smile.

"Ach, nothin' of the sort. A stranger sitting in church with a smile so serene as to make the angels envious – ah, now there is a man who is remembering a part of his past with fondness."

"It's true. I was remembering and it was with fondness and, yes, it was a very long time ago," Julian said. "It was not my intention to intrude."

"Intrude in the house of God is it? Nothing could be less likely."

Julian rose and with an outstretched hand approached the priest. "My name is Julian Blessing."

The old priest took the offered hand in his and with remarkable strength greeted Julian. "Oi don't recall a family of Blessings around here, but then Oi am a relative newcomer. Oi only arrived in 1960."

"My people aren't Irish, Father."

"It is none of my business, and feel free to tell me if Oi'm being meddlesome, but what brings you to our village? It can't be the wonders that are St. Michael's Church."

"Oh, I'm just taking a walking tour of this part of Ireland." Julian knew the priest saw that for the lie it was. Julian tried to recover by handing the priest his map. "I'm headed here," indicating a spot.

The priest's smile started at the eyes and infected his entire face. "Walkin' tour of Ireland, is it? Is that a fact? If you are headed for that wee ink spot on your map, then Oi welcome you to Cappel Vale and to St. Michael's. My name is Father Fahey. You have arrived, son."

"Are you sure, Father? This is it?" Julian didn't mean to sound incredulous.

"Mr. Blessing, is it Glocca Morra you were expectin'? In that case, Oi would suggest you get your good self a new map or some strong drink. Sadly, we are all that you'll find under that little fly speck for miles in every direction."

"Father, honestly…"

"Honesty, is it? Now wouldn't that be a grand place to start – for a change." The old priest's eyes were alive with mischief, he had Julian on the ropes, and both men knew it.

"No really Father, I wasn't looking for anything in particular. I just had that map and that spot. I had no idea what I would find here."

"Ah, well then, you'll be a happy man indeed because you have found nothing in particular. We pride ourselves on that actually. We have an overabundance of nothing. In fact we're thinking about exporting it to the wider world."

Julian determined this was a line of conversation that was going to lead him nowhere worthwhile. He changed the subject. "There are very few people on the street, Father. In fact I didn't see anyone except the children."

"Most of the men are off to the fields," the priest continued smoothly. "The women are making themselves busy inside before noon Mass and the little ones are nearly always left to their own devices to cause what devilment they may.

"Have no fear though. The entire village knows you're here. Jungle drums, you know," and the priest winked conspiratorially.

"Father, I was wondering if you would know of a boarding house or someone who would rent me a room for a few days. The ladies at the pharmacy, sorry, apothecary, said I should find the Lord Mayor, but I thought you might know of something."

"Lord Mayor is it! That's rich. No one can say the Hackett sisters don't have a sense of humor for all their craziness. Lord Mayor! Now that is choice.

"Thomas Cahill is marginally the mayor of our little village. He has the job because no one else would do it and now he can't get rid of it. He votes against himself every election, but it does him little good so he has embraced his fate. He would be the first to tell you that his is an awesome responsibility, which is why he is usually taken with the drink.

"Still, Oi suppose if anyone would know of a suitable place it would be our good Mayor.

"Follow the main road until you come to the first house. There you will find the Hagan. She will know where our Mr. Cahill is to be found. If you value your life, however, don't mention that 'Lord Mayor' business or that you talked to me.

"Is that the time? Oi must get ready for Mass. Feel free to attend, Mr. Blessing. You can even keep this last seat in the last pew. God can see you just fine even there."

"That is very kind of you, Father. Perhaps another time."

"Perhaps," the priest said and his face ignited into another smile as though he knew a secret that Julian would tumble to in time.

"By the way, Father, who is the Hagan?"

"Oh, that you'll learn soon enough, and may God have mercy on your soul" said the priest as he scuttled away.

***

At the first house he came to, peat smoke curled from the chimney and Julian felt that this indicated a social call would not be ill timed. He approached the door of a small tidy home. As he walked up the fieldstone path, he noted that some of almost everything was growing in the yard. All the other houses and businesses he had passed had window boxes. Many had lush vegetable gardens, but this was an unconditional riot of vegetation.

Julian set his shoulders, dropped his duffle bag beside him and straightened his jacket. Taking a breath, he knocked. His simple knock on a rustic door opened the gates of hell.

The door fired open and before him stood an older woman whose eyes, pale gray and hard, burned into him. It was difficult to determine the precise age of the householder.

'Older' was all that would fill the bill. The curtains were drawn and a layer of thin smoke floated on the air inside the house obscuring all and giving an ominous aspect to everything within.

"Good morning, Ma'am. I thought you might be able to direct me to Mr. Cahill."

"Liar!" she snarled, as she looked Julian up and down. The croak of her voice was like a rifle shot and her features were as sharp as her voice and as penetrating as her eyes.

"Sorry?"

"Indeed you are. You are also a liar. That nasty little priest told you to come see 'the Hagan'. Don't lie to me again or I'll cuff you on the ear hole, ya eejit!"

"Well, I suppose that is what he said, but he didn't say it unkindly," was all Julian could muster.

"It is my hope that the gods save us from all priests. Yes, and other eejits!" the Hagan exclaimed.

"Yes, well anyway, I was told the Mayor would be able to direct me to some type of lodging..."

"You saw the barracks house as you entered the village this morning." It wasn't a question and neither was her knowledge of Julian's movements since entering Cappel Vale.

"Barracks house?" Julian asked as he tried to translate the word into something he recognized. He received a withering look for his efforts.

"The building that says Garda, ya eejit!"

"Oh Garda – the Police Station. I see, yes."

"And I see you are a bit thick headed. Go there and stay. The Mayor will be along."

Hell's gate closed in Julian's face. He was glad she was gone and with the fear she would return still roaring in his ears, he made his way to the police station to await the Lord Mayor's pleasure.

Perhaps the station was far enough away from the Hagan and its walls thick enough and its Gardaí beefy enough to afford him some protection from her, but he doubted that sort of safety existed anywhere on earth.

As he walked toward the police station Julian tried desperately to convince himself of something. The last thing he wanted to acknowledge was the first thing that came to mind. "No, it couldn't be. Not possible. No one could be that unlucky. Nah, I'm just tired. It's been an emotional day. Yeah, something like that," Julian thought to himself.

***

The police station was the sturdiest building in Cappel Vale. Solid, square, and made of a gray-green stone, it was of obvious government design. The words Garda Síochána were picked out in gold on a finely finished board painted black. A flagstone path led to the building's only door.

He knocked and when his knock was met with silence, he opened the door. The single room was remarkably spacious. Three cells stood to his left. One of the cells had its door removed and had been curtained off from the adjoining cells to make sleeping quarters, presumably for the local constabulary. The sleeping area was furnished with a chair, a bench at the foot of a full sized bed and a dresser. There was a modern bathroom beyond. Against the far wall in the main room there was a large stone fireplace.

A desk of utilitarian design and Government issue sat nearly in the middle of the room. A nameplate on the desk announced "Desk Sergeant."

In front of the fireplace sat two new rocking chairs separated by a low table. The fireplace had never been used and the entire room was free of dust of any kind. It wasn't so much that the room was empty; it was as though it was waiting someone's arrival.

Julian sat in the desk sergeant's chair and could see clearly up and down the main street by turning his head slightly and looking through the windows on either side of the front door. He had left the front door open to announce his presence to any and all passers-by.

***

"He is a strange one to be sure."

"Is that a bad sign? Bad for us? A good sign then? I thought you could tell when, well, you know..." the Mayor said.

"Tell? There was a time I could. But that was one of the first things I lost. Too soon to tell about much, but have a care. That one, it is lost he is right now, but when he finds his way that will be a different matter," said the Hagan. "He is capable. No special talent needed to see that."

"Capable of much good or much bad?" the Mayor asked.

"We shall see. Good I think. He is stumbling right now and so, likely to knock things over in his clumsiness," the Hagan answered. She looked and felt tired.

Julian had been preoccupied by the Hagan's pronounced sharp features and her pale gray eyes, but now in the kerosene light without the shawl over her head, she was a woman out of the ordinary.

Unruly hair combined with ivory skin to imbue her with a sensuousness that was at odds with her stern and startling bearing. She was possessed of an intelligence no one would dare doubt and a type of beauty no one could explain.

"We'll just have to keep an eye on him, won't we?" the mayor said.

The Hagan continued with a statement of fact. "What do you know about anything? You're drunk."

"Oi am always drunk. Oi can't remember a time when Oi was ever fully sober. Saints above, what a world it would be if Oi ever had to be completely sober. Life wouldn't be worth living. Oi suppose Oi should go see him."

"Let him stew awhile. I have some thinking to do so sit and eat your oatmeal. I'm hoping the raisins I put in it may absorb some of that alcohol."

"Oatmeal is it? Oatmeal you may call it but I know what is really in your heart, woman. You'll be the death of me with all your rapacious demands, but Oi suppose you can't help yourself. The power of me office is a potent aphrodisiac."

"Shut up you old fool," Moira Hagan said. "If they were giving you away with free mackerel for life there's no one who'd have the offering. I've put up with you as a friend for over thirty years. Count yourself lucky." She smiled and a softening came into her face and eyes.

Chapter Six

Shadows lengthened as late afternoon turned to twilight. Groups of men entered the town talking in the subdued voices of men who had put in a full day's labor. These were workingmen for whom there was seldom any real hurry. Life, they knew, was best met head on and with a steady, tireless pace.

Greetings were exchanged and good-natured banter ensued as someone approached the men from the opposite direction. Footsteps neared the flagstone path leading to the front door of the police station. Julian sat behind the desk and waited.

A ginger haired man in his 60s in a suit and tie with a bowler hat and a satin sash running across his chest like a bandolier filled the doorway. The Mayor of Cappel Vale, all five foot four inches of him, actually took up a fair bit of space. He peered into the gloom of the police station like a myopic bat until his eyes lighted on Julian.

"Ah, sur, it is full of apologies Oi am. The press of business kept me busy all the day and even then, Mrs. Hagan neglected to tell me of your presence. It was a good talking to Oi was after givin' her for this oversight."

Julian could smell the whiskey coming off the Mayor from across the room.

"I am glad you could make the time to see me, Mr. Mayor."

The Mayor beamed and seemed to draw on hidden resources to push him to a full height of five foot five inches.

"And who would it be me honor to address?"

"My name is Julian Blessing."

"Blessing. Blessing. Oi believe there may have been a family of Blessings in the village of Flicks, but that was many years ago."

"My people are not from Ireland. I am just visiting."

"It is odd visiting you would be doing to find yourself in a place like Cappel Vale. You may have noticed we are not exactly the sun and fun spot the Western World claims we are."

Julian smiled as the Mayor continued. "Mrs. Hagan – the poor dear woman is distraught over the tongue lashing Oi gave her – mentioned you were in need of accommodations in our little village. Oi must tell you that nothing springs immediately to mind, but if you would like to repair to me office, mayhaps a thought will come to me. Leave your things here and come along with me."

Shadows had lengthened into night and a chill was in the air. Julian picked up his jacket and towering over the Mayor, the two headed up the narrow main street now lit from the edges by the lights of the village pubs and cottages.

"We'll go to O'Gavagan's and a lovely pub it is too," the Mayor said as he took off his sash and folded it neatly before depositing it in his suit coat pocket.

"Which one?" Julian asked.

"Which one what?" the Mayor answered.

"O'Gavagan's Pub – which one? I noticed there were two."

"Doubtless you noticed there are a number of such establishments in our small village. Some of the village people congregate at O'Gavagan's Pub while another group gravitates to the other O'Gavagan's Pub. Still others will be seen at Mulherin's Pub."

Confused, Julian looked for clarification. "There are two pubs…"

"Well there are three pubs actually, but let's not quibble."

"Three pubs and two of them are named O'Gavagan's. Are they owned by brothers or something?"

"Lord, no," the Mayor chuckled good-naturedly. "If they were owned by two brothers one would be Tom's and t'other would be Sean's don't you see?"

"Well then, who owns O'Gavagan's?"

"O'Gavagan does. Pardon my sayin' so, but I was led to believe you might be somewhat brighter than this, lad. And wasn't it I who defended you when Mrs. Hagan said you might be an eejit of some sort?"

Julian knew there had to be sense hidden somewhere in the Mayor's logic, but he would be damned if he could find it. "So the same man owns two pubs and each one is called O'Gavagan's. Then if someone were to say, 'I'll see you at O'Gavagan's' how would either know where to go?" Things were becoming murkier by the moment and Julian found himself looking increasingly like the idiot others claimed him to be.

"Forget O'Gavagan," the mayor said. "He doesn't matter. What does matter is which O'Gavagan's one goes to after a long day of physical labor.

"Some families have gone to one O'Gavagan's for decades and would never think of stepping foot into the other O'Gavagan's. Anyone who knows you knows your family and knows which O'Gavagan's is yours. Then again, there are those who frequent Mulherin's. They would rather be found dead in a ditch than in either of the O'Gavagan's even though O'Gavagan might be a distant relation. It is all a matter of who you are, who your people are. Don't ya see?"

"So which of the pubs do you frequent?"

"Oi'm the mayor. Oi have to spread me patronage around lest Oi be seen to play favorites."

Julian felt that somehow there was an odd reasoning at work in all of this and so followed the little mayor into the first pub they found. It was called O'Gavagan's.

***

O'Gavagan's was a spacious room with dark wood on the walls and floor. The bar itself was nearly black with age and the top was polished to a glass-like finish. A turf fire burned in the fireplace and the smell of peat smoke and pipe tobacco wafted in eddies throughout the room.

Village men and women crowded all the tables and children ran around any open floor space. The babble of voices ran the range from quiet conversation to raucous laughter. This was Cappel Vale's answer to prime time television. The community drew together, talked, listened, laughed, shared, ate occasionally and even drank a little.

The Mayor entered the pub and approached the bar while Julian secured the door. He turned and managed one step into the room before all noise stopped and all eyes turned to him.

The Mayor called out, "God bless all here. Now get back to your business!" and that, much to Julian's amazement, was exactly what happened.

The Mayor handed Julian a pint of beer and said, "Pay the man. Oi've gone off and left all me money at home." He then picked up two pints for himself and headed for a vacant table in the deepest corner of the pub.

Once seated Julian tried to get right back to the point, "Mayor Cahill, I've been told that you can direct me to a place where I might find room and board. I am willing to pay of course."

"To be sure. Oi've been giving this more than a little thought. We are a small village and of boarding houses, we have none. Oi do have a thought though Oi don't know how it will be received by your fine self.

"No family has a room to spare though Lord knows they could all use the money, but there is one entire building sitting unoccupied at the edge of town. We could arrange with one or two of the village women to provide you with a light supper per day for a modest fee. Any other food or drink you may require could easily be taken care of by one of the three establishments we have for such purposes."

"That sounds ideal. How much do you suppose the owner would want for rent?"

"Rent is it? Oi wouldn't worry about rent. It has all been paid for by the good citizens of the Irish Republic." The Mayor took Julian's look of confusion for one of interest and continued.

"I'm speaking o'course of the police station."

Julian's mild confusion turned to stark befuddlement.

"Jimmy Grogan!" The Mayor bellowed and a red headed boy of seventeen appeared.

"Jimmy, this is Mr. Blessing. He will be staying with us out at the police station. Run there, get a fire started and the hot water tank up and runnin'. Then lay some peat in so he'll have some extra to throw on the fire as needs be.

"Mr. Blessing's things are already there and if you, Jimmy Grogan, disturb any of them Oi'll take a stick to your worthless back and your father – God rest his soul – would be thanking me for it too.

"Mr. Blessing, give young James here a coin. Off you go Jimmy and do as I say."

The boy took the coin, bobbed his head and was gone.

"When you get back to the station, go through your things and make sure none of 'em are missing. Jimmy Grogan is a notorious thief, but bright and will follow directions up to a point."

"Mayor Cahill, how can this be alright with the police? I mean I can't just take up residence in their station. It doesn't seem reasonable."

"It stands like this, Mr. Blessing. This being Ireland, reason has very little to do with it." The Mayor made a show of clearing his throat. "Oi would be happy to tell it to you of the matter, but me throat has gone powerfully dry it has. Be so good as to fetch us a few more pints."

Julian hadn't touched his, but the Mayor had dispatched both of the ones sitting in from of him.

Julian returned and set two more pints in front of the Mayor.

"What a good man you are! Well then, as Oi was saying, in their infinite wisdom the research branch of the Garda Síochána decided there was not enough of a police presence in this part of the Republic. They'd after be sayin' somethin' about community policing, although Oi'm not at all sure just what that means. They'd made noise, but we thought nothing of it. Then without a word to us they arrived one day with heavy equipment, building materials, and workmen and proceeded to take a month to erect that lovely station."

"They appointed said police station as you have seen it. They then discovered three small facts that had been overlooked during the planning phase."

"First, we have no need of representatives of the Garda Síochána. The occasional dust up, some cattle or sheep thieving and some school boy pranks, but nothing that would take a police force to handle. Oh, there was the time when Lawrence Donnelly tried to rob Flynn's store with a hammer. I can tell you, walking into a store with a hammer is an exceptionally bad idea when the stock in trade of the store in question is hammers and the owner is a man who isn't afraid to use them. It ended in tears of course.

"Second, the Garda could find no group of lads who would work in our little corner of paradise and third, the Garda didn't have the money to pay salaries and expenses even if they could find someone daft enough to take the job. Slight oversights all, I'm sure.

"That is how we came to have a police station without the policemen who usually inhabit such establishments. It really is the best of all worlds," the Mayor said as he finished his fourth pint.

Julian still had only sipped his, but he went to the bar and returned with another beer.

The Mayor looked dejectedly at the lone pint but became resigned to his fate.

"Mayor Cahill, I have operated in the business world all my working life. On the one hand, I wouldn't feel right about taking advantage of your offer gratis. On the other hand, I know nothing is ever gratis. What is it you want in return?"

"Ah, but you are a man of affairs and a man of the world. Oi could see it right off. In faith, Oi have no idea what rent to ask. I'm sure we will be able to work something out. What do you have?" the Mayor asked. "And don't say money. We are a poor, sad village and you could doubtless buy the lot of us and put it on your credit card.

"No, your money has very little value here except for the occasional pint. Oi'm sure Flynn, for one, down at the store would be happy to be off the barter system and go to hard currency. For the most part your money is not an inducement, however, as Oi say, Oi'm sure we will be able to work something out.

"With that, I wish you pleasant dreams. I will be making my way home. It would seem you are bad company because you have got me terribly drunk," the little man concluded and lurched to his feet.

As the Mayor headed one way, Julian turned toward the police station. Lamplight issued from the windows and smoke rose from the chimney. Jimmy Grogan was nowhere to be seen.

Julian followed the Mayor's advice and quickly sorted through his few belongings in the duffle bag. Everything seemed to be accounted for. Julian sat before the fire and in time nodded off to sleep. His last thoughts were of the Mayor's parting words.

"I'm sure we will be able to work something out." Slightly ominous, but Julian had handled ominous things before and had always won. He wondered what there was to win this time.

Chapter Seven

"You!"

From a sound sleep, Julian bolted out of his chair. The fire had gone out and the room was chilled and now occupied by a woman who seemed intent on ruining his day.

"You!" she spat out again.

Standing at the door was a woman of middle height, slim and in her early thirties with soft chestnut colored hair. She was dressed out of character for the village in dark slacks and a tan silk blouse.

"Attractive if she weren't breathing fire," Julian thought as his mind began slowly gathering data and his other senses came online.

The woman was framed in the doorway as bright sunshine washed in behind her. The force of her personality struck Julian of course, but there was something else. She seemed decisive, professional and accustomed to making hard decisions quickly.

There was nothing pretentious or squeamish about her though her femininity was undeniable. Nerve impulses fired throughout his brain at breakneck speed, encapsulating his observations in less than a second.

For reasons he could not explain, Julian found himself thinking about this young woman in ways wholly inappropriate to the situation. He could not remember ever having been drawn to a woman so spontaneously – or so stupidly. He tried to will himself to concentrate but it wasn't working all that well.

"Are you deaf or just an eejit? And don't you be glarin' at me or it is sorry I'll make you," the young woman barked at him and took a step closer.

Her accent was different from that of the villagers. The one point of commonality between the Hagan, this woman and no doubt the villagers at large was their liberal use of the word eejit in conjunction with the name Julian Blessing.

"I'm sorry, how can I help you?" Julian tried to ask in a reasonable tone, although his voice sounded thick and gravelly. The room felt like it was getting stuffy and confined. He was as hot as a mouse in a wool sock.

"'How can I help you', is it? I'll tell you how you can help me. You can stop trying to seriously maim the children of this village. You are responsible for the grievous bodily injury of a young boy. Do you know Jimmy Grogan? Well, you nearly killed him you stupid man!"

"What are you talking about?

He continued with an edge to his voice that he did not intend, "I met Jimmy last night at O'Gavagan's. I never even spoke to him." Julian had no idea who this woman was – a relative perhaps? A teacher? He had no idea what she was talking about. He had no idea of how he had nearly killed anyone. He was fresh out of ideas.

"You gave Jimmy Grogan a deadly weapon and he managed to nearly sever two of his fingers. He could have bled to death if someone hadn't found him. It is that kind of thoughtlessness and stupidity that infuriates me."

"Deadly weapon? I gave Jimmy a little money for starting a fire here. What deadly weapon? Please start from the beginning. I really don't know what you are talking about."

The woman's features hardened from simple anger to deadly fury. Her hazel eyes turned pitiless as they narrowed. She took a step further into the police station as she shouted, "You gave Jimmy Grogan a bloody great knife and he damned near cut a couple of his digits off you immense fool! How many times do I have to say this?"

The conversation with the Mayor the night before raced through Julian's head. He moved quickly to the desk, snatched up his duffle bag and emptied the contents of the bag onto the desktop. With eyes and hands, he quickly inventoried the contents. The Swiss Army Knife was missing.

The woman in the doorway watched as a slow comprehension inched its way into her mind. It was too late now to turn back. She was nearly certain she had made a mistake, but there was nothing to do but to see how it played out.

"Listen," Julian said, "the Mayor sent Jimmy over here last night to get a fire going. Mayor Cahill told me to look through my things, as Jimmy was known to, well, borrow items from time to time. I did take a quick look around and I honestly didn't notice the knife was missing. Even if I had, I don't know that there was anything I could have done."

Julian made a gesture of haplessness. "Where is he? I'll just wash up some and go see him right now," Julian continued. "Maybe we can take him to a local hospital where he can get the right kind of care."

"Not another step will you take," she stated with force, but the fire was gone. Still, something he said rankled. She could see it all clearly now though. Jimmy had stolen the knife. It was just the sort of thing he would do and had done many times and probably would do all his life.

She looked at the target of her rage. He was perspiring and seemed short of breath. She noted that and intensified her examination.

She saw a tall man with dark hair shot with gray at the temples. His deep set eyes were a silvery blue tending toward gray, warm and kind. He seemed the sort of man one could confide in and who could be trusted to keep confidences. She noticed his high cheekbones, straight strong jaw and sensuous lips.

She was near enough to see that when he gestured his hands were strong and expressive. The woman felt a long forgotten warmth wash over her as her gaze continued to take him in.

She shouted silently to herself, "What in the name of God do you think you're doing? You must be mad. These are not the thoughts to be having now of all times."

Julian's visitor said with less intensity than before, "You will keep your distance from him and I shall advise every family in this village to keep their children away from you." This last was added for effect. She had no intention of following through on the threat, but she'd reached a point where there was no graceful way of extricating herself.

This stranger was innocent of all the things of which she had just accused him. She knew it and she was pretty sure by now he knew it too. Still, he wasn't innocent of everything and judging by the shortness of her own breath, she wasn't either.

She walked to the station's wooden desk. The knife was in her hand and the blade open. She buried the tip of the blade in the desktop, turned, and strode through the doorway slamming the door behind her. She felt mortified as she walked down the fieldstones and into the street. She decided since Jimmy Grogan hadn't died of his wounds she would kill him for putting her in this awkward position

***

Julian studied the closed door and wondered what had just happened. He reflected, "A bit volatile but damned attractive. Even an eejit can see that," and he exhaled heavily remembering he had sworn off women forever – for the time being. "Time for a cold shower or to go for a walk," he said aloud.

***

More than anything, Julian wanted to know if the woman in the doorway would make good on her threat. At any moment, he expected mothers to rush their children indoors at his approach.

It didn't happen. A sizable number of young children followed him at a discreet distance. Not as discreet as yesterday, but still an acceptable distance.

Father Fahey met Julian along the way, greeted him warmly, and walked with him up the main road and through the warren of cottages.

"Jimmy Grogan was injured last night," Julian said flatly.

"So Oi understand. He stole the knife and hurt himself foolin' around with it. There t'wasn't anything you could have done. Doctor Dwyer stitched him up and now we have to wait and see if there will be any nerve damage.

"Still, I shouldn't worry, Jimmy has nerves of steel and will be back to his thievin' ways before long," the priest said as he gave Julian a sidelong look. Father Fahey's blackthorn walking stick matched his pace perfectly as it struck the ground precisely at every third step.

"Don't you think it would be worthwhile taking Jimmy to a town with a hospital and top notch surgeons?" It was a mistake and he knew it as it left his mouth. He had said this to the woman who had been breathing fire in the police station. This time it sounded much worse.

Father Fahey cocked his head to one side and said, "Do you want your head handed to you boyo? If anyone in this village but me heard you say that, your teeth would be on the ground about now.

"Dr. Dwyer is like a saint to these people and they will not hear a word otherwise."

"I am sorry, Father. I meant no disrespect."

Before he could finish, Father Fahey cut in, "Oi know what you meant. You wanted the best for Jimmy, as do we all. What we know and you don't is that he has the best right now. Dr. Dwyer is top notch. There is not a hospital in all of Ireland, and a few outside too, that have not tried to add our good doctor to their staff. A finer physician and a finer person you will never meet."

"I'm sure that is true and I look forward to meeting the doctor. I'm sure he is an excellent physician." As Julian said this he glanced at the priest and noticed an odd, nearly cunning look about him, but having impugned the reputation of the village doctor, he didn't feel it would be wise to go looking for other hot buttons to press.

The two men continued to walk slowly through the village. Children would, from time to time, run up to the old priest and grab his cassock so that they could have their hair tousled by him or a cheek pinched.

Julian encouraged the priest to talk about Cappel Vale and its citizens. It was with melancholy and pride that he obliged.

"The village is dying. Farming and livestock here have been a way of life for many hundreds of years, but that is all changing. Cattle, sheep, crops and pigs are all expensive ventures and lack the lure of technology.

"The young people want to get away from here and the sooner the better. Many of these farms have been passed from father to son since time out of mind. Those days are finished now, I'm afraid."

"There is nothing to be done? There is always something," Julian said gently.

"Oi believe you are a kind man, Mr. Blessing, otherwise you would not ask a question you knew the answer to as clearly as I do. You did it politely and it did buoy my spirits for a moment, but sadly, the village of Cappel Vale will soon be no more.

"There simply is nothing to sustain it. But there's more. The people here are troubled in their minds. They all know the village will fall away soon enough, but that process is being hurried along."

"What do you mean?" Julian asked and concern etched his face.

"We've had a sudden spike in crime and some of it violent. Unusual for this part of Ireland. Acts of vandalism, mysterious digging in the area no one seems to understand. We've had a couple of rather vicious assaults and something else, but…" The priest considered.

"But?"

"Ach, it makes no difference to a man who is only visiting now does it? No matter, it will pass in time. All things do."

The priest talked of people he knew as no one else knew them. He talked of the gentle and the dull, the bright and the bold, the angry and the agreeable. There was no one in the village who could escape his acquaintance. With real warmth and depth of feeling, the priest painted a picture in broad strokes of the inhabitants of his portion of Ireland.

He talked of his early days, those he knew then and of those whose graves he tended now. He spoke of the living and the dead in a way only one who approaches life from the spiritual viewpoint can do.

All the time, Julian knew no real secrets were being given away. Everything he was being told was common knowledge. No violation of the confessional seal would take place today and Julian knew it never would. Secrets, real secrets, were safe with Father Fahey. Julian felt for the first time in his life he was talking with someone who could be trusted.

Julian was walking beside an old priest for whom trust was his world. He was no innocent though. Father Fahey knew people. Through his faith, he knew that people were at once frail and strong, dauntless and timid, calculating and innocent. He knew people and he managed with equanimity to love them all.

Julian asked about the woman who had accused him of giving Jimmy Grogan the knife, but received little information. A widow with a son who came from Dublin was all the priest would say.

"Tell me about the Hagan," Julian said and watched as a shiver passed through the priest.

"She is a witch of course, but then everyone knows that. If they didn't, the poor woman would be posting a signboard outside her door stating the fact. They say she practices the old religion and has the knowledge and powers that entails.

"Although Oi've never been able to confirm it, Oi believe she comes from one of the ancient families of Ireland. There'll be no 'Ach' and 'Oi' coming from one of those. She is frighteningly intelligent and well bred. She does everything in her power to hide it from view, but that kind of mind is impossible to hide – except in a place like this." The priest raised his eyebrows and smiled.

"Here there is almost no distance a'tall between a nimble mind and magic. We are funny that way."

"She knows things? Has powers?" Julian prompted and his eyes narrowed in concentration. He knew someone else like that. He would not have attached the title witch to Bridget Bragonier though. He would not have associated her with ancient religions either. "The Hagan," he thought to himself. "She fits the bill to a tee, I just haven't seen her caldron yet – but Bridget?" Things were falling into place in ways he did not want them to fall at all.

"Oh, know things she does. Oi wouldn't go so far as to say she predicts a thing will happen, but at some basic level, she simply knows it will. Oi have watched her from time to time as Oi watch any of my little flock. It isn't as though she 'sees' things either. Oi don't know what to call it really. The villagers say 'tis the Darna Shealladh. Oi don't hold with such things meself."

"You mean Second Sight," Julian said and knew instantly he had made another misstep.

The priest's face was darkened in deep concentration. "Mr. Blessing, Oi find it passing curious a man like you would know a thing like that." The priest's eyes were narrow and penetrating as he looked up into Julian's face.

"Oh," Julian began to back peddle. "I talked to a man once who knew something about it. I've probably also seen some mention of it in a book or brochure or something." Julian held his breath to see how far that explanation would get him. "Note to self – admitting to any knowledge of Second Sight is a distinctly bad idea you eejit. Admitting to knowledge of anything else doesn't seem to be working well for you either," Julian thought to himself.

Sarcasm dripped as Father Fahey said, "Or something, Mr. Blessing? Would that be the best you can do? Oi've been after hearin' confession for more years then you have teeth. You don't think Oi know when someone like your good self is being economical with the truth? Oi tell you, sor, you will have to improve mightily. Oi know school children that can out-lie you.

"No matter, that is something we'll discuss during your confession. Hopefully, you'll have concocted better lies by then. Still, we were talking about Moira Hagan.

"When something comes to her she is simply there – so they say. She doesn't see it happening; she is there while it is happening. Past or future, it seems to make no difference. Often times she comes away with fragments and nothing more. Other times she is able to produce details with alarming accuracy.

"The people of the village go to her. She is a witch for all seasons if you don't mind me bending that phrase. Sometimes they come so that she can find a missing sheep or to see who stole a goat. Sometimes they bring their children to her to be frightened.

"It's true. People need to be frightened from time to time. Sometimes they come to her for things they believe are too big or too small for Dr. Dwyer to deal with or meself or our school principal, Sister Eugenia, for that matter.

"The Hagan heals too – at least that is what the local people believe. Still, there is more to her than that. Oi don't know what it is and Oi don't want to know. The people here about believe, no, they know, she protects this valley. This troubles me and has for many years."

"But you don't believe in her ability?" This was an important conversation to Julian and he had to keep it going.

"She practices, as Oi said, the old religion and because of it, God has a soft spot in His heart for her."

Julian looked surprised.

"Do Oi believe? Oi believe she is here and there is no shakin' her loose. Oi believe she does good work in her own way, but that she has a robust dislike of Holy Mother the Church in general and priests in particular there is no doubt. Oi believe that God loves her as he loves all of us. Is there more in which Oi need to believe?" Father Fahey shrugged.

Very little additional information emerged and Julian was left with unanswered questions. By noon, the men found themselves in front of the police station again having toured the entire village twice.

"I would offer you tea, Father, but I've not laid in any supplies. I have many other questions," Julian said.

The priest smiled warmly, "Oi'll give you time to settle in and the next time Oi'm in the area Oi'll stop by for a visit and we can talk. But please, something a wee bit stronger than tea would be called for. Conversation is thirsty work." The corners of his eyes crinkled with mischief and Father Fahey continued down the main road and back toward St Michael's.

Julian sat in one of the rocking chairs and stared into the cold fireplace. His thoughts drifted and soon he was recounting all the firsts that had occurred during his day in Cappel Vale.

"First witch who may be more or not. First Lord Mayor. First time at facilitating a young man nearly cutting off some of his fingers. First time yelled at by an exceedingly pretty and exceedingly strange and angry woman. First time being followed by herds of children. First time being chastised by a priest for denigrating a village doctor," Julian thought.

"Overall," he thought, "things could be worse." He didn't doubt there would be more firsts but he hoped they would be better firsts.

***

When the door of the police station burst open, he was seated at the Desk Sergeant's desk studying his map.

"Sor, the Mayor says for you to come quick!" a ten-year-old boy shouted from the threshold.

"Why?" Julian asked.

"No time, sor. Just come quick to Mulherin's Pub! There's to be trouble with Sean Maher. He is with drink taken. The Mayor says you're the only man who isn't out in the field, and he needs all the help he can get. Besides you're the police." The clearly thrilled boy had gone at a run back up the street. Julian pushed back from the desk and picked up speed as he reached the road and followed the little boy to Mulherin's Pub.

CHAPTER EIGHT

A swarm of women and children had gathered and were peering in the windows of Francis Mulherin's establishment. The front door hung by its hinges at a sharp angle. Julian worked his way through the crowd and stood in the doorway.

A huge man stood against the bar and shouted, "So, ya little toad, you've called a filthy police constable!" as he pointed at Julian.

"Now Sean Maher," the Mayor began, "There is no need to be testy." Mayor Cahill was at the opposite end of the bar and gave Julian a beseeching look.

"I'm not from the police, Mr. Maher. I'm just a visitor," Julian said and with a remarkable grasp of the obvious noted the larger man was slightly drunk and built much like a rhinoceros. Even Julian, with only his book-learning knowledge of the natural world, understood an ever so slightly drunk rhinoceros was a very dangerous animal indeed.

"No, Sean. Mr. Blessing is the police. Don't listen to his denials. He is but a modest man. He lives in the police station as you well know…" The Mayor was cut short by simultaneous glares from Sean Maher and Julian Blessing. Their looks were filled with equal parts rage and disgust. The Mayor looked to Julian with deep pleading, but found little sympathy.

In the low, nearly inaudible voice he saved for business negotiations that had reached a delicate stage Julian sighed and said, "Please tell me the problem."

Sean Maher roared, "That is the problem!" and pointed at an old man cowering behind the bar. Francis Mulherin is the God rotting problem!"

"Mr. Mayor, are there some details Mr. Maher has left out?"

The Mayor swallowed hard. "Sean believes Landlord Mulherin here has watered his beer and thus is selling an adulterated product which Maher says is not fit for the beasts."

"Believes is it. Believes! Be God, Oi believe the lot of you would look better if Oi pulled your bloody heads off!" Maher took a step toward the Mayor and Julian interposed himself and smiled as he faced the big man.

Maher was a head and shoulders taller than Julian. The man's biceps were as large as Julian's thighs, he had no discernable neck. His hands were ideally suited for pulverizing stone or strangling cattle.

Julian did not move but called over his shoulder. "Mr. Mulherin, if you please? Pull me a pint, but don't top it off." The Landlord trembled and shook his head indicating that he would sooner drive a fork into his eye than meet the terms of what was being asked of him.

Julian faced the barman and repeated himself, turning a request into a demand and dropping the smile. Mulherin pulled a light pint and with trepidation pushed it across the bar toward Julian. The Landlord then jumped back and resumed his cowering. He seemed remarkably good at cowering.

Julian took the glass and raised it to look at the color. He then set it down and looked from Maher to the Mayor. Maher's look was one of smug, undisguised disgust. For the big man, watered beer was a sacrilege. It was the sort of unspeakable act whose reward could only be unprecedented violence.

The Mayor's eyes showed ferret-like quickness mixed with fear. His look told Julian this had better go the right way or things were going to turn ugly very quickly and that activity in the pub would turn vicious.

Julian pushed his shoulders back and lifted the pint. First, he plunged his nose into the glass and inhaled deeply. He set the glass down on the bar and exhaled. Maher's lip twisted into a snarl.

The crowd outside went silent.

Julian hefted the glass again and lifted it to his lips. The amber beer slanted as the glass touched his moth. He took a mouthful and seemed to chew the liquid all the while looking thoughtful, his eyes tight in concentration.

He swallowed.

Everyone waited.

The glass was gently set back on the bar.

Julian Blessing, the great Solomon of Cappel Vale, spoke.

"This beer is watered," Solomon said.

"HA! You milky bastard, Mulherin! Jaysus, Mary and Joseph! Even a feekin' policeman and not even an Irish one knows you watered your beer!" Maher barked.

"This is a serious offense Mr. Mulherin," Julian cut in, "and one that should not be dealt with lightly. For the next three days, or as long as it lasts, you are to serve your beer free of charge to any adult customer who comes into your establishment during your normal hours of operation. You can, of course, continue to sell your food and sundries as usual."

"You heard the police. You'll be ruined with everyone rushing in here to drink up all your nasty profits," Maher cried gleefully.

The Landlord's eyes turned into a squint as he calculated his potential losses. His forehead furrowed as he thought over the punishment. His eyes locked on Julian's as realization set in.

There would be no loss. Mulherin would close down both of O'Gavagan's Pubs as people flocked in for free watered beer. He would more than make up for his losses on the bar side from the profits on food and sundries. The entire thing was flawless. This policeman was a genius, something of which most policemen could not be accused. The Landlord made a note to find out what sundries were and then get some quickly.

With gratitude, the Landlord winked without changing his otherwise ashen appearance. He then closed his eyes looking every bit the broken man.

The crowd outside erupted in laughter and shouts.

Sean Maher did a drunken jig and began repeating the refrain of a song he had just recently created, "Mulherin is a bastard. Mulherin is a bastard, Mulherin is a bastard." It was a song short on lyric qualities, but sung with real feeling.

"But," Julian said.

Singing, dancing and laughter faded away and all waited for the words of the great Solomon, wellspring of all wisdom and lawgiver without equal.

"Even for watered beer it isn't half bad."

Pandemonium erupted outside as the crowd picked up where it had left off. Nothing had changed. Everyone got free pints and, by all reports, rather good pints at that. The Mayor slumped and smiled knowing that much tragedy had been averted.

"What! What do you mean not half bad!" For all the racket, it was hard for Julian to hear Maher over the bedlam. "It's watered beer. Do you know nothin'!" the big man roared.

"Mr. Maher, watered or not it was good enough to get you a little unsteady on your feet," Julian tried to shout above the crowd's raucous celebrations.

"Unsteady is it? I came into this rat hole of a pub in that condition. I'd been drinkin' at O'Gavagan's across the street most of the morning."

"Oh," said Julian before looking toward the Mayor. "Oh," was the last thing Julian remembered saying before his head bounced off the floor.

How he got to the floor was something of a mystery to him. He was vertical one moment and horizontal the next. What happened to cause this perplexed him. There was a roaring in his ears, but he assumed that was just the noise of the crowd. From this angle the wood planking on Mulherin's floor seemed remarkably straight, smooth, and only slightly uncomfortable to lie on.

That is what Julian thought before the floor faded into gray and then black as his eyes rolled back in his head.

****

Father Fahey and Sister Eugenia arrived at Mulherin's Pub and shouldered their way to the door through the now silent crowd.

The priest moved immediately to Julian's prone body. He felt for a pulse and finding one that was strong and regular, nodded to Sister Eugenia. The stately nun picked up Father Fahey's blackthorn walking stick, stepped over Julian and strode up to Sean Maher who had retreated to the end of the bar after having pole axed Julian.

The punch to Julian's head had been delivered to an area between his temple and his left ear. Sean Maher had delivered it at half speed and at half strength and was as surprised as anyone when Julian didn't see it coming and kissed the floor with what appeared to be real gusto.

At the nun's approach, Sean drew himself to his full height and towered over her. If he thought this either intimidated Sister Eugenia or afforded him some sort of protection he was much mistaken, but he would soon find this was not to be his only regrettable mistake with this nun.

"Did you do this?" the nun's diction was impeccable and the implied growl was palpable. She was a slight woman, but her bearing made her appear every bit as large as Sean Maher. She held the walking stick in her right hand and tapped it rhythmically into her open left palm.

"What do you mean, Sister? Oh that? Well, yes. Just a wee bit of horseplay. Ach, 'tis nothin' to get worked up about and that policeman would tell you the same. But you'll be excusing' me, Oi have to get back to the fields."

"You, Thomas Donnelly," the nun said never taking her eyes off Sean Maher's face. The runner who had brought word to Julian appeared. "Yes, Sister," said the boy as he ran to the nun's side.

"Liam McMaster employs Mr. Maher does he not?"

"Yes, Sister, he works for Farmer McMaster same as me Da," the boy said and began to suspect he was about to be given a starring role in this production.

"Good. Go tell Bobby McMaster's father that Sean Maher will not be able to return to work today. Go now and be quick."

"Now wait just one minute!" Maher bellowed.

When exactly the big man realized his error was hard to calculate. It could have been when the nun caught him behind the knees with Father Fahey's walking stick. Taking Maher's knees out dropped him to a convenient height so that the nun could take hold of his entire ear. That might have been a dead giveaway of the magnitude of the blunder Maher had made.

However, it surely must have dawned on him that something was amiss when she bent near to his face and with the sort of menace he had seldom heard, the nun said in a language he understood clearly, "You, Sean Maher, will come with me and it is sorry I will make you if you offer even the slightest trouble." She measured out each word with painful slowness. "Resistance will only embarrass you and shame your family in front of the entire village. Now, come along you great thug."

With the big man bent in half and the nun holding onto his ear like a limpet, Sister Eugenia walked Maher through the silent crowd. The beginning of a snigger was heard and the nun wheeled on a girl from the 6th grade class. Later in life, she would claim Sister

Eugenia had frozen the blood in her veins on the day Sean Maher knocked down the policeman.

Having quelled that, and any contemplated disturbances, the nun and her prisoner moved off toward the police station.

Father Fahey had two of the larger village boys remove what remained of Mulherin's front door. The priest and the boys then rolled Julian onto the door. Using it as a stretcher they too trotted off to the police station.

***

Julian woke slowly to a world devoid of all light and only a slight rustling sound of nearby movement. He had been undressed and found the bed covers tucked in tightly underneath him, pinning his arms to his sides. He made an odd gurgling sound and moved only slightly.

"Shhhhhh. You're to stay still." The voice was a woman's, soft, slow and gentle. It sounded dimly familiar to Julian.

The voice continued, "Do you know your name?"

"Of course I know my name," Julian said as he tried to sit again. "What I don't know is where I am or who you are or how I got here or what happened. How long have I been this way?" Nausea swept over him and he lay back on the bed exhausted by his efforts.

"You will just have to lay still for now. As for the other, politeness forbids me from speculating on how long you're been the way you are," the voice said and chuckled.

"Tell me the last thing you remember," the voice whispered.

"I was in Mulherin's Pub. I must have tripped on something. I don't remember falling down. I do remember my head hitting the floor, but that doesn't make sense and God, my head hurts." He tried to think more slowly and connect the dots one at a time, but his thoughts wouldn't slow down.

"It is true, you were in Mulherin's Pub, but you didn't trip." The Irish-English accent sounded musical to Julian. The voice continued, "You were knocked down. Sean Maher struck you. The room has been darkened and you have a compress over your eyes as a precaution."

"Precaution against what?"

"Well, a blow to the side of the head could have done nasty things to your eyesight temporarily, but, as easily, it could be far worse – a detached retina, although I seriously doubt that. You could have a concussion for all we know, but I doubt that too. There really is no way of knowing right now. Symptoms could show up immediately or a week later. Any punch delivered by Sean Maher is always serious business."

Julian tried to focus. It wasn't working. "If it's a concussion. I'm not supposed to go to sleep because I won't wake up. I heard that somewhere."

"Then you listen to odd things from even odder sources," the voice said softly. "Concussions happen when your brain violently bangs the inside of your skull. One of the primary symptoms of a concussion is fatigue.

"Your body," the voice continued, "is experiencing fatigue in order to tell you that your brain needs rest. Rest is, in fact, one of the best possible ways to treat a concussion.

"Not to worry though, we'll have you taken to a proper hospital where you can receive proper care from a top flight specialist," the voice said leaving acid in its wake.

"That's okay. I'll take Dr. Dwyer's opinion for what should be done. When can I speak with him?" Julian said.

Julian felt the woman move closer to him. Her voice became softer still and low as though she were sharing an intimacy. He could feel her breath on his ear and smell her hair. She whispered, "You are."

"Are what?" That voice, there was something about it. "Sweet Jesus!" He thought suddenly as he placed the voice. "She hadn't been whispering when she came to the station to tell me what an idiot I was!" He tried to sit up, but the doctor pushed him down.

"You have Dr. Dwyer's opinion for what should be done. I don't know if you noticed, but I am not a he," she said. My name is Ailís Dwyer, Doctor Ailís Dwyer if you like or Doctor Dwyer or just Doctor, whatever pleases you, Constable Blessing."

Julian tried to repeat the doctor's name. Doctor and Dwyer came out well, but the first name was a jumbled mess. His tongue was thick and his mind even more so.

"EYE-lish," Dr. Dwyer corrected. "You'll get used to it."

Julian weakly insisted he was not a policeman just before he lolled to the side and fell into a deep and dreamless sleep.

Dr. Dwyer smoothed back her patient's hair and then inspected again the lump on his head. She followed the contour of his cheek with her long fingers and admired the plane of his face, the broad forehead and the strong jaw. She smiled when she thought of her first encounter with him. She looked at his lips now and decided she was having decidedly undoctor-like thoughts again.

"You're a fish out of water, Julian Blessing, but a rather handsome fish I think," she said in a voice just above a whisper. The doctor smiled.

She moved from Julian's bedside into the station proper, drawing the curtain behind her. "Moira Hagan! What are you doing! You can't do that. Leave his things alone this instant," the doctor said. She was trying to keep her voice down. A whispered shout loses much of its power to persuade.

"Well, dear," the Hagan said, "what does it look like I'm doing? I'm searching the man's things. Fortunately, you kept him busy so I wouldn't be disturbed with my work. Don't worry yourself though, I'm nearly done. If you come help we'll be done all the sooner." The older woman was meticulous in her examination of Julian's belongings and had them spread over the entire top of the station's desk.

"You'll not get me mixed up in this outrage. The man is entitled to his privacy. Besides what difference does it make, he'll be moving on soon I'm sure," the doctor responded sounding indifferent to the matter.

"Will he?" the Hagan said and looked up sharply, "I have the feeling he will be with us for a while yet. That should please you some, eh?" As an aside the Hagan added with a pleasant smile, "By the way doctor, when did you decide to take up fishing, or is it still fishing if the fish is out of the water?"

Ailís Dwyer stiffened at the older woman's remark, but said nothing.

"You saw his shirt of course when you took it off of him – along with everything else. By the by, that's unusual treatment for a head injury, but then you're the doctor, aren't you, darlin'," the Hagan said pointedly and grinned.

Her hand rested on one of Julian's neatly folded dress shirts. "Now why do you suppose a man would tramp around Ireland in workman's clothes wearing a shirt that cost a workman's monthly wages?" the Hagan said thoughtfully. "And isn't it fun we'll have finding out the why of it and more importantly, the who of this Julian Blessing."

CHAPTER NINE

With a dull ache throbbing behind his eyes, Julian sat on the cot in Sean Maher's jail cell. The big man was a picture of wretched dejection. Earlier he had said he felt sure a pint of porter would lift his depression somewhat, but Julian remained adamant that they needed to concoct a plan before any pints would be consumed.

Maher wasn't good at making plans and felt this one flaw would leave him parched throughout eternity.

"Let's go over this again," Julian said softly.

Sean sighed. "That great brute of a bastard, Liam McMaster, has given me the boot and now Oi've no job and no one will hire me because Oi'm a convict and me wife and children will starve and I'll be forced to go to some filthy place like Cork where Oi'll be worked to death by a money grubbing bastard who is an even bigger money grubbing bastard than Liam McMaster."

Julian had to admit it had all the elements of a middling Shakespearian tragedy or a country-western song. It lacked literary force, but Maher's impassioned telling of the tale made up for that.

"You really have to stay away from depressing thoughts like that," Julian said.

"Why?" Sean asked. "I'm Irish, it's what we do best."

"Well, let's move along. What can you do?" Julian asked kindly. "If you had the choice, what would you like to be?"

"Oi've always worked in the fields. Oi don't know anything else. It was out of the school Oi was at an early age because Oi got into fights, Oi wasn't very smart, and the nuns hated me. Never trust a nun. They will do you unto death and never think twice about it and that's for sure."

"Sean, Sean, Sean, let's get back to the subject. If you could do anything you wanted, what would it be?"

Sean Maher had to give this some thought and the effort was wearing him out. He screwed up his face and bit his lower lip. He took deep breaths that would draw his massive shoulders up to his ear lobes. The exhalations were nearly as dramatic. In the end, he had to give the whole thing up. Thinking this through was beyond him.

"Oi'm just not smart like you Mr. Blessing."

"We went over this before, Sean. You can call me Julian and you are plenty smart. We just have to figure out the best fit for you.

"Why don't you go home to your wife and children? They've not seen you in three days and your sentence is up," Julian said.

Sister Eugenia had tried, convicted and sentenced Sean to three days in lock up. The nun had decided to go for the upper limits on the cruel-and-unusual-punishment scale by not allowing the prisoner any alcohol. It was the worst torture imaginable for Sean Maher. "Hard labor from a hard nun," he called it.

"Oi can't go home for the shame that is on me," Sean said.

"What shame? You did the entire village a huge favor."

"Oi brought shame on meself and all of me family, Mr. Julian."

"It's just Julian. Sean, it didn't happen that way. You discovered that Mulherin was diluting his beer. The entire village now knows he is a man who can't be trusted. All of that led to your fellow citizens being able to drink up all the pints they wanted for free for three days."

"True. True," Sean Maher said as he cocked his head and tried to look thoughtful once more.

"Of course it is true. Go home. Hug your wife, hold your children, and know that the entire village knows you for the hero you are. We've got to find you a job, but we'll figure that out later."

"Julian," Sean said as he rose from the cot, "about that pint? Mayhaps not a pint so much as a dram?"

Julian was distracted, but said at last, "Huh, no, do as I say and go home to your family. Then you can send someone to the pub to bring you back a pint. You're to stay out of pubs for awhile." As Julian spoke, the germ of an idea was beginning to sprout.

* * *

Liam McMaster wasn't an imposing man. He wasn't a smart or even a clever man. He was, however, cunning and as cunning men are wont to do, he was backing the winners and trashing those likely to lose.

"'Tis exactly as Oi've told you, m'Lord. The village has a constable and that eejit, Sean Maher knocked him down. Oi had the pleasure of firing Maher too. The man won't work again."

The Pale Man sat behind the desk and steepled his fingers as he listened to McMaster. He thought for a moment and then asked, "Not an auspicious start for the policeman. Who is this new constable? What is known about him? How did he come to be in the village?" His eyes narrowed and he continued, "What is his agenda? Why is he here and why now?"

The man's voice was cultured with barely discernable Irish English cadences. He was an Irishman, but one of substantial means, highly educated, well traveled and well read. He was a man who knew his business, a man who had secrets and a man who inspired fear.

McMaster should have guessed the pale man behind the enormous carved oak desk would have questions. Still, he was prepared to appear knowledgeable without actually knowing anything at all.

"M'Lord, these are all questions that have occurred to meself and Oi am busy getting to the bottom of 'em now. Oi will have answers shortly. Oi have spies throughout the village. Oi can tell you the man's name is Blessing."

That much was true, but the rest was a tissue of convenient lies. McMaster had no inside sources. He had overheard someone mention Julian's last name. McMaster was a man not at all well liked in the village. Even Father Fahey didn't like him and Father Fahey liked everyone.

Liam McMaster always felt Father Fahey was listening to him in the confessional, but only begrudgingly. It didn't really matter. McMaster made up the sins anyway for the benefit of the old priest and any parishioners who would see him enter and leave the confessional box. "Hell with 'em all!" McMaster thought, "'tis nothing but jealously that Oi am prosperous and they are dirt poor. That is why they all hate me."

This man behind the desk – that was different. If McMaster was prosperous, this man was wealthy beyond words. He had leased a large manor house some distance from the village and staffed it entirely with people from the big cities of Dublin and Wexford and Cork. The staff, McMaster knew, had instructions not to mix with the locals and that included him.

***

Julian slept late into the day and awoke with an appetite and a plan. He showered in what turned out to be quite a modern facility. He shaved, and quickly dressed with every intention of putting his plan in motion. His head still throbbed and when he closed his eyes lights still popped behind his eyelids. Still, things were looking up.

He opened the door and found a young man sitting on the police station's stoop. The young man seemed fascinated as he watched a bird in a nearby bush.

"What can I do for you?" Julian asked cheerfully, but the last word caught in his throat.

At Julian's feet sat a young man of perhaps seventeen. Handsome in every way and as big as a bull, the young man had a distracted smile and his eyes held the iridescence of a child. He hadn't suffered the ravages of living in this world because he lived in a world of his own. Julian saw this and more and he knew.

He sat down next to the young man and asked his name.

Through the obstacle of a pronounced stutter the boy said, "Brendan Maher."

"Would Sean Maher be your father?"

Julian winced as the young man worked on and finally forced the simple answer out.

"Yes," he said.

"Well, Brendan, you should be very proud."

"Me da got free beer for the village." Each word from Brendan's lips was an effort and each pulled at Julian. The boy capped his stumbling sentence with a child's smile.

"That's true. But far more than that." Julian glanced around conspiratorially before he looked into the simple handsome face and sparkling blue eyes of Brendan Maher, "More than that he is a good man and being a good man is one of the most difficult things to be."

There was a moment of incomprehension as though the words were somehow disconnected from their meanings. Then what was said seemed to settle in. Brendan sat up taller, pushed his broad shoulders back, and smiled with a pride beyond compare. A guilelessness unknown outside of absolute innocence illuminated the boy's face.

For all his life, it had been like this. Things were said, words spoken, but very few of them involved him. In Brendan's world things were simple if not always easy. Sometimes he had to try very hard to be good and not fight even when some of the village children tormented him for his simple ways.

The perverse delight children take in torturing their own, although well documented, is little understood. As real and as serious as children take their playing, they seem to take no heed of the damage they cause, and the damage they cause to the damaged is a cruelty beyond words. It flails alive those with scant defenses and bores into the marrow of those whose frailty is demonstrable.

The cruelty of children is Darwin's theory taken to the extreme – not only do the strongest survive and thrive, but they do so at the expense and heedless of the tears of the beautifully innocent.

"Brendan, I need to go up the street and visit someone. Will you be alright here?"

Brendan closed his eyes and pushed the words out one at a time again. "Should Oi sit here?"

"You can if you want. I might be gone for awhile though so make yourself comfortable."

***

The lush vegetation grew wild in the Hagan's front yard and Julian had to pick his way with care up to the front door. His knock had an authority he did not feel. The front door opened slowly and Julian glimpsed a back door on the opposite wall closing hurriedly before the Hagan came into view. Her strong, stark features looked out onto Julian and she let an uncomfortable silence hang in the air like drifting smoke.

"I would like to see the Mayor," Julian said. The Hagan could tell he wouldn't be put off as before.

"Would you? I've not seen him in," the left corner of her mouth twisted into something like a smile and her eyebrow arched, "awhile." She closed the door and left Julian steaming.

He knew what she meant. The Mayor had dodged out the back door only moments before and the Hagan's "awhile" meant anything from three days ago to three seconds ago.

Julian hammered at the door this time. It opened again with greater speed, but before she could speak Julian said, "My business is not entirely with the Mayor. I am here to see you."

Again, silence hung between them as she barred the door to her home. Her features softened, she turned her back and walked toward her turf fire.

"By all means then, come in. When our village constable wishes to see a citizen, why 'tis that citizen's duty to comply." She sat in a chair by the fire and indicated another chair to Julian.

"My business with you touches only slightly on my business with Mayor Cahill. I will catch – that is I will *find* him later when it is," and Julian paused, "convenient." It was his turn to arch an eyebrow and the Hagan smiled slightly and inclined her head.

***

An hour later, he returned to the police station and found a young boy sitting with Brendan Maher on the stoop. The boy was about twelve years old, had red hair sticking out from under his cloth cap and freckles across the bridge of his nose. The boy rose but indicated to Brendan that he should remain sitting.

The boy approached Julian. At a respectful distance, he stuck out his hand and announced that his name was Timothy, and that he was a friend of Brendan's. The boy's hazel eyes were clear and spoke of spirit and intelligence. To Julian, he couldn't quite place it, but there was something familiar about the boy.

"May I talk with you Constable Blessing, sor? It is regarding Brendan so you wouldn't mind if we stood over there, would you?"

Julian attempted to look suitably grave as he stifled a smile at the grown up language and manner of the young boy.

"Sor, did you tell Brendan to wait here for you?" The boy's manner was direct and efficient.

"No, Timothy, I did not. I told him I would be visiting with someone up in the village. He asked if he could sit on the stoop and I told him that he could and to make himself comfortable."

"Oi thought as much," Timothy said. "You see, sor, it sits like this. Brendan is me best mate in all of the world, but he is simple as you can see. When you said he *could* wait he understood that he *should* wait. It seems he waited too long though."

Timothy and Julian turned to look at Brendan who shot to his feet and as he did the matter became perfectly clear.

"He's pissed himself you see."

Indeed Julian could see a large spot on the front of Brendan's pants. Julian motioned for Brendan to sit down which the young man did.

To Brendan Maher the matter was a simple one. An important man in the village had told him he would be back. After fifteen minutes of watching a thrush in a thorn bush, Brendan became aware of a need. The important man would return soon and tell him it was all right to use the toilet in the station. He had told Brendan to make himself comfortable, but what if while making himself comfortable he missed the important man's return. These conflicting instructions played back and forth in Brendan's mind to the exclusion of all else.

After an additional thirty minutes with his fists clenched in excruciating frustration there was no choice. Brendan urinated on himself just as his friend Timothy spotted him from the road and waved. Brendan waved weakly back and Timothy approached and saw at a glance his friend's predicament.

"Oi'm sorry," Brendan had said to Timothy and tears had welled up in Brendan's eyes.

"'Tis nothing," Timothy responded and bumped up against his big friend. In an easy silence, they both sat and watched Julian approach the police station from the far end of the village. While they waited, these two friends watched the thrush in the thorn bush.

"It stands like this," Timothy said. "If you will sit with Brendan, Oi will run to the Maher house and get him some fresh trousers. Then he and Oi will walk home as Oi'm to have supper with the Mahers tonight. If Brendan doesn't change his clothes he will be in for no end of ribbing as we make our way home and frankly, he and Oi can't afford to get in trouble again for fighting."

Julian looked puzzled.

"Brendan and Oi get into fights because of the way he is and because we are best of friends. Oi don't often win. Oi never win really, but Brendan always does and he tells me Oi get too angry to win – oh, aye, and I talk too much."

Julian nodded his understanding and his approval of the plan and walked back to Brendan as Timothy ran up the street.

Brendan pointed out the thrush to Julian. Together they admired the small, plump, bird as she constructed her cup-shaped nest.

Before long, Timothy was back with a tote sack. Brendan went into the police station, and changed his pants. As the boys left, Julian told them that they were both welcome anytime. He also told the boys they were welcome to use the toilet in the station at any time. Julian had not moved from the station's stoop.

He thought to himself, "Knowing that would have made it easy for Brendan. I'll make sure he understands." As an afterthought, Julian called out, "Timothy, what is your last name?"

Timothy stopped in the street and answered, "Dwyer, sor."

Julian closed his eyes and slowly shook his head. "How many Dwyer families are there in this village?"

"Just us, Sor," Timothy said while cocking his head to the side. The boy had his mother's eyes and smile.

"Why doesn't that surprise me?" Julian thought. "Timothy, please tell your mother I am an eejit, would you?"

"Oi would never say you were an eejit, even if you were and Oi'd certainly never say it to me Ma."

"Oh she knows by now," Julian thought.

***

In the darkness from a position where he could see all three pubs, Julian sat and waited. Time was on his side.

Shambling down the street in the shadows, Mayor Cahill cut round a corner too quickly and clipped the end of a fence. After cursing the darkness for allowing such a thing to happen, he cursed the householder for living there, then moved on to the fence builders followed by the lumberjacks who cut and milled the lumber and finally the tree itself. He would have followed this line of reasoning further, but cursing God was a sin and it just brought bad luck. Besides, he had lost interest by then as he targeted O'Gavagan's Pub.

Straightening himself and squaring his shoulders, Mayor Cahill opened the door and the interior sounds of friendly voices spilled out into the street only to be muted again when the door closed. Julian smiled.

Within minutes, the pub's door was torn open and Mayor Cahill bellowed into the darkness like a wounded animal, "O'Gavagan, you are a rogue and no Christian!" Thomas Cahill drew himself up and marched with all the majesty his office could afford to the steps of Mulherin's Pub and Julian smiled again.

Moments later the mayor emerged. "Francis Mulherin is an even filthier scoundrel than O'Gavagan!" Cahill roared into the empty street. He staggered to the second O'Gavagan's only to discover the full impact of his predicament.

"The world is full of nothing but bastards! Not one of them will sell me a pint of ale or a thimbleful of whiskey. Why is God doing this to me?" Mayor Cahill's lamentations were painful to watch. They were painful for everyone except Julian Blessing who had now moved to a position within striking distance of the mayor.

"So, no one will sell you a drink." The Mayor had fallen heavily into a chair by the front door of the last O'Gavagan's. Julian's voice sent Cahill into a panic and he nearly escaped, but Julian got hold of the back of the Mayor's coat. "That seems to be a dreadful shame. Why do you suppose that is?" The sugar oozed in Julian's voice and the Mayor sat very still.

Julian continued. "You know, of course, why none of the pubs will give you a drink. Although I am paying them for not giving you a drink, they would have done it for free just to see you suffer. Cruel men are our local pub keepers, don't you think?"

"What is it that you want?" Julian had torn away the Mayor's only comfort and support in this life.

"The village needs a new constable. I'm not the man for the job. Tomorrow before mass, you will appoint a new one. You see, if you don't, you will never touch another drop of alcohol in Cappel Vale again." The Mayor thought Julian's was the voice of purest evil although it never rose above a whisper.

"We have no one to appoint. Nobody will take the job," the Mayor said.

"I shouldn't worry about that. Tomorrow you will introduce Constable Sean Maher to the entire village," Julian said.

"Maher! You're mad!" The Mayor shot out of his seat and was as rapidly propelled back down. The wail that went out of the Mayor was pitiful indeed. "You don't know what you're saying. Sean Maher is an eejit. God forbid we should ever have a crime. He would just start beating people until he found one to confess.

"And old scores? In the name of Christ, Maher'll be settling them by the score he will. And who is going to pay him? And, and, well, he's an eejit!"

"These are not problems," Julian said. "I'll be nearby to guide him when he needs it. I'll even be an assistant constable so I can still have a place to stay for the time being. I'll talk with him about settling old scores.

"He needs a job after McMaster fired him. I will pay him myself – but understand me, he is never to know that. If, by some accident, he finds out – follow me closely here Cahill. If he finds out – your fault, anybody's fault, nobody's fault, everybody's fault – it will be the driest year of your life."

"It doesn't matter, he won't take the job," the Mayor said and brightened somewhat.

"Really? Not even if The Hagan had a vision?" Julian said.

"You're a viper! Oi took to you like you was me own son a*nd* gave you a place to sleep. And how am Oi repaid? How! Oi'll tell you how..."

"Oh, shut up. The equation is a simple one – appoint Sean Maher and have a drink. Don't and don't. Your choice, Mr. Mayor," Julian said with a malicious smile.

CHAPTER TEN

Alone in a cold study in the quiet manor house, the Pale Man studied a topographical map of the area and wondered. Here? There? Where? In his left hand, he turned a small tarnished coin over and over. He stopped and began to rub the coin in his long fingers hoping it might act like a divining rod over the map.

He selected a book from a stack on his desk and began to read, stopping to look at the map from time to time. Here? There? Where? What he sought could be almost anywhere, but he was close. He knew it. He could feel it.

He said, "Enter," a moment before there was a quiet knock on the heavy oak door.

A tall, austerely dressed man opened the door and advised his employer of a visitor.

"Farmer McMaster, Sir."

"You have something for me, McMaster?" There was no real expectation that the farmer would lead the Pale Man to what he sought, but McMaster did occasionally bring bits of information that were of value.

"M'Lord," McMaster said as he removed the cloth cap from his head. "That numbskull Cahill has appointed Sean Maher to be Village Constable."

"So the American has moved on? That is good. Maher will make a fine policeman for my purposes."

"Well, sor, the first Peeler, the one from Amerikie, Cahill made him assistant constable."

"How many constables does that village need? At this rate they'll have more policemen then Galway City."

"Sor, if'n I might ask?" McMaster said as he gave the slender man a sidelong glance.

"Go ahead," the Pale Man said, but he knew what his visitor was about to say.

"Your honor said Maher would make a fine policeman for our purposes. What are our purposes?"

The Pale Man had been leaning over his books and maps. He straightened and turned his slight frame to face the beefy farmer.

No older than thirty and with eyes so pale they looked as though he had no eyes at all, the Pale Man took a step forward and the larger, more powerfully built McMaster retreated two steps.

The Pale Man smiled, but rather than softening his sharp features, it only made him look sinister. "McMaster, I have purposes and you may be assured they are not your purposes at all. Your purpose is to serve me. I do hope I will not have to make this clear to you again."

McMaster recoiled as if from a blow. "No, sor. No need for you to make it any clearer."

"Good. If that is all you have, you can go." The slender man turned his back to Liam McMaster and bent over the maps and books again. "McMaster," the Pale Man asked over his shoulder. "Do you remember Donny Pearce? His head exploded not a dozen meters from where you stand now. I did that once. I can assure you, I can do it again. Remember that, won't you?"

"Yes, sor," McMaster said and ran from the room.

The Pale Man smiled. He had a gift for inspiring fear in others.

***

These were early fall days, days of morning ground fog when softly veiled wisps would steal along the valley to inhabit the low areas. The mornings were thick, quiet, and intimate, and Julian enjoyed them immensely.

He would rise early, dress and with a mug of hot tea sit outside and watch the fog, listening for the bark of a dog in the distance or the clop of a dog cart as it trundled up the main road.

He sat and he listened and watched as the fog swirled around the village houses and shops.

There, on the road in front of him stood the Hagan. He was sure she hadn't been there a moment ago and he hadn't seen her coming. The fog wasn't so thick that he wouldn't have seen her. Yet, there she stood looking at him. She said, "Walk with me."

Julian set his mug down and walked down the flagstone path to the roadway. Wordlessly, she took his arm and walked him out of town and through the thick forest that surrounded Cappel Vale.

She led him along a narrow path skirting peat bogs and outcrops of rocks, up a small hill and across a flat pasture until they stood looking down into an adjacent valley. The Hagan relaxed visibly, let out a contented sigh and smiled lazily. "Have a look. That is the Ireland I've loved so much for so long.

"The pasture land and the lovely shade of the lake along with that glen on the far side of the valley with its army of trees that have endured for a century or more – all of it blends together seamlessly, naturally," the Hagan said and sighed again.

Julian saw a small, still lake that sat at the bottom of the valley. Pastureland had encroached and left the edges of the lake in soft focus. Cows grazed nearby and in the distance a thick stand of trees stood tall and straight. Sheep could be seen just beyond that.

The fog continued to hug the sides of the hills and obscure and soften the valley below. The bleat of sheep could be heard hushed in the distance. Moira Hagan looked into the valley and then took in the near horizon. She sat on top of a broken low, thick stone wall and indicated Julian should join her.

This was a different woman then the one he first met or the one with whom he conspired to persuade Sean Maher to become the Village Constable. Perhaps it was the time of day, perhaps it was the fog, but something had softened her features.

She stared at him frankly and smiled. Reading his thoughts she said, "I come here daily and it is the place I am most alive."

"You're her, aren't you," Julian sad flatly.

"You know I am. You've known from the first."

"Why didn't you tell me sooner? I thought there was some God awful hurry."

"Keep in mind, laddie, I needn't explain myself to you – or to anyone. I will on this occasion only so that you will know how wonderful a person I am," she sneered.

"I wanted to watch you. You aren't interesting enough to study, but you are worth observing. We're short on entertainment here in the country so your comic value alone was worth watching."

Julian wasn't pleased, neither was he in a position to do or say anything. "So you are supposed to be my teacher and I am to be your student. Cozy."

She let the sarcasm slide off easily and asked him, "Disappointed are you?"

"No, of course not. Doesn't matter to me in the least. However, I should point out…" Julian tried to sound matter-of-fact.

"Liar," she interrupted. "You are indeed disappointed. You wanted someone who would speak softly to you and answer all your questions patiently. If your teacher turned out to be someone as winsome as the good and pure Dr. Dwyer well, money for jam, eh?"

The Hagan held up her hand. "Don't bore me with your pathetic bleating. And don't lie to me anymore – or yourself. I know the truth of it and you know I know."

"My mentor or sponsor or friend or whatever, said you would be different from her. However, I..." the Hagan cut him off again.

"Well, then you are lucky a wise woman found you. Often we don't get what we want, boyo, but what we need. Believe me, I am what you need," the Hagan said.

Julian was insistent. "As I've been trying to say, I have to tell you, as I told my friend, I'm not sold on any of this yet."

Julian's companion let the last sentence hang heavy in the air. "May I ask you a question?"

Julian smirked and answered, "Would it matter if I said no?"

"Not a bit. I would pretend I didn't hear you and ask my question anyway. Perhaps I wouldn't even bother to pretend. In any case I will ask and you will answer, because, you'll never let no-answer answer for you."

"Then I suppose you should ask. I'm ready when you are," Julian said while he chuckled.

"It may seem an easy question, but don't be fooled. I ask few easy questions."

Julian smiled broadly, "I stand warned."

"Warned you may be, but ready you are not," she smiled and continued. "Do you believe in what you cannot see?"

The question wasn't difficult on the surface, but it wasn't what he had bargained for. He needed time to think. "I suppose I do," Julian answered tentatively.

"You don't know? Don't be daft, of course you know."

"Alright, I do believe in things I can't see. I'm here and I can't see the Empire State Building, but I know it's there."

Moira Hagan shook her head slowly. "Nothing gets by you, now does it. Do you have any more of those? I certainly hope you won't continue to spout off about the sorrowfully obvious. In any case, I'm not talkin' about the physical, but the incorporeal.

"So we've established two things thus far. The first is that you do believe in what you can't see. So much so that you gave up the safety and security of your way of life to find your way. You, son, are committed to finding the things you cannot see in the hope they will change you for the better. The second thing we know for certain is that you're an eejit."

"Thanks awfully."

"It is my pleasure. Now let's see if you are willing to understand what you can't rationally explain.

"The supernatural, the unexplained, do you believe in those? Do you believe in things that seem like a dream but are not? The mysterious, the miraculous, the magical, are those on your list of beliefs? You have been living an illusionary life. Are you willing to believe in an extraordinary life with a truer sense of reality?"

Julian sat looking into the valley below. The pastureland was a ribbon of deep green stretching up the valley. The stand of trees drew his eye. The abundance of trees and their variety matched the profusion and range of his thoughts.

Moira Hagan snapped her fingers in front of Julian's face. "Did you forget I asked you a question? Are you going to be all day thinkin' up some feeble answer? I'll take my answer now if you please."

"That my life was an illusion I can't really accept. It was all too real. Still it never felt genuine somehow. It never felt like it was the life I deserved or the one I was meant for. It's true, I believe in and want a life that gives me more than I have, that will make me more than I am."

"Stop right there before you compound your stupidity. There is a life waiting for you that will do nearly what you describe if you are willing to not only believe but also take hold of it.

"I say, nearly what you describe, because nothing will ever make you more than what you are. The object is to be all that you are. To an eejit like you that may seem to be a difference without a distinction, but it isn't, so follow along and see if you can learn something useful," the Hagan said and Julian snorted.

"Don't think to get cheeky with me, Blessing. You can't afford to know what I can do when I receive sass from the likes of you – little man.

"We, you and I, are in the knowing business," she continued. "Part of what you're required to know is the reality of reality. The mysterious, the miraculous, the magical if you will, are all real to be sure, but for you, separating reality and unreality is what you need to learn."

She continued. "But for now, you must believe. For now, you need to disregard your senses. Close your eyes on what you know. Those senses and the knowledge you brought with you from your old life will do you no good here. Distrust them for they will distract you. The only sense you need is your sense of self. Trust, but not the man you used to be. Trust the man you want to be, need to be, will be.

"You have a task and it is an important one, this I know. How you handle this challenge will have far reaching… What is it you find so humorous, eejit?" the Hagan snapped.

Julian shook his head and chuckled. "Well, this has all been very pleasant – if a bit odd – but you will have to deal me out. I'm not in need of any sort of paranormal supernatural mumbo jumbo. Not today. You need somebody to fight a dragon, but that someone isn't me. You need a knight-errant to find what must be found? Well, you'll have to find someone crazier then me.

"Granted that won't be easy given the way I feel just now, but maybe you can place an ad in the newspaper. I'm sorry, that was flippant and uncalled for. You take this seriously and I must respect you for it.

"Mrs. Hagan, if this is a disappointment to you, I am sorry. I am sure you are very good at whatever it is you do. The woman who brought me into all of this, well, I hate to disappoint her. She really is a lovely lady. Still, I'm not the guy for either of you.

"Been great talking to you, but I've got to go." Julian said.

Moira Hagan let the moment dangle. "Where?" she asked mildly and looked bored.

"Pardon?" Julian asked.

"I asked where you planned to go. 'Tis a simple enough question, surely."

Julian was silent.

"No answer? Oh well, be that as it may, I can see by the look of you that you are tired. Best we are going. Why don't you lead the way?" Julian looked into the dense forest and the dark lake below with its lush pastureland framing the scene.

"I'll miss this," Julian thought. "It really is very beautiful, restful somehow but this isn't the place for me." Submerged in his own thoughts he turned and started back to the village of Cappel Vale. The Hagen followed, a small smile touched her eyes and lips.

As they approached the village Julian felt rather than heard a whisper. His had reached a point at which whispers brought only bad tidings, but he had become resigned to them.

"Go back and look. Go back to where we sat just now and look again. Look at what you saw, or thought you saw."

Julian turned. The Hagan's cool gray eyes were penetrating and locked on to his. Her smile was crooked and cunning.

"I won't delay you further, but go back and look hard at what you see." He heard it as clearly as if she had whispered it into his ear. Her smile turned kind and she swept past him toward the village. *"Hush. Quiet your thoughts. Go back and look. You'll understand – at least you'll begin to understand. We'll talk again."* With that, she left him in her wake.

***

Julian stood at the stone wall. He stared into the valley below. None of what he now saw made sense. Then he heard it. The Hagan's voice was unmistakable and not a whisper this time. *"We don't really need you to prattle on about what you do and don't believe in and what is and isn't real, do we? You can save your protests and your puny notions. I said we were in the knowing business. I think we've established a simple fact – you don't know anything.*

"Until you do know something, let's play it this way. If I tell you a thing – take it as read. If I say there are dragons, there are dragons. If I tell you, you have a task, then a task you have. If I mention warlocks, magicians, soothsayers, alchemists, sorcerers or, yes, knights-errant – not likely I would of course – but you are to believe. If I tell you Brian Boru and the Queen of England popped in to see you while you were away, you will only say, 'Oh, what did they want?' Do we have an understanding?"

Julian didn't understand, but she was right. He had made a start at understanding. Stretched out across the valley were plots of farmland separated by low stone walls. Sturdy men in each field harvested their crops.

It was all farmland from one side of the valley to the other and from end to end. It had been this way for hundreds, perhaps thousands of years.

There was no lake, no pastureland, no cattle or sheep, no stand of trees.

There never had been.

Chapter Eleven

The days in Cappel Vale settled into a pleasant routine. The weather remained clement and the people of the village, with some trepidation, accepted Sean Maher and Julian Blessing as their police force.

There was the Case of the Missing Sheep, but that turned out to be nothing more than a drunken shepherd and his lazy dogs allowing the flock of sheep to wonder into the rocky, thickly forested area just north of Cappel Vale.

O'Gavagan's Fight began as an interesting case, but quickly evaporated when Sean Maher arrived, hung up his coat, stood in the middle of the pub and wordlessly started to roll up his shirt sleeves as he whistled a happy tune. Everyone suddenly became the best of friends and remained that way for the remainder of the evening.

The Digging had to be put into the unsolved case file though. It was the thing everyone in the valley and the village talked about in whispers.

A local farmer, George Sullivan, had sent for Julian and Sean. George had given them some Wellington boots and walked them to a field some distance from the farm buildings. The land rose sharply on each side of the field leaving a rich level bowl of land in the center.

On one side of the field, behind a small stand of ancient trees where the land arched away from the level plain, the hillside had been deeply scarred. There was evidence of heavy boots in the soft ground and pick and shovel marks gouged deeply into the hillside.

The area wasn't large, perhaps only twenty feet long, but it sheared the hillside showing clearly the different strata of earth that had settled over millennia.

Julian and Sean were not the first on the scene. The farmer had found the dig and notified Father Fahey. He and Sister Eugenia had looked over the site and came to no conclusion. Next, Dr. Dwyer had been called. She too declared the unexplained digging a mystery suggesting it might just be children having some harmless fun, but even she didn't believe that. That pretty much took care of Cappel Vale's intelligentsia. Farmer Sullivan thought there would be no harm in calling in the two new policemen to stomp around the crime scene.

"Digging peat to sell in the village?" Julian asked Sean.

"Don't be daft."

"Why dig like this then?" Julian asked.

"It makes no sense," Sean said. Still, there had to be a reason. The problem niggled at Julian and, reminiscent of his dog-with-a-bone days in New York, he knew he wouldn't let it go.

They all made their way back to George Sullivan's barn and choked down a jar of home brewed poitin.

Sean and the farmer had a lively discussion where each called into question the ancestry of the other. They moved on to a debate about whether the product was "Potcheen," "Poteen" or "Poitin." They were able to agree on a number of basic facts. First of all, they all needed another jar. Secondly, the product was at least 90 proof.

Next, poitin had been outlawed since the 16th century which was a slight against God perpetrated by the Godless British and, finally, that this discussion should be taken up again when they had more time to devote to the scholarly study of strong drink.

Julian declared they could have his share as the concoction had singed the hair out of his nose, burned his throat and landed with a thud, the concussion from which promised turn him inside out. Potent stuff was George Sullivan's poitin.

After very little thought, it was decided Sean and the farmer should reconvene soon and that Julian would be excused. The motion carried unanimously and the meeting was adjourned. The farmer came away from the encounter with the thought that the police were not such bad sorts. Sean had developed a deep and abiding brotherliness for all men and Julian knew that, although momentarily happy, if he didn't lay down soon he would probably die standing up which could be awkward.

On the edge of a farmer's field behind a stand of ancient oaks a scar still exposed the earth and no one was any nearer to finding out why.

***

Returning to the police station, Julian found Brendan Maher and Timothy Dwyer sitting on the front stoop. Between them sat a very tired young dog.

"Well, gentlemen, what kind of animal do we have here?"

Brendan stuttered, "She's a d-d-dog" and smiled. Timothy explained Brendan had traded one of the local cattlemen a week's labor for one of the farmer's dogs and Timothy had brokered the deal. Having just come from the farmer, the boys and the dog were tired.

Julian went inside and invited the boys and their companion to follow. He sat them down around the big desk and laid out some Irish tea cookies one of the local women had baked, and gave the boys large tumblers of milk.

He then poured water into a shallow bowl and set it before Brendan's dog who immediately stood in the bowl and lapped the water noisily until she could take no more onboard. She then stepped out of the water bowl and settled herself between Brendan's feet.

The boys were ravenous and had managed to make a fair dent in the cookies before Julian said, "Brendan, that is a very fine dog and you will, I know, take good care of her."

"I-I-I will, Mr. Julian. I will." Brendan had adopted his mother's habit of calling Julian 'Mr. Julian'. It was easier for Brendan to say too.

"Timothy, if you would please give your mother my regards."

"Aye, sor. That I will," Timothy said and smiled mischievously.

They left it at that. The boys walked up the street with a very contented dog trotting beside her new best friend, Brendan Maher.

***

For the most part, the nights had been so pleasant for his entire stay in Cappel Vale that Julian had moved the rocking chairs from their place before the fireplace to just outside the front door. He and Sean would sit and rock. Sometimes a passerby would stop for a chat.

Tonight Julian sat alone and reviewed all that had happened during his brief stay. His encounter when overlooking the valley with the Hagan had shaken him. She had met with him several times since and while some things were brought into the light many more remained deeply in the shadows.

The second time he and the Hagan met, he demanded, "How did you do that?" Her answer was quick and hard. "Apparently, where you come from, petulance is tolerated. I can tell you I simply will not wear it. Here you ask questions. You do not demand answers!"

Julian took a deep breath. "You are right. That was rude of me."

"And petulant," the Hagan added.

"Yes, and petulant."

"And insolent and pig headed and stupid," she chimed in.

"Alright, yes those things too." This was making him out of sorts.

"What things?" the Hagan said sweetly.

Julian took a deep breath, squared his shoulders and with the taste of gall in his mouth said, "And insolent, pig headed and stupid. Alright? Anything else? Hmmmmm?"

"If I think of anything I'll be sure to tell you. Now what was it you were asking?"

Julian's words came out one at a time. He felt to do otherwise would inevitably lead to his strangling this woman. "Please. Tell. Me. How. You. Did. That."

"Did what?" Moira Hagan sad flatly then cackled wildly.

Julian felt his head would explode.

The Hagan was breathless and said, "Oh, my, I've not had this much fun in dog years. I'll be thanking ya for that."

Julian was able to eek out through clenched teeth a strangled, "My. Pleasure."

The Hagan went on to explain, "Oh, that business at the stone wall? Nothing much to it really. I wanted to show you how easy it is to swallow a lie. I pointed and you filled in the rest. I put a suggestion or two out among your thoughts and from there, you saw what you wanted to see.

"Oh, there was a bit of stagecraft, but I just gave you the paints and the canvass. You painted the picture yourself. That you were not seeing what was really there was plain enough. Nobody looks at a bunch of squalid dirt farms and grins like you did.

"I know you are all atwitter to learn how to be a wizard, but trust me, my young eejit, being a wizard is not in the cards for you. This isn't magic spells and cauldrons. Here, you use your mind to accomplish what needs to be accomplished.

"Now, back to the subject. The thought I let loose in your empty noggin was the easiest way I knew. I took the easy way because you are more than a little dim and timid."

Julian was incensed. The old woman was baiting him. He knew better but he couldn't stop himself. "A little dim! Timid! I just want you to know..."

The Hagan shot back. "You want me to know what exactly? What is it you think you can tell me about anything that matters? Don't be looking daggers at me, little man. I said you're dim and timid and so you are. I told you I took the easy way with you and so I did. Let me tell you a little something," she said as she gathered steam.

"Had I taken an active role in the vision you created for yourself of the valley, it would not have been a pretty picture you painted. I could easily have planted in that thing you call a brain your worst fears. Believe me boyo, I could have had you runnin' away like a little girl. Pay attention when I tell you, an image could have easily been put inside that empty skull of yours that would have rendered you barking mad for the remainder of your days."

Julian took a number of deep breaths. Each reinforced the certainty that there would be no winning. "So," he said. "No wizard stuff."

"Not for you." Moira snorted and hid her smile.

***

A few lessons later, he asked Moira Hagan to explain something to him. Julian approached the subject with trepidation. He had been experiencing something and it made him uncomfortable.

"I feel unbelievably stupid saying this. I've never felt this before, but I'm getting a sense of people. I wish I had the words to explain. It's as though I can feel them or sense them somehow. Not everyone but some and some more than others. And the list is growing.

"I'll give you an example. I was sitting in the station reading last week. I put my book down, walked over and opened the door. Then I put a pot on to boil. I picked up my book again, sat down and said, "Good morning Sean. Water will be ready for tea in a minute or so. I looked up and Sean was standing in the doorway. I don't know who was more shocked him or me."

Julian continued and the Hagan didn't try to explain, but let him go on. "The next day I was walking toward St. Michael's. I stopped under the big elm tree near the Hackett sisters' place. I don't know why, but I just said, 'Jamie Purcell, you be careful up there. Your mother will be angry if you fall out of that tree.'

"Jamie climbed down and stood and stared at me before he took off home at a dead run. I hadn't seen or heard him, but I could sense that he was there. This is so frustrating. I don't have the words to make this make any sense.

"For Christ's sake this is the twenty first century. I'm a sophisticated man, well read and world traveled. I'm not supposed to be saying this stuff."

With patience and care, Moira explained how what he was sensing was tied directly to what she had been teaching him. His questions and her explanations lasted well into the night.

For Julian the shadows were being pushed back slowly. Understanding was taking the place of conjecture.

***

He sat on the station stoop in his rocker. He didn't see her, but suddenly and inexplicably he said, "Good evening, Doctor. I don't often see you out at night." A moment later Julian saw Dr. Dwyer approach from the heart of the village. Her usual brisk pace had been left behind somewhere and she walked with a slow, stiff gait.

The doctor stopped at the foot of the police station's flagstone walk. She looked puzzled for a moment then shrugged and said, "I just finished with my last patient. I needed to get out."

Julian stood at her approach and indicated Sean's usual chair. She canted her head to one side and looked at the rocker with real longing. She eased into it and let out a contented sigh.

The doctor turned her head and looked at Julian. "How are you getting on, Mr. Blessing?"

"I have no doubt you could answer that a fair bit better than I could," he said. "I'm sure the villagers think I'm crazy. For my part though, I am enjoying myself, learning a great deal and find myself baffled most of the time."

The doctor chuckled, "I wouldn't let that bother you. If you weren't baffled, you wouldn't be in Ireland. There is something else that might help you. Ireland is populated almost exclusively by lunatics. Don't worry, they don't think you're crazy." She reached out and absent-mindedly touched the cuff of his shirt. She bit her lip trying to suppress her curiosity. Who and what he was had plagued her thoughts since he arrived. She remembered Moira Hagan rifling through Julian's things.

"Why do I have the feeling you're not telling me everything. If not crazy, then what?" he asked as he watched her.

In a distracted and matter-of-fact tone she said, "They consider you to be pleasantly strange, that's all. This is lovely material." She touched his cuff a last time and slowly put her hand back on the arm of her rocker.

"Well, thank you. These shirts were the only things I kept from my former life. I was," he thought a moment then continued, "I was in an industry that required such things. These were just part of the uniform. Still, I liked them so I hung on to them."

Ailís Dwyer said, "They fit you very well." That was what she meant, but it isn't what she intended to say. She blanched and tried to cover her forwardness by smiling pleasantly. She continued to look appreciatively at his shirtsleeve while she formulated a distracting follow up question.

"You know it's strange," said Julian interrupting the doctor's thoughts. "Strange or odd, I really don't know which, but my shirts seem to be a rather hot topic. Mrs. Hagan asked about them too," he said simply. "Yes, she wanted to know all kinds of details."

The doctor swallowed hard. Her eyes followed his sleeve over his shoulder to his collar. Hesitantly she raised her glance still higher and found the last thing she wanted to find. He was staring at her and his look was enigmatic. His pale silver eyes were penetrating and unrelenting. She smiled as innocently as only a guilty woman could smile.

He looked away and smiled a smile of his own. It softened his face and made him look kind. To the doctor's relief, Julian changed the subject. "How go things for you, Doctor?" She relaxed. He could have made the moment uncomfortable for her and she admired his restraint.

She considered his question and her smile turned ironic and her mood suddenly somber. Ailís Dwyer shook her head. "I have been stuck in my examination rooms from early this morning until just awhile ago. The children are constantly in need of inspections for head lice. It is a common occurrence. Can't be avoided in the country.

"I just needed to get out of that place for awhile and get some air. Too many late nights and too many early mornings."

Julian looked thoughtful and concerned. "Doctor, you don't seem like yourself tonight. You seem tired, but also angry. If I'm off the mark, please forgive me. If I'm not, is there anything I can do to help? I listen well if you would like to talk."

"Angry and tired," she said without emotion. "I've been more and more like that recently. I get so frustrated with myself, with my patients, with life in general. There is always so much to do without a moment to myself. Sometimes..."

Ailís Dwyer's hazel eyes glistened and then welled with tears as she spoke. A single tear coursed over her cheekbone, hung and then continued down her cheek. She sniffed and tried to regain her composure, but another tear followed the first and her eyes burned.

Without looking at her, Julian took out a clean handkerchief and offered it. She took it and nodded her thanks, but did not use it to staunch the flow of tears. She clutched the handkerchief tightly in her hand instead.

The doctor closed her eyes and set her head on the rocking chair's high back as she willed herself to stop crying. Embarrassment washed over her face. "No one should see me like this, least of all him," she thought.

Her eyes burned even more and the tears wouldn't stop. Julian could sense her anguish and more, he felt the deep ache inside her. She had been running on adrenaline for too long. She hadn't taken a break. She had watched her workload increase. She was exhausted. Slowly, even the tears were too tired to seep from her eyes.

"It will be okay," Julian whispered slowly, emphatically. "It has to be." His smile was soft and kind. "Doctor, there really isn't another choice. Oh, maybe not tonight or tomorrow, but soon, I promise."

He reached out his hand slowly, gently and offered it palm up. She took it and felt relief wash over her. She felt she could, even if only for a moment, set her work and her worries down. Sheltered in the lea of this strange man's tenderness and compassion, a moment was enough.

She squeezed his hand. "Thank you," was all she whispered in return. Then, with a nearly painful slowness, she rose and made her way back to her office. Julian watched her go and ached inside for her.

* * *

The doctor turned off lamps as she moved through the practice, then climbed the wide stairs to the living quarters above. She looked in on her son, kissed and covered him and made her way to her own bed. She undressed and got under the covers. Her sigh wasn't from comfort, but from fatigue.

Julian had, she felt, dealt with her with surprising compassion and kindness. She could hear a quiet strength in his voice, although he said almost nothing. She could still feel the warmth of his hand. She felt rather than heard his words and knew they were true for him and for her.

"It will be okay, it has to be," he had said. She knew it as a simple truth. There wasn't another choice. She couldn't let it all spin out of control. Timothy and all too many people depended on her. She not only had to be present, but also at her best.

"Was this American what he seemed to be?" She wondered. "What does he seem to be? What is he doing here?"

She smiled and thought to herself, "I have to remember to poison Moira Hagan for dragging me into that whole silly shirt business." With that thought, she started to drift and then added, "But first, I have to find out what she found out."

Julian's handkerchief was still clutched tightly in her hand and his words whispered, "Maybe not tonight or tomorrow, but soon, I promise." She had no reason to, but she believed him. She fell into a deep and dreamless sleep with that thought.

Julian continued to sit alone in the dark with only his thoughts for company. He could not explain why he had said what he said or acted the way he had with Dr. Dwyer.

He had never been a man tuned in to people. He understood what motivated them. He knew the scores of reasons they did one thing and not another. But he knew them only in an academic sense. No feeling, no emotion, no attachment or connection to or for anyone. His failed marriage proved that. His clients loved him and his ex-wife hated him. What more was there to say?

Tonight he knew, sensed and felt it all. He had known the doctor would appear. He sensed her frustration. He felt the deep pain inside her although she tried to cover it with light conversation. He smiled at that thought.

Then Julian's smile turned melancholy as he wondered why things happened as they did. Why had his life led him here? What was causing him to experience these unsettling events and feelings? He tried to put that aside for a moment but could not stop his wondering.

Why was a woman so kind and generous as Ailís Dwyer constantly on the verge of exhaustion? Why did he feel drawn to her? Finding no answers and with a slight wind chilling the air, he went inside.

* * *

Days flowed into an agreeable sameness as summer drifted day-by-day toward fall. The village streets were empty of playing, happy children as the scrubbed versions of their summer selves were marched to school at St. Michael's.

Julian made it a practice to get to know the names of the people of the village, but he learned little else. He was frequently met with the phrase, "You've not been long among us." He didn't take this as a slight, but only as the way of the villagers.

* * *

One Sunday, as he left Church with the Mahers, Julian asked Sean about an ornately carved pew that sat empty every Sunday. The pew was on the Epistle Side of the transept and seemed to inspire reverence.

"That's for Squire Lanigan that is," Sean whispered as he and Julian dipped their fingers in the holy water font out of habit and each man crossed himself automatically on the way out of church.

"Squire Lanigan? Who is he? Has he been away? I've never seen anyone in that pew."

"Ah, Julian aren't you are a great one for the questions. This is only one of the many reasons you will always be Chief Constable. Why you are a regular Sherlock Holmes while, poor Sean Maher will be nothing but your student forever."

Pleasantries were exchanged with Father Fahey and Mayor Cahill at the front door of the church and within three feet Julian whispered, "Sean, just a couple of things if you don't mind. First, I'm an assistant constable and second, a man more full of shit than you, I have never met."

"For that Oi'll be expecting to see you at the Confession next Saturday Julian Blessing," Father Fahey said in a voice that was directed with surgical precision to strike Julian in the back without ruffling anyone standing nearby.

Sean looked on in mock horror. The priest continued, "And isn't it Sean Maher you'll be bringing with you?"

"But good Father Fahey, amn't Oi as shocked as your goodly self at the harsh and intemperate language used by this sinner."

"Trust that there are not enough confessional hours throughout all the world that would allow you to catch up on your sins, Constable Maher."

Sean mumbled "Look what you've doon now," but Julian was too busy laughing to hear. Not so busy, however, that he didn't feel the slap on the back of his head delivered by Kathleen Maher. Sean laughed and his wife took a menacing step toward him. He retreated instinctively.

"Any two children in this village behave better than the two of you," she said and marched her own children home without a look back.

Chapter Twelve

The inside of the manor house was cold. No fires burned in the fireplaces and the wind blew across chimney tops causing the house to feel hollow and lifeless. Seated in a wingback chair before the dead fireplace, the Pale Man sat with a map across his knees and scowled.

Clutched in one hand was a coin from a time long dead. He rubbed his thumb across the obverse of the coin, turned it over and rubbed the reverse side. It would be his soon. He knew it. There had been a time when he would have said he could feel it, but his feelings had long since been covered over.

Thought and knowledge were all there was. This time the prize would not elude him. This time the trophy would be his and others would pay a mighty price. He knew it and that thought gave him no joy at all.

"Enter," he said a moment before the deferential knock on the door. A servant entered and said, "Sir, your appointment has arrived."

The Pale Man nodded and without warmth said, "Show him in."

Tom Lynch, a large man of middle years dressed in a barn coat entered and removed his cloth cap out of habit rather than respect.

"Lynch, your men have yet to find what I want them to find," the Pale Man said.

"Beg yur pardon, but me men wouldn't know if they found it or not. You've not told us anything but to dig. It is a funny business and Oi don't like it," Big Tom Lynch said.

"You are not paid to like it. You are paid to do as you are told," the Pale Man said as he got up from his chair. "If you would rather take on employment that better suits the inquisitive minds of you and your men I suggest you do it – now. Either that or don't bother me again about what you like and don't like. That I like it is enough for me and that I pay you is enough for you."

"Where's the map?" Lynch asked barely able to mask his distaste. The Pale Man smiled and in his smile there was no warmth to be found.

***

It was early morning and the fog spun in lazy swirls along the dirt lanes of Cappel Vale. Julian sat on the front step of the police station and thought through the things Moira Hagan had told him.

"There are things you must come to grips with and you must do so quickly." Moira's tone had been serious. "There is something approachin' you like a locomotive. In order to avoid being smashed flat and taking others with you, you must work on your talents and be strong enough to take on what the future will bring. You are a strong man in many ways, Julian," she had said. "But the kind of strength this task will take is not the sort you have just yet."

Not for the first time, Julian asked, "What task? What talents?" and Moira answered flatly that she had no idea. It wasn't like her not to know something, especially something like this. It was ominous, that much she knew, but the where or when or what of it was a mystery to her.

As for his talents, again she said she knew he had them, a few had surfaced already, but she had no idea what they all were. She had said, "You ask questions only you can answer. I can only imagine your fear, frustration, and confusion, but in this area, you must find your own truths in your own way." Julian was sure that of all the things Moira did not know, his level of confusion and anxiety had to top the list.

***

Moira sat on a bench in her garden watching the same tendrils of fog churn through the village and eddy around the houses. Like Julian, her mood was reflective.

She had watched her student with care. He had, she knew, worked diligently from the first, even when he didn't know what he was working on or why. He had made progress and she took a harsh line in measuring his efforts and accomplishments. If his work had been anything less than his best, they would have started over. Half measures, she knew, would not do.

***

The detail on the coin when seen through the jewelers' loupe was remarkable. To be sure, it wasn't newly minted, but the detail was nearly perfect. Although it was not exactly round, the coin had been struck hard and the images were clear.

It had a green-brown patina and some smoothing in its fields. The Roman Emperor Vespasian, radiant in right profile, strong and full of power, stood out in hard relief on the obverse side. On the reverse, Pax stood holding a caduceus and olive branch and resting on a column. The words PAX AVGVSTS C were easily legible in clear, clean letters.

The Pale Man's fingers flipped the coin forward and back and forward again. He never tired of looking at this coin. Every detail was familiar to him, every ridge and shadow was known.

He felt the coin's weight in his hand and calculated again the exact market value of his treasure; £55.24. Not much really unless one multiplied it by 400,000. That was his estimate of how many coins like the one he held in his hand awaited him, and that was just the face value.

The real value rested in the story behind the coins and he felt he knew that story better than anyone. He could name his price for the priceless and there were those who would gladly pay.

He gritted his teeth and his grimace seemed almost like a smile. It might have been had not a certain sheen developed over his eyes. "You will soon be mine," he said quietly to the coin as the malevolent grimace set itself more firmly on his face.

In a cold study in a bleak manor house some distance from Cappel Vale, madness waited.

***

Miles away six men in heavy work boots hacked at a circular earthen outcrop as the sunlight faded. A large man in a cloth cap and barn coat stood by and supervised the work. It was night and only a sliver of the moon illuminated the digging.

"Put your backs into it or we will be here all bloody night, ya eejits," the large man barked and the pace of digging increased.

***

The darkness of evening settled over Cappel Vale in dark hues like an Irish chain quilt. Julian found himself drawn to St. Michael's Church. He had essential thoughts to pursue. He had been tacitly accepting the changes he experienced, but now was the time to start making well-reasoned choices.

He felt he was ready to leave behind the notion that life just happened. Life, he was finding, was a series of conscious decisions. St Michael's, not for the first time, was the place he chose to sort through his thoughts and his choices.

He was going there more often lately, always at night when no one was about. Infrequently he would encounter Sister Eugenia or her assistant, a young nun named Sister Gertrude. Sometimes Julian would run into Father Fahey as the old priest dozed in the front pew of the church. Usually though, Julian timed his visits so he could be alone.

He entered the church and walked quietly to a rear pew. Julian could have been in that position in his pew for five minutes or two hours. Time meant very little in Cappel Vale.

He was aware of her before he either heard or saw her. He opened his eyes to see the lone figure of Ailís Dwyer move quietly to a pew ten rows in front and to the left of Julian's. Dr. Dwyer crossed herself as she genuflected then stepped into the pew and sat down. Julian expected to see her bow her head in prayer, but rather she seemed to stare at the tabernacle on the high altar with her chin tilted up and her eyes open.

Julian closed his eyes to resume his contemplations, but before long he sensed her again. He knew she had turned her focus away from the altar. He opened his eyes to find the doctor staring at him.

"You've been there all along," she said with a slight edge to her voice.

"Since before you came in, yes. I didn't want to startle you so I just went back to what I was doing. There seemed to be plenty of room for both of us here."

Her features softened as she smiled. "I suppose there is. You don't seem like the praying kind," she commented as she left her pew.

"Somehow neither do you," Julian said.

"You go first," she said as she slid into his pew. "What are you really doing here?"

Julian thought a moment then said, "Well, like many complex things, it started out quite simply. It is quiet and there is a pervasive sense of peace here. My hope is that being here will help me find what I'm looking for."

The doctor said, "What would a man like you be looking for, I wonder?" she asked with a smile. "You needn't answer that of course."

"A man like me, you said. I'm glad you have a handle on that, because I sure don't." Julian said and smiled easily while the doctor looked embarrassed.

"Anyway, I don't mind," Julian said. "I've never discussed it with anyone actually. I guess you could say I come here to think. I wouldn't characterize it as meditation exactly. That seems too grand a word for what I'm doing. Reflection or daydreaming would be more accurate. It sometimes starts off by my trying to think through a problem, but soon my mind starts to wander and before long I am – well, this is embarrassing really but I'm led to a solution.

"Suddenly, the situation becomes more clearly defined with hard edges and sharp corners and I can see it all with amazing accuracy. It never lasts long, but occasionally long enough to catch a glimpse of what the solution might be."

Julian chuckled softly. "If anyone had told me a few months ago that I would be talking this sort of nonsense I would have called the police and had that person committed for his own safety. It is just that the world changed for me or at least the part of the world I used to occupy did. It happened quickly and I lacked the wits and words to cope with the changes, so I apologize to you for my clumsiness," Julian said.

"Enough of me though. How about you? What brings Dr. Dwyer, the woman of science, to church in the dark of night?" He smiled warmly.

"Clumsiness? If you say so, but you need not apologize for something I never noticed. I will keep a sharp eye out for it in the future though," the doctor said and she and Julian shared a smile. "As to what I'm doing here, that is a story that might take some time to tell and it isn't all that interesting."

"Sorry. That wasn't the deal. With the candor at my command, I told you my story. Now it's your turn. I have all night if you do."

"Well, in fact you have not told me your story. You told me a part of a story, so don't for a moment believe I haven't noticed your oversight. No matter, I will tell you my story," she said in the hushed tones reserved for churches. "The reason for my coming here has changed over time, but maybe I should give you some background."

"I can't tell you how refreshing that would be," Julian said. "No one ever tells me anything here that isn't either common knowledge or common sense, so something of substance would be marvelous."

"It isn't that they don't want to tell you, Mr. Blessing, it is just..."

"It's that Oi've not been long among us," he finished for her using his improving mock Irish English.

She laughed at him and with him. "I'll share with you because I am an outsider too and have spent a long time 'not being long among us' as you are now." Her gaze moved slowly from Julian's face to the tabernacle. A sadness entered her and after a moment she spoke.

"I had finished medical school and was doing my residency when I met and married a wonderful man. Now, medical residency is not conducive to relationships of any sort. There simply is no time. You don't have time for yourself, and any time you make for another is time you have to take from something else. Still, we were happy – blissfully, to use the cliché.

"He was trying to get his start as an architect, but it was hard in Dublin at the time. The economy was in a poor way and architects were sitting around in abundance. I said we had no time together. That wasn't altogether true. We did have a little time alone," she said and smiled.

"I became pregnant. Pregnancy was the last thing I wanted or needed. I never really pictured my life with a child in it. I was happy, professional, and proud of what I was doing. I thought a child would detract from that.

"In any case, I worked up to the very end. Early in the pregnancy, my husband, William, talked me out of going to the U.K. for an abortion. I wanted to, but he was persuasive and I loved him so." She took a deep breath and her chin trembled.

"Doctor, you needn't continue. I have stupidly intruded and I don't want to cause you any distress," Julian said gently.

She took a moment and her thoughts were far away. "You didn't intrude. I have heard other people's rendition of this story, but have never had the chance to tell it myself."

Minutes passed before she continued, "I gave birth to Timothy. I had delivered babies before. After hours of excruciating labor, I would wrap some bright red, squalling, squirming infant in a towel and place it in its mother's arms.

"Without exception each mother, sweat soaked and fatigued beyond words, would coo and fawn over their hideous creature and tell me how beautiful little Patrick or Megan was and I would grin and agree, because that is what doctors are expected to do.

"My labor wasn't that difficult, but still I was a wreck and weak from the effort. They handed Timothy to me and I beheld perfection for the first time. He was so beautiful it hurt. I thought my heart and my head would explode with the joy and love that was inside me. William felt the same. In some ways more so I think.

"I stayed home for as long as we could afford it – which wasn't very long – and then we were suddenly face to face with reality. There were three of us and we were in need of money. Timothy presented unique logistical needs that were hard to meet.

"My husband gave up looking for a job as an architect and it nearly broke his heart. He was good at his profession and he loved it so much. He went into the building trades as a carpenter - he had done that sort of work on and off while putting himself through university. He would work days and I would work the night shift.

"The feedings, the getting up during the night, all of it conspired against us. We were both exhausted all the time. We worked extra hours to try to save a little money and we consoled ourselves with the idea that it wouldn't always be this way."

Julian studied the doctor's profile and listened closely as she spoke. The texture and timbre of her voice, and the way the words fit together – this was a story she had gone over in her mind many, many times before. The church's subdued candlelight glinted off her chestnut colored hair whenever she slightly moved her head.

Her jaw was straight and strong as that of any statue. Her nose was delicate and complemented every aspect of her face, as did her pale complexion. Her eyes and her mouth were her most expressive features, but her voice was more a caress, a tender, loving touch rather than just words spoken in the half darkness.

She continued. "William would often come home from work and find me on the Chesterfield asleep with our son on my chest. By the same token I can't tell you the number of mornings I came home from work and found him in a chair holding our son in his arms – both sound asleep."

"On one occasion I came home and found them like that. I put Timothy in his crib, packed a lunch and woke my husband so he could go to work. I could see the weariness in his eyes. His fatigue was palpable.

"One day around noon I was getting ready for bed. Getting up and going to bed get all turned around when your schedule is upside down. I answered a knock at our door and found my chief of staff, Dr. Gaddis standing there.

"He was a stern man with little warmth or charm, but he was a first class physician and he knew how to teach. Still, it wasn't like him to drop by the apartment of a mere resident. I invited him in, but he didn't move. His eyes were on mine and I couldn't look away.

"It was then that the penny dropped.

"'I have something to tell you, Dr. Dwyer. It is your husband. He was killed in an accident at work,' my chief said. He was a very formal man and referred to my by my title even then.

"The next thing I knew I was sitting on the chesterfield with Timothy in my arms and Dr. Gaddis sitting beside me. The shadows in the room told me it was late afternoon. I don't remember sitting down or how Timothy got into my arms or how long I had been there."

"'Mr. Dwyer was working on a roof. He lost his balance and fell off. It wasn't a great height, but he died instantly. They brought him to the hospital and one of the staff recognized him. Your husband's superintendent was going to tell you, but I insisted I would be the one,' my chief said.

"I remember his words so clearly, but little else.

"He used the telephone and had one of the pediatric nursing sisters sent over to be with Timothy. At first, I wouldn't give him up, but Dr. Gaddis took my face in his hands and looked into my eyes. 'You have much to do. Phone calls to make, things to arrange.'

"God I remember that old man's words and felt his compassion and the softness of his hands. At that moment everything I knew about medicine and life and death and people and thoughts and emotions changed.

"I realized that this lonely old man, whom I had cursed under my breath hundreds of times for the harshness he had shown us residents, could feel what I felt and still remain clear headed enough to know what had to be done.

"The nursing sister took Timothy and as I looked into the old man's eyes and with my heart broken, I sobbed. He folded me into his arms and I cried until I had no more tears left in me and then he whispered, 'You have work to do.' I nodded my head and picked up the telephone to start calling our families.

"Months passed then years and I developed two passions – Timothy and medicine. I wanted to be not just a good doctor, but the sort of doctor Dr. Gaddis showed me it was possible to be. I passed out of my residency and went to work with a large and well-regarded private practice in Dublin.

"The experience I acquired was invaluable, but it wasn't the sort of medicine I wanted to practice. I made more than enough money to provide everything Timothy needed. I went to work and came home during normal hours and when not working I would spend every moment with my son.

"Still, I was not practicing Dr. Gaddis' kind of medicine. The IPH – sorry, the Institute of Public Health – wasn't what I wanted. I wanted to know my patients. Spending four and a half minutes per patient and having more patients than anyone could handle, wouldn't do. That much I knew.

I went to Dr. Gaddis and we talked about my future at length. That is I talked – you've noticed I do that a lot – and he listened. In the end he simply said, 'I'll look into it'.

"One day the old man called wanting to know if I was still interested in a different kind of medicine. I told him I was and he simply said, 'Good' and rang off. The next day there was a letter pushed under the door of my flat."

"Seems a little farming village in the northeast of Ireland was looking for a country doctor and here I am. But that doesn't explain why I'm here in church which is what you asked," the doctor said.

"At first I came here every night to ask God and my late husband to watch over Timothy. He was and still is everything to me and I begged them to intercede on Timothy's behalf and not let anything happen to him."

She chuckled and repeated, "'Asking God and my husband to watch over Timothy.' Not very sophisticated of me. I am supposed to be well educated and enlightened. I am supposed to know science is the new religion and that religion is nothing more than superstition encased in dogma. Still, there it is. I would have prayed to the devil or sacrificed goats if it would keep my boy safe.

"As time went on, the visits to St. Michael's to beg for protection became fewer and fewer. Having pled my case, now I come to express my gratitude that my son is safe. Every day with him in my life is a wonderful gift."

The intensity of her words showed in her eyes. "I love Timothy so much. I can't imagine life without him. And so I come here because I don't know what else to do."

They sat in silence in the dim light, softened further by flickering votive candles and with the faint smell of incense in the air. The old stone church had served for baptisms, confirmations, confessions, communions, weddings and funerals.

This church had heard countless supplications, helped to heal loss and provided shelter when it seemed no other safe harbor was available. It had given people a place where they could talk with their god. Now in early winter, it offered sanctuary to two souls.

Ailís Dwyer said, "You are a strange man, Julian Blessing." She had moved closer. Julian could smell her, see her eyes clearly, feel her warmth and her humanity tinged with sadness.

"There was no reason for me to tell you all of that. You asked a simple question and I could have given you a simple answer. But for some reason I felt I could tell you a story I had never shared with anyone – a point of view not previously heard."

The doctor reached over and distractedly picked a thread from the sleeve of Julian's sweater. Her movement was relaxed, effortless, graceful and infinitely slow. Julian watched her and marveled. He knew her thoughts had taken her to a place he could not go. Still, she seemed to include him with her simple unguarded act, unguarded and unbelievable intimate.

"I wonder what it is about you that could have caused me tell you so much," she continued.

"Doctor, I believe we all have a need to tell our story." Julian said. "Keeping the story to ourselves keeps it safe to be sure, but it's in the telling that we connect with each other. We reveal the depth we each have within us. In admitting how fragile we really are, we are demonstrating how very strong we are. That is a position to which I have recently arrived. Most of my life I have believed the exact opposite.

"I am glad you are comfortable talking with me," he continued. "I am honored really and feel fortunate to be here with you right now. Our stories come bubbling up to the surface. We can suppress them temporarily, but we can't hold them back forever. In time, those stories, if felt deeply enough, will be told."

He continued. "Maybe in telling our stories we free ourselves somehow. It is perhaps the only time we can be more than we are because in telling, we touch another and in that moment maybe we become more human.

"I don't know. I have so many more questions than answers. I really don't know much about anything anymore. Funny really, all of my life I thought I knew and understood everything worth knowing," Julian said with a sad smile. "What arrogance."

The doctor thought a moment then said, "I think you sell yourself short. I believe you know far more than you think you do. You have clarified a few things for me tonight. And you have been a tremendous help. I mean that sincerely.

"Possibly what you said earlier applies to all of us. Maybe we can find our real selves not in the answers to the questions we ask, but in the questions themselves and in the asking of them," she said in a whisper.

"Oh, my, did I actually say that? I certainly hope not." He smiled and she laughed.

"Well, it might have been something like that," she said.

"May I walk you home, Doctor?" Julian asked.

Her gaze had moved to the front of the church again. In a distracted voice she said, "No, but thank you. I think I'll stay a bit longer. There are some things I would like to think over." She looked back to Julian and her eyes held his. "Ailís, Julian. My name is Ailís."

He was silent a moment as he looked into her hazel eyes. "Good night then, Ailís."

"Good night, Julian. Sleep well."

He smiled warmly and kept that smile until he fell into a restful and soft sleep.

Chapter Thirteen

Julian's lessons continued even as the morning fogs disappeared and the weather turned brisk. Still, the mornings were clear and pleasant. If it rained, Julian and Moira Hagan would sit in the police station. If there was a respite from the rain, they might sit in Moira's garden. On this morning, they slowly walked the lanes of the village.

"I have lectured enough," Moira said. "Now it is time for you to tell me in your own words what you know." A farmer on a donkey cart passed them and shot the pair a concerned sidelong glance. For his efforts, Moira Hagan terrified the man with a look that sent him on his way.

Julian marshaled his thoughts, and began. "We talk a lot about darkness and light, the lie and the truth. The darkness we speak of is a physical manifestation. Light, like our thoughts, is infinite. Darkness and the convenient lies we tell ourselves are not. In order to progress, I need to pull aside the curtain. If we let in the light, the darkness is gone.

"I've learned many truths and am developing some useful talents. But what I work on daily has nothing to do with any of that. You give me exercises to perform and I work on them all, but I always seem to return to the same concept.

"I need to find a way to take hold of what's important in my life. Life, the light, my thoughts, true reality – they're all the same. I know this and know also that everything is available to me, but I only know this stuff on an academic level. I've yet to find a way to incorporate it into my life, to make it real." Julian stopped and again tried to get a handle on what he was learning.

"Why are you looking so pained?" Moira asked.

Julian snapped back. "I am not looking pained. I'm looking thoughtful."

"Is that what that is? For a bit there I thought perhaps you'd tucked into a bad potato or had gas or something. I'm glad to know it is just you looking thoughtful," the Hagan goaded to lighten his mood.

Julian said "Yes, thoughtful, you should try it sometime," and smiled an ugly smile.

"Don't give me any of your jaw, boyo. I may be old, but I can still do you a mischief whenever I like," Moira said and suppressed a smile.

"Now, back to business," she continued. "Nearly everyone is bathed in the mist that obscures their lives. They remain sightless because that is all they know. We reject that entirely. We understand that if we open ourselves, our minds, our spirits more fully, the light is all there for us. We come to our place of understanding by employing a clear conscience, an open mind, and a pure heart.

"Understand or even try to understand the light, and the darkness around you vanishes. That's when we are most able to help others." Moira stopped and watched Julian. She thought to herself, "He is so close now. I can see it in him. He's come so far. If he can get through this obstacle then we can begin."

Julian was breathing rapidly now. "That's it. That's the problem, the reason I can't come to grips with all of this. God, but I am stupid." His heart raced and perspiration beaded on his forehead. His hands were clammy. Something she said or he felt had given him a sudden insight.

"I can't be in two places at the same time. In this game, the players are all in or all out. In order to see clearly, I can't accept any part of the mist. That's what's been holding me back.

"Moira. I have to go. I'm sorry, but there is something I need to work on." And with that, he set off at a quick pace. He crossed through the trees, across the pasture and toward the broken wall. He scrambled over it and began to run as the rain began to fall.

Moira Hagan closed her eyes and in her mind watched Julian and she smiled with some satisfaction and said to herself, "Good for him to run," she thought. "He has too much pent up energy and he needs to get rid of it before he can begin to see clearly.

"Now he and I can get on to the serious business," she said aloud as a field hand passed by looking nervously at her.

"Look at me again, like that, boyo," Moira barked. "And I'll make sure things start to fall off your body and your Misses won't like that one bit!" The farm hand decided to follow Julian's lead and run. Away.

***

Epiphany is not an easy thing. Although it is said to be a sudden grasping of reality, no one ever told Julian it would hit like a punch in the head from Sean Maher.

The things the Hagan had been teaching him, they weren't on the periphery. They were clearly in sight. He needed only get closer to be able to see it all. Somehow, all that Moira Hagan had said was beginning to come together.

The essential nature and meaning of it all was within his grasp and as he ran, the thunder and lightening were illuminating his discovery. Julian took what seemed like the wisest and best course of action. He ran as it rained. He ran and the freedom of it cleansed him and calmed him and cleared his mind.

***

He slackened his pace as the thunder and rain relented. He basked in the rainwater that ran in rivulets down his face and soon he was walking slowly with the broken wall still on his right. He had walked and run nearly all the way around the forest that surrounded Cappel Vale on three sides.

Shotgun pellets coursed through the treetops near Julian. Another shotgun blast quickly followed the first and even more quickly came a string of profoundly original profanity and the frantic barking of dogs. Julian followed the sound.

Two beautiful Irish Red and White Setters bounded into the forest nearly colliding with Julian. He knelt down and both dogs determined this was something worth investigating.

Julian had very little experience with animals of any sort but his time in Ireland had been an education in horses, sheep, goats, cats, dogs and cattle. Brendan Maher was talented when it came to animals and he had taught Julian how to introduce himself to each type they encountered.

Brendan's dog, Dunla would accompany Julian and her master when they walked through the countryside. With difficulty, Brendan explained that Dunla was pronounced *Dun-laith* in Gaelic and meant brown lady. And a lady she was with an elegant gait even for a puppy, and a glossy coat Brendan brushed daily. Through her, Julian learned that a gentle hand and a soothing voice would have her doing anything for the opportunity to please. She loved openly, freely and with an innocent intensity she shared with her master.

The setters approached cautiously and with tails flat out. As Julian slowly turned his palms out to them, both tails came upright and began to wag. Tongues hung out and both dogs bounded around him.

"By the wounds of the sweet living Christ, I am going to shoot those two worthless dogs!" a voice in the near distance intoned. "When I find you – and I will find you both – your mangy, fly blown, flea-bitten heads will be on pikes before sundown today. God's balls, but I hate those dogs!"

Julian whispered to the dogs, "Sounds serious, guys. We better go find him." Both dogs cocked their heads and danced around Julian as he rose and walked toward the voice that boomed impending dog destruction through the forest.

"Don't shoot," Julian called out as a man in his early 70s stepped into a clearing about ten meters away. The man stopped. He was wearing tweeds with a barn coat and Wellington boots. A shock of white hair stuck out from under a cloth field cap. The dogs saw their master and began running between the two men.

"Who are you? What are you doing here? And why are you all wet?"

"I'm sorry to intrude, sir. My name is Julian Blessing and I was out for a walk and got caught in the rain storm."

"You are the American fellow who lives in the police station."

"Yes, sir," Julian said grateful the man didn't accuse him of being a policeman.

"Well, come up to the house and we'll get a drink into you and set you by the fire. Perhaps we can roast a nice dog," the man said as he gave the nearest dog an affectionate rap on the skull.

The two men walked in silence out of the woods and across a field. Over a rise, a substantial, dignified manor house came into view. It was by no means large, but it was the largest dwelling Julian had seen since arriving in the valley.

The hunter entered the house through a side entrance that opened into a mudroom where the man removed his boots. Julian sat on a bench intending to do the same, but the man waved him off.

"I do this out of habit. Keep your boots on for now. You can take them off by the fire."

Julian walked through a kitchen where an old woman was bent over a stove. She spun around and said, "Don't track up me floor!"

The man shouted, "Shut up you nasty old crone and get some lunch ready for our guest!"

The woman turned having only heard the word 'lunch'.

They had arrived at the library before the old man said, "She is deaf as a haddock, of course, but a hell of a cook. If she could hear a tenth of what I said she'd have quit years ago or murdered me," the hunter said. "Take a seat by the fire. Brandy?"

"Yes, thank you."

Drinks were poured as Julian took off his boots and stood before the fire admiring the room. It was paneled in mahogany from the floor to the high ceilings. Bookcases lined several walls with well-thumbed copies of leather-bound books.

Two wing back chairs faced a fireplace in which a man could stand upright. The hearth and fireplace surround were lined with granite. A black draped painting hung above the fireplace. Between the two chairs sat a table with a small tobacco humidor and a rack of expensive pipes. Wood and pipe smoke gave a champagne patina to the ceiling.

The hunter brought over two tumblers half full of a dark amber liquid. He reached over to a sideboard and removed a throw rug with which he covered a chair. He then invited Julian to sit and handed him a glass.

The man stood tall and square shouldered in front of Julian and said, "My apologies. I don't get many guests anymore and I've forgotten my manners. We have not been introduced. I am…"

"Squire Lanigan," Julian said and smiled as he shook the man's hand. Although the hand was smooth, the fingers long and slender, the handshake was firm and the eyes that took Julian in were piercing and steady.

"Padric Lanigan, but Squire if you like. So, they still remember me in the village. They are good people. Not because they remember me, but because, well, just because.

"What brings someone from America to Cappel Vale, Ireland? It can't be the weather. Perhaps it was the intellectual cut and thrust our little valley has to offer? Do tell."

"I was on a walking tour of the countryside and found my way to Cappel Vale. One thing led to another and here I am sitting among the gentry."

The Squire sat in the other chair, thought for a moment and said, "That is a load of shit which is truly beyond all redemption. There is little that goes on here that someone doesn't know something about and eventually I hear it all. Some of what I hear is nothing but an old piss pot full of jumbled suspicions. Ultimately I sort the good from the bad and find out the truth."

"Then what am I doing here?" Julian asked and smiled easily.

"That, young man is the mystery isn't it. A walking tour it isn't. You arrived from the M1 road by car. There was a woman with you, but on that subject, I have no more information. That is in itself strange. You walked a couple of miles to the village. A very short walking tour, eh?

"Let's see, what else is there. Oh, you handed that 'on a walking tour and need a place to stay' malarkey around until our good mayor put you up in the police station. It is a good use for a useless police station, by the way. His mistake was in not charging you a handsome rent – which you would have paid.

"That is what I've been told, but now having seen you, I know a good deal more," the Squire said.

"I'm enthralled, please continue," Julian said. Through much of his life, he had dealt with men like the Squire. He had found them to be individuals one did not underestimate twice.

The Squire smiled and set his tumbler down and warmed to his task.

"You are educated, well traveled and well read. You spent just a bit too long looking at the book titles in my collection, by the way. I would say you squirreled away a sizable fortune, which you've had for awhile. It is your money, not inherited, although there may be some of that too. I do hope I am not being indelicate, but I mention all this for a reason."

Julian smiled and said nothing. He knew far from being sorry, the Squire was doing what he could to be as indelicate as possible to draw out his prey.

"People who inherit money seldom know how to use it. Those who work for it do. You are a man who understands money, both in large numbers and in small and how to use it. You have been a source of hard currency revenue for the village since your arrival.

"The villagers overcharge you with some regularity of course. You know this and you don't mind. In fact, you are pleased to help. Unlike many tourists, you do not throw cash around but deposit it where it will likely return the highest profit.

"You mix, but not easily with the Ach and Oi crowd and you are able to blend with our rather limited educated class and now," the Squire bowed, "with the gentry. Nice shirt by the way. Did you have that made for you in," the squire thought a moment, "London? No, wrong cut. New York, I think, but I've been out of that world for a long time and so may be wrong.

"By the way, your shirts, for reasons passing understanding, have been the cause of much discussion. You feed that mystery of course, as it tends to distract others and obscure the reason for you being among us. You have a singular talent for saying much while revealing very little.

"People tend to leave your company believing they know something vital about you when in fact they are no better informed than when they arrived. All of this creates enough of a distraction to allow you to go about your business unnoticed. Well played, I say. Shirts for the love of God. That takes imagination," the Squire said with a smile.

"Since your arrival you've supplied one and all with a little welcome respite from the drone of country life. As to why you are here, I honestly haven't a clue, but if there is a reason, I will learn of it. I'll let you know if you would like."

"Please do. I often wonder why I am here. I am glad I've been able to add a little comic relief though," Julian said with a fixed smile.

"No sense being chapped about it. Life in the country is deadly dull most of the time. You are a celebrity. That whole thing with Maher was really something. The free beer was a masterstroke, but I'll reckon you didn't figure on being hit in the head by that monster.

"Still, you came out of that just fine and managed to slough off that village constable rubbish onto the one man who can knock down anyone in the county. Really masterful in a queer sort of way. How am I doing so far?"

"Quite well, considering. Do you mind if I ask a question?" Julian asked.

"Ask away, son."

"Does anyone like you, Squire?"

"Oh, I do hope not. I am the most feared man in this valley and I've done almost nothing to engender that. I am one of the most respected men in the country too. Archbishops and functionaries from the government and other rogues seek my blessing for anything they want to do in this part of the world. I've never thought to ask for more."

Julian thought for a moment, savored his brandy and said, "You, Squire are a man who knows much about many things and you are obviously well connected. I will have to become better acquainted with you if only to keep you from making up any more facts about me.

"You have had a go at me so may I return the favor? No need to answer. I won't bore you with the details you are all too familiar with. I doubt, however, anyone would confirm them to your face," Julian said.

"My opinion is that you are one of those rare men who are unprincipled without being unethical. You are a gambler, but you would never cheat or swindle. In a different life, you would have been a pirate and a good one. But, hey, the good news is you are a rascal and a distinctly bad influence. Squire, I believe you and I can do business."

Squire Lanigan laughed until tears ran down his cheeks. "Blessing, you are a cheeky bastard and, God forgive me, I like you."

"FOOD!" the cook announced from the doorway.

"She is a woman of few words, but wait until you tuck into her shepherd's pie. It is eloquent!"

The men repaired to the dining room and sat next to each other at the long table and, as advertised, the meal was superb in its simplicity.

Julian asked, "Squire, there has been some odd digging going on at some of the farms in the valley. Do you know anything about that? It is a subject that has the residents of the valley on edge. They don't say as much, but you can feel their anxiety."

"I have heard of it of course," the Squire answered. "But in truth I do not know anything about the how or why of the thing. That anxiety you mention isn't just worry. It is fear, lad. They try to minimize it, mask it with a brave face and a good joke. It is the Irish way and always has been. Believe me though, they are afraid, and why? Because they don't know why they are afraid or of what. That is the worst kind of fear.

"There is more though," the Squire continued. "As you know, there have been assaults and not of the pub-on-a-Saturday-night kind. People are being hurt and badly. It is my fear that whoever is doing this will go too far. I have put out feelers and will report whatever I can discover."

Julian followed the thought. "The level of violence and other activity is increasing and it worries me too. I appreciate any help you can lend. Still, as you noted, I was a man of business, Squire, and so can't take something without giving value in return. I will make you a trade. Use your resources to look into that matter and I will have Sean Maher's son come up and work with your dogs."

"Maher's boy? The slow one? He has the way about him with dogs, does he?"

Julian bristled, "Some say he has a nearly mystical gift. I've seen what he can do. Would that we were all so slow, eh?"

"You're right, that was stupid of me. You get that boy to work with my dogs and that will make it more than an equitable trade. If he can do anything with those disgusting creatures, that would be something to see. You, Mr. Blessing, have a deal."

Over lunch, the Squire commented briefly on the notable residents of the area and Julian asked him about an expression he had used earlier.

The squire smiled and nodded his head, "Yes, the Ach and Oi crowd is it? A term of my own creation. It easily identifies Ireland's rural working people. I'm sure you've heard enough 'Ach, but 'tisn't it Paddy who said,' and 'Well, Oi'll beed thinkin' Oi' amn't about to go ta market this day,' to last you several lifetimes.

"Mind you I do not use that term disparagingly even though it may sound as if I do. Although my manners are appalling and my point of view jaded, I know and respect my fellow Irishmen. The working people, the laborers, the people of the land – Blessing, I value them more than you could ever know. They may populate their speech with a liberal dollop of the ach and the Oi, but even the rudest among them wield the language with true artistry. Moreover, they are good people.

"They have an oral tradition that spans thousands of years. I'm an educated man Blessing, as are you. I know the words, but these people, understand them and through those words they understand and can deal with a very hard life head on," the Squire said.

"As for the educated class and the gentry, language is always the give away, of course. Father Fahey is an exception. He and his flock are strictly salt of the earth types. Have a care when you deal with him though. He may play the cartoon Irish priest, but don't be fooled. Untutored he may be, but he's been around, he is quick witted and nobody's fool. Lie to him at your peril.

"That nun, Sister Eugenia, that woman had it all. In her day, she was a looker, she is still a handsome woman actually. Her family was old money of course. Went to the finest schools but gave it all up. Give her a wide berth. With an angelic and innocent smile, that woman could murder us all and still make it all right with Almighty God.

"The good doctor?" Julian asked.

"I was waiting for you to ask. According to the local busybodies, you wasted no time in making her acquaintance, eh, ya rogue. She is as fine a bit of fluff as I've seen in many a year. Lovely shape on her, but she has a blistering temper that I frankly doubt will improve with age.

"She is respected enormously by her peers throughout the country, which is why I had her brought here. If she knew that bit, she would be livid. If she knew I paid her salary or that she lived and practiced out of a house that belongs to me, she would be rabid. Of course there isn't a person anywhere around here, except me, who wouldn't cut off a limb if she asked."

"But not you?" Julian asked

"I like my doctors male, somewhat marinated and within a score of years of my age."

"You've not mentioned Mrs. Hagan."

The squire picked up a spoon and polished it with his napkin. "Formidable to be sure, but then you know that don't you." The squire smiled and looked closely at Julian. "You, in fact, have good reason to know that. But beyond that I really couldn't say."

The men talked of the likely demise of the village and the surrounding countryside and the squire invited Julian to play chess some evening soon.

Lunch was, as promised, eloquent.

Chapter Fourteen

The storm clouds had blown away leaving only a slight bite to the fall air and the unmistakable fresh just-after-rain smell.

Having dried out some at the Squire's, Julian walked to the village and found Sean on the main road. Together the two walked down the street stopping to talk with Edmond Flynn from the general store. Julian waved to Francis Mulherin while Sean just spat. They nodded to the Hackett sisters who sniffed and went inside their shop in a huff.

Dr. Dwyer was standing outside her practice looking into the sky. As he passed, Julian said, "Good afternoon, Doctor."

"Ah, well if isn't it Constables Blessing and Maher, and by the look of you, a slightly soggy Assistant Constable Blessing. At least it can be said that Sean Maher has sense enough to get in out of the rain," she said and winked at Sean.

"None of that now. Although he is but a modest man and insists he is an Assistant, it is Chief Constable to the likes of you, Doctor," Sean said and smiled broadly.

"Quite right. Modest, ha. Still, my apologies, Chief Constable." She stressed the Chief hard, smiled and continued. "Why ever would you be out in this morning's weather?"

"Just felt like a stroll and it was really rather pleasant. One crosses paths with the most agreeable people while one is out for an amble," Julian said.

"And whose path did you cross today?" the doctor asked, her smile radiant and playful.

"Well, yours of course. Don't you find it strange that when you come out the rain clouds blow away?" Julian said teasingly.

"Go on with you," she said while Sean Maher rolled his eyes.

"And I met Squire Lanigan. Charming fellow."

The smile was gone in a heartbeat. "Well, thank you for that! You would lump me in with the Squire? If I thought you were going to be insulting I wouldn't have bothered myself talking to the likes of you."

With a mischievous twinkle in his eye, Julian said, "Now what could it be about the Squire that upsets you. You both have a fine aristocratic bearing. Both of you are well educated. Both of you have a deep attachment to the valley. You have so much in common."

"Oh, you forgot to mention the man is an ass. If you didn't notice that speaks volumes about you too." She seemed ready to spit nails. "Never was there a more arrogant, self-righteous, selfish, scoundrel. The man is a rogue and a villain and… There are no words to… I can't even tell you… Just the mention of his name makes me…" Dr. Dwyer sputtered.

"He was perfectly charming to me. I can't imagine what he could have done that would have caused you to bear him such ill will," Julian goaded.

"Julian, we have to be going," Sean said.

"Charming is it! He called me '*woman*'!"

"Well, you are a woman, and a very attractive one if you don't mind me saying so." Julian was beside himself trying to keep from laughing as Ailís Dwyer sputtered and fumed with her fists clenched and the bit fully between her teeth.

"Julian, we have to be going – now," Sean said and looked nervous.

"You are as big an ass as he is!" the doctor fired back. "He didn't say I was a woman, you nit! He called me 'Woman.' I was treating him one day and when I was done he dismissed me. Me! Imagine!

He said, 'It is time you went about your business of having babies and such so, on your way, woman.'

"He actually said that – Neanderthal! Can you imagine! The man is insufferable. He is an oaf. If ever there were a man who deserved gout, it's that old reprobate. He needs to suffer and not in the next life – I want to see it in this one!"

"Julian, we have to be going – right this minute!" Sean said sensing the doctor's boiling point was fast approaching.

"Oh my, I will have to think about the things you've said, Doctor. Perhaps I have misjudged one of you," Julian said and started down the road toward the police station with Sean Maher leading him by the arm.

"Arrrrgggggggggggg!" Dr. Dwyer cried out as she searched desperately for something heavy to throw at the head of Julian Blessing.

"Did you really have to annoy her that way?" Sean asked and the irritation could be heard clearly in his voice.

Julian stopped in the street and faced his friend. "You mean there is another way to annoy her? Why don't I ever get the memos on these things? It is your duty, Sean, to keep me informed about the many ways of annoying people." Julian found that uproariously funny.

"Julian, be serious. Why do you do such things? That poor slip of a girl was going to have a stroke and you the cause of it and with a young son to raise all on her own. How would you have felt if she had fallen into a fit and left the poor child an orphan?"

"Oh, she is healthy enough. She looked like someone who needed a little emotional exercise. I was doing her a favor. Can you imagine the next male patient she sees though? That will be a very ugly examination I can tell you," Julian said and began to laugh again.

At last, Dr. Dwyer located and threw a metal pail, but Julian was too far out of range. "You will pass this way again and I will be ready," she thought to herself as she stormed back into her practice.

***

The wind spun in lazy circles among the heather. Fall had turned to winter. The night was cool and crisp, but most of all it wasn't raining. Julian needed to get out and get some exercise. The roads were dry so he took his official police bicycle and flashlight out along the lonely country lanes.

The half moon silvered the night and illuminated his path. If he was careful and didn't ride too fast he should be able to ride seven miles easily and still make it back before nine o'clock.

He rode on in the silent night, alone with his thoughts and feelings. It had been a week since he had seen the Hagan. Their meetings were becoming less frequent. He was given assignments and they would meet to discuss the results.

Still something bothered him. Moira Hagan was drawn, tired and slower than he had ever seen her. She seemed sad to him somehow and oddly distracted. He had felt it in her for some time. With the skills he had developed, he was able to analyze his past feelings clearly. He had to admit, he had felt his teacher's loss of force from the beginning.

"You know as much as I can tell you – for now," she had said to him without emotion. "You may ask questions of course, but for my part I've given you what I can. We'll hope it will be enough in the time remaining."

Remaining until what he wanted to shout, but refrained, knowing she would only look sadly at him as though he were a particularly dull student.

Four bright flashes of light went off in a field to Julian's right. He estimated the distance could be no more than two hundred meters from the road to the position of the flashes. He stopped and two more flashes exploded about two seconds apart. Julian leaned his bike against a tree and made his way to the edge of the farmer's field, jumped a stone fence and began trotting toward the flashes.

The ground was broken and the going hard. Men's voices were carried on the cool night air. At seventy-five meters, he heard the sound of a vehicle engine starting. He broke into a run and arrived in time to see the vehicle's tail lights merge into each other in the distance and the engine noise disappear.

Julian switched on his flashlight and panting heavily, surveyed the area. Men's work boots and the tires of what he assumed to be a small truck beat down the pasture grass. Shining the light in front of him he encountered mud – more mud than there should have been in a pristine pasture. He shone the light up and found the face of a round hillock had been hacked away. He lowered the light and backed away so he could take in the entire scene.

He stopped at a distance and began to follow the tracks of the truck as they approached the site of the digging. He could see where the truck had stopped and suddenly he could see the men as they got out of a white truck. It wasn't as though he was imagining it. He felt he was standing there watching them work. The feeling was unsettling.

They removed their picks and shovels and started for the hillock. They had sheared away the face of the hill and then he couldn't see anything more. It was there. He could feel it. "What did they do next?" He asked himself. But the mental picture wouldn't come back.

The flashes. He remembered the flashes. How many? *Four and then two.* Yes. They had stopped digging, walked back to the truck and put their tools away. Julian shone the light at his feet and between his muddy boots lay a photograph taken with an old fashioned instant camera.

It was a picture of what the men had done.

Julian tried to work it out in his mind. "But what had they done? They had dug away part of a small mound of earth. So what? To what end and why was it so important they would take half a dozen pictures of it. What were they going to do with the other pictures?

To whom would they show them?" Questions without answers presented themselves to Julian.

Chapter Fifteen

He sat on a bench outside the Hagan's front door. Julian knew she was at home. He could sense it and his sense of her was his primary concern. He felt her draw near the door before he heard her open it. He was about to prove or disprove his theory and his feelings. He hoped he was wrong but feared he was not.

She stepped out into her front garden and found the day glorious. The bright sunlight and a bite to the air refreshed her physically but did nothing to lift her spirits. Moira stood and looked into the heart of the village. She had lived in this house a very long time. She knew these people, her people. She knew them in ways no one else did. Perhaps, she thought, it was time someone else did. The sentiment lowered her spirits further and Julian could feel it.

"You can't help them anymore." She felt Julian's words. He had been projecting his thoughts for several weeks and had gained control of that talent quickly.

She closed her eyes. He was near. That she knew, but no more. She took a deep breath and exhaled as she looked at the last of the wild flowers growing on the path at her feet. She heard him stand and she smiled. Moira turned, looked at Julian and said softly, "Come inside."

They sat in front of the low turf fire. The light played upon her face, sharpening her features and Julian could feel the strain in her.

Moira began, "You're right of course. I can't help them anymore. I can't help anyone any more, least of all you. Not in the way I want to, the way I should be able to."

"What's happened?" Julian's asked simply, softly.

"Julian, I don't know, I simply don't know. It started happening well before you arrived. At first, I thought I was growing old and tired, but that felt wrong somehow. I've thought on it a great deal as you can imagine. For us, losing abilities isn't like a head cold. It isn't something you simply get over. No, no 'tis far worse.

"For us it is about control. We take the raw talents we are given and through practice, we develop the skill necessary to discipline our thoughts and so guide the use of those talents."

She continued. "As I told you before we do not change or manipulate the universe about us. This is not about bending the laws of nature to our will. We see what is real and what is illusion and so we are able to act accordingly. At a very deep level, you know this. I can feel that in you. Sadly, I can feel little else.

"That control I spoke of, in my case, is now in question and so the talents themselves are no longer reliable. As a result, I can do very little without running a terrible risk, a risk I'm not willing to take. People get hurt when we get it wrong, Julian."

He did not understand her loss fully, but he could feel her sadness. In a voice touched with tenderness, he asked, "What can I do to help you? How can we get back what you've lost?"

The old woman smiled thinly, reached out and touched Julian's hand. He closed his eyes. Where once she could have left that hand tingling at her touch, now there was just the softness and warmth of a troubled woman.

"That's what I find so worrying. It isn't as though I've lost it. It feels as if it is being taken. I'm afraid I don't know how else to say it. At first, it was small things, but now more and more of me has been taken. Now, there is little left, I'm afraid." Moira said and looked deeply into the fireplace.

"Then is there a way we can protect you from whatever is robbing you of your abilities? Is it something here? If you left the valley for a while, would that help? Is there someone we can call on for assistance? There must be something we can do." Julian bunched his fist in frustration.

"Listen, Moira, you have been good to me – in your own odd sort of way." The woman chuckled and Julian continued.

"If you're worried about me, don't be. I'll be fine. I'll continue to practice and I'll be as ready as possible when I need to be. I know someone who can come take you away from here. She is like you. She's someone who understands and who can help. Maybe there is another teacher who can watch over me while you're away if that would make you feel better. Let's not just sit and do nothing."

"Julian, you are a dear boy – in your own odd sort of way," Moira said not unkindly and it was Julian's turn to smile.

"When you came here you needed my help. Now I need yours and everything is wrong about that. It is outside the natural order, don't ya see?" Moira went quiet as she looked into the fireplace. She closed her eyes and drew a ragged breath, let it out and turned to look into Julian's eyes.

"My place is here. I don't know why, but I know I'm to stay here and I know no more than that. It's not clear what we can do, but we will find a solution. It is up to us, Julian, to find the truth of things and understand it fully. We are the only ones here who can do anything. So, it's you and me, boyo.

"I'm tired, so run along to your lessons. Julian, I am so dreadfully tired," she said.

In a world of thoughts and feelings, knowledge and experience Moira Hagan was lost to Julian. He rose quietly and let himself out.

***

For the next weeks, he practiced harder, longer and with sustained concentration. The efforts left him drained but satisfied with his progress.

***

Brendan Maher watched the trees as they bent in the breeze. By constantly exposing both sides of their leaves, the trees displayed a riot of changing color exclusively for Brendan's delight.

As he sat at the tree line looking across a farmer's field to the other side, he had an unobstructed view of rows of potato plants and the trees. He could smell the damp earth beneath him and could feel the light breeze on his face and through his hair. He saw it all through half closed eyes as his hand rhythmically stroked Dunla's fur.

She had grown and could no longer sit on his lap, but she enjoyed having her head and front paws across her young master's thigh and to feel his hand on her shoulder with an occasional foray up to her ears.

The sounds and smells that left her master content were the same ones that came to her, but her ability to instantaneously calculate their subtle meanings was instinctive and unerring. Although the dog had her eyes closed and breathed heavily through her nose, she was alive to everything around her.

Unlike a person, Dunla had no need to weigh the relative value of the things around her. Danger was the only weighted value. The sound of the leaves, the smell of the earth, the feel of the wind lightly rustling her fur, the love of her master – all were simply facts.

She felt it before she heard it and long before she would have seen it. She tensed and began to rise, but Brendan held her in place and spoke soothingly in Gaelic to her. He knew there was no danger. A truck was coming along a farm road on the far side of the field. The vehicle was a small white pickup truck driven by a large man in a cloth cap.

Brendan whispered to Dunla, "No need to worry my little lady. It is only a truck – a farmer probably," he said in Gaelic and the dog heard not a stutter or stammer, only her master's calm steady voice. This was the voice she knew. This was the voice never raised to her in anger. This was the voice that calmly cautioned her when she misbehaved. This was the voice that lavished praise on her for the simplest activities. The boy watched the truck not understanding what he was seeing.

It passed level with them and stopped near a small hillock a short way up the road. The man in the cloth cap did not get out, but the passenger door opened slowly and a very thin man in a dark suit emerged.

The man scanned the area for activity from the sheltered side of the truck and seeing none, he began to slowly walk around the circumference of the mound while the driver pulled forward and turned the vehicle around. The man in the dark suit stopped from time to time to inspect things near the mound. He returned to the truck, spoke to the driver briefly, got in and they drove off in the direction they had come.

***

While Brendan and Dunla sat and watched the day unfold from the base of the trees, in the village, Julian questioned Sean Maher.

"Why are there all these mounds? Why are these people digging into them? What are they looking for?"

"After forcing me to consume unreasonably large quantities of porter last night, is it you who would be asking me questions that would hurt the head of a saint? For the answers to these questions, you would have to consult the Hagan. She knows of the mounds. I think they were being made a thousand years ago when she was a girl," Sean said sourly. "Still, as to the digging, Oi wouldn't think she knows anything. Still, with witches it is best never to underestimate what they know and what they don't."

"Good suggestion. Let's go ask her."

Maher looked stricken. “Let’s? As in you and me? ME? You are daft. Oi’ll not be seen conspiring with witches. Oi have me reputation and my immortal soul to think of!”

“Are you going to be a big sissy about this? How many times do I have to tell you, she is not a witch. There are no witches. None,” Julian stated.

“If you were not such a vast friend of mine and if my head did not hurt so from the porter, Oi would simply knock you down, Julian Blessing.”

“There, then it’s settled. Let’s go. It is off to see the Witch of Cappel Vale.” Julian laughed.

With a groan, Sean set off with Julian and found Moira Hagan working in her garden.

“Well, the entire police force of Cappel Vale has come to arrest a poor old woman. Is that what the world has come to? Doubtless, Sean Maher has brought his rubber truncheon to beat me while you, Julian Blessing, break me down with your towering intellect,” Moira snorted. Julian noted that she might have lost use of many of her powers, but she had retained her sense of humor and her acid tongue.

“We simply seek the assistance of a law abiding citizen, Mrs. Hagan,” Julian addressed his teacher formally.

“And, should I not be able to render such assistance, well, then ’tis I who will be introduced to the rubber truncheon?” she asked.

“Only if that is what pleases you somehow,” Julian said while Sean tried to hide his massive frame behind his considerably smaller friend.

“We are wondering about the mounds,” Julian said, but Sean cleared his throat. “I am corrected. I am wondering about the mounds. More specifically I am wondering what you can tell me about them.”

"You know the Squire of course," Moira Hagan said and Julian nodded.

"Go to the Squire and ask to borrow his automobile and meet me by the crossroads east of the village near the holy well. Forty-five minutes should give us all enough time. Oh, and bring your field glasses if you have any. If not, borrow some from the Squire," Moira said.

"Good. Now that is settled I'll be on my way," Sean Maher said and his mood brightened considerably.

"Absolutely correct, Sean Maher – indeed you will be on your way with Mr. Blessing to fetch the automobile. You will then accompany us on our outing."

"But..."

"But what?" Moira Hagan snapped and her glance chilled Sean's bones.

"But Oi'll be going with Julian to fetch the Squire's automobile," Sean said resigned to having his soul burn throughout eternity for fraternizing with a witch.

***

Julian brought the Squire's ancient black Land Rover to a stop moments before Moira Hagan shimmered out of the forest and onto the unpaved roadway. Sean looked at Julian and said, "How did you know? The crossroads isn't for another kilometer."

Julian smiled, was thoughtful for a moment and said simply, "Just a lucky guess." And this answer satisfied Sean Maher not at all.

The Hagan stepped to the passenger side front door, cocked her head and squinted at Sean who quickly relinquished his position and clambered into the backseat. "Straight until I tell you. Then we'll take a right turning onto a path where the pasture begins. From there drive until I tell you otherwise."

They drove on in silence. Julian watched the road intently trying to anticipate and avoid the ruts in the road. A goat path appeared and, although it looked just like the four they had passed already, the Hagan told Julian to turn. The path rose steeply leaving the road to Cappel Vale and the valley far below and to the right.

It seemed every variant of green was possible in this impossible place. The breeze, gentle and measured in the village, had become a full wind blowing unimpeded off the Irish Sea. Although not at gale force, the wind buffeted the Land Rover and Julian had to hold on tightly to the steering wheel to keep it on the goat path.

"This path will crest in awhile. There will be an outcropping of trees at the top to the right. Stop there. We will walk the rest of the way. Did you bring the field glasses?"

"Yes," was all Julian said as he fought to keep the back end of the vehicle from losing traction and getting them all mired in the soft earth on either side of the path.

"You didn't think to bring anything to drink did ye?" Sean croaked in a choked panic stricken voice from the back seat. He was a man of the land and didn't much care for automobiles. He looked at them with only slightly less suspicion then he did airplanes, submarines and trips to the moon – not something for a proper Christian.

"Is it porter you would be talking about, Sean Maher? If you weren't crouching there on the floorboards you would at this moment be intoxicated by the beauty that surrounds you, you great oaf," the Hagan said with a half snarl.

"The back of me hand will be something that'll intoxicate ya!" Maher mumbled and Julian's hand shot to his mouth to hide the grin that materialized there despite his best efforts.

"What did you say? And you, what exactly do you find so funny?" the Hagan said as unkindly as possible.

"Me?" Maher said. "Oi didn't say anything, but Oi mayhaps have mentioned that your good self was probably quite correct."

"Funny? Me?" Julian joined in. "No, I'm just intoxicated by the beauty that surrounds us."

"If I didn't have other things to do I'd stop this automobile and beat the both of you eejits for your insolence. As you will remember, 'tis I who am doing you the favor and not the other way round, but even if it were the other way round I would probably take the time to beat you both just for good measure. It would do you both a world of good and make better men of you!"

The remainder of the trip was conducted in silence.

***

Julian stopped the Land Rover at the crest of the goat path and got out. His fingers were stiff from gripping the steering wheel so tightly. Sean slithered from the backseat grateful to be on firm ground. Moira Hagan sat in the vehicle. When she didn't appear both men turned and were horror stuck.

Although outwardly tranquil, the Hagan communicated a wordless message that could not be more clearly understood. It seemed to say, "If one of you eejits doesn't get over here and open my door and hand me out of the vehicle NOW, I will make you both wish your mothers had become nuns!"

The flurry of activity as each man trotted to the passenger side of the Land Rover was remarkable for its comic clumsiness. Maher wrenched open the door with nearly enough force to tear it off the hinges. Julian extended his hand and took the Hagan by the elbow with the other hand to ease her to the ground. After smoothing her long dark skirt, Moira Hagan reached up and patted Julian on the cheek. As she stepped around the door, she touched Sean's hand and smiled at him. Julian and Sean shivered.

"That was very nicely done boys. It is good to know your mothers taught you well. Now shall we go?"

She led them to the very edge of the outcrop. The Hagan sat down on a comfortable rock and pointed into the valley. "What do you see?"

Julian was stunned. "Mounds – lots of them. I didn't realize there were so many."

"I suppose this is why you are a policeman and I a mere woman citizen of our little village," she said and sarcasm dripped from her voice. "Of course there are lots of mounds ya eejit.

"You! Maher. I don't suppose you will do much better, but you have lived here all your life so I am expecting something from you, boyo. Tell friend Blessing what he is looking at."

"They're burial mounds lined up between here and the coast, Oi think."

"Well, you think correctly or nearly correctly. Let's begin with what we know of their beginning." Moira Hagan settled herself, closed and then with heavy lids opened her eyes again. Her shoulders relaxed and she began.

"Although nothing of Ireland exists that can be dated before the sixth century, burial sites are an altogether different matter.

"Four thousand years ago, give or take, the people of this area of Ireland constructed these earthworks. Although known as burial mounds very few of them were. Some of the earthen mounds were hollow inside with the resulting chambers being decorated with carvings and paintings.

"There are 300 so called passage-tombs here in Ireland with the largest being at Knowth, Newgrange and Dowth. These mounds are huge and are surrounded by a dozen or more smaller ones. Those smaller mounds are much more like the ones you see below in the valley.

"Still, in spite of the similarity of size, ours are somewhat different. Rather than surrounding a larger structure as in those other places, ours run in a perfectly straight line. No one living today knows why. They start at the base of the mountain where we are and run east for some way before they reach the sea. Still they do not terminate at a larger mound, as one would expect. Are you two paying attention?" Moira snapped and then continued.

"A number of the mounds were found to have served as burial chambers or tombs for Celtic nobility, others acted as storehouses, some were just mounds and as such solid through and through with no seeming purpose a'tall," she said.

"They are all protected these days by the government, but there was a time when they were freely plundered by the visitors sent to conquer us – that would be our English friends.

"Little good it did them as no real wealth was ever found. Ours is a poor country rich only in culture, history and heritage – nothing that would interest the English," she said.

"Since then the farmers of this valley have simply worked around the mounds. They are not trees to be cut down or boulders to be moved. They are a past to be honored because it is an Irish past."

"So, is it possible someone is still trying to plunder them?" Julian asked. "Is it possible someone came into possession of information that one of the mounds contained something valuable?"

"Possibly, but farfetched and frankly a lot of work for little profit," the Hagan answered. "It is the proverbial needle in a haystack even with access to information. Even if it's true, it is pretty certain whoever is digging doesn't have an exact location."

"Maybe the digging is experimental. You know, testing to see if a given mound is of one type or another," Sean said while Julian scanned the row of mounds through the field glasses.

"That is possible also," the Hagan answered. "It is thought a palisade of plank boards or wooden stakes originally surrounded the mounds. Years of erosion would have washed down over that and your diggers may be looking for that sort of evidence.

"Still, even if such portions of a palisade did still exist it would prove nothing. Farmers built their houses along the same lines using the same tools, methods and architecture," she said thoughtfully.

"Hello," Julian said.

"What is it?" Sean asked and reached for the binoculars.

"Count out eleven mounds and tell me what you see."

"Seven, eight, nine, ten... Shite, oh, sorry. It's the white truck! A man has got out and is walking around the mound. Damn, we are too far away to make out any detail. A driver and at least one passenger – that's all Oi can see," Sean said through teeth clenched in frustration.

Both men turned and found the Hagan seated on her rock with her eyes closed and her face gray as ash. They rushed to her and as they each took an arm, she seemed to come to herself.

"You have seen what you've come to see and I have seen more than I want. We must be off. I need to go home." Julian was horrified. He helped her up and she felt small and frail. His sense was that her strength was fast leaving her.

"Sean!" he called out.

"No!" the woman's bark was short, sharp and emphatic. "That lummox will not lay hands on Moira Hagan this day or any other. Understand me, boyo!" Julian nodded his head and waved Sean away.

Chapter Sixteen

After the truck had gone, Brendan stretched out his hand and began to stroke his dog's silken cheek under her eye. Soon her eyes closed and she began her slow rhythmic breathing again. Brendan watched the branches move effortlessly in the breeze and saw the clouds streak overhead.

"Dunla?" Brendan whispered. The dog sat at attention looking into the boy's face. He smiled, stroked the dog's ear and continued in Gaelic, "Time to go home and clean up for supper." The dog's tail wagged in understanding that she and he would be off on another adventure. Being with her master was always a series of adventures and a source of endless pleasure.

As they entered the village Brendan and Dunla were passed by the Squire's old Range Rover carrying Julian and Brendan's father. Waves were exchanged and Dunla barked at the passing car.

Trouble stepped into Brendan Maher's path and Dunla was the first to sense it. Bobby McMaster appeared in the road, a bundle of belligerence.

"Why do you think you're an eejit, Maher?"

Fully a head shorter than Brendan, Bobby McMaster imagined himself larger than he was, as only a true bully can do. Had it stopped there, Liam McMaster's son would have been merely an annoyance. But the boy had a vicious streak – not just cruel in the way children can sometimes be – he was ferociously sadistic and more than anything, he relished the feeling he got from inflicting pain on others.

His father was prosperous and had always been able to buy his son's way out of one scrape or another. But the torments Bobby McMaster visited on others were escalating.

Dunla locked her eyes on the malignancy before her and began a low, rumbling growl.

"Oi asked you a question Maher. Why are you an eejit?"

Brendan's eyes narrowed and he set his mouth. Dunla sensed more than felt the imperceptible shift in her master's weight. She stepped forward and displayed a row of teeth that bore nothing but ill will.

"Do you think that cur frightens me? That thing is hardly worth killing. It looks as stupid as you." Dunla moved forward another step and set her weight into her hind legs bracing for the attack.

"No Dunla."

"Oi think you're an eejit because your Da is an eejit. What do you say to that?" McMaster snarled.

"Let's g-g-go, Dunla," Brendan said.

Normally quick to respond, Dunla held her ground.

Brendan stepped past Bobby McMaster, but close enough to let him know this had nothing to do with fear. Still Dunla held fast.

McMaster pushed Brendan away and faster than the speed of human thought, Dunla launched herself and was firmly attached to McMaster's pant leg and was pulling him off his feet. Brendan assisted this by grabbing the shorter boy's shirt and forcing him backwards. Once McMaster was firmly on his back Dunla was called to heel and she obeyed immediately, but without ever losing sight of Bobby McMaster.

"I'll have you for that Maher ya feekin' eejit and that vicious mongrel too! I'll tell me Da and he'll sort you out!" Bobby McMaster screamed at Brendan's back.

A dirt clod broke on the ground at Brendan's heel. He stopped and turned around to see McMaster, another clod in his hand, standing in the road, impotent rage etching his face.

"Home, Dunla," Brendan said and both dog and boy turned as the second dirt clod broke harmlessly on the ground behind them.

"Good girl," Brendan said and Dunla knew he was right.

***

In a cottage beside St. Michael's school, Julian Blessing and Sean Maher took tea with Sister Eugenia and her assistant, Sister Gertrude.

"Sisters, which of the children is the best artist in school? There is something I need drawn. It isn't anything complex, but I want it to be as realistic as possible."

"Always happy to be of assistance, gentlemen," said Sister Eugenia. "That would be Grace, don't you think Sister Gertrude?" The nuns agreed Grace was the most accomplished artist and Sister Gertrude went to get her.

The delicate teacup looked like a thimble in Sean's enormous gnarled hands. The cup clattered in its saucer. Sean was afraid of very few things in life; the devil, witches and nuns and not always in that order. Determining which was worse boiled down to which was in front of him at the time. Sisters Eugenia and Gertrude, a plague of nuns, was really more than a good, strong, God fearing man should have to endure.

"Will you have more tea, Mr. Maher?" Sister Eugenia's question nearly made the big man jump out of his skin. It was a civil enough question, but after long and painful experience, Sean knew nuns would exercise civility only as a set up to hoisting one's vitals on a stick.

"Thank ye, Sister, no more for me."

The nun said with a smile, "Mr. Blessing, while we wait for our little artist to arrive would you be so kind as to indulge an old woman's curiosity?

Julian found himself bracing for a blow from a ruler of the thin, regal woman of undetermined age seated across from him. After long experience in school, he knew you had to watch out for the wiry ones, they were the fastest with a ruler.

"It is perhaps a personal question. Do you mind?"

"Not at all, Sister. If I can, I'll answer any questions you have," Julian answered. Sean issued a high-pitched whimpering sound and the nun shot him a glance through narrowed eyes.

She turned her attention back to Julian. "The other day, I was conducting some business in Mr. Brady's establishment when you walked in. You saw me and developed that 'Oh-sweet-Jaysus-a-NUN' look. That look is, in my experience, unique to some of those of the worst sort who have been educated in Catholic schools. For some reason you would like me not to know that. I wonder why that would be, but we can discuss that another time."

The smile was frozen on Julian's face and Sean's whimpering grew strangled.

With the expression of someone who was inquiring about the weather, Sister Eugenia asked, "How horrid a little creature were you at school?"

As best he could, Julian tried to transform his smile to a look of sincere innocence before he said, "I was an altar boy, Sister."

"Oh my," the nun said, the calm smile still lighting her face. "I somehow should have known. In my experience, it is a testimony to the fortitude of Holy Mother Church that she has survived altar boys these many years. Do you not agree Mr. Blessing?"

"Well, Sister, I can not speak to that, but I was quite good. I never got into trouble." Julian gave her his best innocent, yet modestly pathetic, look.

"Good, you say? Really? Never got into trouble? Would you not say a more accurate statement is that you were seldom caught?"

The nun smiled and inclined her head slightly, her eyes bright with innocence. It was the innocence available only to those who have spent a lifetime dealing from a position of moral superiority and spiritually hellacious firepower.

Julian suddenly recalled being in grade school, kneeling in the corner, the corduroy of his uniform pants feeling like razor blades under his knees. He tried to perfect his pitiable look but said nothing.

The nun's eyes narrowed slightly and she fixed them on Julian like an entomologist would pin a bug to a corkboard. Julian Blessing, man of the world, a man of affairs, a man of rare importance and wealth swallowed hard and felt remarkably bug-like.

"Tell me honestly Mr. Blessing, how many times do you suspect you and your fellow altar boys got into the altar wine? How many unconsecrated hosts did you and your gluttonous compatriots consume?"

"Sister Eugenia..." Julian was about to lie his protest.

"Ah, Sister Gertrude, you are back just in time. Our Mr. Blessing was preparing to be exceedingly untruthful? Mr. Blessing, would it not be a shame if a large black lie were to sit on your soul and corrupt your spirit?" Sister Eugenia said and looked horrifyingly angelic.

"Mr. Maher, you seem to be unwell. No? You will understand my concern. With the teacup rattling in your hands it has become difficult to hear. But it is those odd mewing sounds coming from you that have me most concerned."

"No, Sister, Oi'm fine," Sean mewed.

"That is so good to hear. In any case, Mr. Blessing, I am following my line of inquiry in order to, as I said, satisfy the curiosity of an old woman. You see, your companion Mr. Maher is, of course, well known to me. Isn't that true, Sean Maher?" she said and withered Sean with a frosty glance.

She continued. “Well, that leaves only you Mr. Blessing. So you will understand my curiosity is simply to gauge the level of mischief I can expect from you.

“Ah here is our little Grace. Sister Gertrude and I have things to which we must attend. Grace, please assist these gentlemen.”

Sean hung his head after the nuns had gone. Soft moaning sounds could be heard from him as he sat in shame and rocked gently back and forth.

Julian held a plastic smile on his face as he said softly, “Jesus! That woman is truly frightening.”

Twelve year-old Grace looked at the two grown men and pitied them. They didn't know the half of it.

***

Grace, a reedy girl with glasses, drew a very real likeness of the white pickup truck. Julian supplied the description and it all appeared under the single word WANTED. Sean had his fill of nuns for one day so was glad he and Julian could escape.

After making copies on the school's ancient spirit duplicator, the men papered every flat public surface with posters. They made plans for a door-to-door campaign throughout the valley looking for information on the vehicle, its owner or any sightings.

It wasn't much, but it was something. After being on the defensive for so long over all the digging, not much was just enough. To Julian, taking the initiative seemed the most important work of his life.

***

Julian's daily routine was forming itself around demanding, self-directed study and occasional intense discussions with Moira Hagan. This he would follow by breakfast and forays into the valley to call on the local farms. In the evening he would return tired from his day's efforts, have supper and, when the village was dark and still, he would walk the main street visiting with those he met.

He would end his night in his rocking chair either on the stoop or before the fire if the weather was chilly. He contented himself with the fact that no further assaults had taken place recently, but the digging continued and the feeling in the valley had turned dark.

The lessons with Moira Hagan had sharpened Julian's senses. Even without her daily assistance, his universe was expanding by the moment. His sense of the real and the counterfeit was also becoming more clearly defined. He was more attuned to things around him, things that had gone unnoticed in his past.

Julian had been sensing things before he saw or heard them since his arrival, but his ability was now more accurate and detailed. He constantly surprised himself with this new talent and found it served him in many ways.

There was a game the village children played with him, which he felt was a good practice exercise. The youngsters tried to sneak up and catch him unaware. At first, his batting average was poor and they were able to get the drop on him easily but as time went on this changed. He found he could feel their innocence hiding in the bushes along a road. He could sense their unrestrained mischievousness concealed in a tree.

Over time, he could sense individual children before they appeared and would call them by name. This pleased him and sent them into fits of laughter at having been caught out.

Adults were even easier to sense. Julian knew before he saw him that the Mayor was approaching and could judge the degree of strong drink the man had onboard.

Sean Maher was an open book. He could sense Sean's big and childlike presence before the man appeared. Julian sometimes delighted in making the large man uncomfortable by identifying his mood before a word was spoken.

"Thirsty, Sean? Let's have a pint," Julian would say in the middle of the day. This, at first was disconcerting to Maher. He felt as though Julian was inside his head. Recently Sean Maher had taken to crossing himself whenever Julian's senses were too sharp.

Julian made a special study of Ailís Dwyer. He could tell if she was inside a building as he passed by outside. After some practice, he had been able to read her moods and occasionally he felt he was reading her thoughts. This last bit of information he tried to blot out of his mind. He was comfortable with Ailís and didn't want to risk spoiling that after their rocky beginning.

Easiest of all had been Moira Hagan, but his awareness of her had changed as she weakened. In the beginning, he would sense her presence but this sense was becoming weaker in ways that he did not understand. Sometimes she felt very near, but other times even when talking with her he felt she was somehow ephemeral and not really with him at all.

She would smile knowingly when she sensed his confusion, but never explained what was happening.

***

One evening when he was snug in front of the peat fire of the station house Julian looked to the door and called out, "Come in Moira."

She entered and he felt what she was thinking. The sense was weak and distant, but it was there. *"You really have become very proficient at that."* Julian smiled. It wasn't so long ago that voices in his head made him question his sanity.

His teacher continued with a pleasant voice, "In some ways your talent surprises me; in other ways it does not," she said as she crossed the threshold of the station. Julian rose, indicated the second rocking chair. Moira said she would rather sit near the fire and took her place on a long wooden bench that ran perpendicular to the hearth.

"Why does it surprise you? Do you think I'm too thick for such things?" Julian asked. "Plodding and soulless creatures like me can't attain any sort of wisdom?" he asked and smiled broadly even though he remembered clearly the source of those words, the letter from his ex-wife.

"Plodding? No, I don't see you as that. You may wander about without much sense of direction from time to time, but I wouldn't call that plodding. You have discovered bits and pieces of yourself and your abilities, so that doesn't apply.

"You are the tiniest bit too bright to be considered thick. But wisdom, well I do wonder if you'll ever attain that," Moira Hagan said with a smirk as she looked into the fire. "No it surprises me you have grasped the ability to project your thoughts. It is a talent that most acquire last. The difficult you seem to do with amazing ease. The easy things, like quieting your thoughts, are nearly impossible for you."

"Nearly impossible for now," Julian said.

"Alright, I'll go along with your, 'for now,' but let's hurry it along. I don't plan on living forever just to prove you right." Moira and her student shared a smile.

The fire illuminated half of her face giving her next words added gravity.

"Julian, I do have a rather important question to put to you. You need not answer now, but you will need to answer soon."

"Yes?"

"What frightens you?" she asked.

Julian closed his eyes and let his chin rest on his chest. He took a very deep breath, exhaled and his thoughts took over. "*I knew you would ask that eventually. I had in fact practiced some very snappy replies, but they were all lame and shallow – even for me.*"

"No, Julian. I want you to speak the words and I want to listen as you say them," his companion said softly.

He continued aloud, "I have given this a lot of thought since I started working with you. I have examined the thing from every possible direction and discovered something.

"The complex answers I concocted always ended up looking a lot like rationalizations while the simple answers all pointed to the truth. Moira, I am afraid of nearly everything."

Moira continued to stare into the fire as Julian fell silent. She turned to look, not at him, but into him when he continued.

"I am very serious. I am afraid of both sides of everything. I am afraid people will know me – the real me and I am afraid I will die unknown. I am afraid to be happy and am terrified I will never know happiness. I am afraid of being a friend because I don't know how to be one and the thought of losing one is terrifying to me. I am afraid to love because I don't know how to receive love or what to do with it. I am afraid of being intimate with someone and afraid I will never be truly close to anyone.

"Not in the things we practice of course, but I am afraid of not being good enough all the while hoping people don't believe I think I'm too good. I am afraid I will never get a handle on all that you have shown me and that what little I have grasped will somehow slip away."

Moira listened to him as he continued the litany of his fears. She looked deep inside the man and knew the measure of his sincerity. After a while, Julian went silent, spent from the effort of summoning up his personal torments.

"You have not mentioned the one thing people fear most, why is that?" Moira asked.

"Why is that? I have not even plumbed the depth of how much I don't know. I have no idea what people fear most."

"Death, boyo. They fear death in all its many ways and means, yet you mention it not a'tall. Why is that?"

"That, Moira is sadly simple. It is the one coin of which I fear only one side. I'm not afraid of dying. I am afraid of living."

Teacher and student sat in silence while the firelight painted the walls. Shapes and shadows lingered and merged, softened and disappeared.

"It is time to face those fears of course, but then you know that," Moira said. "You have told me something of your life before you arrived. In your old life, your risk-taking was always calculated and when the reward out-weighed the risk, you rolled the dice. Winning and losing was based on your ability alone to read the financial tealeaves, but rearranging the tealeaves a bit worked too. In your own way, you could win if you could direct, redirect or predict the course of life. Would that be a fair statement?"

Julian nodded.

"Well, my young friend, it is time for you to learn the sort of power that awaits and the protection it affords you. Time for you Julian, to discover you are in league with life rather than fighting to outflank it.

"The best way to gain the knowledge you need is for you to risk without the least hope of a reward. It is a thing that is more important than you know. It will be hard for you, but you must do it and keep doing it until it becomes not second but first nature. You see, you must know when calculating your risks is necessary and you must know when to risk all for no reason at all other than you know it to be right.

"To some degree you have come to know the people of the village and the valley. What do you suppose would happen if you made it a habit of telling each exactly what you thought of them?"

"You're joking of course," Julian said wrinkling his forehead in consternation.

"I am not. This isn't your former life. These people are simple as is your life here. A simple truth will not offend. What would happen, do you think, if you went around and told each of them your observations of what they meant to the village, or what impact they had on you? The short of it is you have a debt to repay and that is an easy first payment.

"These people are Irish and so they hold a foreigner like you at an arm's length, but you've grown on them over time and so they have softened toward you. They have allowed you into their lives even if only to a small degree and they have given you a place to rebuild yourself.

"In the short time you have been here you have done some good already. You have given these people a view of a world that exists outside of their own. That is a wonderful gift, but you can give more and in so doing, you just might come to grips with your fears.

"You've an outsider's eye. Think of Sean Maher and Ailís Dwyer. Think of that priest, Fahey and Thomas Cahill. Think of what they mean to the village and then think they will never know it unless you tell them. Share your observations so they can see what you see. Sharing yourself will follow naturally. Don't be afraid to be human, Julian. They'll see you are not as foreign as you appear and I think you'll come to know the truth of that yourself," Moira said.

"You may gain from this experience. You may not. But this much I do know, this time there is no way to calculate the odds.

"Remember, Julian, by taking time to connect with another human being, you are connecting with the life inside yourself. With that connection will come a freedom from fear.

"Know this, you are coming to a time when you must be devoid of your fears if you are to be able to invoke the power and the protection you'll need. You must face your fears now, but how you face them is really up to you," Julian's teacher said.

"I will leave you to think on these things, Julian. I know you will come to find within yourself the best course of action. Good night to you."

Julian continued to stare into the fire as Moira Hagan rose, crossed the room and left, closing the door quietly behind her. The sun rose in the morning and found Julian still gazing into the remnants of the peat fire. He got up slowly, took a shower and went to bed. He had work to do and he would need at least a little rest before he started it.

107

Timothy Dwyer waited under the twisted birch tree in front of St. Michael's school for his friend Brendan Maher. As usual, Brendan was hustled out the front door of his family's home right on time and hard on his heels was Brendan's dog Dunla. Timothy smiled and waved and his friend waved back and picked up the pace.

"So Dunla is on her way to school then," Timothy said and laughed.

"DDDon't be daft. She waits for me here," Brendan answered his friend.

Brendan laid out a small blanket under the shade of the birch tree, and then took out a tin bowl he had brought which he filled with water at the side of the school building and brought it back to Dunla.

Brendan communicated with Dunla by gesturing with his hand that he wanted her to lie down. Once she was settled, Brendan put her water down beside her. "Oi know you will, but be a good dog. Oi'll be back soon," Brendan said in Gaelic and he and Timothy hurried inside the school.

As they made their way to class Timothy asked, "How is it she knows what you want? It's like she was a person. She seems to understand you perfectly."

"AAAAnimals are like that, but Dunla is sssspecial. She is the best ddog ever."

"That she is, Brendan. You're lucky and so is she."

* * *

Bobby McMaster was late. He was nearly always late, but he carried a stock of plausible excuses. This time he was late for school and his excuses were wearing progressively thin with Sister Eugenia.

As he hurried to school, he passed the big birch tree. Although he hadn't seen Dunla, she had seen him and moreover she had remembered. She stood at Bobby McMaster's approach, head down, hackles up, teeth bared. Only the low rumble of her growl made her presence known and McMaster skirted the tree mumbling curses under his breath.

"Mister McMaster!" Sister Eugenia barked as the boy entered the schoolroom.

"Sister?" the boy responded.

"You are late and doubtless you have another fanciful explanation."

"It wasn't my fault, Sister. It was Brendan Maher's dog. She chased me, Oi fell down, and I had to fight her off."

"TTTThat's a lie!" Brendan said jumping to his feet.

Bobby McMaster turned away from Sister Eugenia and toward Brendan and smiled maliciously.

"McMaster, take your seat. Brendan, please see me after class."

"BBBut, Sister," Brendan stuttered.

"But nothing, Mr. Maher, you will see me after class. Now sit."

After class, Brendan and Timothy approached Sister Eugenia's desk. The nun continued writing in her lesson plan as the boys stood uneasily before her. Although Brendan and Timothy were not in the same grade, she knew to expect Timothy at Brendan's side.

She set down her pen, sat upright in her chair, and addressed Brendan Maher as though Timothy Dwyer wasn't present at all.

"Brendan, I have a choice for you. Either leave your dog at home or secure her to that tree outside school. I do not say this to be unkind, please understand that. You can go. Mr. Dwyer you will stay."

With his eyes burning with tears of frustration at the injustice, Brendan left the schoolroom.

"Timothy, I asked Brendan to see me after class. Under normal circumstances I would have chastised you and sent you on your way for your presumptuousness in staying with him, but Brendan is a singular case. I know you are a special friend of his. I know you are able to influence him and so I allowed you to stay. I have kept you behind now so that you will be able to show Brendan the wisdom of my decision."

"But Sister, Dunla would never have chased Bobby McMaster. She does nothing without Brendan saying so. Honest, Sister. She is innocent and this is wrong," Timothy said.

"That is enough!" the nun said slapping the top of her desk with the flat of her hand in a way that made Timothy jump. She took a long slow breath and continued in a calm voice.

"You are a bright boy, Timothy, but no amount of brightness will take the place of experience. I realize the dog is a good one. I have seen her at Brendan's side all summer and never have I seen her act out of turn. I only wish my students were half so well behaved.

"You must realize this and, more importantly, you must make Brendan realize that by leaving that dog unsecured Brendan is playing right into the hands of the Bobby McMasters of this world.

"I could have had McMaster here in front of me instead of you and your friend, but Brendan gave that great bully McMaster the perfect excuse to escape punishment. So now, he is out on the playground tormenting one of the other children and you and Brendan are here.

"Do you understand, Timothy? Do you understand that all of our choices have consequences intended and unintended. Sometimes the purest motives and intentions bring us great grief, but the grief from our unconsidered actions is more bitter still. Give Bobby McMaster no further excuses," Sister Eugenia said.

"Yes, Sister," Timothy said without conviction.

Brendan had gone home, and brought back a length of cord. He wound it loosely around the tree so Dunla would not become tangled. With tears in his eyes, he knotted the other end of the line inside the dog's collar. He spoke to her in Gaelic so he would not stutter, "It isn't that I don't trust you, but Sister is making me do this."

Brendan Maher with both fists clenched then went looking for Bobby McMaster.

Chapter Seventeen

It had been a night and a day, another night and now on the second day after Moira Hagan's visit to Julian, he emerged with a plan.

The first stop on Julian's list was Edmond Brady's shop. Julian had never known anyone so versatile, so accomplished, and so confident in his abilities. Brady's sign told it all – Brady the man to see to fix anything. Julian decided he would take that truth-in-advertising concept a step further by letting Brady know his true value.

Julian's analysis was detailed and far-reaching.

Next on the tour was Flynn's General Store where Julian stated his observations of the man and the importance of his business to the village and the valley. He explored with Flynn the financial state of the man's store.

Julian catalogued each aspect of village life that was being supported by the store and how Flynn could play an even greater role in the future of the valley.

It was a short walk to the Apothecary and the bells above the door tinkled as Julian entered.

Julian waited until both of the Hackett sisters appeared behind the counter. As always, they were dressed in gleaming white, starched blouses, black jackets and long black skirts. Each was replete with an identical watch on her jacket above the breast pocket just as they had when he first came to Cappel Vale.

"Ladies, I am a stranger here and as such I am conflicted. I bring a unique perspective with me. I can see clearly things that you may not have noticed. At the same time I feel a certain reluctance in discussing my findings with you." This introduction had been a formula he had practiced on both Brady and Flynn and it had easily hooked both crafty men.

"Do continue," the sisters said with more excitement then he had ever seen them demonstrate.

"It stands like this, ladies. You and your shop are integral to the life of this area. I know you are meticulous in dispensing the medications Dr. Dwyer prescribes, but there is more to it than that.

"Not everyone takes his or her ailments to the doctor. People depend on you two, on your establishment, to give them the advice and help they need. It is you who provide the herbs and poultices, the compresses and the wisdom. It is you who blend your knowledge and your care into every remedy and it is you whom the valley loves.

"Ladies, with time we all fade away and find our final reward elsewhere. I am telling you it is imperative that you do not allow your shop to follow. The people's needs must not be abandoned. Modern medicine does much to alleviate suffering to be sure. You know this as well as I do, but the folkways must not be forsaken and neither must the people, your people.

"For the love the people have for you and you for them, you owe the Apothecary's continuation to them. Perhaps I have said too much. I will leave you now to think about this and to not think ill of me for having said it." With that, Julian nodded, turned and walked out the door. Both of the Hackett sisters stared open mouthed after him and then turned to each other in stunned silence before tears began to roll down their cheeks.

Julian worked his way through O'Gavagan's Pubs – he had to visit both before he found the elusive O'Gavagan. Done there, Julian crossed the street and dealt out the cards face up to Francis Mulherin at the pub of that name before he closed on St. Michael's Catholic Church.

Father Fahey was just coming out of the rectory as Julian approached the church.

"Julian Blessing, saints be praised, would you be here for confession? Is that what brings you to the church at midday?" Father Fahey asked.

"No Father, it is you who brings me to the church today. I come with a message especially for you. I'm afraid confession is not my purpose today. No, I come on another mission altogether.

"I am here to tell you a story about a young priest who joined St. Michael's in the 1960s and about the love and respect he imparted and engendered."

Julian left the church half an hour later leaving a shaken Father Fahey in his wake.

Thomas Cahill was next on the agenda and the Mayor of Cappel Vale felt drained and fully sober by the time Julian was done.

Julian continued his relentless door-to-door campaign of telling people how important they were to the valley until he ran into Sean Maher.

"May I speak to you in private a moment Sean?" Julian asked when he met his friend on the village's main thoroughfare.

"Never fear, friend Julian. Oi always have time for you even though Oi was about to make time for a pint."

"Well, that's important business, so I'll get straight to the point, Sean. I envy you."

"Oi'm sorry, you were saying something, but Oi must have got it wrong," Sean said.

"I envy you. You are a man who has it all and I unabashedly covet what you have," Julian said with a warm smile.

"Julian, you envy me. Is that what you said? What in the name of God do Oi have that would be of the slightest interest to you?"

"You have a warm and welcoming home. You have a wife who loves you. You have the twins, your daughters and your son Brendan who all adore you. You have your honor. You are a man who lives a simple and abundant life. You have everything, Sean.

"The people of the valley respect you. One need only mention Sean Maher and people know, not who you are, but what you are. You are known, loved, respected. The valley would be a far poorer place without you," Julian said with terrifying sincerity.

Sean Maher had taken all of this in while looking at his shoes. "Julian. Julian?" He looked up now to see the back of his friend as he walked away. "Julian?" he said weakly. Sean's next thought was, "Now, Oi really need a pint!"

* * *

When Moira Hagan entered Mulherin's Pub looking for Thomas Cahill she was greeted by a sight of soul eviscerating devastation. Seated at one long table were Sean Maher, Jimmy Grogan, Ailís Dwyer, Edmond Brady, and Old Man Flynn.

Sitting in a curtained off section of the pub in an area called the tearoom sat Sisters Eugenia and Gertrude at one table and the Hackett twins at another. O'Gavagan was leaning on the bar staring into a pint of bitter while Francis Mulherin absentmindedly washed glasses behind the bar.

Father Fahey entered and strode to the bar and ordered a whiskey neat. The time was eleven o'clock in the morning.

The priest downed his drink and ordered another. Mulherin arched an eyebrow and the priest looked murderously at the landlord who poured a second drink in order to save his own soul. Father Fahey joined the long table and after a wary nod to Moira Hagan, he took a seat.

"Who is the wake for today?" Moira joked.

"He envies me and people respect me," Maher said quietly.

"He? Who?" Moira asked even though she had a sinking feeling she knew the answer.

"Mr. Julian says the valley needs me," Brady added.

"Without me the valley might survive, but never the village," Flynn chimed in.

"What have we here?" Moira Hagan asked then answered her own question. "A thinking priest. It is a terrible thing to behold truly. What say you priest?"

"As God is my judge I felt like I was in the presence of a minor saint. The man reminded me that my life and my soul were precious gifts and not to be used frivolously. He caused me to think hard about what Oi represented to the people of the parish. He spoke with absolute humility and he humbled me in the process."

"He has gone mad of course," Sean Maher said.

"Would that we were all so mad," Flynn added.

"True, 'tis true," they all chorused with murmuring voices lost in thought.

"Jimmy Grogan, you've not said a word," the Hagan remarked. "What says a nasty little piece of work like you?"

The young man's eyes brimmed with tears before he spoke. "He told me I didn't have to be a nasty little piece of work. He said I was made of sterner stuff and that the world expected more from me and that it was time I started to deliver the goods."

"Good advice. Perhaps we have all underestimated our Mr. Blessing, eh?" Moira said quietly.

"Aye, perhaps we have, but I'll not underestimate him again. I believe he is blessed or mad or both," Father Fahey said for them all.

Moira Hagan sat and studied the group closely. Their thoughts ran in similar veins. She could see those thoughts mirrored clearly on each face. Each finished his drink slowly and left the pub lost in a private world of thought and emotion.

"Doctor?"

Ailís Dwyer looked up and then looked around the nearly empty pub. The landlord continued to clean glasses and put them away. Moira Hagan was seated directly across from the doctor.

"You've run into Mr. Julian have you not?" the Hagan asked.

"I have and if called on I would have made something up. I could never tell the truth of what he said."

"There are only we two now." Moira looked concerned.

"Like the others, he told me the contribution I was making made a difference in the lives of people, but he went into detail – great detail, very great detail. He knew things he should not have known. He had individual examples and he covered each in turn.

"There was something compelling about what he said and the way he said it that forced me to listen. His voice was so soft I had to strain to hear him. He wasn't just being honest or sincere though. It was as though his life depended on what he was telling me. When he was done, I felt wrung out, shell-shocked. I was exhausted, but he wasn't."

The doctor continued. "He looked into my eyes as though he could see clearly into my soul. His eyes – those soft, deep-set, warm, gray-sky eyes mesmerized me. I couldn't look away from him. I tell you I was paralyzed. I couldn't have moved if I had wanted to."

The doctor went on more slowly. "I'm sure you wouldn't believe it, but he told me he cared a great deal for me. Then he just smiled, took both my hands in his. At his touch, I could feel some kind of shock, yes an electric shock, that was it. He looked at me for a full minute. His smile was so gentle, so, I don't know, intimate, tender. I don't think I drew a breath for the whole time.

"Then he turned and went on his way. He left me standing there literally speechless. And there was something more, something odd. When he let go of my hands, I could hardly feel them. There was this strange gentle, almost tender tingling sensation. I looked at them and my hands were shaking. I can't explain that. I can't explain any of it. I've not been so shaken in my life. I was moved and stunned and frightened and touched and honored and could hardly breathe all at the same time.

"Do you think he is crazy?" the doctor asked.

Moira patted the doctor's hands, "Perhaps he has lost his mind a little," she said at last, "but I believe he has found something far more important and so have we."

Each woman sat and reflected on all that had been said and thought and felt. They were silent and still for a long time. The clinking of Francis Mulherin's glasses as he put them away was the only sound that marked the passage of time.

Moira recovered herself first. "Let's talk about you, shall we? Ailís, do you mind if I give you a prescription?"

The doctor gave a puzzled look, but said nothing.

Moira smiled kindly and with a gentle knowing voice continued, "I want you to go home. Darlin' you have an aching inside of you. 'Tis an ache you have carried for too long. You need to go to your room, get comfortable and, well, do something about it. You know what to do. It will only be a temporary fix, but it will hold you for now if you keep at it."

"What?" Ailís Dwyer shook her head and began questioning if not her sanity at least her hearing.

"What? What! What are you saying? I have no idea what you're talking about. Are you mad too? No, the whole world has gone mad!" The doctor was flushed, but the color rose higher and she found her face burned and her breath was coming in shorts shallow gasps.

"I have no idea,' is it? Well then do an old woman a favor, would you?"

Ailís was mistrustful. Her ears felt absurdly hot. "What is it you want then? But I'll not have any more of your conclusions regarding my personal health. My very personal and very private health, mind you Moira Hagan."

"It was sheer poetry the way you put it. The Irish are a poetic lot, don't you think? Tell me again about his – what did you say – 'soft, deep-set, warm eyes like the color of a gray sky?' And I believe you mentioned he left you with a, what is it you said, yes – a tender tingling. Tell me again about the gentleness and the intimacy you shared with that man.

"You just think about that when you see to yourself, eh lass." Moria's lips broke into a small perceptive smile. She had struck home with the doctor and both of the women knew it.

Ailís let out a quiet, staccato high-pitched moan and her face tightened. "Enough, I have a practice to attend to. I'm sure I don't know what you are saying and I don't want to know. Best you leave it before you embarrass yourself further."

"Embarrass myself, is it? It isn't I who've begun to sweat like a draft horse – yes, just there on your lovely forehead. It isn't myself whose face and neck look to be about to combust at any moment. 'Tisn't I who is losing her mind with need."

With that, the doctor launched herself to her feet. She felt her legs would fail even as her pulse raced and a wave of lightheadedness washed over her. She clutched the table and straightened herself.

It is difficult at the best of times to look dignified while seeking any solid object for support. For Ailís Dwyer this was not the best of times. Her attempt at a majestic exit was stunningly unsuccessful.

Moira Hagan smiled and her eyes were on fire with mischief and then her thoughts turned to Julian. The distance between mischief and malice is very short.

On unsteady legs, the doctor made her way to her office. She climbed the stairs to her bedroom above the examination rooms. She closed and locked the door, then crumpled onto her bed. The doctor panted as she struggled to breathe and closed her eyes willing her head to clear without success.

The young woman rolled onto her side and doubled over with a sustained whimper and an acute longing to be touched, to be caressed, to be held, to be wanted. Ailís Dwyer could still see him. Soft, deep-set warm gray eyes… a gentle tingling... intimate…tender… shared… That was the thought Ailís held in her mind as she found the relief she so desperately sought.

***

Julian was returning from what he viewed as a very productive if somewhat peculiar interview with the Squire. For his part, the Squire thought it somewhat less satisfying. He would say in the future, this was the day Julian Blessing became unhinged.

Julian was feeling light and refreshed. He seemed to be attuned to every breath of wind, the movement of every tree branch, the rustle of the leaves beneath his boots. Before he rounded a bend in the road he knew Moira Hagan would be waiting for him. He felt she was troubled. What he should have felt was that she was about to trouble him.

"Hello," Julian shouted as he waved at his teacher sitting on a large bolder. She said nothing.

"Are we brooding a bit today?" Julian asked.

"Brooding is it? Not a'tall. Brooding is something one saves for those times when things are unsure. I am feeling quite sure just now. I am sure in fact that I gave a very simple assignment to an eejit and like any good eejit he carried it off like a most excellent eejit would!"

“What?” Julian said shocked. “I thought about what you said and I took your advice and now you are berating me for it!”

“Blessing, you went at this like a job of work. If I weren’t such a lady I would simply smack you in the gob and have done with it.”

“I still don’t understand.”

“That is the only – I repeat the only – reason I have not cuffed you,” Moira snarled.

“That and your being a lady of course,” Julian added.

“Tempt me not, Blessing. I can change my mind at any moment, you great bloody fool. I gave you work that would nourish your spirit, feed your soul and you went at it like a construction gang. Did you have to run through the entire village like a dose of salts? Did it all have to be done in one day? I am only surprised you didn’t try to work ’em all before early mass!”

Julian came back hard. “Hey, you are the one who said I had a unique perspective that people needed to hear and that I had a short time to get my affairs in order – or words to that effect. ‘If it were done when ’tis done, then ’twere well it were done quickly.’”

“Lovely and an appropriate quotation, little man, but you may remember that was Shakespeare’s Macbeth, plotting murder. I had something a little less ghastly in mind,” the Hagan said with some heat.

“…” Julian said.

“Ahhh…” Julian said.

“Err…” Julian said.

“Oh. Well, perhaps I could have approached this a little differently.”

“You mean differently from leaving your fellow citizens feeling as though they had been run over by a train?”

"Well, yes."

"Odd as it may seem, even through your own unique, blisteringly stupid way, you seem to have accomplished what needed to be accomplished."

"Oh, thank you," Julian said. "What is it that needed to be accomplished again?"

"You were overcoming fears, transcending other people's expectations and ideas about you."

"Well, good for me then, right?"

"Oh, yes, you did indeed face at least one fear that I know of. You were afraid of not being known. Well boyo, it would be safe to say you are known now. It would also be safe to say you have transcended other peoples' expectations too."

"Terrific. I've been a success."

"Oh yes. And aren't they all quite sure you are mentally disordered and therefore capable of doing the queerest things imaginable at the oddest times possible? Oh yes, people know you all too well now."

"Oh. Hmmm. Someone told me the villagers think I am pleasantly strange. I rather liked that term. You think they've changed their minds about that?"

Moira's hand went to her forehead and she snorted, "What do you think, ya eejit?"

"Not the success it might have been, eh?"

Moira Hagan drew a breath and let it out slowly. "Not quite. But we can work with it."

Chapter Eighteen

Tom Lynch, hardened, tall and broad shouldered with a barn coat and a cloth cap stood in front of his employer's desk. He had worked hard all his life. He feared none, liked few and respected the thin Pale Man not at all.

"Why is it you and your people will down tools at the slightest provocation?" the Pale Man asked.

"We was caught out by one of the local farmers. He happened upon us while we was at it and there 'twern't anything for it, but to make ourselves scarce," Tom Lynch said.

"A farmer? Do I have this correct? A farmer frightened you and all your men away?"

"You told us we were not to be seen. He must have been waiting for us he was on us that quick. Still, we got away 'afore he sawed anythin'."

"Ah, but you have already been seen." The Pale Man took one of Julian's wanted posters off his desk. "You've been seen and now people are looking for you. A dirt-poor farmer runs surveillance on his property and manages to nearly capture you and your lot. For the love of God, you are pathetic." The Pale Man held up his hand and said, "Enter" a moment before his servant knocked and announced another visitor.

"Oi came as soon as I got your honor's message," Liam McMaster said as he rushed into the room.

"Do not take another step," the Pale Man said slowly. He looked beyond McMaster to the open door behind the farmer. "You, boy, step to where I can see you." Bobby McMaster sullenly lurched into the doorway.

"What is that?" the Pale Man said through gritted teeth. The man's anger was palpable.

"Ach, that's just me boy. Bobby, say hello to his honor." The boy glowered and said nothing.

"Bobby, that is your name, correct?" the Pale Man said with a plastic smile. The boy said nothing. "Well, Bobby, get out or I will kill your father." The boy shrugged.

Liam was thunderstruck. Tom Lynch suppressed a smile and looked away. The Pale Man said, "So much for filial loyalty, eh McMaster?"

The Pale Man's voice was hard and low, his mouth twisted into a hideous sneer, "Bobby, get out or I will kill you." The boy shrugged again, turned and left. He closed the study's big door with a bang and sat in a nearby chair in the hallway.

"McMaster, you are truly unbelievable. You brought your son here. Here! I trust you will make it perfectly clear to that little animal the consequences of any lack of discretion. Up to now I've not cared if you lived or died. I am starting to rethink all of that and it's not looking good for you." The Pale Man shook his head and said, "Back to business. I believe I was about to give you both a good bollocking.

.

"I think we were talking about neither of you being so much men as rabbits, running away at the slightest noise. Maybe I am not providing the proper motivation. Perhaps you are not the right men for this job, eh?" The Pale Man rose and paced in front of the cold fireplace before he sat in one of the wingback chairs flanking the hearth, crossed his legs and steepled his fingers.

"What do you think? Is there a reason I should keep you on?" he asked.

"Oi would keep meself on, your honor. Oi have value," McMaster said.

The big man snorted. He stood just off the carpet and with a flinty look in his eyes said, "Me and me men we'll get the job done. You needn't fear on that account. The American can paper the moon with posters if he wants, it won't bother us a'tall."

Tom Lynch sneered as he watched the Pale Man and considered snapping his employer in half should the disrespect continue much longer.

Emboldened by anger Lynch said, "Now if we can be pointed in the proper direction rather than spend our time digging away at one dead end after another…" He let the statement hang in the space between them.

The Pale Man smiled maliciously and then rocketed to his feet.

"I plan and you dig. It is a simple division of labor. I think and you do." His face reddened and he continued. "Most of all though what you never do is question me, my plans, my motives or anything about this operation that does not concern a spade and dirt.

"You, McMaster are even less beneficial to my cause, but I live in the hope you will someday get your thumb out and do something useful." McMaster cowered.

The Pale Man went on, "I want to make certain I am perfectly understood. I pay you to do what I tell you to do. Your rabbits do as you tell them to do because I suffer to pay them too and because you are supposed to put the fear of God in them.

"If I want them to turn over all the turf in Ireland that is what they will do and you will make sure they do it or I will find someone who can. Do I make myself perfectly clear?" The Pale Man was shaking with rage and his voice was raised.

"I will now give you both a new task. I require you and your men to spread a little terror in our little part of Ireland. I do not want to put too fine a point on this, but it seems I must.

"If you chance upon someone or they happen upon you, now follow along," the Pale Man taunted, "I want you to maim that person.

Badly. I want you to continue this policy until the general population stops seeing fit to disrupt my activities.

"Please, understand this applies equally to men, women, children, priests, nuns, the lot. Burn the village if need be. Is any of this sinking in? Don't look stupid, McMaster, this applies to you as well."

Big Tom Lynch said nothing. His knuckles ached for the opportunity to mutilate his employer. McMaster nodded his agreement with the plan, although he was unsure of what the plan was exactly.

The Pale Man continued. "You may not think it amounts to much, but those two idiots in the village, Maher and that American, have plastered nearly the entire county with these handbills. I hear reports they are circulating more widely than that. I do not need this distraction. Employ that amount of violence necessary to stop further interference with my plans." The Pale Man was pacing and shouting. His face had nearly taken on some color.

"I want this valley to ache. I want people to suffer. I want this part of Ireland to get what it deserves."

"What it deserves?" Lynch questioned. He did not look so much puzzled as wary.

"That is what I said! I will have what is mine. Kill anything that gets in your way," the Pale Man screamed. Servants in the hall outside stopped what they were doing then resumed their duties more quietly and elsewhere. Bobby McMaster, however, had a ringside seat.

The Pale Man stopped pacing. He took several deep breaths and tried to gain control of himself. He turned and smiled. McMaster took the smile as a positive sign. Tom Lynch went to an even higher level of alert.

"Gentlemen," the Pale Man said, "we will be finished soon. We will then evaporate like fog. The American will have questions without answers and little else – if he is still with us. We will stop as quickly as we started and we will all be far wealthier – that is if I can get you two to do your part." His smile lacked warmth, humor, pleasure and fellowship. It was a smile that wasn't.

"Do you have any questions." It wasn't a question.

"In Cappel Vale, that witch, the Hagan," McMaster said, "'tis she who protects the village. Muckin' about with witches, Sor, is bad business."

The Pale Man let out a noisy breath. "I would point out three things only. Business, bad or otherwise, is my business not yours. Next, I've worked a little something of my own. The witch isn't able to protect herself right now let alone anyone else."

The Pale Man walked slowly across the room and faced his employees. "The last thing is something I urge you never to forget. Mention that woman's name in my presence again and, well, let's just say, you will beg to die. Either of you or both of you – it makes no difference to me. But know I will kill you." The pale man walked to the window turning his back on his visitors. "You understand all of this?"

"Aye." Lynch felt his employer would not hesitate to try to kill whatever got in his way. He had done it before, he would do it again. He thought over the word that made all the difference. Try. The man smiled, turned and walked toward the door.

McMaster reached the door first, pulled it open as he repeated the Pale Man's words. "Kill anything that gets in me way. I understand perfectly, Sor." He collected his son who looked cunning and sullen. Tom Lynch slapped the back of Liam's head causing him to stumble into his son on their way out the front door.

"What the...?"

"Do not speak to me, McMaster. You are as thick as shite and not even half as useful." Lynch snarled and left the manor house. McMaster slapped his son hard for laughing.

The interview was complete. The Pale Man, his colorless complexion restored, returned to the maps spread out on his massive desk. He rubbed the coin in his pocket and plotted the next dig site. The idea of murder calmed him.

***

The thin, Pale Man sat before a cold hearth and relished the hatred inside him. The room was cold, but he didn't feel it. He didn't feel anything beyond anger, hatred and the need for revenge. The drapes were pulled and he didn't see anything but the target of his rage.

He closed his eyes and cast his mind into the darkness.

***

In the pasture beyond the grove of trees, Julian stood and tried to pierce the veil of the reality he knew for the other reality he knew was out there. It was early morning, well before sunrise and the time he found it easiest to focus.

Suddenly the ground seemed to shift beneath him and he felt dizzy. He looked to the grove where Moira was sitting to see if she felt it.

His teacher's face was ashen and she was trembling. Her right arm and shoulder twitched violently. He ran to her, took her hand and then did what he had no reason to do, no way of knowing he could do or should do.

He closed his eyes and relaxed. He opened his mind and gave Moira Hagan a place to hide. He tried to construct a barrier between her and whatever was gnawing at her, clutching at her, attacking her.

He could feel a violent, malicious, consciousness leaching Moira's abilities, draining her. Julian's hands began to shake uncontrollably with the effort to hold back the attack. His fingers began to tingle.

He took a deep breath and suddenly his mind focused. The world went painfully white and intense. Everything went quiet. Reality shifted, but only slightly. Then he saw it, felt it. He was there at the source of the blackness.

A reed-thin man with an unnatural pallor sat in a chair in a darkened room. Julian could sense him, sense his loathing, his malice and the horror his spirit had become.

To be successful required more energy and skill than Julian knew he possessed, but he turned all his power to protecting his teacher. He relaxed again and opened himself to all the resources true reality could offer. He concentrated his thoughts, narrowed the intensity to a single spot, to a single moment in time. He waited. He waited for the slightest opportunity, the smallest chance.

It was there. He could feel it approach. The Thin Man paused to gather his thoughts for what Julian felt would be a final onslaught. Julian attacked with all the ferocity he could manage. To save his teacher he had to stop this man. The student remembered his teacher's words, "People get hurt when we get it wrong." Julian's world went whiter still.

The man in the chair began to shake. His body went into spasm, his face contorted, he shrieked in pain and then went slack and sat panting. His eyes were unfocused, unseeing. His mouth was slack and open. His breath came in short sharp gasps.

Julian was back in the glade. He took up maintenance of the shield, but no further attack materialized. The breeze felt cool. His arms and legs were suddenly heavy. Each breath was an effort, every movement painfully slow. Moira watched as his eyes fluttered open. He tried to speak, but she held up her hand to stop him.

For an eternity, they remained frozen in time and space - an eternity in a moment. Slowly, Julian stood, lost his balance and fell to his knees. He tried again, swayed but remained upright.

He looked at Moira, smiled the best he could and thought to her, *"I'll go get Sean. He can carry you to the doctor's. I would do it, but I'm not feeling quite myself.*" He chuckled and Moira Hagan smiled her appreciation of his concern if not his plan.

She had lost the capability of transmitting her thoughts so she said aloud, "Julian Blessing, you go get that ox, Maher. You just do that, boyo. If he lays hands on me, it will go very badly for the pair of you. I don't have much left, but I'll wager I can make life unpleasant for you both.

She chuckled. "Indeed, the very idea. I'll not be manhandled through the streets of the village. This experience has left you more than a little addled! Come here you great bloody fool. Help an old woman up," she said not unkindly. Julian smiled and did as he was told.

"What happened?" Julian thought to his teacher. The effort needed for speech was beyond him.

"It is too much for you to absorb, too much for either of us. Tomorrow night or the day after maybe," she said. "We need to digest this." Julian understood completely and didn't understand at all why or how things were changing so quickly for him.

***

"Sean Maher, the Squire would be after sending me to get you." Sean recognized the boy before him as belonging to the family who tended the Squire's flocks of sheep. It was getting light. The sun would be up soon spreading light but no heat. Sean shivered slightly and indicated with a nod that he would be ready to go with the boy in a few moments.

While many others would be ablaze with questions, Sean Maher's mind was unfettered by what might be and concentrated instead on what was right in front of him. Right in front of him right then was a pale, blond boy who led the way to the Squire's home and did so with a dreadful state of glee plastered on his face.

The walk was a brisk one and terminated at the side door that led into the squire's large brick house through the kitchen. Sean deposited coin with his young guide and smiled benignly.

The messenger peered into his palm in stark disbelief and then looked upon Sean Maher, Protector of the Right. "Oooh, all for me? Sure you can afford it, m'lord?" the boy said, his voice soaked in sarcasm.

Sean looked confused, but then the fog of incomprehension lifted and he was able to beam a smile of unimaginable brightness onto his little friend. Reaching his large paw down with lightening speed he snatched up the coin.

"Hey! Whatcha do that fer?" the young man shouted.

With remarkable cheerfulness Maher said, "See, me boyo, first you had me thanks and a lovely coin. Now you have me thanks, but unless you take yourself off right now, you'll have me boot up yor buttocks."

Sean sighed deeply and thanked God for being born a poor country fellow. He was secure in the knowledge that his young guide would receive a flea in his ear from his father for having lost the coin through cheekiness.

Sean chuckled to himself and entered the Squire's mudroom leading to the kitchen. "Good day to ya, Cook. 'Tis the master wishes to see me on a matter of grave importance," he bellowed.

"Speak up, you eejit. Did you say 'matters of importance?' With the likes of you, Sean Maher? The Squire may be in his dotage, but he would never be such a fool as to talk to you about anything of value," she shouted.

"Ah, your kind words warm me soul as only a lovely woman such as your fine and upstanding self or a jar of poitin can. Although Oi believes Oi'll take the poitin first, the better to look upon yourself. Oi do thank ye and will be seeing myself into the presence of his Lordship."

"Bahhhhh!" the cook said. "The devil take you for all Oi care."

Sean followed the dark hallway from the kitchen into the formal dining room and from there into the house's foyer. Sean was faced with three sets of closed doors and a wide sweeping stairway leading off to the right to the upper reaches of the house. Light drifted from under one of the doors and it was this door Sean opened.

The Squire was pulling shut a black drape over a picture that hung above the large fireplace. A boisterous turf fire warmed the room and cast a limited radiance in a half moon around the hearth.

"Maher, come in. It is good to see you or as good as it can possibly be to see a large ugly creature like yourself," the Squire said with a smile. "Pour yourself a brandy to warm your bones and come sit by the fire. It is conspiracy and treason we'll be talkin'."

Although the day was undeniably underway, it was still undeniably too early to be drinking. Still, Sean figured, it was at the behest of the Squire who was simply offering his brandy for medicinal purposes.

"Since 'tis you what asks, Squire, and since me poor old bones do have the rheumatics, I'll do them a kindness."

"That's a good fellow. Now sit yourself by the fire.

"You are a direct fellow, Maher. I like and respect that so I'll waste neither your time nor mine and so come to the point. Your partner, Mr. Blessing, has been busy."

"Now, Squire, there was just that one incident when he became a little tetched in the head and said a lot of nonsense to a lot of people…"

"No, not that. Truth be told, his nonsense made more sense than anything I've heard in a long time. It is a discussion for another time of course, but it escapes me entirely how a man like Blessing can be so bright while not having the sense God gave a duck."

The squire continued. “As I say, that is for another time. For now it has to do with his handbills.”

“Handbills – aye, the drawing of the wee white truck.”

“The very one. Well, little escapes me as you know and as I explained to Mr. Blessing, he made me a proposition and I accepted. I would keep my antenna out for information and in return he would talk that boy of yours into training those filthy beasts of mine.” At this the Squire pointed toward the shadows at the side of the fireplace. His two dogs lay on a neatly folded blanket alert and alive to any word from their master.

“That son of yours is a wonder. He worked but for a short time with my dogs and now they will hardly draw breath unless I give them leave. And where I would have tried to accomplish the same by laying a birch switch liberally about their hind quarters until my arm fell off, what does your boy do? He simply looked or whispered a word and those animals turn to liquid. Speaking of liquid, will you have another?” the Squire asked.

Swelled with pride, Sean shook his head and said, “Thank ye, but no, Squire.”

“Well then you won’t mind getting me another. I’ve not yet warmed my bones sufficient to the task of getting up.”

Sean smiled, took the Squire’s tumbler and refilled it from the sideboard.

“Thank ye, Maher. Now to the matter. I don’t have anything firm yet, but your white truck has been seen frequently on the furthest edge of County Louth right on our shared border with Meath. It is only a matter of time until I get the exact location from my spies.

“I want you and Mr. Blessing to know something. Those handbills don’t come without risk or cost. You are meddling in the affairs of others and they’ll not thank you for your thoughtfulness.

“Sadly, Ireland is a nation of heroes, poets and spies,” the squire said. “Thanks be to God we’ve always had more of the two former than the latter. It's the spies who will run a copy of your handbill directly to the – what should we call them – culprits? I warn you to have a care Sean and to pass along the warning to your Mr. Blessing. Mark my words, there'll be ugly and violent business before this is over."

"It's a mystery to be solved, Squire, and laws to be upheld," Sean Maher said.

"True, true, but be careful how you go. I'll contact you when I have more information. Thank you for coming."

The audience was at an end. Sean rose from his chair and asked, "Should I be freshening that for ya?" indicating the Squire's drink.

"It's a good man you are, Sean, but no. Sadly my bones are now warm enough to take me through another day." The Squire smiled, but not fully. Sean nodded his good bye. The big man was headed toward the kitchen when the sound of the Squire's voice reached him.

"Yes, Squire?" Sean said sticking his head back into the library.

"Maher, it is by the front door that you will enter and leave this house," the Squire said.

Sean raised both eyebrows and stood for a moment in stunned silence.

"Sean, boyeen, you are the law in this tiny bit of Ireland. It's not as a tradesman or tinker you are pulling your forelock and asking to see the Squire at the kitchen door. The law is not a handmaiden who slinks in by the servants' entrance. The law is a handmaiden to no one."

"Ahh, sure the Squire has the learnin' on him and words to do his bidding while Oi am but a poor Irishman. Still, sor, 'tis a slight disagreement Oi will have to make with ye."

The Squire's eyes narrowed to slits.

"It is the front door Oi will use and wish you to know that you honor me greatly. Still, the law is a handmaiden to justice, yor Worship," Sean ended with a flourish and a smile.

"Is that from your unaided wit or from over much association with Julian Blessing? In either case, it is as I said, Maher, 'heroes, poets and spies'. Pick your poison. But take some advice, don't you and Mr. Blessing make heroes of yourselves. Ireland has enough dead heroes, eh?"

Chapter Nineteen

An hour after breakfast, Sean approached the police station to meet with his friend. This was a ritual; it was something they did every day of the week except Sunday. Sunday was a day for other rituals and St Michael's Church supplied most of those.

As Sean advanced on the flagstone walkway leading to the station, the front door snapped open and Julian seemed irritated, "What's kept you? You're five minutes late. Not like you."

The men arranged themselves before the station's fireplace with their mugs of tea. The turf fire's soft warmth was comforting. Julian asked, "Sean, how was your interview with the Squire?"

The big man's eyes narrowed and he answered with a reserved, "Foine."

"Why don't you tell me about it? Leave nothing out. I wish to know everything," Julian smiled. He had discovered another ability.

He had watched the scene unfold in his mind. It happened after he left Moira at her home to rest after the assault. The scene had happened as he saw it happen. He didn't need proof. He didn't need it – he wanted it.

Sean gave a brief recital of the morning events at the Squire's home.

"Haven't you missed something?" Julian asked.

Sean shook his head knowing there were small pieces that had been intentionally left out in the retelling.

"Really, Sean, nothing else?"

Again, Sean shook his head and looked at Julian even more narrowly.

"How about being forbidden the kitchen entrance to the manor house? You're to use the front door according to the Squire. I believe that is what he said. Anything else now?"

A visible shiver ran through Sean Maher and the big man wrung his hands and said slowly, "No, nothing else, Julian. You've got it all."

Julian left the warmth of the fire and looked out the front window for a moment. He turned, stared into his friend's face and said softly, with kindness, "Sean, how about heroes, poets and spies?"

Sean Maher, with his skin crawling and his mouth hanging limply open, said the only thing left to say, "Holy Mother of God protect us all." He closed his eyes tightly and crossed himself. There were two witches in Cappel Vale and his friend was one of them.

* * *

Sean and Julian walked the streets of Cappel Vale. The big man was deep in thought and it was a painful thing to behold. He was afraid for his friend and so needed to devise a clever way to warn him of the dangers one faces when dealing with things otherworldly.

Sean realized Julian was a cultured and sensitive man whom it was necessary to handle with more than a little care. One had to use diplomacy and tact to explain a matter of this gravity.

Julian and Sean came to rest on the remnants of an ancient holy well in a clearing leading to the sea. The wind was down, but the air was crisp and cool. The well was one of the thousands that dotted the Celtic world. Each was situated to foster tranquility and contemplation.

Sean turned to his friend and with all the fellow feelings, all the tact and diplomacy he could muster, grabbed Julian by the shirtfront and shouted, "Julian, you are a feekin' eejit!"

"Do you mean just on general principal or is there something specific that prompted this observation?" Julian remarked with a smile as he hung in the big man's hands like a rag doll.

"It isn't unkindly that Oi say this," Sean answered unhanding his friend. "That witch has you muckin' about with things that, well, shouldn't be mucked about with; unnatural things, ungodly things."

"Sean, I am touched by your concern, really I am, but I don't think you have anything to be concerned about."

"Really? Being able to know things you shouldn't know? Seeing who is on the other side of your door before they knock? These things don't seem even a little unusual to you? Maureen Tracy says you read her mind and left her with impure thoughts, although that one I doubt as that ol' trout has always had impure thoughts. But what about Tommy Gallagher? He says you turned him blind and then gave his sight back to him not two minutes later!" Sean shouted.

"That Hagan creature has you bewitched. And isn't it she who is putting your immortal soul at risk? Don't you see it? She'll have you turned away from the bosom of Holy Mother Church and doing her dance with the devil before you know what's happening."

Sean continued with force. "It is the way with witches. A small thing here, a tiny thing there and before you know it you are caperin' neeked around fires in the woods at midnight with all her familiars!"

"Sean, it isn't as if I'll be wearing a goat-head hat, sacrificing virgins, or putting babies on spits any day now. There isn't any witchcraft. No pointy hats, no broomsticks, no hairy warts, no spells to make your tender bits shrivel up – none of it. Get it? No witches. No witchcraft. So take it easy."

Sean Maher visibly shuddered then exploded. "Julian, listen to yourself! Jaysus, Mary and Joseph – how is it, Julian Blessing that you think of such things? And isn't it you who says them like they are normal. Tender bits, goat heads, and, as if the rest weren't blasphemous enough, babies on spits! By God!"

Both men became lost to their respective thoughts, but Sean announced his first. "For the love of God, Julian - babies on spits," he said, "That's just proof of how diseased is your poor soul!"

* * *

"Who is that young girl?" Julian asked Kathleen Maher. He indicated a young woman who followed the Hackett sisters like a skiff in the wake of two ships of the line as they made their way down the main thoroughfare.

"Ah 'tis Gwyneth Kirby and a shining success she is, thanks to you," Mrs. Maher answered. She and Julian stood side by side in front of Flynn's general store.

"Pardon me? Shining success thanks to me? I have no idea what you are talking about."

"Would you be remembering the talking to you gave the Hackett sisters? That was the day you were more than passing tetched. If people are to be believed – and they are, but only about half the time – you convinced the Hacketts they had a duty to pass along their knowledge to a younger generation."

"Well, I did mention something like that." Julian looked embarrassed.

"Indeed and rightly you did. Sure it would be a pity for the two of them to take to their graves – for that can't be long off since they are each a hundred and fifty years old – before passing on the wisdom they have gathered to themselves. It would deprive us of the various medicaments we depend on. We can't be bothering the sainted Doctor Dwyer for every little thing ya know," Kathleen Maher said.

"Okay, in a way I might have suggested it would be a good idea to train an apprentice. So that's what they're doing with that girl?"

"You're quick as lightening, Mr. Julian. 'Tis the Hacketts' youngest cousin's daughter up from Wicklow way. She is a bonny lass, strong and anxious to please, bright as a penny and pretty besides."

At the mention of her name, Gwyneth Kirby looked up as she crossed the street and Kathleen Maher motioned for her to join them. Gwyneth whispered to her aunts who gave their assent. The young girl ran to join Mrs. Maher and the stranger.

Mrs. Maher introduced a red haired young woman of about seventeen years with egg white skin and a smattering of freckles across the bridge of her nose. Julian noted she was a beckoningly pretty girl with a soft smile and eyes alight with the potential for mischief.

"Gwyneth, this is Mr. Julian Blessing. With my husband, he provides safety and security not only to our village, but also to the entire area here abouts. He is an important man of vast experience and learning. Should a problem present itself which your sainted aunts can't answer, present yourself to Mr. Julian and he will find a solution."

The young woman curtsied and Julian inclined his head and smiled.

"'Vast experience and learning' is it, Kathleen Maher?" Ailís Dwyer said. Julian spun around to find the doctor standing behind him. "Is it our Mr. Julian you would be talkin' about then?" she asked and smiled slyly.

"Good morning, Doctor," Julian said with an enthusiasm he did not intend to show.

"Why, Oi am honored that such a weighty individual as your fine self would see fit to talk with but a poor country doctor," Ailís intoned with a mocking broad, flat Irish brogue. "Sadly, I have little time for idle chitchat right now."

Just then, a group of village women surrounded the doctor and spirited her into Flynn's store. Julian looked on as she left and grinned at the doctor's playfulness.

Kathleen Maher and Gwyneth Kirby's lips formed subdued, but knowing smiles, heavy with meaning and rich in understanding.

***

"George Sullivan is altogether dead," Jimmy Grogan declared as he ran into the police station.

Julian, Sean and Father Fahey were seated around the desk playing a card game whose chief feature was lying and cheating. But the lying did not end with the playing cards. The score was being kept in turns and each scorekeeper unabashedly shaved points from his opponents and added them to his own score.

"That's forty-eight points for me," Julian said.

Sean said, "Forty-eight" and wrote down twenty-eight adding the wayward twenty points to his own score bringing it to fifty-five.

"Saints be praised," Father Fahey said. "I have forty-eight also. What a coincidence." Father Fahey leaned out of his chair and watched as Sean attempted to turn the thirty-eight he had put down for the priest back into a forty-eight. Father Fahey raised an eyebrow and looked at Sean. Sean looked at his pencil as though it was an instrument of the devil.

The rules for scoring were simple. Laymen could be cheated as freely as one's conscience would allow. Priests were cheated less enthusiastically. If one was a scorekeeper-priest, it was permissible to cheat with abandon all except bishops. Bishops did not, it was assumed, cheat cardinals and so on.

Father Fahey did not breathe the rarified air of bishops and cardinals so did not concern himself with such matters. But as much as it was his obligation to cheat while playing and scoring, it was his holy duty to caution his flock about fudging the numbers on the score sheet. He reconciled this as being for their own good. And his.

"Were you hearin' me? Auld George Sullivan is dead," Jimmy said again.

"That's a total of five hundred fifty points for meself, five hundred forty-eight for himself, Father Fahey, and one thousand one hundred…"

"That's one thousand eight hundred for me," Julian corrected.

Julian had invented his own way of scoring. He kept the numbers in his head and would correct the score sheet when it was passed to him. This didn't keep his opponents from re-correcting it later, but in the end Julian always won by such a large margin that he thought it churlish to argue over a few hundred points.

"Nine plus four, carry the one, naught from naught equals naught, seven plus nine take away three and carry the two…" Sean intoned. "It is right you are, one thousand six hundred…"

"One thousand eight hundred," Julian interrupted.

"Right. As I said, one thousand eight hundred points," Sean announced.

"Is it deef as stones you are? Does no one here care if a Christian has died?"

"Shut your gob, Jimmy Grogan and it is a civil tongue I would be thinkin' you should keep in your head or a knot Oi'll put on you that ye won't be forgetin'," Sean said. "Besides, chances are he isn't dead this time either ya ugly little creature."

"Well, if you're so sure, take me bet," Jimmy said. "Oi'll bet a hundred you are wrong and for another thing, the likes of you wouldn't recognize me true beauty if it bit y'r arse."

"Jimmy Grogan, you would bet on a bag of dead pigeons in a horse race, ya eejit," Sean enjoined. "But you say truly, I know little of beauty. That said, ya ugly spud, Oi do know you have a face on ya as would drive rats from a barn."

"How dead is Farmer Sullivan? Oi've said the rosary over him four times this year and gave him last rights twice more besides. Each time they were ready to put him under the earth. Each time it was so George could get some porter under his roof," Father Fahey added.

"No, but Father, a hay bale fell on him and crushed his head like a gourd! As Jaysus alone is my judge, George Sullivan is surely dead this time."

"It isn't takin' our Lord Jaysus name in vain that'll save ya because if Oi find this is more of your filthy lies, Jimmy Grogan, you'll be prayin' to all the saints to save you from me," Father Fahey said. "Oi suppose we should go have a look though just to make sure."

The three men walked out of the station with Jimmy bringing up the rear and closing the door behind him.

They all walked the mile out of the village to the Sullivan farm where they found George Sullivan was good and truly, altogether dead this time.

***

While the mourners gathered for George's wake, Julian and Sean inspected the barn where the farmer had died. Walking into the barn, Julian doubled over in pain. He staggered, then stumbled into the lee of his friend. Julian was beset by an aching melancholy and in the next moment, he was there. He was watching George Sullivan die.

Julian lost all color in his face, his hands shook and his eyes looked as though he was witnessing pure horror. "Get me out of here, Sean," Julian managed to say.

That evening's wake going on inside the farmhouse was an event that demanded hushed tones and temporary decorum. Alcohol flowed with abandon. It was explained to Julian that strong drink was necessary to toast the newly departed and to put the living in a reflective frame of mind to better consider their individual mortality.

Julian thought it was an excuse for getting drunk.

He sat on the back porch, pale and exhausted from what he had witnessed in the barn and got profoundly and reflectively drunk.

CHAPTER TWENTY

Dr. Ailís Dwyer wasn't pleased. It was near noon as she hurried from her practice to the police station without knowing why. Jimmy Grogan had arrived at her office with an urgent request from Sean Maher.

"That's all he said?" the doctor asked.

Out of breath from his run up the street, Jimmy answered, "Aye, Doctor. Sean said to come quick. That's all I know."

The doctor pulled her wool shawl close around her slender shoulders and, with a sharp breeze biting her face, continued on toward the station house.

Arriving, she raised her hand to knock, but before her knuckles could touch the wooden door, she heard Julian's voice softly calling for her to come in. Ailis forehead furrowed and wondered how he always knew she was there.

She entered and hung her shawl by the door. The station curtains had been drawn. The only light was from a turf fire. She overheard Sean say, "I really wish you wouldn't do that! I've told you, knowing who is at the door before you should know anyone is at the door, well, it isn't the sort of thing a Christian gets up to."

Both men were seated in the rocking chairs before the fire. Ailís approached and welcomed the warmth of the fireplace. She took a seat on the long bench and turned to ask the nature of the problem. Sean motioned her to stay still and nodded toward Julian.

Julian sat transfixed. His eyes were heavy lidded as he stared into the fireplace. His face wore a weary and painfully sad expression. He was distant and distracted.

Ailís sat a long time watching Julian. The only sound in the room was the occasional pop of the peat and the ticking of the station's wall clock.

She moved to him slowly and knelt beside his chair taking his wrist as she did. "Julian," she said. She had no difficulty locating his pulse, it was fast and matched his rapid shallow breaths. "Look at me." He shifted his attention from the fire to focus on her face. His smile was slow and slight.

"Tell me what has happened. When did this start?" She exchanged a look with Sean who only made a hapless, concerned gesture.

"I've asked, but he won't tell me. He wasn't well at George's wake yesterday. He took the death hard and he had the drink on him by the end of the evening. I left him here in the chair last night and he was this way when Oi got here this morning. We were going to talk about Georgie Sullivan, but, well you can see for yourself," the big man said.

Julian's voice was low and slow. "I'm fine. Really. Probably just tired. I'll be okay after I get some sleep. Please, don't worry – either of you. There is no reason to talk about George though."

"What do you mean, Julian?" the doctor asked, but he did not respond. "I want you to come with me. Sean, help him up," she said. Julian continued to look into the fire as though he hadn't heard. She saw something, a flicker in Julian's eyes. She relented and shook her head when Sean began to move to his friend.

"Julian," she said with whispered softness. "Do you know something about George Sullivan's accident?"

With an aching slowness, Julian said, "Wasn't an accident. George was murdered. Three men beat him nearly to death. The hay bale didn't fall. It was pulled down onto him." The way Julian said it was definite. He said it with absolute assurance. It was as though he had just read it in the newspaper or seen it on television. For reasons neither could explain, Ailís and Sean believed him. They were troubled before, but Julian's friends were nearly frantic with worry now.

The room was warm, but Julian rose slowly and threw more peat on the fire. He sat and distractedly looked at the doctor, then looked back to the fireplace. Julian said, "That will be for you, Doctor. You'll need to go quickly. He is in a great deal of pain and he is very weak. Sean, go with her, please. I would like to rest if you don't mind. I feel so desperately tired."

Ailís's concern was palpable. Sean was afraid for his friend. "Julian," Sean said gently, "What are you talking about?"

Julian never looked away from the fire. He raised his hand and pointed casually at the station door.

A young boy pushed the door open without knocking causing Ailís and Sean to jump. "Come quick, Doctor. There's Farmer Monahan and he's hurt bad. They've taken him to your surgery. He's bleedin' somethin' awful."

Ailís turned slowly and looked carefully at Julian. His features hadn't changed. He sat and stared intently into the fire with the hope the flames might burn the images he saw from his mind.

The doctor and Sean started to leave and Julian spoke again. "You'll need to stay at your office, Ailís. Another injured man is being brought to you. I think it is Tommy Ryan. He'll be here shortly. Sean, you'll want to be there. Both men have been attacked.

"They've been set upon by the same three men who killed George." He closed his eyes tightly and pain was etched deeply on his face as George's death scene played out before him again.

Sean Maher, a man afraid of very little, crossed himself and was afraid for his friend. He held the door for the doctor.

"Julian," Ailís said as she gathered her shawl from the peg by the door, "we'll talk about this later."

He looked up and smiled kindly, almost tenderly, cocked his head and said, "Talk about what?"

CHAPTER TWENTY-ONE

"I watched a man die, Moira. George Sullivan – I watched him die. The images wouldn't stop coming. I feel like I'm stuck in some endless loop. I've been watching him die over and over," Julian said and closed his eyes trying to will away the images in his mind.

"There have been other assaults and I've seen some of those attacks, but never so close and never in such detail. I was there this time. If this is a talent, I don't want it."

Moira had been watching Julian intently since he entered her house and sat down. With palpable compassion she said, "I'm sorry, Julian. I'm sorry you have been thrust into this position so soon. I am sorry I can't take the bitterness away. As for the other, sadly, lad, the return window is closed.

"Under normal circumstances you would not experience anything close to this for many years. Even then, it would have been slight and you would have built up to it. You have come so far, farther than I thought possible for anyone. I was fully three years getting to where you are now and I was considered lightening quick."

"Is this the Sight, Moira? I'm serious, if it is I honestly don't want it."

"The Sight is it? What would the likes of you know of such things?"

"I've seen it. My friend in Dublin has it. You have it. I don't know how you live with it," Julian said.

"Well then, it is time we put some things to rights. As to your friend, I can't say if she possesses the Darna Shealladh or not. If she does, she is one of the few. As for me, there you are mistaken. That is a gift I do not possess and am thankful for that. It is something a person is born to and a dreadful responsibility it is. It takes a person of rare character to bear it.

"I see things, 'tis true, but what I see are bits and pieces only. Sometimes I see it all very clearly. At other times, I see scenes or an image and nothing more. Honestly, I've found it useful at times but a great distraction for the most part and like you, sometimes what I see has been agonizing.

"As for your good self, you may trust me, you do not possess that gift. You may be able to see only into the past. Some can only see into the near future, while some see nothing at all. It is different for everyone,"

Moira said and then continued. "I'm mindful of what you said, son. Seeing a horror like this is not easy. It will not get easier. If it does, if ever it isn't painful to you to witness the suffering of another, quit. Get out. Set your burden down and never pick it up or speak of it again.

"If you had the Sight you would be there. You would have heard all and felt everything. You would have walked around watching everything with no way to stop it or change its course. They say the Sight is a thing nearly past enduring.

"It's not all darkness though. You saw it happen. You saw the vipers that did this. That is a start toward finding justice for George, aye and the others."

"I wish that was the case," Julian responded. "I couldn't move. I was in a sort of fixed position so I couldn't see their faces. I couldn't hear their voices. I could only watch as George's life was snuffed out over and over again."

They sat in silence for a long time. The evening shadows began to fall across the village. Men returned from the fields, meals were prepared, tables set, families gathered. The pulse of life continued unmindful of a man who sat and wept in the company of a woman who understood.

***

An hour passed. Moira made no attempt to move or speak. She wanted Julian to set his own pace. Julian rose without a word and walked into the garden. Moira followed.

"The attack on you, what was that? How did it happen?" Julian asked and let out a ragged breath.

"That is for you to tell me." Moira smiled and continued, "I was distracted." Julian snorted.

"I was going through an exercise," he began. "I'd done pretty well and was preparing to move onto the next step when it happened. I suddenly felt unsteady. I'd never felt anything like it before. I looked back to see if you felt it and, well, you weren't in very good shape.

Moira nodded and watched her student carefully.

"I ran back to the grove. The closer I got to you the stronger the…" Julian groped for the right word.

In a soft gentle voice Moira prompted, "The stronger the – what?"

"Hatred," Julian said. At the word, Moira's eyes narrowed. "At first I wanted to think it was something else, that I was mistaken. Hatred is the right word though. The intensity was painful. More painful was watching what it was doing to you. Then it happened. I don't know how, but I knew exactly what to do and I did it.

"Listen," Julian said. "I know I am talking about this in the wrong way. I don't know the words that would frame this in metaphysical terms."

"Don't worry about the words, son, just use the ones you know," Moira said.

"I deflected the attack or as much of it as I could, then started an attack of my own. I can tell you at first my efforts were pretty poor. Anyway, I focused and somehow was able to follow a sort of mental pathway to the source of the attack." Julian went quiet for some moments.

"There was a man, Moira. He was filled with hatred and he was alone – no, not alone, empty. His anger had pushed everything in him aside. That's just the way it felt, but there was something else. I don't know what and wouldn't know how to explain it if I did."

"We'll leave that for now. What did you do next?" she asked gently.

"At first nothing. I had trouble maintaining the wall I'd put around you while watching the attacker. That was taking everything I had. Then I felt it. I literally went blind, but not in the way I think of blindness. My world didn't go dark, it went stark white. That's when it happened. I felt this surge. I let it build up in me. Then, just for a moment, he faltered. It was as though he was taking a breath before mounting another assault.

"I'm sorry, but I went with a feeling that came to me. You were right, I acted without regard to reason or logic or analysis. If I'd been wrong it would have been bad for us both, but mostly for you." Julian drew a breath and said, "I dropped the wall and focused everything on him.

"I could feel the confusion in him. He couldn't reconcile what was happening. He was disoriented and bewildered. Moira, just for a moment he was afraid, terrified. That was replaced quickly by an unbelievable rage. I never imagined one person could carry so much hatred.

"I had no idea someone could be so consumed with malice. Never have I seen raw evil and madness, but I saw it then. I didn't think that kind of intensity existed. I concentrated everything I had in me and it broke his focus I guess. I waited for a moment, but he didn't move.

"I called off my attack to get back to the wall. I knew if it fell completely, I wouldn't have what it took to build it again. If the wall was down and he had recovered and renewed his assault on you, we would have been good and truly screwed." Julian lapsed into silence.

Moira Hagan was shaken. It was Julian's description of the hatred. That made this attack a personal one. She had witnessed attacks before, but they were nearly clinical in their execution. This one was bristling with malevolence.

She already told Julian he had come a long way along his path and done it quickly. When she had said that, she never imagined he had already arrived.

She watched her student and smiled. Julian was rough. There were sharp edges to his thoughts. His application of what he had learned was overly muscular. He lacked finesse. He hadn't had the luxury of time. He hadn't spent years studying and years more as an apprentice.

She knew Julian had done the only thing he could think to do. He had grabbed the ancient wisdom by the throat, wrestled it to the ground then rifled through its pockets to extract everything he could.

"Good and truly screwed," Moira Hagan thought to herself. "Colorful to be sure. I can work with that."

***

Johnny Doyle, a local farmer's son, had been attacked in the same way as the others. Ailís sent a note to Julian outlining the extent of Johnny's injuries and giving her opinion. Based on the damage done, she felt it was the work of the same men who had assaulted the other two farmers.

Her note went on to detail her frustration and concern over Julian's condition. She wrote, "We will talk about your physical and mental condition and I'll not let you get away fobbing me off with answers that aren't really answers at all."

Julian knew this time she would not be put off. He thought it prudent to avoid the doctor for the time being. He reasoned that if he could stay out of her way long enough, the problem would go away of its own volition. He reasoned wrong.

Chapter Twenty-Two

Julian ratcheted up his efforts. He blanketed several valleys in all directions with flyers describing the suspicious activities and the white truck that has been seen in the areas of the digging.

He talked to everyone who would talk with him and received information on new dig sites for his efforts. He drew a map of the area and marked excavations and sightings of the people doing the digging.

He organized nighttime patrols and when no one would go with him, Julian went by himself. He and Sean bicycled to opposite ends of what they defined as their territory and haunted the areas around the mounds. At every opportunity, Ailís Dwyer went looking for him. Each time, he escaped. Barely.

***

Three times the digging team had been out and three times they had been chased off. Four more farmers had been punished for their interference. But three sites had been left only partially explored. That was more than a man intent on pillage was willing to endure.

The Pale Man whose long, cold fingers manipulated the coin in his pocket had come to this part of Ireland for the purpose of securing a treasure and his progress was being blocked.

The coldness of the manor house fed his icy rage. The drafts of chill air that wafted through the high ceilinged house whipped up his frustration and deepened his hatred. The influence of this meddling American was going to have to be removed permanently. Nothing less would satiate this fury.

***

The wind drove in from the Irish Sea and bit hard against Julian's face. Arriving earlier than his teacher, he had already begun his mental exercises. He was meticulous in the application of his skills.

Julian stood in the meadow and the wind shrieked down on him. He set his hands away from his sides slightly, closed his eyes and exhaled fully.

At first, Julian felt the wind as short, violent jabs that stung his face and tore at his shirt and pants. As he stood in the exposed pasture, the wind roared down causing his ears to ring.

No part of him was unaffected. The smell of the sea, the bite of the cold, the sound of the wind screeching in his ears, all tried to blot out his senses. "There is one sense you can not touch," he said to the wind and little by little that single sense lifted him out of the din.

It wasn't through an act of will. He did not raise himself above the tumult through the force of his mind. Rather his spirit, his true self as Moira called it, found a space in time and reality that was set aside from the forces of the physical world. For a fraction of a moment, his world went brilliantly white.

He dropped his hands to his sides and opened his eyes. The tall grass was bent with the wind as were the tops of the trees, but he could detect no sound or movement. He turned and looked back toward the grove and saw Moira Hagan looking at him with a curious expression on her face.

He walked toward her and called out, "What's happening to me?" Moira did not respond. Julian noticed her glance never wavered and she continued to stare as if she were frozen looking at the place in the meadow where he had been.

When Julian reached the shelter of the trees the wind suddenly rose again and the familiar din and smell returned to him. The Hagan seemed slightly startled to find him standing next to her, but she smiled. "Sometimes I think you're too fast for your own good. I must remember to watch you with more care, my boy," she said.

"Watch me, why? What just happened?" he asked again as they sought shelter deeper in the woods.

Moira thought awhile before she said, "It is difficult to explain. On the one hand, you could think by what you experienced that you had frozen time, but that didn't happen. It would be silly and arrogant to think you could. Closer to the matter would be that you, just for a moment, perceived the true nature of time."

"Using the senses of your spirit and not your mind you captured your place in the universe. None that I know of are able to hold it for long, but you did right well today," she added. "Today's experience – now that was of real importance. For you that was truly a step forward – far forward.

"You have advanced, though without understanding and that we cannot allow. What you've glimpsed today is too important, too vital to your purpose to allow it to go without a full understanding." Julian nodded his head in agreement.

He thought, *"I need to know what just happened, how it works and how and when it is to be used and how in hell it can be controlled."*

Moira heard Julian's thoughts clearly. She smiled and said aloud, "To be sure, you are making progress. There in an instant you have asked every important question. Do you realize a few months ago you would have been rushing around thinking you were losing your mind on the one hand and on the other wondering how you would use this talent to spy on your delectable Ailís Dwyer?"

Julian looked at the ground suddenly like a schoolboy caught out. His ears were aflame.

"Think nothing of it, my boy. Wasn't it I who was just pointing out known facts. That is, they are facts known by everyone but you and her. That's right, a greater set of eejits I doubt there ever has been. You are perfectly paired."

Julian tried to look incensed, but it was no use. Moira just laughed at him and said, "As for your impure thoughts with regard to the doctor, anyone who doesn't know about that for two valleys in any direction, well, is either pickled in alcohol or simple minded. But that is all a discussion for another time, eh?"

"In fact," Julian said, "it is not a discussion for another time. There is no truth to it. We are good friends and nothing more."

The crack of the Hagan's laugh set birds high up in the trees flying. "Good thing for you your Catholic God does love a simpleton, otherwise he would strike you down for the liar you are," she said and continued to laugh at Julian's expense.

"No matter, no matter, let's get back to the subject at hand. I'll not have you drawing me off with stories of your sordid love life," she said and grinned devilishly.

***

After taking his supper with his clan gathered about him, Sean Maher decided to stroll through the village. Wives and children were fine, but there were times a man needed solitude. He walked the streets of Cappel Vale rattling doors and making sure everything was locked up for the night. This had been his habit since he took on the mantle of police work.

At the far end of the village, he recognized Julian walking slowly toward the police station with his jacket over his shoulder. Sean called to his friend who turned and cocked his head.

Julian's condition had improved, but Sean saw the changes. His friend was more deliberate, more thoughtful and occasionally not as much fun, but that was improving steadily. It seemed that Sean only blinked and when he looked again, his friend was gone.

"It is a lovely evening, Sean."

The big man nearly soiled himself. Standing behind him was Julian Blessing with a pleasant smile on his face and an evil look about his eyes.

"What!" Sean shouted, his fist cocked back and ready for battle.

"I commented on the fact that it seems to be a lovely evening." Julian smiled.

"Wouldn't Oi be knowin' what you said. How is it you were there and now you are here?"

"I don't know what you mean. You waved and I thought I would join you on your rounds so I walked up here."

"'Tis a lie! It is deviltry you are up to and for it you will surely burn, Julian Blessing. I'm begging you. Come with me now to see Father Fahey. It is sure I am that he can drive the devils out of you before your immortal soul comes to any more harm." Sean was so sincere and the sentiment so heartfelt that Julian had to chuckle.

"Fine. Dance to Satan's tune and 'tis the fires of eternal damnation that will be roasting you. Then we will see how funny you think it is. Still, me and mine will look down on your sorry condition and shed a tear for the man who was my friend in life," Sean said in a huff and marched off to O'Gavagan's with Julian's laughter singeing his ears.

The big man took hold of the pub's doorknob, but it was as if knob was welded in place and the door wouldn't budge. He turned the knob and pushed again, nothing. Julian stood in the road at a distance of fifteen meters watching his friend do battle with a door Julian was holding shut. With feet set wide apart and his arms crossed over his chest Julian thought, "This is so cool! I am never gonna get tired of this!" He smiled broadly, turned back to the police station and released the door as Sean gave it one more try and found the knob turned easily. He turned and saw Julian wave over his shoulder.

***

"I've been watching the two of 'em peelers for weeks just like you told me. The American knows Georgie Sullivan was kilt. Oi knows he contacted the Garda, but they said they was busy. In any case, the Yank is going about investigatin' on his own. Maher is a lazy, drunken swine and so is no help. It's that Yank who is the active one."

The Pale Man walked to the tall windows, pulled aside the heavy drape and looked into the gray-green countryside toward Cappel Vale. "The American has become an inconvenience. Although you've brought me no news, what you say confirms what I already suspected. Ireland would be better off without one more American tourist."

"Ach, your Lordship is right as always. I'm glad to be of service. I can say nothing takes place here abouts without my knowin' of it within minutes," Liam McMaster said with the chest thumping pride of one who tells the truth only by accident. "That's what makes me so valuable if you know what Oi mean."

The Pale Man turned toward his visitor, "I wonder, McMaster, do you have any principles at all? Is your loyalty all bought and paid for? Never mind. It was just an idle thought. I really don't care." He knew very well what motivated Liam McMaster – greed and fear. Either, applied correctly, would elicit the desired response.

"Oi was thinkin', yor honor, that a man of my talents might be of real use to you if Oi would be knowin' a bit of the plan."

The Pale Man's eyes turned to granite. "You seem to have an unnatural desire to know my business. If you knew my plans what would keep you from selling me to the highest bidder? I've dealt with quislings like you before, McMaster. I know all about you. I know what you will do and when you will do it and I always understand why you will do anything you do.

"Do you know when I will share my plans with a little prick like you? Never! Now get out and count yourself lucky I don't just pop your head like a grape."

"Didn't mean to give offense, yor honor. Only trying…"

"I know what you are trying and would suggest you never try it again with me or you will find yourself in a ditch on the side of the road. After you suffer some, of course. For now, keep an eye on our American friend."

Liam McMaster backed out of the room without further prompting.

As McMaster left, Tom Lynch entered the study and stood before his employer.

"You heard of course."

"Oi did."

"See to it."

With those three words, the fate of Julian Blessing was irrevocably fixed.

CHAPTER TWENTY-THREE

After supper at O'Gavagan's, Julian walked Ailís Dwyer and Timothy home and then began a methodical inspection of the shops and buildings that made up Cappel Vale.

He had done this scores of times, but lately something had been different. Julian could feel an unfamiliar presence, dark and heavy. He sensed Jimmy Grogan was nearby too, but this other presence was back again and with it there was an edge Julian had not sensed before.

He had a tangible feeling something was wrong and he knew it in every fiber. Still he walked his beat, perhaps with more care than usual, but he did his duty from one end of Cappel Vale to the other and back again for good measure. The last of the lights emanating from the cottages had gone out when Julian ended his patrol at the police station.

After he removed and hung up his coat and kicked off his boots, Julian said, "Come in Jimmy." The knock on the door landed a millisecond later.

"Mr. Julian, Oi wouldn't bother you so late if it wasn't important."

"I know you wouldn't, Jimmy. Come in, please," Julian said.

Jimmy Grogan had grown since Julian's arrival. He had been known as the village liar and thief, and although some of that reputation still clung to him, he was now being seen as a young man with potential.

He had come to Julian many times seeking advice on various matters and displayed an agile and capable mind. Julian promised that if Jimmy would apply himself to his studies, there could be a scholarship in it for him to Trinity or University College Dublin if he preferred. Although not wild about school, Jimmy could see that an education was his ticket out of the small village and a life as a farm hand or shopkeeper.

"Oi stayed to help O'Gavagan clean up so Oi left the pub after you did."

Julian sat in one of the rocking chairs and indicated the other to Jimmy, but the boy declined preferring to deliver his message standing.

"The wind was up so Oi had gone round to the lee of the pub to light me pipe when Oi saw you walk by on the main street."

Julian remained silent.

"You got about forty meters up the street when Oi saw it. Nothing but a shadow at first, but then he moved. You was being followed on your rounds. Oi didn't think no good could come of this so Oi followed the one that was following you.

"'e didn't do anything but hang back and watch. Every time you stopped, 'e stopped. Every time he stopped, Oi stopped. Oi had to hang back a fair distance and when you came back here to the station, well, the one what was following you just vanished. It's the truth, Mr. Julian. Oi wouldn't lie to you, sor."

"I know you wouldn't, Jimmy," Julian said and looked intently into the peat fire.

***

The next night Julian watched the clock as it ticked off the minutes until he would start his rounds. The time came. Julian opened the station door and was swallowed by the cold, wet night.

***

His rounds completed, he returned to the police station, stripped down and changed into dry clothes. He then sat down before the peat fire and waited for Jimmy Grogan.

Julian had the same feeling as the previous night, still he could not put a name to the presence.

Jimmy Grogan came in with a grin on his face. Julian knew from experience what success looked like and Jimmy had that look.

***

Jimmy had monitored the dark figure following Julian on his rounds. From the pub, up the main street, down the village's few side streets, his surveillance continued up to St. Michael's and back to the police station.

Several times the shadow slipped and fell in the mud. Jimmy said, "Mr. Julian, Oi near shit meself with the laughing. The fool might as well have brought a brass band."

Once Julian was inside the station, Jimmy reported, the dark figure snaked its way outside of town and was gone.

Jimmy had no trouble following because of the rain and mud. The figure met with four men standing beside a white truck. As the stalker struck a match to light his cigarette, Jimmy saw the face of Liam McMaster in the match's flare.

***

"Well then, let's just go pinch his head off," Sean Maher said matter-of-factly the next morning.

"We can't do that. You see, I wasn't going to tell you at all, but we are partners and I felt you would be hurt if I didn't share this information with you. On the other hand, I knew that if I told you, violence would soon follow. You see, we can't let him know that we know what he is up to," Julian said.

"Well at what point can we pinch his head off?"

"Later. After this has all played out, but even then I don't know that it would be such a good idea," Julian offered.

The frustration was building for Sean. "Oi just want a simple answer; when can we pinch that bastard Liam McMaster's head off for spying on you and, like the Judas he is, selling you out to our enemies?"

Julian said, "We know what he is up to and he doesn't know we know. We are ahead of the game."

"We'll be ahead of the game, son, when Oi've delivered a headless Liam McMaster," Sean Maher said.

"Not to worry, it will all come soon enough," Julian said. "It would seem they are interested in when we stay in the village and when we patrol the valley. My guess is they are trying to figure out when it is safe to dig. Don't worry, my friend, we'll have a long chat with Mr. McMaster sooner rather than later."

"Julian, do you ever worry you could be wrong?" Sean asked.

***

Julian met Ailís and Timothy again at the pub for supper. On walking her home he said to Ailís, "Did you notice Gwyneth and Brendan?" Julian asked. "I thought she was interested in Jimmy Grogan."

Ailís cocked her head, smiled and looked up at Julian, "It has been Gwyneth and Brendan from the moment they set eyes on each other. It is refreshing to watch young love. Where have you been that you didn't notice it before now? You're the police, you're supposed to notice things."

"Doesn't it surprise you that I've managed to live this long while being delightfully unaware of what is going on around me? I think it is one of my more endearing qualities, don't you?"

The doctor laughed and shook her head. "You are such a very odd man."

"Thank you. Oi can't remember being more pleasured by a compliment, but what else should Oi expect from such a lovely creature as your fine self," he said in passable Irish English. She had suspended for the time being her interrogation of Julian.

She felt she would sort it all out in due course. Questioning him only caused him to avoid her. She had grown to like having him nearby. They were able to be easy in each other's company and both liked it that way.

"Go on with you. I mean it. In some ways, you are stunningly, almost frighteningly aware of things and of other things you are worryingly unaware. What is to become of you I wonder?" Ailís asked.

"Believe me, that is something I ask myself all the time." He had become more serious. "How do we ever know; I mean really know? I don't mean how do we know we have become the person we are meant to be, but how do we know we are even on the right path to becoming that person?"

"We don't and we never will," Ailís said. "I don't think we were ever meant to know for sure. I think we were designed to keep going through doors, finding our way along life's various hallways."

They had arrived at the doctor's front door when Julian asked, "What corridor are we in, Ailís? Is there a door you and I are supposed to go through?"

His question and his stare were piercing. She reached up, touched his cheek, and said, "I don't know."

Julian's gray eyes arrested Ailís. She held her breath as he gently lifted her chin with his fingertips. His movement was slow and gentle, relaxed and without hesitation.

His kiss was soft and lingering. Her body went taut for the smallest part of a moment before she leaned into him. His next kiss was hardly a kiss at all. His lips hovered over hers without fully touching and his fingers moved through her hair.

She made a noise that was a mixture of frustration at being teased and insistence that he give her more. When she kissed him, it was firm and resolute and it lasted for a moment suspended in time for them both.

She followed easily with a kiss that was firm without being demanding. One moment, two then three and she stepped back from the kiss slightly and her tongue softly, slowly touched his lips. She leaned away from him, touched his cheek again with her fingers and mouthed the words 'thank you' as Timothy pounded down the hallway behind her.

Julian's eyes were heavy lidded with his desire for her and his pulse continued racing as he stepped back, smiled slowly and turned away into the night leaving her with her arm around Timothy's shoulders and a smile on her lips.

***

Julian began his patrol at the end nearest the police station and worked his way slowly to St. Michael's Church. The pubs emptied quickly and people made for home and turned in for the night even more quickly. The village was dark and still. The dogcarts that took people to their farms no longer echoed back from the valley. There was no moon and the sky was vacant of stars.

He had given Jimmy Grogan the night off. Julian could not feel the presence of Liam McMaster or anyone else. He was alone in the streets of the village and no one that Julian could detect followed or watched. Everything seemed right, but an indefinable something felt wrong.

Edmond Brady's shop was locked as were both of O'Gavagan's pubs. Flynn's General Store and Mulherin's Pub were buttoned up along with the Hacketts' Apothecary and the livestock feed store. Since the digging had started, people had begun locking their doors and Julian and Sean took it upon themselves to rattle the doorknobs each night without exception.

He passed the residences of the villagers and admired the staunch simplicity in which they lived. The lights were out at Moira Hagan's house and Julian rounded her home and saw a short distance up the dusty road that all the lights from St. Michael's Catholic Church were ablaze.

Normally the church closed but never locked its doors. Father Fahey always dimmed the lights promptly at 8 P.M. Tonight it was nearing ten thirty and every light in the church shone.

Julian began to run.

Chapter Twenty-Four

Father Fahey lay on his back near the altar rail on the left side of the church. Julian ran up the center aisle and knelt beside the priest. There was a gash in the old man's forehead that was bleeding freely. The prone figure opened his eyes and tried to speak, but Julian silenced him with a gesture. The priest raised his left hand and pointed as the first kick caught Julian in the ribs taking the wind out of him. A second kick from the opposite side made sure he didn't recover from the first.

Two men on either side of Julian stood him upright. He found his breath and raised his head. A loan figure stood at the altar rail to the right of the altar and motioned for his compatriots to bring Julian forward. In a dragging, stumbling, shambling gate Julian was brought to the waiting figure.

Clearly, this man was in charge. The malice in the man's voice and face was plain enough. "Georgie Sullivan wasn't enough of a warning to you? How about them other bogtrodders we visited with a bit of pain? You should have taken the hint, mate?" The man pulled on a pair of leather gloves.

"Time for you to join poor dead George, Oi'm afeared." That was all the man said before his fist landed in Julian's midsection. Another blow landed in the same place and the man spoke again, "We need to make a suitable example of you so we need to make you look, well, not so pretty. That way those who go to your wake 'll see no good 'll come of muckin' about with us."

While his companions held Julian upright and immobile, the leader proceeded to pour punches into Julian in a stomach-ribs combination and sprinkled it with backhands to his face. It all served to keep Julian unfocused and in constant pain.

Every time he looked like he would pass out, his captors would drop him and he would fall to his hands and knees where he would nearly catch his breath. They stood on Julian's hands grinding his knuckles under their boots while they launched kicks into his ribs. They grabbed him by the arms and started the process over again.

In the end, Julian found himself on his hands and knees in a pool of his own blood and vomit. He was taking a far worse beating than George Sullivan had. A hand took him by the jaw and landed another punch below his left cheek. Blood flew from his mouth and face forming an arc to his right. His eyes cleared as his chest heaved for breath.

With his thoughts scattering, his mind in disarray, his brain jumbled and running in slow motion, he thought of Ailís. "I'll never kiss you again. I should have done it the first time I saw you," Julian whispered.

The three men who were sent to murder Julian took this as a sign of resistance and mockery and they rained relentless punches and kicks onto him as he lay on the stone floor of the church.

To Julian, time meant nothing. They could have been beating him for five minutes or two hours. Time may have meant nothing, but pain filled Julian's world to overflowing.

As his eyes started to roll back in his head he thought of how disappointed Moira would be with him for not being ready, for not being able to sense the danger, for not being good enough. A tear seeped from one eye.

"I'll do better next time," Julian said with a mouth full of his own blood.

With that the leader took Julian by the chin. "Next time? You've got a good sense of humor Oi'll give you that. There won't be a next time for you, son."

Julian watched as the man pulled his gloves tighter then drew back his arm. The fist rocketed toward Julian's face and he turned his head a fraction. The knuckles glanced off his cheekbone catching him on the outside of his right eyebrow drawing blood and closing that eye. Each man then landed a solid kick into Julian's ribs. The leader said, "Finish him."

Julian whispered the only word that meant anything to him. "Ailís."

The leader knelt beside Julian. The man's mouth twisted into a venomous snarl. "You don't give up easy," the man said, then spat in Julian's face. The leader drew back his fist and Julian was unable to avoid the blow that opened his right cheek leaving an ugly gash in its wake and covering him in his own blood. "You heard me, finish him!" the leader hissed at his men.

Julian felt the man on his right side kneel. He was a large man and he took Julian's chin in his big hand. The man positioned his other hand on the back of Julian's head. He had no doubt what would come next. With blood dripping from his face and mouth Julian breathed the word again, "Ailís," and another tear formed at the corner of the only eye from which he could see.

There was a loud noise at the back of the church as the doors opened followed by a roar from Sean Maher that rattled the choir loft. The three men ran for the side door, but the leader slowed long enough to kick over a table of votive candles.

Julian could hear Sean's heavy boots pound up the center aisle, but also became aware that the votive candles had splashed against the old, tinder dry curtains that hung at either side of the nave of St. Michael's statue. Soon the flames were climbing the drapes.

As Sean reached the intersection of the center aisle and the altar rail, Julian got to his knees and pointed to Father Fahey and managed to gasp, "Get him to the doctor now." He added, "Forget them. See to the priest."

With murder in his eyes, Sean turned to the unconscious priest, picked him up as if the old man weighed nothing and ran for the doctor's house.

Julian slipped and fell in his own blood, stood and launched himself at the drapes as the flames licked at the wood paneled walls of the nave. He found a portion of the curtain that wasn't burning and pulled hard. His arms hurt from being pinned behind his back, his hands were nearly useless from pain and swelling.

Every muscle in his stomach and chest cried out and his ribs shrieked for relief. His eyes were nearly swollen shut and rivulet's of blood flowed from every wound on his face until his shirt was soaked with blood.

He pulled once – nothing. He pulled again, harder – again nothing. He took a deep breath, gasped in pain and pulled harder still. The heavy velvet drape gave way and fell, pooling at Julian's feet. He dragged the red curtain into a heap on the marble floor in front of the nave and away from the carpet and began to beat the flames out. Smoke and cinders filled the air as he continued to beat at the curtain.

As soon as Sean broke through the church doors with Father Fahey in his arms he had raised the alarm with a bellow that woke everyone in the village. By the time he came out of the doctor's surgery half the village was at the doctor's front door. The other half was in or on its way to the church at a run.

The villagers stood in a loose semicircle around Julian as he continued to beat out the remainder of the cinders from the smoldering drape.

"Sean, we can't make him give over. Do something," Edmond Brady pleaded.

When Sean knelt next to his friend, Julian was nearly unconscious from the pain. He was breathing in quick, jerking, shallow breaths.

Sean looked at the face of Julian Blessing, the face he had seen every day for months and he hardly recognized it. Julian, the big man concluded, had taken a thorough going, vicious and very professional beating. This wasn't to be a murder, this was designed to sow terror by leaving a body so bloody and broken there would be no need for any further messages. "Someone will pay an almighty price for this," Sean whispered.

Tears ran down Julian's cheeks and mingled with his blood. His beating of the curtain had turned to ineffectual flailing with arms grown weary and useless. Julian could, if he squinted, see Sean Maher kneeling beside him. The big man captured both of Julian's wrists and stilled his arms.

"You've put out the fire, old son. It's time to go," Sean Maher said softly.

"Father Fahey?" Julian mumbled through broken and swollen lips where bubbles of blood formed.

"He is fine and resting at the doctor's surgery."

"Sean, I feel so very tired and it hurts so bad," Julian said in short sharp breaths.

"I know. Let's have the doctor patch you up. Why, she won't take but a minute then we'll go find us a couple of pints of the black stuff."

"Please Sean, she mustn't see me like this; no one should," Julian pleaded.

"She's a strong and capable lass, that one, and has seen far worse. Besides, who said you look so bad? Not as handsome as my fine self, but then who is?" Sean whispered and gathered Julian up to help him stand. The circle of villagers parted and all bowed their heads as Julian, leaning heavily on his friend, passed by.

***

Ailís looked down at the nearly unconscious figure on her examination table. Julian's once handsome features were red and bloated with swelling. It had taken all Ailís's strength to look at him as Julian winced in pain with each breath. She closed her eyes, steadied herself and with the clinical detachment of an excellent physician, she set to work repairing Julian's battered body.

His left eye was swollen shut. His right was just a slit. She thought "I lost myself in those gray eyes." She had been able to straighten his nose. She looked at Julian's lips. Those same lips she had found so soft, tender and gentle when she kissed them such a short time ago were dry and cracked and there were vicious wounds elsewhere on his face where fists had met skin.

A deep gash ran from below his cheekbone to his jaw. Her sutures were as small and tight as she could get them. Still, she knew even plastic surgery would never fully repair the scar.

She had no doubt but that he had many cracked ribs and she had wrapped his chest tightly. There were deep blue bruises all over his upper body. The bruising around his kidneys was especially worrisome.

Her eyes traveled to his face again and found that he had forced his right eye open somewhat. He swallowed hard, parted his lips and said, "Hurts" in a strangled whisper, before his head rolled to the side and he slipped into painless unconsciousness.

Ailís wept.

* * *

Julian was transferred from her surgery to one of the upstairs rooms. Ailís sat with him for several hours as he struggled to breathe. The least swollen of his eyes opened slightly and the foggy image of Ailís Dwyer appeared. Her smile was mixed with equal parts sympathy and relief. Through gasps, Julian said, "Ailís, please, don't cry," he pleaded. She stood up straight, drew a long breath and let it out slowly. The act served to let her gather herself and remember who she was.

"Timothy, go and get Mrs. Hagan and Mr. Maher. They are in the parlor. Tell them he is back among us," Dr. Ailís Dwyer instructed her son standing outside the door.

***

Sean Maher approached the bed, "These vipers were serious. Why Julian, old son, this was the work of professionals. By the look of you, there were sap gloves involved. I know these things and few would have survived such a beating."

Julian blew air through his dry lips to part them and said, "Lucky me. Sap?" the word 'gloves' was more than his mouth could stand.

"Sure it is. Leather gloves with led shot sewn across the knuckles. You could pulverize bricks with those on. Good thing your head is so hard, eh?" Sean said and tried to grin.

Moira Hagan slapped Sean on the arm and said with a snarl, "Chair, you oaf!" The big man rushed to the corner of the room and brought back a straight back chair.

Julian lay in bed and panted fearing the pain he knew would follow if he took a deep breath.

"Well," Sean said to Julian as the big man returned with the chair and sat down, "it is good to say that you gave as good as you got, eh?"

"Not for you, ya great fool. The chair is for the doctor," the Hagan snapped.

Julian looked like he was trying to work something out in his mind. At last he gave up trying to form the sentence and just settled for a mumbled, "What?"

"Your knuckles. Judging by the shape they're in you smacked a few of 'em in the gob."

Julian started to laugh, but the pain settled him quickly and the torment of it showed on his face. The doctor, Moira Hagan and Sean all winced.

Julian took the deepest breath he dared and then mumbled through cracked and broken lips, "They stood on my hands while they kicked me. I never landed a punch. Sorry, Sean." Julian tried to smile as a tear ran from the corner of his eye.

The big man said quietly and as gently as he knew how, "Hush-a-bye now, it's no matter we need to be paying to that. First we'll get you well and then we'll hunt these filthy creatures down and scores will be settled."

Ailís approached the bed with a syringe in her hand. "Moira let me get in there. This will settle the pain and help him sleep."

"Not now," the Hagan said.

"What! This is my practice. I am the doctor here. He needs rest and a lot of it. That is the only way he is ever going to heal, so out of my way," the doctor growled.

"Maher, help the doctor take a seat. I don't want her upsetting our patient."

Sean let out a groan, "Now, doctor darlin'. Here's an idea – let's the two of us rest over here. Oi know, let's have a nice chat, shall we."

"One more step Sean Maher and it is you who will be gettin' the shot. After that, believe me, you…"

"Maher! Don't make me repeat myself," the Hagan snarled.

"Yes, Mrs. Hagan," Sean said unhappily. Women, Sean decided, would be the death of him.

The big man feinted right, captured the doctor's wrist and removed the needle easily. Picking her up with one arm, he walked with Ailís to the chair and deposited the enraged young woman. He positioned himself behind her and eased her back into the chair when she tried to stand.

"Enough, the both of you!" the Hagan roared and the room fell silent except for Julian's short rasping breaths.

"I won't lie to you, boyo," Moira said. "This is going to be painful, but nothing you can't endure and it will be over in just a moment. Then you'll rest easy. Do you understand me?"

"No, don't! You can't afford it. Save it for yourself. You may need it more than I…" Julian whispered.

"It's fine, son. I've been working my strength back up. There've been no more attacks and so I'm gettin' myself back."

"Moira, he thought to her, *that is a lie. You can't afford this. I'll be fine. I may need it later. So save it for now."*

Her ability to project her own thoughts came and went, but she felt his words clearly enough. The attacks had continued, although not as concentrated as the last. She was weak and getting weaker.

"This is going to be hard on you, my dear, but it's for the best," Moira said tenderly.

Julian resigned, nodded and braced himself for more pain. *"Moira?"* Julian thought, *"I'm sorry I failed you."*

The old woman rubbed her palms together slowly, reached out and set her right hand on Julian's chest over his heart. He stiffened, arched his back in agony, and drew in a deep breath through his nose as the electric shock shot through him. His back arched again, the veins in his neck were distended and he let out a low cry of pain.

Ailís screamed, "Get away from him. Don't you see what you're doing?"

Julian settled back onto the bed still and stiff. He had felt a slight version of this once before when Bridget Bragonier, had touched him. The intensity had been nothing like this touch.

Ailís stood, knocking the chair backwards. Sean made no attempt to restrain her as she made a dash for the bed.

The doctor reached to push Moira Hagan away, but was silenced when Julian grasped her wrist gingerly. Sean Maher crossed himself, but took a step forward prepared to do battle with the witch if she hurt his friend again.

Julian seemed to go limp. His shoulders dropped and his head sank back onto the pillow. Moira took her hand away and Julian stopped panting and took a deeper first breath followed by another and another. These were not normal regular breaths, but they were better and Julian was grateful for the relief from pain.

"Now you two pull chairs up closer to the bed. We mustn't ask our Julian to shout as he recounts what happened."

"That isn't necessary," Ailís said angrily. "We must let him rest."

"You'll soon find out how necessary, girl," the Hagan said with a bleak smile.

***

With eyes closed, Julian was led through each detail of his ordeal by the firm, even voice of his teacher. She told him that he was not experiencing the events he described but observing them and reporting what he saw. In a featureless voice, he was able to describe each blow and more. The details painted a horrifying picture, but one with clues.

"Two questions. The man you describe as the leader, how tall was he in relation to you?" Moira asked. "How did he feel to you, what was your sense of him?"

"Not tall, under five foot eight inches I guess," Julian murmured as he concentrated not on the pain that still wracked his body, but on his attackers. "Thinking on it now, he felt dark and angry, but not with me. I was just a punching bag. He was angry with whoever ordered this."

Moira Hagan motioned for Sean to ask the next question. "Was he right or left handed?"

"How would I know? He was hitting me with both hands," Julian answered. "And it all hurt."

"Keep him talking," Moira mouthed to Sean and he nodded once.

"Which hand seemed to have the most power behind it, boyo?"

Julian thought hard and tried to picture the man's stance. "Left-handed, he was left-handed. There was less force behind the punches from his right."

The Hagan nodded to Ailís Dwyer who had no idea what question to ask or why. At last, she said, "What color was his hair?"

"Red. Dark red. Sorry, I should have mentioned it before. I wasn't thinking," Julian answered wearily.

The doctor probed further. "Any marks, scars, anything? You said he rolled his sleeves up before," she swallowed hard, "before he began."

Julian's forehead furrowed in intense thought and then cleared and he attempted to smile. "A tattoo of a spider on the inside of his left wrist. I saw it when he pulled on his gloves. I should have mentioned that too. I'm not very good at this. I'm afraid I'm a bad policeman."

Sean smiled evilly. The information Julian provided would make finding the leader easier, but not easy. The spider was a prison tattoo. It was a start. "Julian, lad," Sean began. "You said they thought you were laughing at them. Why would they think that?"

"Doesn't matter," Julian said with what approximated to a smile. "That's not true. It does matter a great deal, but it's personal." Sean and Ailís exchanged puzzled looks. Moira Hagan smiled slightly.

He was unable to protect his thoughts and even in her condition, she read him easily.

They had taken him through it from beginning to end. Moira got up from her chair at the side of the bed. "Rest now, my boy. You did well. It is now for the three of us to put this puzzle together while you rest." She bent over him and lovingly kissed his forehead.

Tears seeped from his eyes as he whispered, "I wasn't ready. All your work and I failed you. I'm sorry."

Moira kissed his cheek softly and a tear of her own mingled with his.

Ailís gave him an injection. Moira approached the doctor. "Stay with him. Ask him what he said that was personal. It will take you a few tries, but he'll tell you, darlin' and then you'll know the truth of it. You'll know it more clearly than you've ever known anything."

Moira shook her head sadly as she looked at her student. Julian had thought of her even in his agony and how he had disappointed her. Moira whispered, "You don't know how proud I am of you." She closed the door softly behind her.

***

The door to Julian's room opened a short time later and Ailís joined Moira in the hallway. The older woman looked at the doctor. The color had left Ailís's face and she looked deeply troubled as she bit her lip and said, "What am I to do?"

Moira folded the doctor in her arms and Ailís Dwyer began to sob.

CHAPTER TWENTY-FIVE

The next morning the Hackett sisters and their apprentice arrived with satchels of potions and evil smelling ointments, plasters, and oddly colored poultices. After two hours, they finished and looked exceedingly pleased with themselves.

***

The room was dark when Julian awoke. The house was quiet as was the street outside. He could sense her nearby. He stretched out his fingers and could feel Ailís Dwyer's soft chestnut hair. She was sitting beside his bed resting her head on the covers. Her even breathing told Julian she was asleep.

He gently stroked her hair and with that feeling, he fell away again.

***

For several days, Julian passed in and out of consciousness. Ailís entered his room as he was waking fully. She approached and simply stared at him. "Well," she said grasping for something pleasant to say, "you look, well, festive."

Julian couldn't laugh. What didn't hurt on his body was plastered over or otherwise bandaged. "Festive?" he asked.

"Well, yes, you look very festive. Believe me, that is important. It is far easier to treat people who are colorfully decorated."

Julian tried to angle his good eye to see what she was talking about.

"It is much more difficult to deal with people who have simply been pulped to a natural black and blue state. No, you look much better in Technicolor.

"It can't look as bad as it smells," Julian said.

"I wouldn't say that. You've not seen yourself," she said and tried to smile. "You, of all people, should know there is a lot to the folk ways – and other ways – of Ireland." She looked at him pointedly. "If it works, I'll not argue. And, in truth, if it doesn't work we've not lost anything. The Hacketts do what they do best and I do what I do best. We have a mutual understanding."

"What do you mean, 'of all people'?" Julian asked. "And what other ways?"

"Oh, people talk," she hinted with a small smile.

"And when these people are talking what are they talking about?" Julian demanded. His tongue felt thick and his lips weren't working all that well so his demand was only relative.

"What are you going to do? Threaten me if I don't tell you? Are you going to jump out of that bed and come force the truth from me?" she asked making sure to keep out of reach. "Or is it your wizardry you'll use on me? In any case you'll not frighten me Julian Blessing," she said and smiling mischievously, she sailed out of the room.

***

It had only been a few more days and already he was able to sit on the side of his bed. The swelling in his face and lips had gone down slightly and the deep black bruises had eased with a pale yellow cast. The cuts remained as angry reminders. Sutures had closed the deepest ones while butterfly bandages drew the skin together on the minor ones.

Ailís entered Julian's room and smiled warmly when she saw him trying to get out of bed. "I'll help you. Do you think you would be able to get dressed and take visitors tomorrow?" she asked.

Julian was quick with his answer. "Absolutely. I won't even need much help if I have enough time and take it slowly."

"So you've learned moderation, have you?"

"No, but pain has a way of reminding me that stupidity and excess will hurt like hell. Visitors? The police?"

Ailís looked at him in wonder. "You have lived among us for how long and still you know nothing a'tall. The police is it? Maybe in Dublin or some other big city and even then I doubt it. You are a genuine saint and the people of the valley and village will avenge the wrong that was done to you. The police can have what's left," she said in all seriousness.

"A saint? What are you talking about?"

"You honestly don't know? You've not figured out your neighbors yet? For the love of God, you are a saint all right – the patron saint of eejits!

"I was going to let this wait 'till tomorrow, but let me take a random sampling and show you what I mean," Ailís said.

She tucked Julian back in bed and flew from the room. He could hear her moving through her house and down the stairs toward the street. The front door opened, closed, and opened again a short time later. Shoes shuffled down the hallway toward his room and Julian slid deeper under the covers awaiting whatever fate Ailís Dwyer was bringing his way.

The door opened, Ailís stuck her head in and asked, "Are you decent enough to meet decent people? " Julian shook his head no. "Good, I knew you would be."

She ushered in two pair of sturdy farm people. "Mr. Julian, let me introduce Mr. and Mrs. Clooney and James McGraw and his missus." The strapping men nodded and their stalwart ladies made abbreviated curtsies. "Don't be shy, gather round the sick bed and have your say. You're the first of his visitors so don't hold back," Dr. Dwyer instructed.

"'Tis wonderful to see you alive, Mr. Julian. No one in the village or here about can stop talking about the wondrous things you've done," said Mrs. Clooney.

"Wondrous? Why it was nothing short of a miracle!" chimed in Mrs. McGraw.

"Well, I don't know if it t'wer either wondrous or a miracle like, but what I do know it was two men's share you did that night," added James McGraw.

"You saved us all and it is in your debt we are," said Mr. Clooney and the others chorused their assent.

Julian stared at his visitors and the doctor. His eyes were large and his breathing labored. He was a monument to confusion. "I'm afraid I don't know what you are talking about," Julian said.

Dr. Dwyer smiled indulgently with her most professional doctor-smile and added, "You will understand there is much about that night that is still a little hazy to him what with the nasty business and all."

"Ay, nasty business it was and it is a nasty and dark business that will be visited on them that raised a hand to you, yor honor."

"True, true," the visitors chorused.

The doctor said to the group, "We musn't tax our poor Mr. Julian so if you would like to speak your minds…"

"'Tis tired he's getting and we with our gobs flappin'," Mr. Clooney said. "Say it plain for us all, James."

James McGraw took a step forward, straightened himself, threw out his chest and hooked his thumbs in his waistband. He cleared his throat as though he was about to address Parliament.

"Mr. Julian, it is proud we are to have you with us. You single handed saved the life of our dear old parish priest, Father Fahey, and took a beatin' for your kindness, but without thought for your fine self you saved our church by throwin' your bleedin' and broken body on the flames them godless hooligans left behind themselves.

"For this we thank you and will forever be in your debt. You'll not be forgot for what you've done and thems that injured you will not be forgiven."

"Well said, well said," the chorus echoed and there were many congratulatory handshakes and slaps on the back among the visitors.

"Ladies and gentlemen," Ailís said. "We must now let Mr. Julian get his rest. He must be fully rested, for one never knows when God will place another test in his path." The doctor grinned and stuck her tongue out at Julian.

Ailís Dwyer saw the group out and returned to Julian's room with a self-satisfied look on her face. "No more random sampling could possibly be found. I picked the first group of people I saw on the street and dragged them in."

"But they're wrong. That isn't the way it happened. It was nothing like that," Julian sputtered. "And you know it."

"No? Well you are going to have the opportunity to convince the entire population hereabout of the error of their ways. Mind you, they will only see you as being modest – as befits any good saint. You'll never change their minds, so accept your fate.

She continued. "Sadly, you have no choice now but to live up to their expectations and that won't be hard since nearly everything you do from here on out, no matter how loony, will be ascribed some divine origin," she arched an eyebrow and added, "even your extracurricular activities." She got up, arranged his blanket and started for the door. "Pleasant dreams – St. Julian," she said and her laughter echoed down the hallway.

***

By the end of the week, Cappel Vale's saint was put on display in the parlor everyday between nine o'clock and ten, and the faithful queued up in an orderly fashion to pay their respects.

At first Julian tried to explain that far from being a saint he was an unfortunate casualty of circumstances. He attempted to tell the faithful that he had actually acquitted himself very poorly as witnessed by the yellowing bruises on his face. He endeavored to instruct his visitors that rather than save the church and its pastor he had actually brought this trouble on them. His reasoning was, if he overstated by one hundred percent and people discounted half of it, they would be near the truth. Julian's reasoning, of course, was wrong.

Like people of faith the world over, his protestations only fueled a more fervent belief. They put it down to the humility and modesty that one could ascribe to any of God's anointed. In the end, he gave up trying to change minds and resigned himself to a neutral expression with the occasional shy smile and gentle word.

Dr. Dwyer was right. He needed to accept his fate. In being right, she exercised what Julian told her was an exceedingly unattractive smugness that did not became her profession, her nationality and her sex. His characterization of her only elicited wall-shuddering laughter from Ailís.

Julian even tried to extract the help of Father Fahey. He begged the old priest to read out from the pulpit what Julian saw as the actual sequence of events. In this, he was to be stymied. The priest's recollection was hazy at best and what he did remember tended to support the view of Julian-as-champion rather than Julian's view of himself as a hapless crime statistic.

Otherwise, the days progressed with painful slowness. With each, Julian ached a little less. Each day the swelling and bruising faded a little more. Each day he found moving a little easier. And each day he felt Ailís become more distant. For this last, he had no explanation.

True, Julian wasn't the perfect patient, but he tried to follow her directions and he found that she was becoming more stern with him the harder he tried. It seemed to him that with each advance in his physical condition, each improvement in his strength, Ailís became more cross with him.

He couldn't understand her attitude and attributed it to his inability to understand women in general. In the end, he returned to the notion it was something he was doing or saying. That was the easiest answer. He was very far off the mark. The easy answers are often the wrong answers.

***

"You're disappointed in me, huh?" Julian asked Moira Hagan as she visited him one afternoon toward the end of a week filled with the visitations from the faithful and Julian's discovery that he wasn't indestructible.

"Disappointed? Why ever would I be disappointed?" she answered.

"After all the time you've invested in me it seems to have done no good at all. I should have known I was not alone with Father Fahey in the church. I could have felt it if I had focused on my entire surroundings rather than just a small portion. I should have been able to take myself out of the situation by using my advantages.

"Instead I reverted to being the idiot I was when I arrived. It was as if you had told me nothing, as if I had learned nothing. I made a hash of things from beginning to end and I'm sorry I failed you."

"Failed me, do you say?" The Hagan smiled, cocked her head to one side and suddenly Julian's mind was filled with her words. Her ability to use this talent was unpredictable.

"No, you didn't arrive at the church soon enough to save that old fool of a priest from getting a lump on his pate – that he doubtless deserved. No, you did not detect what must have been an impressively ugly presence

put out by your attackers. No, you didn't keep them from attempting to set fire to the place. No, you didn't use the talents you've developed to turn the situation to advantage. No, you didn't capture the evildoers.

"And no, you did not disappoint me. You were concerned for that priest – although why you should have been, I will never know. He has a head made entirely of granite and the thumping he received has made him the object of substantial sympathy, which he will use to get invited to untold free meals while causing his collection plate to be just a little heavier.

"According to Sean Maher, the men who beat you were cunning in the way they went about their job of work. By the time they started in on you, it was already too late for you to collect yourself. In the end, you made the dual choices of getting help for the priest and putting out the fire rather than let Sean go after your assailants.

"On the whole, you made more right choices than wrong ones.

"Don't be so hard on yourself. What happened, happened. Learn from it and prepare for the next onslaught – for there will be one – on that you may depend, laddie and the consequences may be dire.

"What, nothing to say?"

"No," Julian said out loud.

***

Late that night Ailís looked in on Julian as he slept. He looked better. His color was returning and much of the swelling was down. She approached his bed. Extending her hand, she touched his lips with her fingertips. Her touch was as soft and tender as his kisses had been.

Reaching up she brushed hair off his forehead, then her fingers traced the deep scar on his cheek she knew was under the bandage. The last time she had changed the dressing it had looked better but was still livid.

Ailís Dwyer the doctor, looked at Julian and in assessing his condition had reason for optimism.

Ailís Dwyer the woman looked at this man, this man with the soft, gray eyes and the sensuous lips. She looked at this man with the gentle touch and a tenderness she had not known before and whispered, "I am sorry – for both of us, more sorry than you will ever know."

She leaned down and kissed his forehead as a tear rolled down her cheek onto his.

Chapter Twenty-six

Another week drew to a close and Julian was slowly getting dressed to receive what promised to be the last of those who lined up outside in the brisk November weather to thank him for his efforts.

He was pulling on his boots with some effort when a light knock came at the door to his sick room. Ailís Dwyer in taupe slacks and a cream colored silk blouse stuck her head in. To Julian she was as beautiful as when he had first seen her. He doubted she would ever look differently to him. She asked if he had a moment and with a smile, he motioned her to come in.

She explained that the faithful had been let into the kitchen to warm themselves with cups of tea and that they wouldn't mind if the audiences were a bit delayed. Julian could tell by the way she avoided his gaze that something was very wrong. There was something palpable in the air around her. He knew the feel of her presence. Another presence was in attendance, another Ailís.

She looked at the state of his boots and knelt down to help him by tying his bootlaces. It was a touchingly tender act he felt. She straightened the tongue of his boots, tied the laces and pulled his pant legs down over the boot tops. Although her chestnut colored hair obscured her face, he felt the seriousness in her. She finished helping him and drew a chair to the side of the bed on which he was sitting. He smiled encouragingly and waited.

"Julian, I have a confession to make," she began.

"Ailís, would you like me to send for Father Fahey? My powers of absolution are rather limited even though I am a saint." He smiled and she returned his smile, but only half-heartedly.

"No, there is nothing Father Fahey can do for me I'm afraid. It is a confession I have to make to you only.

"Do you remember – oh, it seems like quite awhile ago – you came to me and explained how the people of the district needed me? You told me all about the high esteem in which they held me and a lot of other things about the people here abouts. Do you remember? You told me a lot of lovely things – lies mostly – but they came when I was down and needed a kind word."

He smiled again and said, "When you and everyone else thought I was crazy – most of all you? Oh, yes, I remember – and no, there were no lies. It was in my truthful phase."

"Yes," she said, "that's the time. Well I have to confess that I am a coward."

"You, Ailís? You must be joking. Never you," he answered emphatically.

"Oh yes. While you were telling me that everyone loved me you showed a remarkable amount of courage by telling me that you were fond of me in a special way. I remember it clearly – you took my hands in yours and said that you had come to care for me a great deal."

She reached out and captured his bruised hands in hers and looked into his eyes for the first time since she entered the room. Julian luxuriated in the soft warmth of her hands and the delicate fragrance that seemed to emanate from her. When his eyes met hers, he felt an ominous weight and the smile died on his lips.

"I should have told you then. Oh, there have been plenty of other times that you've expressed the same feelings for me and never once did I give you the answer I should have.

"Julian, you are a dear man in so many ways."

He suddenly felt an unreasonable tightness in his stomach and chest. Blood thundered in his ears in time to his racing heart. She was about to say what he least wanted to hear and there was nothing he could do to stop her. He pleaded for some intercession –

"Please don't. Please don't. Please don't," he repeated to himself. And then she did.

"But there can never be anything for us. I have tried to pretend it was different. I have tried to live a make-believe life, but I can't – we can't," she continued. "I am your doctor and you are my patient and no matter what I may feel, that is the only relationship we can have. You are here only for the short term and then you will return to America. That is a parting I do not want. It is not one I could endure.

"There is Timothy to think about too. He is very fond of you. He not only likes you, but he admires and trusts you and I won't let my entanglements break his heart. I am sorry for leading you to believe anything else. It was selfish and cowardly of me. In another time in different circumstances, I feel we might have made something, but it simply won't work as it is.

"That doesn't absolve me. When given the chance to act with courage I was unable to rise to that occasion and say what needed to be said." Tears brimmed in her eyes while Julian felt every ache and pain return and all of the strength leave his body.

She let go of his hands and stood. She raised her hand to caress his face. He longed for her touch, for the intimacy, but with his spirit in agony, he turned away.

"Julian..."

He didn't know where he found the voice for it, but he said, "Thank you for telling me, Doctor. I appreciate your being candid with me and I know that this wasn't easy for you to say."

Ailís Dwyer closed her eyes for a moment then turned and left his room slowly.

Julian sat on the edge of the bed, for how long he did not know. At last, he stood and made his way to the parlor to listlessly receive his visitors whose coats smelled of wet wool, peat smoke and ashes.

***

Timothy had been ushering the waiting guests into the parlor from the kitchen. After several of the villagers had come and gone, Julian called Timothy. "When you bring the last of them in, would you please go find Mr. Maher and ask him to come and see me right away? Tell him I need his help."

"Yes sor. Is it something I can help you with?" Timothy asked.

Julian smiled wearily and answered, "No, Timothy, but it is very kind of you to offer." He looked into the boy's face and saw Ailís Dwyer's eyes and smiled. He glimpsed the curve of her mouth and her broad, clear forehead. Julian ached as he felt his soul auger into his own private purgatory of lonely despair.

The boy looked at him questioningly and Julian realized he was staring at the boy and smiling a sad smile. Timothy, with luck, would never need to understand.

***

Julian leaned heavily on Sean as the big man assisted his friend to the police station.

"Are you sure this is alright with the doctor? You're weak as a pint of that filthy Mulherin's watered beer."

Julian winced as he walked, which Sean took for a smile, but otherwise Julian did not answer.

The big Irishman poured Julian into bed, then lit a fire in the fireplace. When he returned Julian was asleep. Sean covered his friend with a blanket and left feeling in his bones that something was very wrong.

***

Jimmy Grogan came by in the evening and found Julian in a rocking chair with a blanket around his shoulders in front of a guttering fire. Jimmy stoked the fire and cut some peat into manageable sizes. Julian sat in a lethargic silence staring vacantly. Jimmy also went away knowing something fundamental in the universe had changed and not for the better.

* * *

Moira Hagan entered the police station without knocking and found Julian sitting on the bench just inches from the fireplace. His face was flushed with the heat from the fire, but he felt neither hot nor cold.

"You are causing concern," the Hagan said.

Julian's expression never wavered as he said in a whisper, "Sorry."

Moira's eyes narrowed. "It has to be altogether obvious if that lummox Maher and the whelp Grogan think there is something ailing you aside from your injuries. That both of them screwed up the courage to come and see me is a testimony to the anxiety you're causing."

In a voice that sounded very far away Julian said, "I suppose we all suffer from our own injuries, no?"

This was not the Julian she had come to know, the one she had worked with for months, the one she had come to love in her own way. She could sense a little of that Julian but there was something else, a profound aching sadness she knew well.

She moved forward, took Julian by the arm, and led him to a rocking chair. She took the chair next to him and asked, "What has happened? Tell me now, what has happened to you? Where are you right now?"

"Sadly, Moira, I am right here. Although I am always happy being in your company I think I will go lay down now and sleep."

"Are you in pain? I'll go fetch the doctor."

"No!" he answered too quickly. "I mean no. I'm fine and don't need a doctor."

Moira Hagan knew in a moment what she should have known at first glance. "I'll leave you," she said. This she did and marched at the double to the surgery of Dr. Ailís Dwyer.

***

"What have you done?" Moira Hagan spat at the doctor

"What are you doing here? I'm with a patient. You can wait outside," Ailís answered with heat in her voice.

"You," Moira pointed a boney finger at the patient and barked, "You're cured; now get out!"

Edmond Brady was seated on the examination table with his shirt off when the thought struck him that it would be a very good idea to go along with the witch's advice and take himself elsewhere. He was suddenly feeling ever so much better and almost anyplace had to be healthier than this place right now. He snatched up his shirt and was gone before the doctor could protest.

Moira Hagan let the door slam behind Brady and the two women were alone in the examination room; a room that was about to become a lot less clinical, sterile and professional than it had been a moment ago.

The women stared at each other for a long time before Ailís Dwyer looked away and said with misery in her voice, "What do you want?"

"I want to know what has happened. I am not going to leave here until I know everything that went on between you two. More is riding on this than you could ever know – for him, for me, for you, for all of us," the Hagan said with force.

"He was falling in love with me – as simple and as complex as that. It isn't something that would have done him any good. I should have ended it sooner, but it was such a pleasant thought and I felt so good when I knew he was nearby. Still, I should have been stronger. My nerve failed me. Now I've done it – I've ended it and it is better this way," Ailís said as the sleepless nights suddenly caught up with her.

The Hagan never stopped looking at Ailís, but the older woman's face softened somewhat. "Tell me no lies, girl. Do you love that man?"

"It isn't as simple as that…"

"It is every bit as simple as that. Now answer the question. Do you love him and be quick with your answer."

"I will only answer that I won't love him," Ailís said and defiance entered her eyes and set her mouth.

"You will let fear kill your chance at love? You will let your heart grow small and cold? You will deny yourself what you deserve." Moira stepped closer saying, "Don't do this. I made the choice you are making and I have asked myself why every day of my life since."

"I have no choice."

"Ah, but you do. Life is full of choices. Let us hope that you are given another chance to choose a different path. I have traveled the one you are on now and I can tell you that you will not enjoy where it takes you. No one ever has."

***

Sean Maher and Mayor Cahill came to visit the saint of Cappel Vale, but the saint seemed to be in no mood for visitors. Julian said, "Enter," as his guests approached the station door.

Mayor Cahill approached Julian, "You're famous my boy. Ach, and isn't it your fame that will be spreading quick as that?" The mayor snapped his fingers and looked pleased.

"Meaning?" There was a snarl in Julian's voice and Sean detected it immediately.

"Me meaning is a simple one. There is a story unfoldin' here in our little village and we are sore in need of a good story that draws in visitors." Julian's eyes narrowed and Sean went on a higher state of alert.

"Why, there is danger and intrigue, hearty stalwarts like our friend Maher here. There is the handsome, valiant stranger and," Cahill said with a wink, "yon fair young widow with her charmin' child. Oi'm tellin' you all the elements are…"

Julian rose quickly from the bench by the fire not feeling the pain the movement caused and crossed to the mayor's chair faster than Sean could react. Julian placed his hands on both arms of the chair and leaned in close enough to smell the hard boiled eggs and cabbage on the man's breath. Sean rose slowly and Julian stilled him with a look.

"Listen to me Cahill, you can say what you want about me, about this village and its people. Tell the story with accuracy or make it up out of whole cloth. I don't care. I will say this as plainly as I know how; mention the doctor and it will be a story that will be remembered always because it will be the last story you ever tell!"

"Julian!" Sean said. He had never seen his friend upset by anything. He wasn't upset now, he was murderous.

"Have I made myself understood to you, Mr. Mayor?"

"Perfectly your honor," Cahill stuttered and swallowed hard trying to get his breath. "Oh, my, look at the time will you. Sean, it would seem we have stayed over long. Shall we?" Thomas Cahill, with eyes pleading for any sort of rescue, turned to Sean Maher.

"As you say, Thomas, perhaps we should be taking our leave."

Julian returned to the bench by the fire as Sean Maher and Thomas Cahill left in silence.

Chapter Twenty-Seven

Julian walked slowly to Moira Hagan's house with the help of a cane Father Fahey had loaned him. He rapped sharply at the door and heard her call his name in welcome.

"It is good to see you up and around. Sitting by yourself in the dark only leads to freezing out your friends and threatening mayors it seems," Moira said.

"I'm here to work," was all Julian said.

"No, you're not. You are here for revenge. The question is on whom, eh? Do you have an answer to that?"

"The men who did this to me won't catch me unaware again. Now, will you help me or not." Julian framed it as a statement rather than a question.

"Ay, I'll help you, but I'll not stop questioning your motives."

***

Bobby McMaster's lips twisted into a cruel snarl. Dunla, Brendan Maher's dog, was tied to the tree outside the schoolyard as Sister Eugenia had instructed. The nun wanted Bobby McMaster to have no more excuses.

A blanket had been laid in a hollow between two tree roots and the dog was content to wait for her master. She was protected from the wind on three sides and could easily keep the schoolyard in view. Her coat, lovingly brushed every morning and every night glowed in the dull sunlight. Dunla had no reason to fear Bobby McMaster, but she was alert to his movements.

Without warning McMaster reached into his jacket pocket and hurled a large lump of coal at the dog. She raised her head in reaction and dodged the first rock only to move into the path of a second projectile. It caught her right eye and Dunla yelped. Bobby McMaster stepped closer to the stricken dog as she tried desperately to escape the tether that held her fast to the tree and her attacker.

McMaster, smiling and laughing, now let loose the third and largest of his lumps of coal that he had taken from the coal scuttle at school. The piece struck Dunla in the ribs and she fell to her side. McMaster moved in picked up the same rock now covered with blood and fur and smashed it into her side repeatedly until she moved no more.

* * *

Brendan heard Dunla's yelp across the noisy schoolyard and began to run. He vaulted the rock fence and ran quickly to his dog's side. Her fur was matted with blood and her tongue lolled limply from her mouth into the dirt.

With infinite care Brendan removed the rope from her neck and gently picked her up. Tears coursed down his cheeks as he ran to the doctor's house. He kicked at the door and Dr. Dwyer answered quickly. She assessed the situation quickly and led the way to her examination room where Brendan lay the dog down.

"Please! Save her, please. Doctor, please." Brendan managed to get out through strangled sobs.

Ailís Dwyer was not unaccustomed to dealing with animals. She took out her stethoscope and listened carefully.

"I need you to step outside, Brendan. Do it now" she said.

"No, please" he managed to say between gasps for breath.

"Yes, Brendan. I need room to work." She ushered the boy to a chair in the hallway as Timothy ran into the house and up the hall. "Stay with your friend, Timothy. He needs to keep out here."

Ailís closed the door and moved to the examination table. She knew immediately that the dog was beyond anything she could do. She touched the animal's side and felt the broken ribs.

Dunla shifted her head slightly, exhaled once through her nose and died.

Gently the doctor began to clean the wounds where bits of bone protruded. Pressing them back under the skin, she began suturing and covering the stitches as best she could with the surrounding fur. The eye lay against Dunla's muzzle. The doctor replaced this too, cleaned the area and stitched the eye closed.

Dr. Ailís Dwyer sat on the stool and patted the soft fur of Brendan's best friend and softly she began to cry. She ached for the emptiness Brendan would feel when she had to tell him that she had done everything she could, but that Dunla was gone. She threw back her head and tried to suppress the sobs that shook her shoulders over her own losses.

The examination room door opened and the doctor stepped out into the hallway. Brendan and Timothy stood there, but any flicker of hope disappeared when the boys saw the doctor's face.

"Brendan…"

"Oi know" the boy said simply. Tears welled in his eyes. "Thank you" he stammered. Brendan walked past her into the examination room, lifted Dunla into his arms and settled her for the last trip they would take together. He came into the hall and both of the Dwyers bowed their heads as Brendan passed. Timothy moved to follow his friend, but Ailís stopped her son.

"Let's give him time." They walked to the front door slowly and looked up the dusty street in time to see Brendan Maher disappear into the woods west of the village.

"Thank you for trying. Oi know you did your best," Timothy said. "But Oi need to go."

Ailís nodded her head and let go of her son's shoulders.

Timothy took off at a run, not in the direction Brendan had gone, but toward the police station and Julian Blessing.

***

"Come quick, Mr. Julian. There has been a murder!" Timothy shouted.

"A murder – who, where? Let's go." He grabbed up his cane, but hadn't made it as far as the flagstones leading to the road before he stopped, clenched his fists and shut his eyes tightly. Timothy looked back in alarm when he heard a strangled cry escape from between Julian's clenched teeth. "Please God, not that!"

He sighed in resignation as he watched the scene unfold. He fell to his knees in the dusty road, covered his eyes and wept. The sobs shook him as he witnessed Dunla's death.

He felt Timothy next to him and knew the boy's jumble of emotions. Julian reached out, and drew the boy to him. He was still kneeling in the street,

From the doorway of her practice Ailís watched the scene unfold before. She felt his heartache as Julian reached out and drew her son to him. She witnessed the man she loved and the child she adored.

Still on his knees, Julian wept until he had no more tears left to give.

Leaning on Timothy, Julian made the best progress he could. His ribs ached and burned with each step. They reached the tree and silence pervaded the area. The schoolyard was empty and the school was hushed.

Julian saw the three lumps of coal and picked up the smallest of the three. The coal dust came off on his hands and he brushed them on his pants as he surveyed the place of Dunla's execution – in his mind, there was no other word for it.

In that moment he felt it, he watched it happen again in more detail. And he saw clearly Dunla's executioner. And he saw more, much more.

Julian picked up the dog's blanket and covered the bloody ground. After kicking the three stones under the blanket, he looked down at his hands and at Timothy standing beside him looking expectant. Coal dust permeated the crevices of Julian's still raw hands.

"Timothy, go back to class and tell your teacher you were helping me. Tell her I will explain later.

Julian stayed near the tree and let the scene play out until he was able to stop it. He entered the school and knocked lightly on Sister Eugenia's classroom door. Puzzlement crossed her face as she opened the door. Julian followed the nun inside. The smell of sweaty children was pervasive in the closed, overheated space and Julian wondered if smell had always been the same throughout time.

He cupped his hand and whispered into the nun's ear. She turned her head and looked at him. His face was set and his eyes were ablaze.

"Bobby McMaster. Come here. Now." Julian's voice was level and low.

"McMaster! Are you somewhat hard of hearing?" Sister Eugenia barked.

Julian's eyes locked on to those of Bobby McMaster. The boy's eyes never wavered and the sneer never left his lips. Julian looked into the boy and what he saw frightened and sickened him.

"Come here, boy," the nun said and McMaster rose, pocketed his hands and shuffled to the front of the room. Julian pulled the boy's hands from his pockets. Coal dust was etched deeply into both hands and under his fingernails.

"What does this mean, Mr. Blessing?" the nun asked. Julian only answered with another question.

"Warm day don't you think, Sister? Too warm for the likes of Mr. McMaster here to be wearing a coat indoors." Julian grabbed Bobby's jacket and pulled it open, pinning the boy's arms to his sides. His shirt was spattered with blood. The class gasped collectively. Gwyneth Kirby looked terror stricken. Next to her sat the empty desk of Brendan Maher.

"He used lumps of coal to stone Dunla to death while she was tethered to a tree." Julian said simply and without triumph.

Bobby McMaster broke away from Julian and the nun.

"Yes, Oi did it and Oi'm glad the bitch is dead. Oi've had orders from an important man. More important than you'll ever be. Oi'd do it again, orders or no. You should've heard her whimper!" McMaster called out as he ran from the room laughing.

***

When Julian came out of the school Sean Maher was kneeling in the dirt under the tree where Dunla died. He had called for a rake and smoothed the dirt taking care to cover the dog's blood. He had picked up her blanket, folded the stains to the inside and set it on the nearby stone wall that partially surrounded the schoolyard.

Julian expected his friend to have a lethal anger, but such was not the case. He felt a sadness beyond words tighten around Sean Maher's heart.

"Timothy told me Brendan went into the forest. Have you seen him?" Julian asked.

Sean shook his head no.

"Let's give it awhile and then we'll go look for him. It wouldn't be good for him to be on his own tonight, you agree?"

Again, Sean Maher nodded his head.

"We'll have a pint and then we'll go looking, alright?"

Sean didn't trust himself to speak. He just nodded again and followed Julian to O'Gavagan's Pub. Once inside Sean stood at the bar looking straight ahead unaware of the murmured condolences the other patrons offered.

These were farmers, men who understood the value of a working animal. Dogs were just another farm tool, nothing more and nothing less. But to these men, Dunla was more, far more because Brendan Maher was far more.

Sean continued to stand, unmoving. His beer sat on the bar untouched. A deep sigh escaped him before he said, "Tell me Julian, how does this happen? What power makes monsters and puts them among us? And a child, how could a child be so twisted."

"It is an illness, Sean. That's all – an illness."

"Oi won't accept that. A wee creature that never did anyone any harm and brought nothing but joy and companionship to me boy – and you say an illness snuffed out its life? The ability to do that sort of thing just happens without warning?"

"No, it doesn't just happen. Someone with this sickness builds up to it and it goes on building and growing with increasing violence. People like this need help."

"'Increasing violence" is it? Ending the life of an innocent creature in so brutal a way isn't enough? Is anything ever enough for a disgusting little bastard like that? And what help is there that will ever make 'em right? Tell me that, Julian. Tell me there is a way to mend someone who would do such a thing?" With tears in his eyes Sean Maher faced his friend and said, "Please, Julian, for the love of God, tell me."

Julian seemed lost in thought for a moment before he touched his friend's forearm. Julian knew he couldn't speak the words. His words soundlessly entered his friend's mind.

Sean looked startled and confused, but Julian stilled his friend's thoughts.

"Shhhhh, hush, feel the words." Julian thought and paused. *"Please believe me, Sean, if there was a way I could change any of this I would. If I could reach in and take this sorrow from you and from Brendan, I would gladly take it on myself and I would never say a word.*

"There is no sense to be made of any of this. Bobby McMaster is a monster as you say and I do not believe there is any way of ever repairing him. I believe his is an illness from which he will never recover. I don't know if prison is the answer or a hospital is a better place. All I know is that he must be placed somewhere from which he will never be released and from which he can never escape – not just because of this, but for the crimes that will surely come.

"That boy will become a man and his sickness will grow just as surely as he does. He is not someone that you or I will ever understand. He needs to inflict pain. He needs to cause and then observe agony. He places no value on the lives of others beyond their ability to feed his hunger to inflict suffering.

"I lied to you in the hope that I could relieve your anguish. I told you the boy needed help as though such help was available. I don't believe it is. He suffers from something that puts him far beyond redemption.

"But you and Brendan and me and all of us have in one way or another been changed by this brutality. We will live and grow. It has made us sadder, but it will in all likelihood help us to become more human while Bobby McMaster will become less and less so until he is gone altogether.

"He is a great sadness, but he is not someone to be pitied. Neither is he someone to be hated. Emotions of any sort are wasted on him. We must work out a way to identify and protect ourselves from the Bobby McMasters of the world and that we will do.

"Now let's go find Brendan and bring him home. He needs to be with his people." Julian said aloud.

Sean continued to stare at his friend, comforted by the words and confused by how he came to hear them in his head. At last, he said, "And his people need to be with him."

When they turned to leave, all the other patrons rose and shuffled to the door. By the time Julian and Sean made it outside there were twenty stalwart, silent men standing outside O'Gavagan's. With a nod given and acknowledged, the group moved off into the forest west of the village and began their search for Brendan Maher.

***

The searchers swept the wood thoroughly and found no trace of Sean's son. If the boy had been there once, he was not there now and the dispirited men returned to the village as the sun set and darkness settled on Cappel Vale.

Julian's face mirrored the pain his injuries still caused him. He found himself leaning heavily on the borrowed cane. Stopping to catch his breath, he wiped his forehead with his hand. It was a cool day, but Julian felt hot and tired. His muscles cried out for a hot shower and a chance to rest.

Sean approached and asked Julian if he would join the Mahers for supper before they returned to the search. Julian's chest ached and he wanted to unwrap it in the hope of breathing deeply. He thanked Sean for the offer, but said he would just clean up a little and they would meet again in an hour.

Julian made it to the police station with slow, painful steps. He removed his shirt, wiped down his upper body with a wet cloth and lay down, intent on a few moments rest. The shower could wait. Minutes later he swung his legs off the bed, got up unsteadily and grabbed for his shirt.

"Come in, Doctor," he said softly before the knock landed on the door. He could feel her nearly the way she had been. Urgency and fear were intertwined with her softness and caring. He closed his eyes knowing her caring would never be for him.

Ailís Dwyer entered and crossed the room to him quickly. "It's Timothy," she said out of breath.

Julian looked into her eyes and asked more calmly then he felt, "Tell me what has happened."

"He's gone into the woods to search for Brendan. He saw everyone come back and I guess he thought they had given up the search. You must help me find him. He is terrified of the dark, and the thunder and lightning only make it worse for him."

Julian thought for a moment and walked to the open door.

Her gaze followed him. His shoulders rolled forward in weariness. In his profile, she could see how deeply pain had etched lines in his face.

Julian said slowly, "I want you to bundle up some food, find a flashlight and then meet me at the tree line where the woods meet the village. Can you do that quickly?"

"Of course," she answered and ran from the room.

Julian gathered a sweater and jacket. The weather had turned against him and a light mist was falling. The wind was biting cold, blowing in gusts that sent leaves scattering before it down the main street.

When he reached the tree line, Ailís met him with a heavy backpack. She, too, now wore a heavy jacket and scarf.

Julian yelled to her over the wind, "You're not going to like this and I'm not saying it out of any sense of bravado, but I would rather you stay here. The villagers will want to start the search again, especially knowing Timothy is out there too, but we don't want everybody and their brother roaming around the woods in the dark. Keep them here tonight and don't start the search until nine o'clock or so in the morning.

"If Timothy gets back before I do, he'll want you waiting for him even if it means he is in trouble. If there is a safe way of getting back here tonight we will. If not, he and I will find a dry spot and sit tight until morning.

"For another thing, it could be that Brendan didn't come back sooner because he was hurt. If he limps back in, he'll need you around to patch him up. Believe me, if I could I would stay in the village, but you're the doctor. You've got the skill, not me. Make sense?"

She looked frustrated, but nodded her head. "Here is your torch," she shouted over the wind and handed him the flashlight. "There are pain medications in the pack. Please tell me you'll take them if the pain gets to be too much and, whatever you do, be careful."

He smiled tightly, leaned nearer to Ailís and said, "It'll be alright. It has to be. I won't let it be otherwise," and started on his way into the forest. The rain had increased and turned the dirt street at the tree line into a swamp.

"Julian took a step fighting against the wind and then fell down on the slick mud. Working his way back to his feet, he slipped and fell again and the pain was intense. With another try, he struggled to get upright and managed to gain the limited shelter the trees provided where he would begin his search.

Had he looked back quickly enough, he would have seen Ailís fight back the tears. To her mind they were tears for the man she loved, tears for the boy she adored and bitter, bitter tears for herself. He would have also seen her mouth the words, "I won't let it be otherwise."

***

Although soaking wet and muddy, Julian finally gained the shelter of the thicker part of the woods. The trees broke the wind and the branches overhead gave him shelter from the heaviest of the rain. He began to work his way around the woods in a long arc to the right thinking he would ring the forest and then gradually work his way in deeper.

He walked for half an hour, stumbling over rocks and roots, slipping from time to time, but never being able to sense Timothy's presence. Julian saw a sparkle of light straight ahead. "The Squire," he thought and continued on, depending on his walking stick to keep him upright.

At last, he came to the tree line at its nearest point to the Squire's home. Lights showed from the downstairs windows. Thinking the boys might have made for shelter, Julian moved toward the large brick house.

He knocked at the back door and, remembering that the housekeeper was nearly deaf, he pounded harder. With the rain pelting him hard, Julian deferred to practicality and entered the mud room. Calling out he got no answer, so he ventured even further before the Squire's dogs ran to greet him and led him deeper into the house.

Light from the fireplace danced on the wall of the hallway outside the Squire's study. Calling again, and again receiving no response, Julian continued toward the study before he heard a soft humming; the tune was a familiar sad ballad in the way only Irish ballads know how to be. The rendering now was diffused, distracted and filled with melancholy and pain.

At the entrance to the study Julian froze. The Squire was seated in his wingback chair before the large fireplace humming to himself. Hanging above the fireplace was the portrait of a staggeringly beautiful woman. Julian heard the Squire had been married long ago. Because the drape had been drawn whenever he visited, Julian assumed it was a painting of the Squire's late wife.

"Squire," Julian said softly.

"Who's there? Oh, it's you Blessing. I'm afraid I'm in no condition for a game of chess. As you can see, I am quite drunk. What brings you out on a filthy night like this?" the man asked.

"Two of the village boys are lost in the wood that borders your property."

"Let me see if I can be a detective, eh? One of the boys is Brendan Maher. That would make the other one Timothy Dwyer. Dirty business about that dog. That McMaster boy should be put down of course. The father, too, come to think of it."

"I wonder if you would make such a good detective if everything wasn't reported back to you as soon as it happened. I thought the boys might have come here to get out of the rain," Julian said distractedly. The portrait mesmerized him.

"Oh, but I am remarkably well informed. Sadly, I cannot say the same for you," the Squire said. "I see you can't take your eyes off that portrait. She was the most beautiful creature I had ever seen and I worshiped her. Look at the eyes. They could pierce you right to your soul. Her hair was coal black and her skin was as smooth and as utterly flawless as the finest silk." Julian stood awestruck before the painting. He was unable to look away.

"Ah, you too are captivated," the Squire said looking up at the painting. "It is entirely understandable of course. I myself am a slave to that image – and to the memories.

"She was twenty three when that was painted," the Squire said as he indicated the painting with a boney finger. "Her family had been a well placed fixture in Ireland back to the ancient times. Druids, they say, run in her family, my boy.

"There was that, but there was something more. I never knew what, and she never spoke of it." Wistfully the old man said, "You see, she was special in many ways – in so many, many ways. She had a power, and not just over me. No, it just emanated from her somehow.

"And that I suppose was where the problem began. I was young and a more perfect idiot you would never hope to meet. She was younger still and a more headstrong and stubborn creature you could not find.

"We met, married, and at first things were perfect. Our life was a poem, as they say. But an old priest in the village managed to poison me against her. He told me that both of our souls would be damned if she did not give up the old ways of Ireland. He even hinted at witchcraft. According to him, I had an obligation and a right to demand it of her.

"Until then she had balanced the old and the new quite well, but being an ass, I ordered her – commanded her, mind you – to leave off with the old ways of her people. She, of course, said she could not and would not if she could. I told her if she did not, we were through.

"I knew I had gone too far, but my stupid pride would not allow me to take it back. She looked at me, I could see the love that we shared begin to die." The old man's voice tore the air, "and still I did nothing. I could have stopped it, I could have saved our love, but I did nothing. The next morning she was gone from this house and from my life forever.

"I didn't know it at the time, but she was carrying our child. She gave birth to the child and raised him for a short while, but again Father Fahey's predecessor convinced me that the boy was mine and must be raised in a 'proper Catholic home' whatever the fuck that means." Bitterness dripped from his words.

"Being an idiot and having my pride wounded, I lashed out again. I sought sole custody of the boy and got it. Money is a powerful motivator for some and I spread it freely to get..." his thoughts trailed off.

"For decades she and I have lived in each other's shadow and have never spoken a word to one another.

"'Tis a sad story, don't you think? Still, it is a fitting punishment that I should have to live forever beside the thing I loved above all else. And love her still." The older man drew in a deep breath and with eyes closed, let it out slowly.

"Friend Julian, it is the simplest thing in the world to give advice. It is the hardest thing in the world to take it. Listen, son, never willingly let go of love. Never give up on it.

"Oh, yes, I know about you and that girl of yours. I am telling you Julian, forget who is responsible for what and put away your pride. Go to her. Plead, beg, promise anything, do anything to make it right between the two of you. Do whatever it takes to convince her to join you in making a world for the two of you and that boy of hers and tell the rest of 'em to piss off.

"I did not follow the advice I am giving you. It is for that reason I have lived a tormented life. I deserve every moment of it because I forged it with my ignorance and my arrogance. Don't let that happen to you, my boy. Don't do now what I did then. The bounty you reap will be bitterness itself. The cost of that harvest will be suffering that is nearly beyond enduring. I say nearly because your choice will not so easily let you die, and death, my friend, is the only escape from this misery."

At this, the Squire began to hum again softly to himself and before long, he was asleep.

Julian rose, found a lap rug and draped it around the old man's legs. He threw another log on the fire and took a last look at the beautiful woman in the painting. He smiled at the exquisite young woman who had become Moira Hagan.

Julian closed the portrait's drape and let himself out.

Chapter Twenty-Eight

Julian limped through the wind and rain across the small pasture adjacent to the Squire's home and reached the shelter of the woods where he continued his search for Timothy and Brendan.

He walked until his ribs and chest and back ached, but pushed on using the notion of rest as the carrot that kept him moving. Still, he could not sense either of the boys. He came to the northernmost edge of the forest that met the rim leading into the next valley.

He could make out a dark mass at the bottom of an adjacent valley he knew to be another small, but thickly wooded stand of trees. The locals said that area was special. At the word, *special,* the faithful would cross themselves and look deeply pained while Moira Hagan would simply smile.

Julian's endurance of the pain had reached its limit. He felt he had to give up the physical search and allow the boys to find him. The storm raged, but inside the cathedral of trees he was relatively dry. Julian removed his jacket, shook it out, and set Ailís's bag of food down on a rock. He turned his flashlight on and stood it up so that its beam shone into the canopy of trees. He sat, closed his eyes and began one of the drills Moira had given him.

The object of the exercise was to relax his mind and body, but it was also intended to open him to the forces of the world around him. How long he sat there, he did not know, but before long he opened his eyes and said softly, "Hello, Timothy."

Before him stood Timothy Dwyer and the look on the boy's face was one of extreme fascination mixed with instinctive hesitation to engage the unknown.

"You have frightened your mother and are in more than a little trouble."

The boy looked down at the ground and didn't reply.

"Are you ready to go back or would you like to have something to eat first?" Julian asked as he gathered his flashlight and jacket. While sitting there, the night had turned colder and chilled Julian to the bone.

"I can't go back yet," the boy said.

"Timothy, you are causing your mother a lot of heartache so the reason we have to stay had better be a good one."

"Oi can't leave Brendan. He isn't ready to go back and Oi won't leave him behind." Lightening crackled across the night sky and Timothy cringed.

"Well, that is a good reason, but I don't know that it is good enough. Where is Brendan now?"

"This way," is all Timothy said as he turned and headed east toward a deeply crevassed hillside that was a prominent high point in the topography of the region. Timothy disappeared behind a clump of bushes and Julian followed. A path led behind the bushes and ascended the hillock at a steep angle. The climb caused Julian substantial pain.

At one point Julian asked Timothy to stop for a few moments. The bushes seemed to be ancient with well-established root systems and a decent canopy that kept out nearly all of the weather. Julian looked through the thick growth and could easily see for miles to the east, west and north. He knew, however, that he could not be seen through the tangle of foliage that clung to the hillside.

Still out of breath and aching, Julian nodded that he was ready and Timothy set off again. The path continued uphill for another forty meters to the top, but ten meters short of the summit Timothy stopped abruptly, turned toward the hillside and disappeared. Julian was stunned and ran to where the boy had been just seconds before. Julian could sense the boy and followed the feeling to a gap in the rock face where he inched his way in.

The opening was relatively spacious. Julian couldn't stand upright, but the width was ample. He was at the mouth of a cave and the walls were rough sandstone, cool and dry to the touch. He continued along the passageway, but soon found himself crouching down further and then emerging into a large cavern. In the center of the single room was a compact, but efficient fire. Only dry wood had been used so almost no smoke worked its way to a slight opening in the roof of the cave.

Julian was puzzled. This place felt wrong to him, deeply wrong. But he could not fix the cause or the cure.

Seated near the fire, bathed in firelight, sat Brendan Maher. Timothy was kneeling beside his friend explaining something. Brendan nodded and Timothy spoke.

"Brendan says you are welcome in this place, sor. As far as we know, only he and Oi know about it. He could hear the men searching for him earlier and he is sorry to cause a bother, but he wasn't ready to come home. Later on it was too dark and wet to try to get back tonight. He says he'll be ready to go in the morning and face what he has comin' so I guess I will too."

Julian sighed. The boys were right; it was too dark and wet to try to get back without the likelihood that one of them would get hurt.

"Sit tight it is then, but hear me boys – we go back in the morning and no questions."

"Yes, sor," Brendan and Timothy said in unison.

"Good. Let's see what your mother sent along to eat," Julian said as he sat down by the fire and unpacked the bag. He ached everywhere and he was glad to be able to rest for the night.

* * *

The three well-fed campers settled in around the fire in silence, each lost in his thoughts. Julian looked up ten minutes later, smiled and shook his head. The boys had fallen asleep in various tortured positions comfortable only to the young.

Something in a back corner of the cave dimly reflected the firelight and caught Julian's eye. He picked up his flashlight and rose to investigate.

As he neared the object, he first slowed his pace and then stopped. Spilling out of a bag of some sort was a pile of coins. Those exposed to the air were heavily tarnished while the ones underneath still held on to their dull gray sheen. He approached and knelt in the dirt. He picked up a coin and rubbed his thumb over the surface. There, under the covering of fine dust, Julian could clearly see the words that chilled him, PAX AVGVSTS C. He was holding a Roman coin in his hand that dated back nearly two thousand years.

Julian felt, more than heard, Brendan stir. The boy sat up, knuckled his eyes, and stretched. He got up and came over to where Julian was kneeling. He pulled the boy by the sleeve and together they looked at the coin from two opposite points of view.

Julian saw that he was holding a piece of history that dated back millennia. He was filled with wonder, awe, and an ominous trepidation. Brendan looked at the coin as though it were a rock or a fish or some other constant in his natural world.

"Do you know what this is, Brendan?" Julian asked.

"C-C-C-oin," Brendan answered and smiled without pretense or guile.

"Well, yes, but Brendan, this isn't just any coin." The boy nodded his head, then reached deeper into the darkness and pulled out what Julian recognized immediately as a Roman sword.

The grip had long since disintegrated, but the tang and pommel remained in good shape and the iron blade, although corroded, looked serviceable. Brendan used the sword to brush away some the dirt from an area under where Julian had spotted the coin. The boy made a quick stabbing motion with the sword and scores of coins fell away from the dirt mound. Brendan smiled as though he had performed a remarkable magic trick for an appreciative audience.

Deep lines of concern scored Julian face. He had felt more clearly something was wrong, off somehow. Now on the ground in front of him was the cause or a part of it. The air seemed to leave his lungs and the cave suddenly seemed small and tight. At last, Julian said, "This isn't possible."

Brendan smiled broadly and shone Julian's flashlight against another far wall and pointed with the Roman sword to what looked like a low mound of dirt. He drew Julian closer and removed some of the dirt with his boot. More coins spilled onto the dirt floor. Julian used the light to examine the area.

The mound was actually the remains of leather bags full of Roman coins. All but a few remnants of the bags remained. The years it took for the bags to disintegrate were also years when wind and weather deposited a fine covering of dirt on top of them. Julian took the flashlight and sent the beam along another wall of the cave.

He continued to scan the next wall and then over to where he had first seen a glint in the firelight. Bags of coins had been stacked around the entire perimeter of the cave. When and by whom were the questions Julian wanted answered and he knew a man who would have those answers.

"Brendan, may I take a few of these coins and that sword to show a friend of mine?"

Brendan Maher smiled broadly then moved to the back of the cave. He returned with another sword in better shape and handed it to Julian.

The boy then moved back to his bed by the fire and Julian found himself a comfortable place opposite. Sleep, however, was the last thing on Julian's mind.

He could feel them, see them, these men who brought this treasure to Ireland. They were soldiers, and he could sense their honor and their valor. But the scene Julian was witnessing was confused and confusing. His ability to see into the past was improving, but his previous experiences were of recent events. Tonight, he witnessed an incident two millennia into a dark past.

***

The coal blackness of night had given way to a steel gray morning that found Julian staring into the fire pit. He had sat before the fire in the company of Roman Legionaries who arrived in Ireland to fulfill their duty. Now these men of honor sat in abject despair knowing they would never see their homes again and, to their shame, knowing why.

The wind had died down and the rain had stopped. Julian woke the boys and together they finished off the last of the food Ailís Dwyer had packed. They doused the fire and Julian watched as the boys erased any trace of their having been there. They obscured the entrance to the cave and dusted the trail with branches to obliterate any footsteps that would have given away the location.

The path through the woods was easier now that they had rested and could see. Soon they neared the tree line that abutted the village of Cappel Vale. Julian stopped and looked at the boys. Even after a night's sleep, they were tired and ragged and could use a hot bath and a hot meal.

Julian said to the boys, "Now you know you are probably in for it. The entire village was worried sick about you Brendan, and Timothy, your mother was beside herself. It is my advice that you stand up straight, leave off with any sort of excuses and simply throw yourselves on their mercy and hope they don't punish you as you deserve."

The boys looked mournful, but only murmured a subdued, "Yes, sor."

"Right, here we go. Let's try to look like we know what we're doing."

They moved through the tree line and into the village. Sean Maher, Ailís Dwyer and Moira Hagan were on the main street talking together. A number of men were just coming out of the pubs after a farm breakfast and were ready to take up the search again for the missing boys.

With more discipline then he would have expected, the boys stayed with him and marched up to Ailís and Sean. The thunder behind Sean Maher's eyes dissipated when he set them on his eldest son. Julian approached Sean, looked up at the big man and murmured, "I'm not sure I would have done any differently than Brendan and I don't think you would have either."

Sean nodded his head and opened wide his arms to his son. Together they moved off toward the Maher house. On their approach, Kathleen Maher emerged along with the rest of the brood and they surrounded Brendan and spirited him inside.

Julian looked at Ailís and noted she was doing a very bad job of looking stern. Her nose flared and her lips were pressed hard together as she tried to suppress her emotions. Before hugging her son, she took him by the shoulders and said, "You are never to do that again."

Julian approached, his face drawn by pain and weariness. He leaned down and with his lips close to her ear and whispered, "Try not to be too hard on the boy. He faced his worst fears to search for his friend. He did this after he thought everyone else had given up the hunt. That is the kind of strength and courage few have." Ailís turned to look at him. This was as physically close as she had been to him in weeks. Pain seared her soul as she looked at him. There was a haunted look that had swept away the softness of his eyes. Ailís slowly nodded.

Moira Hagan looked at Julian, smiled warmly and was shocked by the knowing and disturbingly frank look she received in return.

Julian inclined his head slightly, nodded, smiled slightly and, with the help of his walking stick, limped the length of the village to the police station.

With history in his hands, he hefted the backpack with the score of coins he had picked up at random and the Roman sword and thought about nothing but a hot shower, a proper bed and sleep.

Behind him, Ailís Dwyer knelt in the dusty street and held her son for a very long time. She thought, "He said, 'I won't let it be otherwise,' and I knew he wouldn't. What have I done?"

***

"Timothy, come along and I'll get you something hot to eat," Moira Hagan said to the boy who smiled. He left his mother and moved toward the older woman.

"I can do that," Ailís said and looked profoundly confused.

Moira looked at her as if she were an especially dull child and said, "No, I'm afraid you can't. There are other things you need to do." She gently pushed Timothy in the direction of her cottage.

Ailís's face, drained of color said, "I don't know what you're..."

Moira looked at the doctor, into her and said nothing. Ailís deflated visibly. "I can't and even if I could it is too late. You saw his face. He hates me and so he should."

"Indeed, I saw his face. Tell me, did you or did you not just see what you needed to see? Did you see the face of someone who overcame every bit of his past and all of his fears in order to love someone? Did you not see the face of a remarkable man who was forced to watch as the woman he loved shredded his soul?

"You are a bright woman, Ailís – a bright woman capable of doing some of the stupidest things imaginable." Moira let her words sink in.

"Don't you see? I can't," the doctor pleaded. "It isn't just about me. I am protecting Timothy. I won't let him have his heart broken."

"Well then, you have been stunningly unsuccessful," Moira spat. "You have played a dangerous and stupid game, my girl. You sat down at the card table without knowing the stakes or the odds. You risked it all not knowing there was never any chance of winning.

"You say you wished to protect Timothy and your lovely self from heartache. Well, you played and you lost and you are only now coming to grips with how much you lost."

Ailís looked at the ground and closed her eyes.

"Since you mentioned your son, let me ask you a question," Moira said. "Timothy looks to you for guidance. That is as it should be. When it comes time to talk to him about love, what will you tell him?

"Will you say, 'Walk away from love, son. Set your foot on a path that will lead to heartache without end. That is what I did in order to protect us both.' Will you say that to him, Doctor?"

Ailís stood in stunned silence, powerless to answer a question that only had one reply.

"You are in pain, Doctor, are you not?" Moira smiled crookedly. Her piercing, dark gray eyes cut into the younger woman. "Just answer me yes or no. 'Tis an easy question, surely."

Ailís had no choice. She nodded yes.

"Ah, but you don't have a monopoly on pain now do you. Timothy is a sensitive boy and he feels the loss of his Mr. Julian's company keenly, as keenly as he senses his mother's sadness. I can feel it in him and you know the truth of it too. But we will put your son aside for the moment.

"You suffer, but yours is a pain that is self-caused. You picked the time and the place with care and you set it in motion by your own hand. Agonizing to be sure, but as I say, you are not alone.

"There is man suffering an anguish that you cannot imagine. He had no control in its cause you see. His is a pain so intense many would lose their minds if they had to endure for a moment the torture he does. And why is this you might ask?" Ailís bunched her fists and swallowed hard as Moira continued her relentless assault.

"His suffering is limitless because he loves you with a passion that is limitless. At the end of this very street is a man who loves you so completely that he does it without the slightest reservation or regard for himself. You see, he is so devoted to you that he will pay any price to assure your happiness even if that price is his own happiness," Moira said.

"You did tell him there could never be anything between you two, did you not? Don't worry yourself, he didn't tell me and wouldn't. It is plain for anyone to see. You saw it just moments ago in his face.

"But it doesn't stop there for him now, does it?" Moira stepped closer to the doctor and Ailís staggered as if struck. "He believes he will have to endure this pain endlessly and not only that, he must do so alone."

Ailís gasped for breath, her shoulders shook with her agony as she screamed, "Stop it. Enough. I can't take any more of this!"

Moira stepped closer still and her eyes flared. "Ah, but darlin', that is the nature of a thing that is endless. It doesn't stop. This pain is limitless. There is no 'enough' don't ya see, either for you or for him."

Ailís stood in the street and said nothing, her lips a thin harsh line, her eyes pleading.

"I will not say you suffer less nor that you love less, but you have Timothy who relies on your wisdom, who loves you and you him. You are not alone and at the end of the day, that is a tremendous comfort.

"At the end of the day the man we are talking about will suffer alone with his only comfort being that he once loved another completely.

"Ailís, the choice is plain. Take yourself home and suffer for your choices or go to this man and offer your love to him.

"I'll say no more. Besides, Timothy and I have a great deal to talk about and we're both hungry." Moira Hagan smiled shrewdly. "Doctor, do see if you can come by for supper this evening. Timothy and I will have something special laid on for the occasion. But," she added and smiled a wicked smile, "If you are somehow detained, ah, but that will be alright too."

***

Entering the police station Julian sat down heavily on the bench near the fireplace. In his absence, Jimmy had stoked the fire. After his night in the forest and cave, the station felt warm and inviting.

He had been arranging his personal papers by the fire before being called away by Timothy for Dunla's murder. He thought again of Timothy and the important place the boy had taken in his life. His spirit sagged at the thought.

He hefted the papers, then groaned at the thought of sorting through them. Stiff and aching, he dropped the stack of documents, removed his boots and the rest of his clothes. He made for the bathroom where he intended on showering until all the hot water was gone.

The water had been searing hot, but not nearly hot enough to burn away the ache he carried. He dried off, pulled on a pair of sweatpants and picked up his razor to shave. Wiping steam from the mirror, he carefully shaved around his scar. He felt, rather than heard, the station door open.

Julian closed his eyes and could sense Ailís. She felt to him like a jumble of thoughts and unhappy emotions. When he sensed her in the past she had always felt clear, focused and without equivocation. Now she was confused, angry and rudderless, but he sensed something else too. Wariness crossed his face, then he relaxed slightly, calmed his thoughts and continued shaving.

Julian emerged into the office and found the station's curtains had been pulled closed and the bar used for locking the door had been shot home.

She sat in the Desk Sergeant's chair. "How can I help you, Doctor?" Julian said with formality.

Ailís looked up at the sound of his voice then closed her eyes tightly. A towel was draped over his shoulders. His chest and abdomen were still covered with the remnants of bruises that varied between light green to dull yellow. The scar on his cheek was still an angry gash.

His face was no longer swollen and the smile she longed to see, the sensuous lips once soft and tender under hers had been replaced by a thin, tight line. Ailís had closed her eyes to shut out what she now saw. The eyes she remembered so vividly as being alive with mischief and deep caring were the same light gray, but were filled with pain.

"Doctor?" Julian said and walked wearily to the hearth where he straddled the bench and sat facing the fire.

He looked up at her for a moment and Ailís's heart ached for them both. She took a deep breath. Her eyes burned and she bit her lower lip hard. She dug her fingernails into her palm to control the flood of emotions that threatened to ambush her resolve.

Ailís stood and walked toward Julian, swallowed and knelt beside him. His eyes never left the fire, eyes that looked ghostly as they reflected the fire's light and the agony inside of him.

"Julian, I need to talk to you. You have no reason to listen to me, but there are things I must say."

He sat, stared into the fire and said nothing.

"Please, tell me you will give me a fair hearing. I'm not asking for anything more," she said.

Julian looked down to the sheaf of papers at his feet. The letter from his ex-wife sat on top, a potent reminder of his failings. Ailís was a reminder of his deficiencies too, but also of his profound loss. "Doctor, go back to Timothy and your practice. Your future is there. I'm asking you to leave all this alone, leave it all in the past. No good will come if you pursue it. Now, please, leave before things are said that should not be said."

A sob escaped her lips. "Please, for the sake of any feelings you may have once had for me, I am begging you to just listen to…"

Julian's eyes blazed, his face contorted not with anger, but with pain. Ailís was stunned and frightened by his intensity.

"For the sake of any feelings I may have once had for you. Is that what you said? Is it? How dare you," he spat. "How dare you come here and say that to me?"

"Please, Julian, my heart is broken. I'm asking you…"

He shook his head slowly and turned back to the fire. "Your heart is broken?" he asked. "When things turned personal between you and me, the last resort became your first response. I have been learning to make choices, but I found that another would make the one choice vital to my life. You chose a path you needed to follow. That choice tore the heart out of my chest." His breath was ragged and his teeth were clenched.

"That day in your home, after you put me back together, you said to me, 'There can never be anything for us.' That was the last thing in the world I wanted but the only thing you could live with.

"I know you did it without malice. You did what you thought best for you and for Timothy. I understand that." He looked down at his ex-wife's letter. "I'll have to learn to live with the only choice you left me.

"I don't say this – any of this to hurt you – I realize I'm not what you want or need, but please know I would rather have died in the church than hear you say there could be nothing for us." His eyes were closed, his face twisted in torment and tears coursed his cheeks. "Go Ailís, please. Being this close to you is killing me."

She crept closer and put her head on his thigh. Sobs shook her shoulders as she searched for the voice to say what she felt so deeply. He looked down at her and ached to be able to run his fingers through her hair. He wanted to hold her, reassure her everything would be fine.

Deep ridges appeared on his forehead. He realized comfort was a road closed to him; he had no hope of getting it or giving it. He would not lie to her or himself. The world, their world, had changed and nothing would be as it had been.

She looked up and met his eyes. She looked for solace there and found only grief. His pain doubled her despair. She pushed away from him. She sat back on her heels and a hard-edged fury overtook her. "No!" she said. "I will not have it. I will not let go so easily.

"You're right, I made decisions but I was not heedless of the consequences. I was willing to accept the cost or thought I was. But I forced the consequences of my decisions onto you and I had no right to do that. I made choices for the reasons you say, but for another reason as well, one of which I am deeply ashamed. Ultimately, I made that decision and every decision leading up to it because I was afraid," Ailís said.

"At first I convinced myself my love for you could never match the intensity of yours for me. That made me feel almost noble, but I knew the truth of it – deep down, I knew. I was terrified you would go away and leave me loving you. I felt that would break me all to pieces.

"Julian, you loved me once, didn't you?" She staggered under the fierce intensity in his eyes.

"You must stop saying that. Don't you know what it does to me?" The fire left his eyes, his body sagged as emotions dragged away the last of his stamina.

Without looking at her, Julian transmitted his thoughts. *"I do not know another way. Feel the words I don't trust myself to say."*

Ailís' eyes went large and fear paralyzed her. His lips did not move, but she heard the words all the same.

"Do you understand?"

The doctor nodded her head slowly once and stared at him, her breathing short and sharp.

He continued, *"You said before, 'for the sake of any feelings I may have once had for you.' Just now you said that I loved you once. I never stopped loving you, Ailís. Never. I can't ever stop. Don't you understand that? Can't you see it?"*

Ailís stood up next to Julian. She took his face gently in her hands, looked into his tortured gray eyes and asked, "Julian, will you help me build a future? Can you do that for me?"

Julian looked at the stack of papers on the floor. There sat the letter he had carried with him and inside of him for so long. He recalled what Bridget had said early on – 'You have a letter. Destroy it now for your own good and that of others. It is poisonous and it will keep you from what you want most.'

He understood, he knew, he felt it – all of his decisions had led him inexorably to what he wanted most. He leaned down, wadded up the letter and tossed it into the fire.

The words that entered Ailís's mind were clear and calm and tender. They carried with them a quiet strength and absolute assurance. *"No, my love, but I can do it with you and for us."*

Her knees buckled and she fell heavily against him. He guided her gently until she straddled the bench in front of him. Together they sat looking into the fireplace. They sat in silence and watched the paper burn, curl to gray-black ash and disappear.

CHAPTER TWENTY-NINE

Ailís let her shoulders drop and she leaned into him so that her back rested against his chest. She needed to be near him. She needed to feel he was close behind her with his strength and his vast capacity for tenderness.

She pushed back again and reached for his hand. She looked at the badly bruised knuckles and the healing skin.

She whispered, "I am sorry. It is very little, I know. I was frightened and took the coward's way out. I said no to your love when all I wanted to say," she lifted his hand to her cheek and then to her lips, "was to say yes."

His arms encircled her, wrapping her in a blanket of gentle warmth. Ailís groaned softly and said again the only word Julian wanted to hear, "Yes."

Her head rolled back and rested against his shoulder. How long they sat staring into the depth of the fire, neither knew. Her breath caught as she felt his lips close to her ear.

He said gently, "Ailís?"

"Yes?"

"I don't know if it's a good time, but as for you being my doctor, you're fired."

"Good," she smiled. "That saves me the trouble of firing you as my patient."

"Ailís," he whispered after a moment's pause. "I have a confession." This, she felt was an odd time for confessions.

"Do you remember the first time I ever saw you? Do you remember that day when you were so angry? It was right here in this room."

She smiled and nodded. "Well," he went on, "the first time I set eyes on you I…"

Her breathing had picked up. "You? You what?"

"Well, I looked at you and had – impure thoughts." She could hear the smile in his voice and she knew lines of mischievousness would be gathering around the corners of his eyes. "The nuns told me that kind of thing would happen, but I didn't believe them."

Her smile turned to a chuckle, then to a laugh. It was such a release that she sagged back further against his bare chest and laughed until tears ran down her cheeks. His arms closed more tightly around her making it difficult for her to breathe. With all of her strength carried off, all she wanted at that moment was to be held in this man's arms.

At last, when she could speak again she said, "Yes, I know. You had, what should I call it, an impressive display of sinfulness. I didn't want to of course, but I noticed and had immodest thoughts of my own. Just think what Father Fahey would say and Sister Eugenia would be scandalized!"

With his lips touching her left ear, Julian whispered, "Ailís?"

There was something slow and seductive in his voice that caused her breathing to quicken again.

"Yes?" was her tight reply.

Julian could feel the heat generated by her body penetrate her silk blouse and warm his chest. He touched his fingertips gently to her shoulders and moved slowly down her arms. His fingers traced the outline of her muscles under the sleeves of her blouse. Past her wrists to the backs of her hands, he moved with agonizing slowness and began to trace over her delicate web of bones and muscles and tendons. His fingers moved easily between hers.

"What do you think we should do to counteract our earlier sinfulness?" She could feel his tongue touch her earlobe.

"Well," she said in a high strained voice, "I suppose I could pray."

Julian removed his intertwined fingers from hers and his hands moved to the outside of her thighs. Her entire body became rigid when his fingers moved slowly over her thighs to her hips and then to her waist. Ailís exhaled a ragged breath slowly and completely.

Julian felt the deep rumble that escaped her lips. It communicated her feeling of stark anticipation and matched his intense need for her. "Oh, Jaysus," came her answer through clenched teeth as she lowered her left shoulder and tilted her head to the right giving him full access to her slender neck.

Julian began kissing her shoulder and trailed kisses back to her ear where he whispered, "Are you sure I'm not distracting you from your prayers?"

"Well, yes but it is helping me to come up with some new prayers so don't stop now."

His arms tightened around her again. He leaned down and gently kissed the side of her neck. She murmured again the brief prayer lovers always murmur, "Oh God, yes."

For Ailís, for Julian, the past faded into the mist and their future became linked in that moment. Both understood that their past was a memory to be learned from and that the future might never come. Each understood the priceless quality of the one perfect moment in which they both existed. Each kiss, each movement, each unique moment they shared was imbued with a sacred quality and a crystal clarity neither of the lovers had experienced before.

Ailís disentangled herself from Julian and stood silhouetted by the fire. He rose with her, took her face in his hands and looked deeply into her eyes.

Julian smiled and said, "You understand the world will never be the same for us."

"I understand now that the world changed for both of us the moment I left Dublin, the moment you left New York and along the way at a thousand different points in time." She placed her hands behind his neck, drew him down to her and slowly, gently and without trepidation, without hesitation, without reservation, she kissed him.

***

Sister Eugenia sat in her office and waited with Sister Gertrude sitting in a side chair acting as witness. The older nun prayed to be given the strength to suppress her anger. She had put off this interview with Bobby McMaster and his father because she felt her rage would boil over onto the pair and scald them to death.

She looked up as she heard the approach of heavy work boots coming down the hall. A light knock and the smiling face of Liam McMaster came around the door.

Sister Eugenia was dumbfounded. "What can this man find to be grinning at?" she thought. The nun did not speak, but simply pointed to the chairs that faced her desk. McMaster entered and sat down and still the smile did not leave his face.

"Where is your son, Mr. McMaster?" Sister Eugenia asked.

"Well, Sister, it sits like this. After the beatin' Oi gave the boy he was in no real condition to be out visiting. He'll be missing more then a few days of his schooling and that's a fact. Took me belt to him Oi did and make no mistake," McMaster replied with equanimity. "The boy did a wicked thing and he needed to be punished."

Sister Eugenia looked at her hands and found they were shaking with rage. She folded them on her desk, looked at a bewildered Sister Gertrude and looked back at McMaster.

"Is it that you do not appreciate the gravity of the situation because you are ill informed or are you as monumentally stupid as you seem?" she said in tones so quiet McMaster had to strain to hear.

"Do you realize what your son has done? Do you realize why? Have you any idea what his actions say about him – and you? You do know he is not coming back to school here not now, not ever."

"Ach, but Sister, the boy was having a bit of fun and it went too far is all. Oi've talked to him about it and, as Oi've said, Oi already beat some sense into him. You'll not have any trouble with him again. In fact, when we're done with our business, Oi'm going to see Sean Maher, if he's sober," McMaster winked. "I'll give him a bit of money to go buy that boy of his – the simple one – a new little doggie."

Sister Eugenia rocketed out of her chair causing McMaster to sit back so fast he nearly overbalanced and fell to the floor. "Listen to me you disgusting creature. You are under the impression this is a small matter. It is not. Your son has an illness.

"I am sure there are lower forms of life on this earth, but right now I can not think of a single one lower than you. But it is lucky for you that I am a nun for if I were not I would never warn you about going to see Sean Maher. If your paths crossed just now, you would not be getting up. I tell you this not to save your skin, but to keep Sean out of the dock charged with capital murder.

"Now get out of my sight. I have people to contact. People in the Government who are charged with providing the type of help your son will be receiving. Are you somewhat hard of hearing, McMaster? Get out now!"

"Sister," Sister Gertrude said looking frightened and coming toward Sister Eugenia.

"Sit," Sister Eugenia said with a voice that brooked no further discussion.

"Look now, you've no right to be talking to mc all bold like you have!" McMaster shouted.

"Don't tempt me," Sister Eugenia growled. "Get out and do it now without another word."

The farmer rose saying, "If you wasn't a nun Oi'd…"

"You would do what, you worm!" the nun exploded. "Take your belt to me too? Well, I would be imploring you to do just that and be quick about it because it is the last thing you will ever attempt to do. You little gobshite, you had better pray God gets to you first. If He does not, trust I will sort you out myself and there is not a bit of it you will like.

"I need not worry though. A time is coming for you, boyo. You are known, you quisling, and you can believe scores will be settled and soon."

Liam McMaster was shaken not so much by the nun's words as by her venom. After weighing the risks and the absence of any possible rewards to be found in striking her, he opted for a hasty departure.

As the door to her office slammed shut, Sister Eugenia sat down heavily in her chair. Sister Gertrude came and stood beside the older nun and put a hand on her mentor's shoulder.

Sister Eugenia reached up and touched the hand of the younger woman. Straightening herself and exhaling deeply Sister Eugenia said, "Well now, that did not go nearly as badly as it could have.

"I'm sorry I barked at you, Gertrude. I hope you will forgive me – and pray for me for I will not be doing any praying for that animal. There is only one thing for which I am truly sorry. I am sorry God didn't strike Liam McMaster stone cold dead. I would have in His place."

***

A thin, pale man with cold dead eyes sat in a lifeless house and dreamed of a future in which he could buy the life he wanted, the life he deserved. He didn't know exactly what that life would be, but he knew it wouldn't be anything like the life he had endured to date. The Pale Man looked up before the knock on his study door.

"Farmer McMaster to see you, Sor," the butler announced from the doorway. The Pale Man pulled a face, rolled his eyes and opened his desk's bottom drawer.

"Tell him to come in."

A red-faced McMaster entered and approached. "They're on to me!" he said.

"Stay right were you are," the Pale Man said. "I like you better at a distance. So, whoever they are, are on to you. And that would be any of my concern because…?"

"Yor honor's business will be in jeopardy," McMaster said flatly.

The Pale Man smiled his cold smile as he watched the farmer cry out as he collapsed to the carpet clutching his legs. They had gone numb from the knees down and he could feel the paralysis moving inexorably higher. "Yor honor! Please!" McMaster begged.

The Pale Man's face was a malicious mask. He said, "I've told you before you don't know my business, so how could anything you do or say put me or my plans at risk? It simply isn't possible. Surely, you see that. In the grand scheme of things, you, McMaster, are exactly no one.

"You are an insignificant creature who would inform on his mates for two pence apiece. I do believe you would sell your mother to the highest bidder – that is assuming you knew who she was or was it your father whom you didn't know. Refresh my memory," the Pale Man goaded and continued.

"You've lost all feeling below your waist by now and it's climbing higher. Soon your lungs will stop working and I'll be able to watch you suffocate. Remember Donny Pearce, the one who shot his mouth off in the pub? I rather liked popping his head like a balloon. You were there, do you remember the look on his face? A priceless memory, don't you think? Your death promises to be far more entertaining, well, for me anyway," the Pale Man said.

"Still, McMaster, killing like this, although entertaining, well, it isn't very satisfying. I would like to perform an experiment." The paralysis stopped at mid chest and feeling started to return to the farmer's body.

"You see, although you knew you were dying, you still had the insane hope you wouldn't. I would like to remove that hope." The Pale Man reached into his bottom drawer and came out from behind his desk. A short-barreled side-by-side shotgun hung easily from his hand.

McMaster fear turned to abject horror. He tried to crawl away, but was rooted to the spot. The Pale Man crouched in front of his victim. The farmer reached out, pleading, appealing for compassion where none existed. He begged for a reprieve.

"People are strange creatures, don't you think?" the Pale Man said. "I possess an unfathomable ability. I need only think it and you will die in hideous agony. That, you sorry shit, is real power. Still, for all my mastery, I must demonstrate what this inanimate object can accomplish with its simple presence. Don't you find that odd?" The Pale Man handled the shotgun casually, the twin barrels never straying far from McMaster's face.

"I can see it, feel it. Hope is dying inside of you. Let's extinguish all doubt and all hope right now, shall we?"

The Pale Man's lips never moved. The words that followed were thoughts unspoken, whispers in the dark and they ratcheted up McMaster's terror. "*Prepare to find out if there is a God, McMaster,*" the Pale Man thought as he enjoyed the death of all his victim's hopes.

He brought the shotgun to bear on the farmer's face. One of the weapon's hammers fell forward; the exposed firing pin striking with a sharp, sickening *snick* that McMaster felt rather than heard. He urinated on himself, at the moment the hammer fell, but there was no bone shattering, tissue tearing, all encompassing, unique moment when life winked out.

The Pale Man stepped back laughing. "Good thing I remembered which barrel was empty, eh? There would have been even more of a mess if I'd got that the wrong way around.

"Don't worry, I won't make you clean up after yourself. You just run along now. Keep your mouth shut and think about what it's like to die. Remember, you fool, there is always the other barrel waiting for you," the Pale Man said aloud.

The farmer tried to stand, staggered, fell and tried again. He waited a moment and tried again and this time succeeded. The urine that stained his crotch and ran down his pant leg had started to cool and shame burned the soul of Liam McMaster. After fumbling with the doorknob, he managed to get it to turn. He lurched out of the study and with a stumbling run made it out the front door, down the steps of the manor house and into his work truck.

The Pale Man followed McMaster to the front door and waved as the farmer's truck passed down the gravel drive. The pale man, with cold, dead eyes, smiled his thin mirthless smile and squeezed the second trigger. The hammer fell. There was no explosion. There was no shell in that chamber either. "I think I'll kill him next time," the Pale Man said and laughed.

Chapter Thirty

Later that afternoon, Ailís Dwyer woke in a state of drowsy contentment sheltered under Julian's arm. She could feel his heart beat. All of her senses were dreamily alive.

Her thoughts drifted to the tenderness he had shown and his maddening control. She smiled as she thought of the slowness he employed to undress her. She recalled the near insanity she experienced at being the focus of his endless succession of building then slowing down to let her senses settle only to stoke the fire again.

She smiled as she thought of how each agonizing cycle made her more aware than before, more alive. She remembered the events as a montage of pleading and bargaining. When she could take not another instant of it, he had fanned the fire until the world inside her exploded.

She floated on waves of that pure emotion until she felt the touch of his lips and he would begin again. "It was just as I wanted it. Like he could read my mind," she said to herself and her eyes narrowed slightly. The thought passed quickly when she felt him draw a deep breathe.

She whispered to herself, "I felt his need. I saw that hunger so clearly. He wanted me, but until he felt sure I was content, he wouldn't let himself go. But when he did, Jesus, I thought I would burn up with the pleasure of it." Her mouth had gone dry. She shivered with the memory and pulled herself closer to him, draping her leg over his, feeling his warmth.

***

He felt her stir beside him. Julian drew a full slow breath as he examined his thoughts. "It couldn't have happened. I have never felt so centered, so focused. I was addicted to the idea of feeling her pleasure. My God, I thought I would die when I felt her release. Each time she drew me closer and closer to her."

He smiled and thought, "I wanted it all. Every sensation, every emotion, the sight of her face, the way she felt, the way she tasted and smelled – I needed all of it."

In lazy contentment, thoughts rolled through his mind. "I wanted it all and she gave it all to me. Her touch made me insane and…"

"You're awake," she mumbled and tucked herself closer still.

"Yes," he said in a soft voice touched with desire, devotion and gratitude. His fingers traced lazy circles on her back and over her bare shoulder.

"I don't want to, but I need to go," Ailís said. "Moira has Timothy and God alone knows what she's putting into his head."

"I understand, but before you go I want to ask you something."

"Yes."

"I have to go to Dublin for a few days. There's some business I need to conduct, but I won't be tied up with that full time. Come with me, won't you? There are people there I want you to meet."

"Oh, God how I wish it were possible. Finding someone to take care of the practice could take up to three weeks," Ailís said.

"If you can't go, please let me bring something back for your clinic?" Julian asked.

"As a matter of fact I can draw up a list of medical supplies tonight and have it ready for you with directions on where to go to find what. It isn't that much. I can't imagine it would take more than a few hours or so, but it would keep you busy and away from thosc wicked Dublin girls." She smiled, looked up and kissed his lips.

She continued, "They are evil by nature and will give you a disease," she said.

"You're from Dublin aren't you? I thought I remember you saying something like that."

"Well, if you are going to be cheeky, indeed I am, but I had to leave when it was discovered exactly how pure I really am."

"Pardon me? Pure? You call it pure to break into a man's home and take advantage of him?" Julian asked in mock horror.

"I am afraid you have that the wrong way around. It is you who stole my virtue. You really are a brute you know," Ailís answered.

At that, he laid his free hand along her cheek. He leaned down and kissed her once, twice, three times on the lips with each kiss growing in intensity. Then he drew back and teased her lips with his. She pushed him away and sat up.

"Just like the brute you are! There you are trying to steal my virtue again. Well, there'll be none of that Mr. Julian Blessing if you please."

Julian looked at her with hooded, mischievous eyes, smiled a wicked smile and said, "Just stay for a few more minutes. I have something to show you."

"Yes, I'm sure you do! You heard me. There will be no more of that – today."

"But honestly, I have a condition and I need your professional opinion. I think its life threatening," he cajoled.

"But you fired me as your doctor, remember?" She swooped in, kissed him quickly than picked up her clothes and ran to the bathroom.

As she turned on the hot water, she heard him say, "Okay, but I'll have to find a doctor in Dublin – preferably one without a disease," and she laughed.

Ailís showered, dressed and looked at herself in the mirror. She considered using his brush to smooth her hair, but today she wasn't concerned with perfect grooming. Instead, she ran her fingers through her hair. She thought the result gave her a reckless look and she liked it. She stepped back into the station to find Julian dressed in his sweat pants sitting by the turf fire.

"You need sleep. Go back to bed. I'll bet you'll sleep through the night," Ailís said.

He said nothing, but took hold of her hand and held it to his lips. He nodded his head. She looked down at him and found tears glistening in his eyes. She knelt beside him and asked, "What's the matter?"

He shook his head and said, "Thank you." He kissed her hand again and continued with a smile, "I am very glad I fired you."

"Not a moment too soon either," she answered, "but I'll bet you've not recanted those impure thoughts of yours."

Freely, easily, comfortably they both laughed.

* * *

Ailís walked with a slow easy step up the central road of Cappel Vale. The lightness of her gait matched her mood. She had to work hard to keep from grinning, instead she selected a self satisfied smile. She greeted residents on the street and engaged in relaxed conversations punctuated with easy laughter. She felt sure they all knew what she and Julian had been up to and she didn't care in the slightest.

Around Flynn's General Store, Ailís fell into step with the village priest and put her arm through his.

"Ach, Doctor," Father Fahey said, "You're looking especially, what is the word I should use? Spirited? You have that look of devilment about you though. Oi don't think you are up to any good at a'tall."

"Father! How could you think such a thing! I'm just delighted to have my Timothy back safe and sound. There's no devilment in that now is there?" she laughed and beamed a glowing smile on the priest.

Father Fahey narrowed his eyes and looked over his glasses at the young doctor. "Ach, now Oi know it! There is deviltry afoot. Confess now, girl. It will lighten your soul and keep you in good standing with the Church."

"Is being happy now a sin, Father? Expressing joy is somehow wrong? Tell me Father, what is it I should confess and I'll do it if only to make you happy. I am very interested in making others happy today," she said and her grin was mischievousness itself.

"Oi have no idea what you've been up to, but up to it you have been. Faith, Oi'll find out. Now, tell me where are you bound?"

"I am going to Moira Hagan's house to pick up Timothy."

The priest looked wounded then outraged. "You've left poor Timothy in the clutches of that, that, creature! Have you lost your mind? What have you been doing that you needed to take such an action? You could always leave the boy with the good Sisters or with any living soul in the village – but the Hagan! You must be mad. Surely, it has only been a few moments. Yes, that must be it. An emergency came up and you had to leave the boy for only a little while."

"I suppose I could give your mind some rest, Father, but I am prohibited from telling a lie to you. In fact, it has been hours and hours – and hours. Timothy has been with Mrs. Hagan from early this morning until – well he is still with her. So, if you wouldn't mind I'll go collect my child. Would you like to come along?"

"Ach! Oi'll have nothing to do with that nasty ol' woman. It is evil she is up to Oi'm sure and our good Lord alone knows what horrors she has exposed your poor son to. Have him come see me tomorrow and Oi'll see if Oi can set him right again."

"I'll do nothing of the sort. You seem to believe Moira would do something to harm Timothy. I tell you nothing could be further from the truth. I shall instruct him that under no circumstances is he to discuss his activities with your good self."

Father Fahey began to sputter. "Keep a civil tongue in your head, woman!"

"Is it 'woman' you just said to me? If it is civil you want, Father, then it is civilly I'll be sayin' good day to you, even though there isn't much of the day left." Her smile turned to a laugh that echoed off the homes and shops of Cappel Vale.

***

Ailís Dwyer strode up the lane a little further, turned in at Moira Hagan's gate and took the crooked path to the front door. The door opened before she knocked and the Hagan stepped onto the threshold. She looked down the lane at an incensed Father Fahey who was still sputtering. She tilted her head and looked down her long straight nose at the priest. The old man raised his fist and shook it at her in impotent frustration. He then turned on his heel and marched off muttering oaths.

Moira snorted, stepped back and allowed Ailís to enter.

"Come into the light," the older woman said. "I can guess what that priest said and he is right, he just doesn't know why, you evil girl."

Ailís blushed and grinned. "I'm sure I don't know what you're talking about. Father Fahey and I were discussing the state of your soul if you must know."

"Liar. He was tellin' you to confess your sins because he suspected you were up to some wickedness. Too bad, he just didn't know how wicked, eh?"

"'Tisn't a thing in what you say. Where is Timothy and what have you been doing with him all day? I do appreciate your help, but it is time I took him home."

"After supper you can take him home," the Hagan said. "He has put a lot of thought into the meal in order to get on his mother's good side again. I gave the boy a hot breakfast and put him down for a nap this morning after you left," Moira said and arched an eyebrow. "Later we read some stories to each other. After that, we planned our supper. He is out in the kitchen garden collecting the vegetables. We've had a rather full day – as I'm sure you have as well my saucy girl."

Ailís smiled, but said nothing as Timothy ran into the house with his arms full of ingredients and eyes wide with excitement.

***

True to Ailís's prediction, Julian slept through the night. He got up early, packed the few things he would need and was ready to set off. He didn't make it through the door of the station before Jimmy Grogan rushed in.

"Pardon, Mr. Julian. Oi've been after following McMaster as you instructed. Oi know the dirty little quisling is after reporting your every move, but Oi don't know who he is telling – yet. Another day should do it though. I feel I'm very near to finding the nest of vipers."

"Jimmy, let's leave off for now. I know you are close, but let's leave well enough alone for the time being. I have a feeling, nothing more, just a feeling we needn't look for them, they'll now come to us."

"To us or for us, Mr. Julian?" Jimmy asked.

"Either way it doesn't matter. Thanks to you we know a great deal about the comings and goings of McMaster and you're right, he is selling us out. I want you to stick close to the village and be available should Sean Maher need you. Go about your business, but take care and keep an eye out for trouble."

"What trouble, sor?" Jimmy squinted and asked.

"I don't know exactly. Just stay alert for anything out of the ordinary. There is something else you can do for me."

After Julian concluded his conference with Jimmy, his first stop was Ailís's surgery. He picked up the list of things she needed from Dublin along with a wish list of other things she wanted. They kissed inside her front door and with reluctance he was on his way.

His next stop was to visit Moira Hagan. His teacher offered him tea, but never asked him what business he might have in the capital city. They were courteous to each other, each knowing a secret about the other and neither having the slightest intention of sharing. They simply smiled and let their eyes communicate the mischief in their hearts.

A visit with Sean Maher was in order before Julian departed. He hadn't seen his friend since he returned Brendan to his family.

"I'm off to Dublin."

"This is sudden. And what would it be that brought about such a trip?" Sean asked.

"I have some business there and will be back very shortly – a few days at the most," Julian answered to deflect further questions.

"Going alone, is it?" Sean asked and smiled roguishly.

"Yes, just me. As I say, it isn't anything, just business. Why, who would I take?"

"Oh, Oi'm sure Oi wouldn't know – ya rascal," and Sean winked conspiratorially.

"I have no idea what you are on about."

"Not to worry old son, y'ur secret's safe with me. Mum's the word, eh?"

"It is a little too early for you to be drinking, Sean, but I'm sure when you sober up you'll feel much better." Julian's ears felt like they would burn to ash any moment, but he continued, "Sean, I want you to swear a holy oath."

"The likes of you would know all about holy oaths with your new-found heathen ways I'd be supposin'?" the big man laughed.

"I know that once you make this oath you will not break it."

Sean Maher looked caught out by Julian's intensity. "Oi would need to know what this oath would be. T'would be a foolish thing otherwise," he continued.

"It will not be easy, but you must swear it. You must swear you will not touch Liam McMaster no matter what."

"Ach! You can't make me swear such a thing for 'tis scores I have to settle with that creature and there can be no stopping it. Oi love you as a brother, but Oi'll not swear such a thing."

"Sean, I am asking as your friend and for the friendship you have for me, please grant me this request. I am begging you not to make me force this issue."

"Force is it? There is not force enough that will save that piece of shit and why are you protecting him anyway?"

"Swear the oath as I ask or I will have you read out from the pulpit on Sunday. Don't worry about the reason. Father Fahey will believe whatever I make up."

"What! You wouldn't."

"I will do whatever it takes. I will involve the church, I will invoke the Hagan, I will talk with your lovely wife, but you will swear this oath, so do it as a friend and we'll have done with it."

"You are a hard and evil man and probably a pagan, Julian Blessing, that you would bring down the saints in heaven and the devils from below and if that wasn't enough you would cause me own wife to lash me with her tongue.

"Hard you have become since you've come among us and evil since you took up your unholy practices with the help of that witch. Not even your most recent activities," and Sean paused for dramatic effect, "seem to have moderated you, now, have they?"

***

Arriving in Dublin, Julian's first stop was the Irish Nationwide Building Society on the Grand Parade. After that, he took a taxi to the Bank of Ireland where his business was conducted in less then an hour. From there, it was only a short walk across Westmoreland Street to Trinity College. After receiving directions, Julian found Professor Reginald Bragonier in one of the vast lecture halls before a packed house.

Julian slipped into a back seat in a top tier and watched as the professor demonstrated how much he loved teaching and how much he cared for his students.

"Mr. Hanraty, I am sure you are a secret Scotsman sent among us to break the spirit of Irish university students and their sainted professors. I know this because no one could know less about Irish history then you. Sit down."

"Miss Fitzsimons, tell us all, if you would, when the first people came to Ireland."

A short, red haired young woman with glasses and a well-you're-certainly-an-eejit look about her, stood. "10,000 BC. The earliest settlers arrived in Ireland in the Mesolithic or Middle Stone Age period. It is believed they crossed by land bridge from Scotland and there is evidence to support that postulation. These people were mainly hunters-gathers who..."

"Ah, that is lovely," the professor said. "Mr. Hanraty, what have you to say to Miss Fitzsimons?"

"I have to say she is a up-sucking little toady who…"

"Oh, do shut up Hanraty. You are a tedious boy." The class laughed with the exception of Miss Fitzsimons.

A bell rang in the distance and the denizens of the lecture hall began to pack up their things. Professor Bragonier raised his voice and said, "Read all of chapters five through seven and be prepared to discuss, in detail, what archeology has to say about these early settlers. I will give you a hint – the Ceide Fields of County Mayo. Now go and be well."

The hall emptied as Professor Bragonier gathered his books and papers and stuffed them into his ancient valise.

A voice rang out from the top tier of the lecture hall that startled the old man. "What is this and why is it in Ireland?" Julian asked and removed the Roman sword from his pack and held it by the pummel with the point down. He was still in shadow but his arm and the sword caught the light from a nearby long narrow window.

The professor peered into the darkness. Although he couldn't see the detail, the unique shape made the sword easy to identify. The professor's manner became guarded. "Where did you get that?" He tried to keep the excitement out of his voice, but Julian could feel the anticipatory thrill building in his friend, the professor.

Julian said, "Please answer my question first, if you don't mind."

"Do I know you? There is something about your voice that is familiar to me. Tell me stranger, what manner of man are you? What is your name?" The professor said.

"Sorry, Professor Bragonier," Julian taunted. "To learn more, you first must answer my question."

Although tired of the game, the professor was drowning in curiosity. "What you have there," the professor said, "is what remains of a Gladius or Roman short sword from the early empire, I should think. Gladii were two-edged for cutting and had a tapered point for stabbing and thrusting. A knobbed hilt with ridges for the fingers would have provided a solid grip. That bit looks to be missing from your specimen. Why it is in Ireland is impossible to tell for certain. I do not trade in conjecture. Facts are my game."

"Well then, it would seem you are the man I am looking for." Julian worked his way from the top tier toward the professor's desk being careful to stay in the shadows against the wall as long as possible. It wasn't until Julian stepped onto the raised rostrum that Professor Bragonier's face split into an infectious grin, and he rushed around his podium to grasp Julian by the hand.

"Friend Blessing, 'pon my word it is good to see you. We had not heard anything from you and assumed the Irish countryside had swallowed you up whole. Still, the good Mrs. Bragonier assured me you were in good hands and I take her words seriously. Although you do look a bit shop worn. What have you done to yourself just there?" The professor indicated the scar on Julian's cheek looking at it through his bifocals. Receiving no reply, he went on, "I must say it gives you that old Heidelberg fencing scar look. Very dashing and rakish I must admit. I'm sure you drive the women mad," the professor said.

"Anyway, this is my last class for the day. Let's go across the street to a pub and overwhelm ourselves with strong spirits while we catch up and you can tell me all about what you've brought me."

"We can do that in a bit, Professor. Do you have an office? We need someplace very private and preferably very secure to talk."

"I do, but what is this all about?"

"It is about history, Professor – discovering it and making it."

"Ah, my dear Blessing, you have been too long among the heathens of Ireland. You've begun to think like them, dribbling out your information with diabolical slowness. I expected you would be able to withstand the Irish onslaught, but alas. Life is a great sadness you know."

Chapter Thirty-One

The professor hurried down a corridor and with his longer legs Julian followed at an easy pace. At the end of the hallway, they found themselves in a small room with a pleasant view of Nassau Street. Within the embrace of the arms of an upholstered chair were stacks of books.

The old man unceremoniously dumped these onto the threadbare Persian rug. He turned briskly and cleared space on his cluttered desk. "Come along, man. I've not got years and years of life left in me. Take a seat and show me what you've brought for I know you've brought me something of value." The professor's eyes sparkled.

Julian again produced the sword. The professor was mesmerized for a moment before caution set in. He moved quickly to the door, locked it, and then returned to his desk and Julian's find.

The old man took the tang between two fingers and carefully inspected the blade. Rust had eaten deeply into the surface, pitting and discoloring it, but still he was stunned into a contemplative silence.

"Professor, a question if you don't mind?" Julian asked.

Deeply distracted, the professor said, "Of course, old man, of course."

"How did something like this find its way to a cave on the eastern coast of Ireland?"

"Huh? Oh, any of a dozen ways really. To be sure this is an interesting find, but it could have washed up on the shore through currents of various sorts then been carried inland by some locals who thought to hide it for later sale. Alternately, a lot of other invaders have come and gone from Ireland. Many of them had dealings with Roman Britain. It is possible it was left when the invaders left, it may have been traded for goods, something like that.

"You've avoided naming the Romans. Did they ever invade Ireland, Professor?" Julian's eyes narrowed.

"Invade? No. At least according to the Irish an invasion never happened. They do accept the Romans may possibly have had trading outposts along the coast though. That might account for your find."

"Professor, what if I told you that I could pin-point a period and state definitively that the Romans were doing more than trading in Ireland? Would that prove helpful?"

"Don't play the jackanapes with me, Blessing. I need facts, my boy, facts."

Julian pulled a small cloth bag from his jacket pocket, emptied it into his hand and stacked up a column of Roman coins on the old man's desk.

Professor Bragonier's hand trembled as he reached for the topmost coin. He scooted around his desk and located a magnifying glass. Easily seen were the motto PAX AVGVSTS C and the profile of the Emperor Vespasian.

"These are in remarkable shape, Blessing. Still this really doesn't indicate anything other than a trading post."

"Come and sit, Professor, I have a story. It is one I need to tell and it is one you need to hear."

***

Julian told his story with an eye to what his audience would appreciate from the perspective of history.

"Two hundred thousand more coins? A dozen more swords? If anyone but you told me this story, I would not believe him. Still, I wonder if..."

"The number of coins is an estimate, but I can say it is conservative. I didn't want to disturb anything I didn't have to. What do you wonder, Professor?"

"Ah, I need to think and we need to conspire. For that we need a pub. Follow me."

***

The professor ordered claret and Julian asked the barman for Guinness. They secured for themselves a table in a dark corner. Julian set the drinks down and found Professor Bragonier staring intently into the middle distance. The old man required every detail, so Julian began his story again.

At the end of the tale, they sat and drank in silence until the claret was gone. The professor rose without speaking and wandered off in a distracted way toward a corridor behind the bar.

Upon his return, the older man was resolute. He had come to a decision – the sort of decision that would make a career or leave it in tatters.

"I've phoned Mrs. Bragonier to tell her I am bringing someone home to surprise her. She was quite cross when I wouldn't tell her who, but that will all be as nothing once she sets eyes on you. As you know she has the Sight, but thank God she can't see everything. I'm still able to hide a thing or two."

Julian said, "Professor, let's assume something I know will go against your grain. Let's assume that what I've told you is all the evidence you have. No research and no resources are available to you beyond what I've told you and your experience as an historian. What do we have?"

Julian's companion took a deep breath, held it then exhaled slowly. "You are a cruel man Julian Blessing. You are right – this goes against the grain. Facts and more facts are what we need, but with a gun to my head I would have to say what we have are several Roman legions at the very least on Ireland's shores. It is either that or one of the most profound mysteries I've met in all my years. And that, my boy, is a lot of years."

The professor stopped speaking and was staring at the glass in Julian's hand. His plea was fervent. "Oh, please tell me you have not developed a taste for that," the old man said indicating Julian's glass of stout.

Julian thought for a moment, grinned and said, "Ach, stout is it? 'Tis like dis it stands w'me, Professor, darlin' an mind Oi'll not be actin' the maggot w'ya. Well den, Oi rightly have a taste o' da stout developed actually. Ween a God fearin' gentleman 'tis tursty, well, stout's your only man. Ah, sure but that's only when Oi can't lay hands on some poitin."

Professor Bragonier sat slack-jawed with a look of horror on his face while looking intently at Julian. "I was afraid something like this might happen. You've gone native on us. Stout is little more than mud in a cup and as for poitin, well it is good enough to run internal combustion engines, but it is not meant for human consumption," the professor said with a shudder and added, "Though that never stopped the Irish."

"Let's be off Julian, before you decide to dance a hornpipe, sing morbid suicide-inducing songs or do something else equally Irish and thus repulsively picturesque. You really have gone native on us, haven't you? Such a shame."

***

Bridget became radiant at the sight of Julian but paled as she embraced him and then took his face in her hands. One slender finger delicately touched the angry scar on his cheek. Julian could see clearly with her one gesture, in that one moment, she knew and felt and saw so much.

"My Ireland has changed you, Julian, and the change suits you. You are strong and fit but there are other changes too. I am so glad to see you. My husband kept your identity a secret from me and for that he will pay a mighty price, but for now let us sit and talk as friends."

"You will both have to excuse me. I have a small bit of research to do before supper. Call me when you are ready to sit down if you would, my dear," the professor said and kissed his wife's cheek.

"That assumes you will be invited to supper, husband. On that subject I am still making up my mind," Mrs. Bragonier answered.

The professor smiled and headed off to his study. The lady of the house began to lead Julian to the best room, but he gently took her by the arm and indicated the kitchen.

"My, but you have been assimilated quickly." Her eyes were alive. "I can see there is to be no parlor for a fine Irishman like Julian Blessing," Bridget said and smiled.

"Not when the warmth of a good kitchen is going to waste. Besides, if there is something stronger than tea it is likely to be hidden away in the pantry," and Julian winked.

"Sit, Julian, and I will fix us tea for that is all you will get before dinner and the fault for that is entirely your own. It will be hours until my husband is ready to emerge from his study unless he has a revelation of some sort. Then it may be days.

"You have set him a task and he will not let it go until he sees the end of it, I am afraid. He has not told me anything about this quest you have put him on, but I will know it all quite soon. While he does his research, you must tell me everything. I must know every detail of what has happened with you."

"First of all, Bridget, it is an indescribable pleasure to see you. I have missed you more than you will ever know."

"Indescribable pleasure? Is that what you said? You have been associating with Irishmen of the wrong sort. Nothing else could explain why you would waste your honeyed words on me."

A twinkle developed in Julian's eye as he remembered how much he liked this woman. He could not, however, afford to underestimate her. He might have played it differently if he had Ailís on the trip with him. But he had secrets to keep and surprises to spring. He dare not let his guard down for a moment.

His companion said, "As you know I am unreasonably curious by nature and simply must know how you have managed to grow into yourself so fully and so quickly." The woman with the silver hair and alluring smile touched Julian's arm and said, "Now tell all so an old woman can have some small enjoyment in her life."

Bridget took Julian's hand in hers and set her free hand on his chest above his heart. The jolt was strong and electrical just like it had been the first time but Julian absorbed it easily and returned a fair portion of it to its source. Bridget's eyes opened wide, the smile melted on her lips and she withdrew startled.

Her eyes narrowed and she said, "Oh my, you are a different man altogether then when we first met, Julian. Different and unreasonably impudent. You should have warned me. I was not prepared for the amount of progress you have made. I will not make that mistake again.

"You have become quite good at protecting your thoughts too. I should have known. When you arrived today, you were indistinct, hazy to me, not at all transparent, as you were when I last saw you. Still, do not think you can get away with it for long. I have ways you can not even dream of and years of experience beyond counting."

Julian smiled and took both of her hands in his. "Bridget, let me tell you a story."

***

Bridget watched Julian closely and noted that much had changed about him since they parted. His gestures were slower, easier, more comfortable and expressive. Even his speech had taken on a fluid elegance.

Many of his sharp and hard edges were gone, replaced by a calm, simple confidence. More than anything else, she noticed his eyes and his speech. When he was being fully honest with himself, his eyes and his voice took on a maturity far beyond his years. He was gaining wisdom. She listened intently as he told his story.

Their tea had gone cold long before he reached the end. Neither had taken a sip. Two friends sat in a warm kitchen each lost in private thoughts.

"You have suffered, Julian," Bridget began slowly. "That much is plain. You have tried to minimize this for my sake and it is sweet of you to make the attempt, but I know the truth of it.

"You may try to keep the memories locked away, but that level of violence and trauma cannot be hidden for long. The experiences of evil, along with the others you have had, have changed you on a fundamental level. That, however, is not the only change, is it?"

She smiled broadly, wickedly. Julian noticed and tried to strengthen his defenses. Bridget continued, "You have come to accept yourself for who and what you are. You have taken responsibility for your valley and its residents. But that is not all that is attractive to you in your little piece of Ireland, is it?" Bridget Bragonier's smile was knowing and turned her face luminous.

"What do you mean?" Julian answered too quickly. He knew she was on to him and tried every trick he had been taught to close that thought down, to hold it away from his friend.

Her smile broadened further and the lines around her eyes deepened into rivulets of enjoyment at Julian's intense discomfort. She took pleasure as she watched his mind work and marveled at his skill.

"Save yourself the trouble, Julian. Although you are really quite good, it is too late and while you spin, turn, and twist you only reveal more to me. You might protect your thoughts, but you did not think to hide your heart from me. Could it be our boy is in love?"

"Who is in love, eh?" the professor boomed as he shuffled into the kitchen. With a smoking jacket on over his shirt and tie, half glasses low on his nose and books tucked under each arm, Professor Reginald Bragonier looked every bit the bookish professor of history.

"That would be our friend Julian," the professor's wife answered while Julian said nothing. His lips were tight and his face felt like he was standing before a blast furnace, but he would not speak and he would not relax his guard.

"What marvelous news, my boy, simply marvelous. Everybody should be in love. The lovely Mrs. Bragonier has been in love with my good self for nearly, what, fifty years isn't it and it hasn't done her a bit of harm. In fact, I would go so far as to say it has made her the woman she is today. By all means, be in love I say."

His wife turned and looked down her long patrician nose. In a tone that stopped the professor abruptly, she asked, "And you Reginald, have you not been in love for the past forty-six years and has it done you any harm? Has it not made you the man you are today?"

Julian exhaled and his shoulders dropped somewhat. He felt drained and was only too happy to let someone else take the force of Bridget's intense scrutiny.

"Of course, my dear, how could you think otherwise?" the professor said and smiled bravely.

His smile dimmed and he took on a panicked look as she asked, "Of course, what, Reginald? Of course you have been in love or of course it has done you harm perhaps?"

"My darling, you are twisting my words and you know that isn't a nice thing to do when we have a guest and…"

"Answer now, Reginald, if you please. You would not want me to misconstrue what you have said, would you? After all, I am but a poor smitten woman, who, it seems, would simply wither if it were not for you. Thank you kind sir for having taken pity on me – and I will take my answer now." Bridget's acid rolled over her husband in rivulets.

"Now my dearest Bridget – Hmmm, what was the question again?"

"So, now you are not listening to me when I talk with you?" she said and arched an eyebrow. It gave her a sinister appearance and with a plaintive look in his eyes, the professor implored Julian to somehow take the pressure off of him.

Julian was back. He was recharged, in control of his thoughts again and better able to protect himself from the probing mind of Bridget Bragonier. "Bridget, on the walk here from the university," Julian chimed in smoothly, "the professor took great pains to explain to me precisely how much in love with you he is and that without you it is he who would be no one.

"He told me he would be some tired, doddering housemaster teaching fourth form history in some third rate public school in Kent."

At the mention of Kent, the professor shuddered visibly. Julian continued, "He told me without you, he would be a fool without either wit or wisdom destined to wander the world in abject misery. It was poetic I tell you. The man was nearly Irish. Why, he was telling me that he – and I don't know if I should mention this – well, he wants to take you away for a romantic holiday to Italy or the Costa Del Sol or wherever in the world it would be that would make you happy. I think that's the way he put it.

"I will tell you it made me jealous and at the same time pleased for his good fortune," Julian said. "This, doubtless, is the emotion you picked up on and thought it was I who was in love." Julian finished, smiled and felt that the mendacity made him Irish by default.

Bridget remained silent and studied both of the men in her kitchen. "Of all the rich traditions Ireland has to offer, Julian Blessing, it is interesting to see you have chosen the path of the world-class liar. My husband said none of those things, but since he is in no position to refute any of them – ever – I will go down to the travel agency tomorrow and find a lovely little holiday. Do you think a fortnight would be sufficient, Reginald?"

"Oh," and the professor ground his teeth and looked daggers at Julian, "whatever it is that pleases you best, my love."

"I thought you might say that and I know you will agree that I will need some new clothes, you definitely need a new suit and our luggage must to be replaced. I am sure I will think of some other items as well."

"Now, the two of you lay the table and Reginald, open that bottle of wine you have been hiding from me," Bridget said.

As the two men left to set the dining table, Bridget Bragonier called to Julian from the kitchen. "Do not think I believed for a moment any of that, especially the part about you not being in love. It is in love you are and I shall have proof of it in due course.

"After supper I will make up the extra room while you confer with the professor," she continued. "Do not keep him up late. We all have much to do before we can be off. I do not want him getting cranky for lack of sleep."

"But where are we going and when?" Julian asked with a look of feigned innocence.

Mrs. Bragonier tilted her head back so she could more easily look down her nose at Julian. She pressed her lips together and snorted lightly. "As you well know, we leave the day after tomorrow. We are going to Cappel Vale of course and your cave full of age-old coins and death."

* * *

Over dinner, the professor talked excitedly and non-stop about his suspicions and theories. He was forming a working hypothesis and it was leading him to ever more thrilling vistas.

His wife hid behind a secret smile. She loved to see her husband animated by his subject and she had never seen him so vibrant. But it was Julian she regarded now.

He had matured during his stay in Ireland but there was more. He had developed a truer sense of himself. And he was in love, of that she was sure. He had tried to keep her away from that part, but it was there and it was healthy and strong.

"Look at him," she thought to herself. "He is smitten beyond words. New love is really a wonder to observe. Looking at him I can nearly remember when I first fell in love with Reginald."

"I'm sure he was a fine figure of a man," Julian said and Bridget Bragonier looked up suddenly and the smile fled from her lips.

"What did you say my boy?" the professor asked.

"Oh, nothing, please continue Professor," Julian said without taking his eyes off of Bridget.

"Well as I was saying that in AD 100, Rome was…" and with that, Professor Bragonier carried on talking and warmed to his subject with each passing word.

"You are a clever boy," Bridget thought and Julian responded, *"Not really. I have a number of delightful parlor tricks. Would you like to see more? I can bend spoons."*

"Do not think to play the fool with me," Bridget thought.

"I'm afraid I can't help it. My teacher likes to say she has discovered my true calling. I'm an eejit, you see. Not much to it really. I can't read minds, but I can sense thoughts sometimes. As talents go, it is pretty useless, but there you have it. Now if I were really clever I could tell you your thoughts before you thought them. I'm afraid I don't have the genes for it though. You see, I am not the one with the Sight," Julian thought.

"You know nothing of the Sight, but let us leave that. What time do we leave for your village?" Bridget asked wordlessly.

"The professor needs to arrange for a substitute at the university and I have some business to conduct so as you said earlier, the day after tomorrow will do perfectly – perhaps first thing in the morning?"

"The professor will want to leave the moment he secures that substitute, but I suggest you put him off," Bridget thought.

"Whatever pleases you, Bridget."

"It would please me to punish soundly all cheeky Americans who go around terrifying old women," the professor's wife thought and looked cross.

Julian smiled. *"There really is no sense being that way about it. Do you remember when I first met you in that park in New York? Well, you didn't bother with a warning before you defibrillated me. After all, what is a little electrocution between friends, eh? Oh, and when you sent thoughts into the head of a man who was already hearing voices – who was terrified then? You didn't seem to mind it though."*

A smile pulled at one corner of Bridget's mouth. *"I will have to pay a great deal more attention to the likes of you, Julian Blessing."*

"And being with the likes of you, dearest Bridget, I can tell you, I have no choice but to pay attention," Julian responded.

***

The next morning, Julian walked with the professor back to Trinity where they parted after making plans to meet for lunch. Julian's business necessitated a number of stops so he was late returning. Because of it, the professor seemed wound up entirely too tightly.

"Time is wasting, my boy. We must be off. I've seen to everything and I am keen as mustard to get to the site."

"Professor, I suggest we have a pleasant lunch then you go home and pack. First thing in the morning we'll be on the road. That will put us into the village well before noon." Although Julian tried, calming the professor was not going easily or well.

"Patience is a virtue I do not have, Blessing. Why can't we be off this afternoon – right now in fact?"

"We are not leaving before tomorrow because I have a few things left to do and your wife will not hear of it. Haven't you dug yourself a deep enough hole on that front?"

"I suppose so. Witched unto death! And you don't fool me. You're no better!" the professor said with an all-encompassing harrumph.

After lunch, Julian went to work on Ailís's list of supplies. He was careful to get all of the items she said she wanted and more. He felt good about fulfilling her wish list and knew she would be pleased to have the goods and equipment needed to update her surgery.

The most fragile items he had packaged so he could carry them back himself. Transportation was arranged for the larger pieces.

Julian purchased supplies for the school and some items for Father Fahey even though no one had asked for anything. For Sisters Eugenia and Gertrude he found some expensive tea. He doubled that order and included the Hackett twins.

He picked up some things for Sean at a police supply store and found something special for the Maher children along with pounds of candy for the rest of the village children. He stopped long enough to select something special for Ailís and Timothy. That alone left him smiling for the remainder of the afternoon.

Chapter Thirty-Two

They made good speed on the northbound M1. The professor was like a child – full of excitement and impatience. Bridget looked pensive while Julian was just glad to be on his way home.

***

In the village children played, dogs barked, cats patrolled the yards and geese floated in tight formation on the pond beside the police station. Before they got out of the car, Mrs. Bragonier turned in her seat. She touched her husband's sleeve while she reached out and took Julian's hand in hers. She looked grave.

"You know me well enough to understand when I am serious. I am warning you both – say nothing about the professor's business here. We are friends you met up with again in Dublin and you invited us here to the village for a little holiday. Do you understand me, Julian?"

"Yes, Bridget, but..."

"That you understand is enough. I will explain later. Reginald, do you understand what I am saying to you? You will hike around some, but for the most part, you plan on taking your leisure. Not one word are you to mention about your Romans. I know it will be hard for you to restrain yourself, but it is important, vitally important. Do you understand Reginald?"

"Yes my dear, not a word."

"There is more at stake here than either of you realize." Bridget smiled and continued. "Now let us all look happy. We are here on holiday, so we are to be the soul of wit, charm and good grace. Now, shall we?"

***

The village children approached the car with trepidation until they saw Julian, then they swarmed round the vehicle with shouts and squeals. As if on cue, runners detached themselves from the crowd and circulated the news. Mr. Julian had returned.

Sean Maher was the first to arrive and he clasped Julian's hand and shook it with painful vehemence. Sean was being introduced to the Bragoniers when Thomas Cahill materialized decked out with his mayoral sash and received his introduction to the Professor and Mrs. Bragonier.

The entire village gathered around Julian and the newcomers and Julian shook hands and murmured greetings, but he never took his eyes off Ailís Dwyer who was standing on her front porch looking at him with a sly smile.

He watched as she descended the stairs and walked slowly toward the tight cluster of villagers. At her approach, the general chaos of the crowd ratcheted down and a path formed that took her to the heart of the mob.

Julian introduced the doctor to his friends. Ailís nodded respectfully and extended her hand. It was first taken up by the professor who beamed. Next, Bridget took the doctor's hand. The smile faded slightly on Ailís's lips, and she paled trying to pull her hand away.

The older woman held on and a smile started at the corners of Bridget's eyes and spread gradually to her lips. Soon Ailís was smiling too and seemed quite at ease as if a soft warm light had suddenly bathed the scene. The spell was broken when Bridget looked into Julian's eyes and her smile turned to a smirk. Ailís didn't understand the look and also turned to stare at Julian.

He just shrugged and tried to look innocent. It wasn't working.

"Well, we should get your things into the station," Julian said.

"What? What do you mean by that, Julian Blessing?" Ailís demanded. "Surely you wouldn't think of putting your friends up in such a place." Ailís turned to the Bragoniers. "You'll stay with my son Timothy and me." Ailís called Timothy and Brendan Maher and instructed them where to put the Bragoniers' bags.

The crowd began to break up and go about their business with calls of "Welcome home" being shouted to Julian. In the important ways, he felt like he really was home.

***

Dinner at Ailís's was a simple meal as it always was – vegetables, lamb, soda bread and a generous pot of tea. It was hot, hearty and filling. The professor's plate had to be filled several times before he gave over. He held forth that there was something about the country air that gave a man a larger appetite, but of coins and swords and Romans there was no mention.

The table was cleared, the dishes washed and put away. It was still early evening. Bridget instructed Julian and her husband to go to one of the pubs for a pint. She and Ailís, she declared, were going for a walk.

During their slow stroll around the village, the two women talked about life in Dublin and how the country had its advantages and disadvantages. Mostly they talked of nothing at all. Random thoughts entered fleetingly and escaped moments before another thought arrived. They talked and laughed, reminisced and commiserated, agreed and disagreed. Ailís felt a level of comfort with Bridget that usually took years to form. Their friendship was being shaped with each step she and Bridget took.

They had nearly reached St. Michael's church when Bridget stopped. "I must leave you here, my dear," she said.

Ailís looked puzzled. "Here?" she asked. "Oh, do you know Moira Hagan?"

"No, but as you and I can attest, it is never overly difficult to make new friends."

"But..."

"No need to fear. I will be fine and so will you since you have that chaperone along to safeguard you," Bridget said and smiled.

"Chaperone?" Ailís asked.

"Yes. On my, you did not know? Come here young man," Bridget commanded and Jimmy Grogan emerged out of the shadows.

Ailís began to sputter and Jimmy tried to explain, but Bridget Bragonier held up a long thin finger to silence them both. She leaned in close to Ailís and said, "Julian asked the boy to keep an eye on you. As a man desperately in love, Julian is inordinately concerned with your safety. Mind you, he has every reason to be, but still there you have it."

Ailís was glad it was a dark night since she could feel her face becoming flaming hot. "I don't know what you are talking about. Julian and I are good friends and he has no right to..."

"To be sure he has no right, but he does feel he has a responsibility. You see, Doctor, he feels he brought trouble to the village even though he did not. However, he now feels it is his duty to assure the safety of all its inhabitants," Bridget said.

"As far as it goes that seems reasonable." The older woman looked thoughtful. "But it all comes off the rails regarding you. You see he treasures you above his own life, but then you know that. You knew it well before he made love with you."

"But..."

"Do not trouble yourself, my dear. I know the truth of it and so do you. Your protestations, that you and he are just good friends, although valiant, are so much silliness. You agree of course. If it makes you feel better, Julian gave it a go too. Sadly, it did not work for him either, although he too still tries to maintain the façade. I am, you see, not got around so easily as that," Bridget said and smiled.

Ailís would have been content to simply dig a hole and disappear, but Bridget pitied the doctor and spared her the need saying, "Now run along and take your chaperone with you. Should my husband inquire, please tell him I am visiting someone.

He will understand and will not bother you with pesky questions." Bridget's smile was broad and knowing and her eyes were alive with mischief before she turned serious as Ailís moved off, followed quickly by Jimmy Grogan.

Bridget walked up the crooked path to Moira Hagan's front door. There was no need to knock. The door was opened as she approached. Bridget simply stepped inside.

Chapter Thirty-three

In the morning, Julian appeared with Brendan Maher in tow. Collecting the professor, the three set off back toward the thick growth of trees at the northwest end of the village. They walked along the edge of the tree line until Julian felt sure they were not being watched or followed.

When he thought the time was right he stopped, surveyed the village and backed up with slow steps. The three hikers melted into the forest and were gone.

Half way to the cave, Julian left Brendan to act as their rear guard. The professor and Julian continued on over the rock-strewn path with the trees towering above them.

At the foot of the mountain where a clear stream passed through on its way to the sea, the two men stopped.

"Is it very far?" the professor wheezed.

"We are only moments away."

"Then what are we waiting for?"

"We have a bit of a climb and I want you well rested when we arrive. It is a sight that will take your breath away, Professor."

The old man grinned like a schoolboy.

Once rested, the men began to climb the mountain. With each step, the view became more spectacular as more of the Irish Sea revealed itself.

Julian stopped and indicated the mountainside. The professor studied the slopes and smiled when he made out how the cave entrance had been camouflaged.

"Follow me, but watch your step," Julian said and together they slipped behind the blind of bushes and into the cave. Once inside Julian secured the bushes from the inside. The men continued down the passageway until they entered the rotunda. Julian removed his pack and began to set up battery-powered lights. It wasn't much illumination, but it was enough to triple the ambient light.

Professor Bragonier continued blinking until his eyes adjusted to the dim light. A sense of wonder began to animate his features as first one detail, and then another became clear. In each moment, he saw a miracle. Thoughts coursed through his brain like a swarm of angry bees. He slowly walked the perimeter of the room. Notebook in hand he entered his observations with an excited hand.

The professor lost track of time and so was surprised when Julian touched him on the shoulder and announced lunch was ready.

The two men settled themselves and Julian distributed sandwiches and cold tea. The professor ate out of habit, lost now in thought while Julian watched him.

"How would you value this find?" Julian asked as he and the professor sat around the cold fire pit.

"Value? You must be joking. It is priceless. What you have here is easily one of the most important discoveries in Irish history. This is the sort of wealth it would take to operate a whole Roman army in the field, not just a legion or two.

"No doubt about that. But had there been a Roman force anywhere on this island, especially one of this size, we would have found evidence by now. That sort of thing can't be hidden. What is valuable here are the answers we shall find.

Julian said, "So, what are we left with, Professor?"

"We do have one piece of the puzzle. It comes to us in a fragment from the historian, orator and general gadfly, Caius Rufus," the professor answered. "Caius tells a brief story. Sixty-nine, C.E. was the year of the four emperors. Galba is murdered by Otho. Otho commits suicide – assisted of course – and is succeeded by Vitellius who is murdered in the Forum by Vespasian's men, whereupon Vespasian becomes the last man standing and thus Emperor. It was a busy, but not especially lucky year for most emperors.

"Anyway, Caius Rufus mentions a slight problem. It seems a ship set sail from Ostia, the main port city of Rome, with a payroll for the legions stationed in Roman Briton," the professor lectured.

"But the ship never made it," Julian added. He was distracted as images came unbidden, soul shredding, painful images.

"Exactly, my boy. Caius mentioned strong seas and the possibility of the ship being swamped and sunk. But there is more in his text and it is far subtler.

"He was careful not to say it in so many words but he hints at the likelihood the legionaries chosen to escort the shipment were not overly taken with Vespasian. More to the point, they were still faithful to dead but not forgotten Vitellius."

"Our reporter, Caius, says no more about that but inserts what seems like a random fact." The professor continued, "He tells us several cohorts of Legio XX – the Twentieth Legion – were removed from Britannia on the quiet for a time.

"You can see how all of this disappearing payroll business would make the escort much sought after and very unpopular. One couldn't go far wrong postulating the Twentieth Legion was sent out to find and return their brother legionaries and the payroll.

Although justice may not always be swift and sure, punishment surely is. Failing in their mission, the Twentieth would have been decimated. Julian, one in ten – over five hundred men snuffed out. Gives new meaning to the saying 'failure is not an option,' eh?

"Julian. Julian?" The professor looked at his friend and was startled. Julian's face had drained of color and his eyes looked haunted. The older man knew that look. He had seen it many times on his wife's face.

It was mid afternoon before Julian whispered, "Misenum."

"What about it Julian?" the professor asked cautiously.

"What does it mean?

"Misenum was the Roman navel base nearest to," the professor stopped, then continued slowly, "Ostia – the port from which the transport departed. Tell me what you see Julian and why Misenum is important.

Julian closed his eyes slowly. "Cur non decedere Misenum – they keep repeating that over and over. My Latin is rusty, but I think I understand the meaning, do you?"

"They who? I don't understand, old boy. 'Why did we not leave from Misenum?' It makes no – oh dear God." The professor was stunned into a momentary silence as a bright light fell upon the dark mystery. "Misenum was a military port. They departed from the commercial port of Ostia."

Julian said softly, slowly, "Can you feel it Professor? Can you feel this place, these men? It's making sense to me now." The older man said nothing, but noted the aching sadness in Julian's eyes, eyes that seemed to darken with understanding as each moment passed.

"The escort, the legionaries, they sat around this pit as we are sitting now. Aside from that one phrase, I can't hear them, but I can feel them all.

"They agree they should have known when their ship departed from a commercial port and not the military port of Misenum that something was gravely wrong. Their orders were simple. They were told to beach the ship, kill the crew, secure the payroll and wait.

"If the Roman army in Britain wasn't paid there would be an armed backlash against Vespasian and the year of four emperors would have been the year of five emperors.

"That was what they were told, but that was never the plan. They went into this thinking they were overthrowing a murderer and a tyrant. They went about their mission out of duty to Rome, but it was all nullified by betrayal."

Julian shifted his gaze from the fire pit to the professor. The man was startled at the intensity evidenced on Julian's face, his eyes troubled to a dark gray, his voice distant and distracted. "It was all so indistinct when I was here with the boys, but I know now. I know so many things now.

"Look more closely at your books, Professor, you will find it there. This cave sheltered men who were marooned and promptly forgotten. Someone they trusted deceived them. Look for the betrayer; you will be seeking a man whose infamy is to be found in his betrayal of these men. But that's not all that makes him important to history.

"Count carefully, Professor. Count as these legionaries did and you will find, as they did, this isn't the entire payroll. Half of it is missing.

The one who deceived them manipulated events and that is why a commercial port was used. Half of the payroll could never have been stolen had the ship been in a military port." The professor was still and pale as Julian drew a deep breath and his eyes began to clear.

"Bridget was right of course," Julian said. "This is a cave filled with age-old coins and death, meaningless, pointless death.

"While they fought with honor for a living," Julian continued, "the other, the betrayer, plotted and schemed for his livelihood. This cave witnessed the deaths of the spirits of men who deserved better and enabled the ascendency of a man who merited far worse."

***

The two men gathered their tools and supplies and secured the entrance to the cave. After making sure they were not being observed, they made their way back down the hill and into the forest.

On the way to the village, the professor said, "I've given some little thought to your illegal excavation problems. My conclusion is not a happy one. The chances are good some sample of the Roman treasure made its way into the hands of our bad actors and they are desperate to find what you have found. Even a fraction of this find on the black market would be worth tens of millions.

"That makes this a dangerous game, Julian. The stakes are high, so have a care. Bridget was right to warn us off even hinting at what we might be up to."

***

They found Brendan where they left him and he reported in his halting way that no one had passed this way through the woods.

Winded from the day's activities, the professor sat next to Brendan on a flat rock. The boy seemed genuinely pleased to be in the company of his friend Mr. Julian and this new man, the professor.

The professor turned to Brendan, clasped him on the shoulder and said, "Young man, I am proud to say I have shared a moment with Brendan Maher, the discoverer of Ireland's Roman Treasure."

Brendan looked to Julian and in that look communicated his fear and his confusion. Julian smiled and shook his head and indicated everything would be all right.

"Well, Professor, it doesn't quite work that way."

"An Irishman and an American; if that isn't a breeding ground for conspiracy and dark work I don't know what is. What are you two up to? What isn't the way what works? Quickly now, I've not the time to waste on you."

"It is like this. You can't share a moment with the discoverer of the Roman Treasure because you are the discoverer. After much consultation and thought, Brendan wishes to distance himself from this project."

"What? But why? Doesn't he understand how important this will be to the world? All of Ireland will know him. He will be," the professor lost steam as the unintended consequences of the find suddenly came into focus.

"Then you see the problem," Julian said. "Brendan is a shy young man. He has no need for accolades or fame or even fortune. His needs are simple ones. A lot of attention from strangers would at first confuse and then frighten him. I can't say I can fault his logic nor can I say I would choose differently if I were in his place.

"No, Professor, you see your marvelous friend from New York, that would be me, was staying in the area very near a location you suspected as the resting place of the elusive treasure you had been researching and chasing for years. You manipulated me into inviting you to the village for a holiday. You are a crafty old fellow it seems.

"You brought Brendan and me out on what you said would be a pleasant walk. What we did not know, but you did, is your exhaustive research pinpointed the cave and thus the treasure.

"Brendan and I were unwitting witnesses to your discovery. However, even you weren't prepared for what you found. After some investigation of the site, you were gob smacked by the magnitude of the treasure and the wider implications. Are you following along, Professor?

"Staggered by the enormity of your discovery, you ran back to Dublin and let the National Monuments Board in on it so a Preservation Order could be put in place and the site protected.

"At least that is the story we shall tell, or rather, I shall tell. As I said, my friend here is a shy fellow. I, however, am not. You can trust I will be able to sell that story to everyone. Don't forget, I was a stockbroker. I am accustomed to selling ideas."

Red-faced, the professor stammered and sputtered, "You, Julian Blessing, are a thoroughly unprincipled person. You – yes and your young friend here – are scoundrels! You can't play fast and loose with the rules and expect there will not be consequences."

"There are always consequences, Professor. Always. I will suffer them and do so gladly, but he will not." Julian was emphatic. He and the professor exchanged glances that were lost on Brendan. The young man lived in a world where the purity of his intentions limited most of the unfortunate consequences.

Chapter Thirty-Four

Julian, the professor and Brendan were lost in the movement on the main street of the village, as men and wagons returned from the fields. Groups shouted greetings and individuals paused to pass a pleasant word or an invitation to one of the pubs.

Men tipped their hats to the professor. An educated man, and one from Trinity no less, was a man worthy of great respect. Brendan refused five Euros from Julian, but in the end took it as a day's wage and went on his way home for supper.

Julian deposited the professor at the doctor's house and continued to the police station for a quick wash and a change of clothes.

The door to the station stood partially open. He knew what to expect before he edged the door open. Seated behind his desk was Ailís Dwyer, one eyebrow arched menacingly and her arms folded across her chest. Where Julian had hoped for a warm welcome, Ailís indicated a chilly reception was in order.

"Well it took you long enough. Where have you been all day? Before you answer that, why were you in Dublin so long? It was those filthy Dublin tarts – I knew it! " Ailís barked. "And you tried to install your friends in this police station – our police station mind you. Where would that have left me?" The doctor had the bit in her teeth now. "I have needs that must be seen to!"

Julian smiled. "I rushed back to you as soon as I could. If there had been another way I would haven taken it, but I regretfully had to take care of my business in person. I did beg you to come with me."

Ailís snorted, but softened somewhat.

"All the time I was gone, I thought about this wonderful, delightful, saucy young woman who has skin as smooth as cream and whom I find intoxicating." Julian was behind her now and he left a light kiss on her neck before she shrugged him off.

"I thought exclusively about how dedicated this young woman is, how she gives unstintingly of herself. My young woman is kind and sweet beyond words." Ailís was allowing herself to be mollified so the second kiss was not shrugged off so quickly. His fingers played lightly along her shoulders.

"My days and nights in Dublin were consumed with thoughts of her. She was the first thing I thought of every morning and the last thing on my mind at night." This time she allowed the kiss to linger and for another to follow.

"Kind and considerate, my lovely one is, thoughtful and talented, strong and independent. She is sexy beyond words and inspires a passion that threatens to consume me.

"Honestly, Ailís, I think you would like her very much," and with that he gently bit her shoulder.

The doctor shot from the chair hissing, "You vile man!" before she stormed to the door. "Supper is in one hour and it starts with or without you."

The doctor could hear Julian's laughter ringing in her ears as her face reddened. "We'll see who laughs last, Mr. Blessing!" she thought and she continued home with a purposeful step and a plan forming in her head.

***

"They really are evil creatures, don't you think?" her houseguest, Bridget Bragonier, asked.

The doctor stopped, shook her head and smiled. Before long, the smile dissolved into a chuckle and then into a laugh which she and Bridget shared.

"They are evil, but how did you know?"

"No great trick really. No woman is ever that vexed by another woman. Women prefer to choose sides and destroy each other from a distance. You had the look of a young lady who would rather see to the matter personally. That left only a man. Men have few options to annoy us – ignore, tease or insult.

"In any case, it could be seen easily enough by the color that had rushed to your face. Besides, you were coming from the direction of the police station. The man who lives there cannot ignore you and would never intentionally insult you.

"He would, however, tease you. I do, of course, mean that as one good friend might tease another." Bridget let the sentence hang in the air. She was too refined for sarcasm, however, irony dripped from every word while she smiled sweetly. "Still it is a mystery to me."

"What is a mystery to you? What could possible be a mystery to you or for that matter that wicked Moira Hagan! And I have more than suspicions about that, that, that – policeman too! The three of you are up to something and I will know what it is!" Ailís was emphatic.

"I must tell you, my dear, how adorable you are when you are cross. Julian was that cross when I first met him, but he has settled down since. He actually has the makings of a proper gentleman."

Ailís snorted and Bridget smiled.

"The mystery is why you and he insist on keeping secret what everyone has known for months now. Still, that is your business. Let us go inside and peel potatoes and we can talk about the dreadfulness of men."

***

Professor and Mrs. Bragonier, Ailís, Timothy and Julian gathered for dinner at Ailís's home on the last night of the Bragoniers' stay in Cappel Vale. The professor and his assistants had made numerous trips to the cave. The preliminary investigation was as complete as possible for now.

For their last meal together, Ailís had insisted on perfection. The dinner table sparkled with her china and crystal. A linen tablecloth and matching napkins graced the table and a centerpiece of heather, hard ferns and gorse set off the silverware nicely.

Ailís had enjoyed her time with Bridget Bragonier and the professor and would be sad to see her new friends leave. The doctor wanted this to be a special evening.

The table conversation was far ranging, intensely interesting and all-inclusive. The professor took special pains to include Timothy and to solicit his opinions on the various topics covered during the meal.

* * *

With dinner finished, the table was cleared and the dishes washed and put away. The professor and Timothy went into the best room. Ailís had some charting to do on her patients leaving Bridget and Julian to wander in the garden and talk.

The older woman looked into the house from the garden and watched with a smile playing at her lips.

Seated in the best chair in the best room, Professor Bragonier was holding forth to a class of one. Timothy sat on a footstool stunned by the idea so much knowledge could reside in one man. Bridget whispered, "It couldn't be helped, but not having children has always been a profound regret of mine."

Julian smiled and took her arm. They both moved away to a swing in the arbor where they sat and rocked gently.

"You have no children, Julian. You should have. I believe you would be a good father."

"What makes you say that?"

"Nothing pleases me more than watching people. Children are just people in the making. You are good with them. You are interested in them, but without losing the unique attitude of benign neglect so needed in their upbringing." She smiled.

"You are such a charmer."

"That I am. In any case, I am an elderly lady now. I am married to the professor on whom my charm is wasted and now dealing with you on whom I would not waste my charm."

"Oh, but I am wounded!"

"You are not and, by the way, if you thought you had changed the subject you have not. You would make a good father. Take Timothy for instance."

Julian gave his companion a sidelong look.

"He is a lovely young boy devoted to you for some reason, as is that Maher boy. Are you ever sad you didn't have children?" she asked.

"Sad? No. When I was young and had the energy for children, I was also too selfish for them. Now that I'm older, I appreciate them more but am too old to be able to keep up with them."

"Oh, but you are not too old. You will find that out soon enough. I would, however, like to change the subject if you do not mind too much – or even if you do.

"You are incredibly fortunate to have Moira," Bridget said. "For you, she is the perfect teacher. It is because she is your teacher that she is unable to tell you what she has entrusted me to share with you. She feels you need to hear it from a source other than her.

"For reasons you understand too well, she has lost a great deal. You have provided her with a shield behind which she can gather herself again. She knows her control has been compromised. She does not trust herself right now with any of the many talents she has developed through the years."

Julian looked perplexed and Bridget quieted him with a smile and continued. "Due to circumstances, she feels she has had to bring you further then she wanted and far faster than she should. She knows you were a reluctant student in the beginning, but that you have tried with passion, discipline and dedication to master your lessons.

"She wonders if she would have done as well in your circumstances and I join her in that. I doubt any of us could have done what you have in the time you have been given.

"She knows you are an extraordinary student, however she knows she has not been an extraordinary teacher. It is hard for her Julian. It is her responsibility as a teacher to nurture and protect you. Instead, it is you who have sustained and defended her." Julian nodded his understanding.

"She has seen something, but not enough. She cannot bring it into focus. She has agonized over this. What she sees is dark and indistinct. Although she cannot see it, she can feel it. It involves the lives of many and the futures of many more. There is, in this valley, a manifest evil. It is both ancient and modern. I know that makes little sense, but better than that, I cannot say and neither can Moira.

"Fighting this malignant force has fallen to you. However, you must know, you must understand this fully, Moira would have taken this task from you. She would have given up anything, paid any price to keep you out of it. She tried everything she knew, but it was not to be.

"I felt the foreboding the first time I looked into this valley. Like Moira, I do not know its source."

Julian looked at his friend. Bridget smiled and he could see those ancient, wise and kind eyes clearly. Now they did not sparkle, they were troubled. She said, "You did not believe me at first when I spoke to you of evil. But it is different for you now. Now you know this evil do you not?"

"Yes," he answered and closed his eyes as he felt again the palpable malevolence.

Bridget continued. "This village of yours, this entire valley, there is a darkness here. I do not have the words that will capture what I am sensing." She stopped, her frustration clearly marked on her face.

Julian's tone was calm and even. The cadence of his words was measured and his voice soft. Without turning he said, "Perhaps I can help." Bridget turned to look at her companion. She watched him closely, but he did not return her gaze.

She noticed his eyes seemed heavy and darker. He blinked slowly and infrequently. The muscles in his shoulders and neck were relaxed. His face wore a placid expression. He seemed absorbed as if his thoughts were far away.

"Please do," she said. Her voice was hushed. She tried to control her breathing and contain her thoughts and feelings. The air around Julian was electric. It rippled and pulsed with subtle energy, but there was a raw vitality to it. She knew she was witnessing something she had never seen, something few had ever seen before. Awakening. The voice was Julian's, but he was removed, detached.

"Please keep in mind my thoughts, feelings and my opinions are worth exactly what you paid for them." He smiled but still did not look at her. She added her own smile.

"Forgive me, I know it is not for a student to say such things to his teachers, but both you and Moira are wrong. Rather than sensing or feeling what is there, you are trying desperately to find what should be there. Your senses report back findings that don't make sense. Rather than investigate the findings, you assume your senses are somehow faulty.

"It is easier for me to see this clearly than it is for you. You both are accustomed to dealing with higher levels of sophistication so you look for what you expect to find, what you have always found. You feel the immense power and so suspect a powerful, dominant force must be its source. You cannot get a clear fix on the source so you expect a certain level of adroitness and vast experience is being used to cloud your vision." Bridget sat stunned.

"Forgive me again." Julian continued. "It is not my wish to play the pedant with you. This is not an exercise in semantics, I assure you. The words we use have meanings and carry with them deadly consequences. I can see that now. The power is raw and immense, I will grant you. It is not a dominant force, however, but a force that needs to dominate. You are looking for a presence that is fully formed. You will not find it because it is a presence being formed.

"You cannot easily define it or get a fix on it because it morphs as it grows and it is growing because it is feeding off Moira. If you were to stay, I believe it would consume you too. Through dumb luck, I managed to deflect a major assault on Moira. This has changed the dynamics of the situation." Julian thought a moment before continuing.

"Dear Bridget, you are not looking for a teacher but a student. He is self-taught and all the more dangerous because of it. He has no discipline, no control. This is evidenced in the viciousness of the attacks. The intensity is maintained by sheer force of will combined with an intense hatred, anger and fear." Julian closed his eyes.

The air was heavy with the scent of Irish dog roses. The creak of the swing was the only noise that breached the silence. After several minutes, Bridget spoke, choosing her words with care.

"You have grown more than you know and so, have made yourself a larger target. Julian, you must guard yourself and those around you. It sounds like melodrama, something seen in a very bad play, to be sure. But you, and those you love, are in tremendous danger. The sharper your senses become, the larger the threat grows," Bridget said.

Julian turned to his companion. His eyes were still heavy and he was tired. "Bridget, I worry about it all the time. I've worried about it from the beginning. Will I be ready? Will I be good enough? Sometimes, like just now, I'm as focused as a laser. I frighten myself actually. At other times, I'm just," Julian paused, his forehead wrinkled heavily as he looked for the words. "Just so off balance, confused, distracted."

"That is rather the point, don't you see? Your confusion is part of the mist that shrouds the truth. Mankind accepted the darkness as light long ago and has suffered for it since. You must not do the same.

"You ask if you will be ready. I tell you, do what you've been taught to do, but more importantly, be fully who you have become. Be as true to yourself as you know how to be," she said.

"Calm your thoughts, focus, listen, and become the moment. Through the mist of false reality, you will hear echoes of the truth. The nearer you get to the source of truth, the more your mind will rebel as it tries to reconcile the dark to the light. However, know that as you approach, the echoes will become louder and clearer.

"It is then you will understand the present moment is what matters Julian, and what you do with it is what counts." Bridget smiled.

"I want you to carry this with you always. At every instant you stand on the brink of a limitless expanse. The past is the past. You would not be here without it. As for the future, you are making it, one moment at a time.

"It begins and ends with you. Right now is what you must claim as your own along with each moment you experience. You, Julian, you are the moment. In this instant, you are everything you ever were and everything you are. Believe and trust in your courage at the moment you are most frightened. Listen for the truth because it all begins and ends with echoes through the mist. You will be as ready as you need to be. However, your vigilance is necessary for you to protect those you hold dear. You may trust me on this."

The older woman touched her companion's face, touched the scar on his cheek again while she looked deeply into his gray eyes. "Julian," she said, "there is no need to worry. Moira has her concerns, but no doubts of your ability. It is right for a teacher to feel this way. Whatever the task, Moira and I believe you are ultimately and uniquely capable of handling it. You are not alone in this Julian. When the time comes, you will find there are others who will lend you their strength should you need it.

"Moira knows there is something crucial that needs to be done but it has been made clear it is not she who will accomplish it. Another had to be found, someone special.

"That did not happen, so when you turned up, she decided you would have to do," Bridget said. The mischief was back in her eyes and she smiled shamelessly.

"That's it," Julian said. "I am going to report you the Irish Tourist Board. The lot of you are supposed to be charming and fun loving and drunk much of the time. You're here to provide me with a bit of local Irish color. I am a tourist. I want a refund."

"This, Mr. Julian Blessing, will teach you not to tease my very dear friend, the doctor."

Bridget laughed and Julian moaned.

***

The night breeze whispered above them and cleared away the clouds, leaving a starless ink-black sky. Bridget Bragonier turned and walked toward the house leaving Julian with his thoughts and the night sky.

When he eventually entered Ailís's house, he found Bridget beckoning him toward the best room. They were all asleep. The professor had dozed off and snored occasionally. Timothy was stretched out before the fire. Ailís slept in her chair with a book in her lap.

Julian smiled and put his arm around Bridget's shoulder. "What a group," she said simply and shook her head. "Can you get the boy?" Julian nodded his head and went to Ailís's chair. He looked at her placid face, and then gently moved a lock of hair aside. She stirred and woke slowly. She smiled lovingly at Julian, then scanned the room. Julian kissed her forehead and then moved off to scoop up Timothy and carry him up to bed.

He heard Bridget say to her husband, "Reginald, I'm afraid we must go to bed so Julian here can go home."

"What? What? I wasn't asleep."

"No, of course. Come along."

"Oh, if it pleases you, I suppose I must."

With Ailís's assistance, Timothy was put to bed. Julian kissed the doctor deeply before making his way downstairs where he checked the doors and windows, banked the fires and secured the front door before he left.

There was something heavy, angry and dangerous in the air. Julian stepped into the street and felt it immediately. Closing his eyes he forced himself to do the opposite of what nature demanded. He let his mind and body relax. Julian was very still for a short time, then opened his eyes and smiled a hard smile.

He thought back on the conversation he'd had with Bridget. Phrases played in his head over and over and through out. There was an overlay of wisdom and the power wisdom brings. This was a wisdom he could use. He knew that for the first time, this power was one he was ready to wield.

As Julian approached the police station, he noticed there were no lights on. The desk lamp had been left on and the turf fire should have been throwing its soft warmth and light.

"Jimmy," Julian said into the shadows.

"How is it you always know, Mr. Julian? You and the professor's wife and of course, Mrs. Hagan?" Jimmie crossed himself. "Nobody else ever sees me. And, aye, it's them no good ones again. You can see their truck parked in the shadows beyond the station. I was just on me way to get you."

"Run up to Sean Maher's and tell him to come quickly. Tell him not to interfere unless he thinks I need help."

"Aye, Mr. Julian, but the last time it, well, it didn't go in your favor overly much."

"Jimmy, last time wasn't this time. Now off ya go."

Jimmy Grogan took off at a run for the far end of town.

"Every instant you stand on the brink of a limitless expanse," Julian said to himself and exhaled deeply as he wondered what the very near future would look like. "Believe in your courage at the moment you are most frightened," Bridget had said. Julian took another breath.

As he walked up the path, Julian could feel them. Three men. He stopped a meter short of the door. Julian cleared his mind, reached out his hand and without touching the door, opened it. He stepped inside the darkened station and the door closed behind him.

Chapter Thirty-Five

"What!" Sean Maher said.

"He told me to fetch you as the three bad'ns were inside the police station waiting for him."

"What!" Sean Maher said as he pulled on his boots.

"Mr. Julian. He didn't seem at all flustered. I was scared shitless, pardon me, Mrs. Maher."

Kathleen Maher nodded without looking up as she knitted in her chair before the fire.

"What!" Sean Maher said as he got into his shirt.

"He said you're not to interfere unless it looks like he needs help," Jimmy said.

"What!" Sean Maher said as he pulled open the front door of his cottage and ran down the empty main street of Cappel Vale with Jimmy Grogan on his heels.

***

Julian could see the outline of his attackers. One leaned against the desk. Julian knew this would be the man with the spider tattoo. Against the back wall stood the man's two assistants.

He could sense them all easily and clearly. The assistants were bigger men, older, sadder somehow, but dangerous and experienced. He remembered them well. The redheaded man was a bagful of vicious thoughts. The man spoke and Julian could feel in every word the rage, the malice and the man's constant pressing need to cause pain.

"Ah, and if it isn't our own little American. How goes it Yank? Oi understand you mixed it up with the wrong sort and came away the poorer for the exchange. Feelin' better now?" The man chuckled.

"Oh, Oi thought Oi might mention it Yank, ya know your little slag, the doctor? Well, Oi'll be givin' her a special medical examination of me own afore this night is out. Don't you worry none. I'll dedicate the first fuck I pour into her to you. And no worries, I'll have her beggin' for more like the cheap whore she is. But you'll be dead long afore any of that."

All three men went silent and their breathing stepped up considerably as Julian leaned against the station door casually. He communicated a thought slowly, deliberately, a thought filled with stark malevolence.

"What a monumentally stupid thing to say. You and I will discuss that later. But first I have to arrest you all. Or destroy you all, which ever comes first."

The voice the men heard was very quiet but the high voltage hum below the surface was palpable and Julian could feel their anxiety and that made him smile.

All three men facing Julian started to move slowly.

Julian thought to himself, "Listen for the echoes through the mist," and with that, he bowed his head, took a deep breath and then he heard it, *"Go now."* When he opened his eyes, his movements were synchronized with the moment. It looked as if time had frozen all three attackers. He knew they were simply moving in a separate reality, one clouded in a thick mist of ignorance and anger.

Julian took another deep breath and stepped back into normal time.

The man who had taunted him seemed disoriented for a moment before he crumpled to the floor screaming, his left knee shattered, his right bent at an acute angle. He clawed the air like a mad thing, thrashing in agony and begging. His companions against the back wall were writhing on the ground, holding their groins and retching.

Julian Blessing, with a pleasant smile, was now sitting on the station's desk twirling the borrowed cane he no longer needed. He turned on the desk lamp and waited for help to arrive.

***

The station door opened and Sean Maher filled the room with an explosive and murderous presence. Jimmy Grogan followed and was fully prepared to mix it up and give far better then he got.

Two steps inside the room, Sean noted the two men on the ground behind the desk. Being an authority on impromptu warfare he knew the men had each been incapacitated, 'nutted' was the technical term, and would be out of action for the remainder of this exchange. "Ach, sorry Oi am lads, but you'll each be pissing blood for a week."

Sean turned his attention to the redheaded man on the floor. The man's face was contorted in terror and an anguish that made Sean wince as he said, "Ah, Julian?"

Julian looked at Sean Maher and Jimmy Grogan and said, "Hey, thanks for stopping by. I'll be with you in just a moment."

Sean closed his eyes and winced again. He could feel this coming. "Jimmy Grogan, if you have sense, turn your head away. You shouldn't have your entire life ruined because of this. It is going to be passing ugly. In fact, I'll join you for the sake of me immortal soul." Neither man looked away. Sometimes you just have to look.

Julian pointed the walking stick at the thug on the floor. The man whimpered in pain and his terror and cowardice were plain to see.

The man felt not only the words but also the force of Julian's malice. *"Now, it is time for you to confess. If it's necessary I'm going to grind my boot into what's left of your knee – just to keep you focused. You see, I'm going to show you all the mercy you showed George Sullivan, Farmer Monahan and Tommy Ryan and the rest."* Julian's thin, twisted smile removed all hope for clemency. *"Let's begin, shall we?"*

Sean and Jimmy had been watching transfixed. The room seemed to hum and pulse with an electrical charge. Julian sat on the edge of the desk and without a word was still pointing his stick at the redheaded man. The lethal smile had not left Julian's lips, but for all the world to see, he had said not a word.

Sean's eyes narrowed and Jimmy's went wide when the panic-filled voice of the redheaded man suddenly blurted out, "Don't do it! Don't! For the love of God, not me leg! Oh God, the pain is something awful. I can't tell you nothin'. Oi don't know! Oi don't know!"

His scream tore the air. "Get me a doctor, please Jaysus, Oi'm dying with the pain! Make him stop. As Christ is me judge, Oi don't know anythin'. We get our orders from Big Tom Lynch. That's all Oi know. He gets his orders from some rich bastard in Loath.

"Please make him stop," the man wept. "I'm sorry I said what I said about the doctor and I kilt George Sullivan, and Oi hit the priest and yes, yes we beat the others too. But those were our orders! We couldn't help it! You gotta believe me! Please, please don't kill me! Please God help me!" The man reached out to Sean and Jimmy for assistance and knew instantly there would be none.

Julian thought it and the redheaded man heard it and horror gripped his soul, *"God is busy, but I'm here. Listen well and never forget. I will forever be in your head. Do not think about the doctor again because if you ever think of me or mine again you will feel far more than this."* Julian smiled a hideous smile.

The redheaded attacker went rigid with an uncontrollable, all encompassing panic. His muscles contorted in pulsing, crippling spasms and he screamed as he entered a cyclone of blinding pain. The horror-filled shriek ripped the air and was thereafter known as the loudest sound ever heard in Cappel Vale.

Sean and Jimmy crossed themselves.

The man with red hair and a spider tattoo passed out.

Chapter Thirty-six

After a comprehensive search for weapons, the assailants were deposited in the cells.

"I suppose we should send for the Garda," Julian Blessing said.

"I suppose we should send for the doctor," Jimmy Grogan said.

"I suppose we should go get a pint," Sean Maher said.

They agreed that before making any difficult decisions, Sean's suggestion was the best course of action so they secured the prisoners and the police station and headed off to O'Gavagan's Pub.

***

"He seemed to handle that well. A bit rough, but 'tis understandable. I don't think he'll need our help, do you?" Moira said.

"You have done a good job. I feel he will handle the next challenge fine without us," Bridget answered.

***

Although it was nearly closing time, O'Gavagan's was still crowded with patrons speculating on the cry the banshee had made. They had all heard the scream, but had decided to have another jar before going out to investigate.

Julian and Sean bellied up to the bar and in uncharacteristically loud voices ordered pints.

"O'Gavagan, old son," Sean called out. The barman eased over to stand in front of his patrons.

"Big Mike O'Gavagan, it is filled with awe and respect, that much that I have for you, that Oi'm about to impart a tale. This regards me friend and companion, Julian Blessing, and the justice of Almighty God."

"Go on, Sean Maher, Oi'm listening. But do not keep this between us. We all of us want to hear your tale."

"Sean," Julian interrupted, "There is no need to..."

"Tisk, tisk, tisk; Oi'll have none of your false modesty, ya beautiful and courageous, and should I say saintly, man?" Sean winked at the barman.

Julian resigned himself and looked deeply into his glass. The room had become as still as a church in Lent.

Sean began to speak. He turned and ran an eye over all of his listeners as any good storyteller would. "You know your fine selves what a most terrible beating our Mr. Julian took at the hands of burly toughs, three or mayhaps four, times his size who had trampled our priest in his own church and who desecrated St. Michael's."

"'Tis true. Oi know this," Mike O'Gavagan said and a grumbled assent went round the room.

"Well, this very night the same Mr. Julian, who up to a few weeks ago was a pathetic ruin of a once great man, due to the said beating he received and the severity of his wounds, prevailed against evil. Anyway, through the craftiness born of a long and expensive education, he laid a clever trap for his tormentors knowing that they would come back to finish the job they started.

"Now Oi would like to say Oi put paid to their evil intentions by me, fortuitous…?" he asked Julian, who nodded that was the correct word.

"...Their evil intentions by me fortuitous arrival at the police station this very night. Where'pon, Oi frightened them away. This Oi would state before God – had Oi got hold of them who commit crimes in churches and mistreat me friends, Oi would be having murther in me heart, surely Oi would. Oi would say all this, but being a modest man Oi will refrain."

Julian blew ale out of his nose and called for a bar towel. Sean looked down upon his friend and sniffed a miffed sniff.

"Anyway, Oi would like to say such is true, but alas 'tisn't. Our very own Mr. Julian it was and he alone confronted his assailants this very night and like a man, he laid them low.

"Boom, boom!" Sean said as he brought his knee up to groin height fast and hard. "Mr. Julian bollocked two of the henchmen mightily."

A collective gasp went up around the room as, involuntarily, men moved to protect their privates and exhibited suitably pained expressions.

"That left only the ringleader who knocked down Father Fahey and administered the monstrous beating to poor Mr. Julian. Aye, and who killt entirely our Georgie Sullivan and who beat the others, too he did. And wasn't it Mr. Julian who subdued the culprit in a flash?" Sean drank deeply from his beer.

The room was thick with a stunned silence as it awaited the next installment. It wasn't long in coming.

"Why, it was the work of a moment and Mr. Julian fully paralyzed the ringleader so that he was on the ground and could not move for the fear and pain that was on him.

"'Tis then that Oi arrived upon the scene with young Jimmy Grogan. We turned up to assist Mr. Julian, but our assistance would not be needed this night, except for a very minor role Oi meself played, as you will hear. It 'twas that friend Blessing, for he is a friend and a kinsman to us all." A noisy concurrence went up around the room. Sean looked to Julian. "Where was Oi?"

Julian rolled his eyes and whispered, "'twas that friend Blessing…"

"Ach, aye. 'Twas that friend Blessing destroyed the evil ones altogether and did it faster then it takes to cross yourselves, it was that fast too. How it t'wer done Oi cannot say for in truth, and I am I truthful man, I did not see this happen. But in spades, I saw the aftermath making evidence of the act plain for all to see.

"Oi will tell you it must have been with a restraint the saint would be proud to have, that worse was not done. Aye, restraint Oi say because our Mr. Julian did not murther the man altogether."

A general agreement circulated again throughout the room.

"To show the wisdom of our Mr. Julian, who is nearly an Irishman for he has that much wisdom and bravery, Mr. Julian says to me, 'Friend, Sean Maher, you and Jimmy Grogan rest yourselves for Oi have a job of work to do that'll take but a moment.'

"Well, Mr. Julian, he looks upon the face of evil that is in a state of misery on the ground afore him. The creature has his legs at unnatural angles, which is often the way of evil creatures.

"Our Julian, he just looks at the creature and before a heartbeat can pass the beast is beggin' us to hear his confession. 'Twas a lengthy confession too considerin' all the pain that was on him."

"Rightly so…" the pub patrons and the landlord agreed.

"Well, after the nasty insect owned up to his sins, Mr. Julian, he just continues to look at the monster. Due to his moral superiority and having right on his side, 'twas that look alone that Mr. Julian employed that caused the monumental howl to rise up from the fiend. And that was the wail you all heard this very night. So much is the power of good over evil." The patrons shivered with the memory.

Julian let his head fall back as he looked at the ceiling and shook his head.

Sean continued, "'Aye, Sean Maher,' says Mr. Julian, 'get Jimmy Grogan to help you deposit these swine behind bars. As both of you are Christians you have nothing to fear from these wicked persons. To the cells with 'em,' says he to me.

"Oi, meself and Jimmy Grogan too did witness these deeds as God Almighty is the judge of us all and 'twas we who deposited hell's imps in the cells of the police station this very night in Cappel Vale.

"And that is me story, Mike O'Gavagan."

"A better tale there could not be – nor a better or more truthful storyteller as we all know." Big Mike cast a questioning eye over the crowd and they quickly agreed. Each patron was already planning his rewrite of history. "And proud it is I am to be able to call you – and Mr. Julian – me friends," the barman said

Julian whispered slowly, "I know it is your pub, Big Mike, but step to the end of the bar if you would."

"Julian?" Sean looked puzzled.

"Mr. O'Gavagan, I said step to the end of the bar. Do it now, please." Julian's tone of voice was calm and low and allowed no further discussion. The barman backed away and looked troubled.

The pub's front door squealed on its hinges and filling the doorway was a very large man with a cloth cap and a shotgun. Without turning away from the bar Julian shook his head, smiled slightly and said in a clear voice that silenced the room, "Welcome Mr. Lynch. Would you join us for a drink?"

"You two!" Lynch bellowed.

***

There was a clear path from the front door to the bar. The barman reached slowly for the shotgun he kept under the bar.

"Enough of that, O'Gavagan," Lynch said and motioned for the barman to back away. "Everybody back up and take a seat," Lynch said. "These two and Oi are goin' to take a walk."

Sean was calculating the distance and began to balance on the balls of his feet. Julian too was calculating. He knew Lynch had his finger wrapped tightly around the trigger of the shotgun. The barrel came up a fraction of an inch and was pointed squarely at Sean.

"Maher, Oi know you by reputation and you're a good fightin' man to be sure. Unless you want your wife to be a widow and your children to be orphans, Oi would stay right where you are. As sure as there is a God in heaven and as sure as you have my men locked in your jail, Oi will spread your guts all over the wall if you move."

"Sean," Julian said still with his back to the intruder, "as Mr. Lynch won't join us, let us drink our drinks without him." Sean was reluctant to take his eyes off the man with the shotgun.

The thought came to Sean in Julian's voice, *"Sean, turn around and drink your drink. It would be such a shame to let good beer go to waste, no?"*

Sean turned slowly to the bar and whispered to Julian, "When we are both killt altogether, it is me hope God remembers which of us is the Christian and which of us is not."

"Turn around! The three of us'll be going now," Lynch said.

"Sadly, I don't think so," Julian responded.

"Don't play the silly arse with me!" the man roared.

"Why don't you set your shotgun down?" Julian turned, rested against the bar and looked at Lynch.

"Why don't I kill you? There are those who would pay me handsomely. You are not very well liked."

"I have been told that in the past, although," Julian turned, smiled at the pub's patrons and continued, "not in a long time now."

To a man, the room stood slowly. Chairs and benches chalked the floor. Julian held up a hand and the other patrons stopped moving and waited.

"Don't do this," Julian said to Lynch. "It isn't worth it." Julian was no longer looking into Thomas Lynch's face. His focus had moved to the muzzle of the shotgun.

"Oi have me orders. Now let's go and get me men."

Tom Lynch looked alarmed. He looked down at the shotgun in his hands. The barrels were beginning to glow bright red and the stock was getting hot. He felt the words.

Julian's thought was calm, clear, and emphatic. *"Do you have orders to die where you stand tonight? You see, your weapon is going to explode in your hands in five, four, three, two,,,"*

Thomas Lynch stepped down the shotgun's exposed hammers and the weapon clattered to the floor.

Julian turned to Sean who, like the other patrons, stood in stunned silence. With a mad grin, Julian said, "Was that cool or what! I never get tired of that sort of thing."

Chapter Thirty-Seven

Jimmy Grogan was waiting in the police station. "This came for you," Jimmy said as he handed Julian a thick package in brown paper. He set the package on his desk and cut the string holding it together. Inside there were several copies of the Irish Times.

On the front page in bold type were the words Julian knew would be there, IRELAND INVADED BY ROMANS SAYS TRINITY PROFESSOR. Julian passed a copy on to Jimmy and the two sat in the rocking chairs and began to read the detailed account.

"Professor Reginald Bragonier," said the Irish Times, "while visiting a friend in the Irish countryside, happened upon a historical site that may overturn previous thinking about the history of Ireland."

Julian read the lead story and the various sidebars and associated articles, then reread them. Jimmy Grogan looked shell-shocked after his first reading.

"Is this true?" the young man asked.

"Well, according to the professor, yes and no. There were Romans here, but I believe the newspaper has taken some license by using the word invasion. Still it makes good copy and sells lots of newspapers."

"But, Romans in Ireland? Bloody hell. Although Oi shouldn't be surprised. Every other sodding country has been here at one time or another."

Julian nodded and both men looked into the cold fireplace and brooded.

"Stay sharp, Jimmy. Things are going to start happening."

"What things, Mr. Julian?"

"I wish I knew. I wish I knew," Julian said as he looked more deeply into the empty blackness of the fireplace and thought about a future he could not possibly know.

***

A tall, thin, pale man seethed as he reread the Irish Times article detailing the discovery made by Professor Bragonier. No real mention of the monetary value of the treasure was given other than to say it was enormous.

The Pale Man knew the professor had found nothing. "That American initiated all of this," he said to no one at all.

He saw his plans in total disarray. His helpers were all in jail, the treasure he had sought for so long had been found by another, there was no hope of recovering any of his losses.

Faced with the futility of the endeavors that had taken up so much of his life, revenge suggested itself as a worthy alternative. To his mind, there was nothing left, but revenge. Killing Julian Blessing would satisfy that nicely he thought.

***

Ailís, Timothy and Julian went to the holy well near the crossroads. It was a pleasant afternoon and a trip to the well and back provided a long but easy walk. For Ailís it was a chance to get out of her office. For Julian it was the prospect of spending time with a woman he adored. For Timothy it provided the opportunity to go for a walk with the two people he loved most.

Although it was mid afternoon when they started out, Ireland's perennial late winter had settled over the landscape softening the edges of everything and putting a chill in the air.

"Tell me about the holy wells," Julian said.

Ailís began. "Well, as is so often the case in Ireland, there are two schools of thought and, of course, those schools are polar opposites.

"One school contends the holy wells were pagan in origin and were co-opted by the Church as a way to more quickly and easily spread Christianity," Ailís said.

"Sounds reasonable and it isn't like the Church hasn't done that before," Julian interjected. "What is the other school?"

"That one believes the holy wells were nothing of the sort. They were Christian from the start and had no trace of paganism about them. They sprouted because there weren't always churches nearby and the wells gave the people a place to come and pray and to join together at special times," Ailís finished.

"Timothy," Julian said. "What does Sister Eugenia say about the wells?"

The boy thought for awhile and then said, "Sister Eugenia doesn't say much about 'em a'tall, Mr. Julian. There are times when she says they are Christian places. Other times she says they are much older. Still, at other times she says they are places where little people and fairies meet."

"What do you think, Timothy?" Julian asked.

Again the boy thought before speaking. Julian liked that about Timothy. "Well, Mr. Julian, Holy wells is..."

"Holy wells, are," his mother corrected.

"Holy wells are special places; places for prayer and protection. The why of it really doesn't matter. That they're here is enough, I guess."

Julian smiled his pleasure and said, "You are a bright lad, Timothy. It is that kind of thinking that will take you far."

Timothy beamed in the spotlight and Ailís put her arm around her son.

Julian decided to pursue the discussion. "So we agree, Timothy, that the holy wells and other holy places can protect a person from harm?"

"Yes, that can happen," the boy said.

"You say 'can happen' as though it doesn't always happen," Julian responded.

"That's right, they don't always protect."

"So what makes the difference between who is protected and when?"

The boy stuffed his hands deep into his pockets, looked at the ground as he walked and thought hard. At last, the answer that came was as simple as it was profound. "Faith."

"Faith in the well or faith in God?" Julian asked.

"Either really. If you believe in the well it is because you believe God has made it special."

"What if you don't believe in God?"

With his forehead lined deeply, Timothy tried to imagine a world without a belief in God.

"Well," Timothy began, "everyone believes in something and everyone believes that something can keep them safe."

Julian said, "Timothy, you are the smartest young man I've ever met. To what do you credit your brilliance?"

"Oi…"

"I not Oi," his mother corrected.

"I would have to say it's because of me Ma," the boy answered without a moment's hesitation and Julian's laughter was unrestrained.

He rested his hand on Timothy's shoulder, but Timothy shrugged it off. He was walking between Ailís and Julian, but stopped and turned to face them. The young boy placed his mother's hand in Julian's and then looked at the two adults.

"Everyone knows, you know," he said as he grinned and with the joyfulness only found in childhood, Timothy darted up the road to explore the path ahead.

Ailís and Julian looked sheepish, but neither would let go of the other's hand. After a few minutes of walking in silence, Julian dropped Ailís's hand and snaked his arm around her shoulder drawing her near. In turn, she ran her arm around his waist, rested her head on his shoulder and smiled.

What started off as a brisk walk in the country had slowed to an intimate amble with neither Julian nor Ailís having a need to talk, but each with a deep need for the other's company.

Ailís said, "You really are quite good with him. Thank you."

"He makes it easy. He really is a remarkable boy and you have done a wonderful job of raising him."

This close to Julian she felt no need to comment. She smiled in his embrace and knew he was right; she had raised a wonderful son somehow.

Julian stopped in the road and Ailís looked at him. Something fundamental was amiss and he could feel it. The presence was dark and oppressive. It was the strongest impression he had ever experienced. The world suddenly wasn't as it had been a moment ago.

All of Julian's senses reached a state of alert simultaneously. The road ahead was clear. Around the next corner, they would come within sight of the holy well. For now the road was straight, trees lined it on both sides with thick beds of dark leafed bracken laying down a carpet of green. Julian held his hand out in front of him. He nearly recoiled at the touch. He could feel it like a wall in front of him. This was malice, hatred and rage. This was evil.

It had arrived. The moment had come and Julian's waiting was, for better or worse, over.

"Ailís?" Julian said softly.

"Yes."

"Do you trust me?"

"Yes," she answered.

"I need to know you will trust me no matter what," Julian said.

"What is this about? You are making me uncomfortable," Ailís said.

"I need to know you trust me."

"Yes, I do trust you, Julian," she said.

The mood was broken. The moment was lost between them. Ailís unwound herself from him, but reached down and took his hand. They walked on together in silence.

She could feel his tenseness. Although he would not transmit it to the hand that held hers, the muscles of his arms and shoulders flexed and she felt something like an electrical charge building on his skin.

They turned the corner and there, ahead of them, was the holy well. Standing in front of it was a tall, thin, pale man. His left arm was wrapped tightly around Timothy Dwyer. The Pale Man's right hand was clutching a very short and very lethal double-barreled shotgun.

CHAPTER THIRTY-EIGHT

Ailís cried out and tried to rush ahead, but Julian pulled her back. "If there was ever a time to trust me," he said, "this is it."

She looked into his light gray eyes, drew a deep breath, nodded her assent once, and said, "I trust you. I don't know what this is about, but, Julian, you can't afford to get it wrong."

He closed his eyes, exhaled and sent his thought out to her, *"I would give up my life before I would allow anything to happen to Timothy or you. Know that. Please, do not move. Please, don't speak. Know only that I love you. Keep to that and we'll be fine."*

Ailís mouthed the words, "I love you," and he could see the pleading in her eyes.

"Come now, you'll need to come a lot closer than that," the Pale Man shouted.

Julian left Ailís, came to within two-dozen yards of the Pale Man, and stopped.

"This is all you get. What is it you want?" Julian said quietly.

"I suppose that is close enough, although I don't know how we are ever going to become the sort of friends we might at this distance," the Pale Man said.

"The question hasn't changed. What do you want?" Julian asked again mildly.

"Want? Oh, it's nothing really. I want to kill you and I'm going to do it. I've not determined if that is a want or a need though."

"Well then, why don't you turn the boy loose and you can satisfy all your appetites?"

"Do you know who I am?"

"No, and strangely I don't really care. It will suffice that you are the man who wants me dead and seems to have the means to make it happen. Oh, I do suppose you are the employer of those gentlemen who were delivered to the Garda." Julian could feel the man's hatred.

"True, but perhaps a better question is, do you know who you are."

"It comes and goes. Sometimes I do and sometimes it is all a bit fuzzy," Julian said.

The Pale Man stretched his thin colorless lips back over his teeth into something approximating a smile and said, "To me you have been a constant irritant. You have gotten in the way of my preparations and in the end you stole from me that for which I have been searching for a very long time."

"I am terribly sorry. What is it I stole from you exactly?" Julian asked. His opponent was becoming darker by the moment and Julian watched and waited.

"You are a funny man or rather, were a funny man. You stole my Roman coins."

"Hmmmm. In the first place, I don't believe the coins were yours and in the second place, a professor from Trinity found them. It was in all the papers. Quite thrilling really," Julian said and smiled.

"There you go being funny again. That old fool didn't find anything. You found them and turned the find over to him." The Pale Man's malice threatened to engulf Julian.

"Let the boy go and he and the doctor can go back to the village. That will give you more than enough time to do what you need to do and still escape." Julian took a step forward and the Pale Man brought the shotgun up to Timothy's head. Julian heard Ailís gasp.

"What seems to be the trouble?" Again, Julian's tone was mild. It was everything he didn't feel. "These two aren't important to you.

I'm the one you want. Let them go and we'll settle what needs settling, eh?" Julian said.

It was there, a flaw, a momentary shudder. The man he faced had power made more potent by his anger, but there was a flaw and Julian could sense it.

"That's rather the point, don't you see?" the Pale Man said. "You are right. They aren't important to me in the slightest. No, these two mean nothing to me, but to you they are the most important things in your life.

"You see, Blessing, I know you. I know who you are and who you are trying to become. You are quite good, but not nearly good enough. I can feel it in you. I can feel your anxiety. Attachments are a weakness. I gave up attachments to people and places long ago to pursue my path. You are unable to do that and that makes you weak.

"I have studied as you have," the Pale Man said. "However I didn't have a harridan in the village helping me, but then I didn't need her to give me her help. I took what I wanted and left you with the rest. I'll destroy you Blessing, and I'll do it in the most painful way possible. I've already started.

"Look at the good doctor. She is nearly paralyzed with fear. I am feeding that fear of course. She knows her son will die and you will be to blame. She will suffer torments beyond counting and she will hate you with a fierceness you cannot begin to imagine.

"I could destroy you with a thought, but why bother? I can use their thoughts to crush you. I know, why don't I kill the doctor and let her son watch. Perhaps his hatred of you for causing that would be greater than hers.

"You took from me that which I valued. Why shouldn't I return the favor?" the Pale Man said.

Timothy squirmed and Julian dug his fingernails deeply into his palm. He relaxed and quieted Timothy's thoughts.

He saw the boy's eyes go wide. *"Timothy, remember what you said? Everyone believes in something that can keep them safe. I want you to believe in the love your mother has for you, that I have for you. The hate this man has inside of him is nothing but a lie. It's love that is the truth. Do you understand?*

Timothy nodded his head once, his eyes filled with barely contained terror.

Julian redirected his thought and continued, *"Ailís, do you trust me?"*

He felt her nod her head and heard her whisper, "Yes."

Julian saw the shotgun in all its terrible efficiency. The man before him had both hammers cocked and his finger caressing the triggers. There would be no easy way to disarm the man. He was protecting his thoughts and countered Julian's every move.

The Pale Man said, "Don't do it, my soon-to-be late friend. That old woman may have taught you a few parlor tricks and you may have a few paltry talents of your own, but none of it will be enough to stop me."

"There it is again," Julian thought to himself. He felt it, he almost knew this man's flaw. Julian took a deep breath and began to close his eyes completely when suddenly he felt something else. A powerful force gathering potency as it grew. He could feel them all. Coming.

His eyes snapped open at the sound of a noise coming from his left. From out of the forest appeared Father Fahey. "Sure, you don't want to be doing this thing, laddie," he said.

"Oi wouldn't do it, boyo. If you do, you had better aim for me and pray to your God that you kill me," said Sean Maher as he emerged from the trees behind the Pale Man. "If you don't or if you hurt me friends, Oi'll make you beg for death."

Julian glanced to his right and saw the Squire and Moira Hagan step in line with Ailís. In a low even voice the Squire said, "Put the gun down now, son. There is no sense making it worse now is there?"

Moira added quickly, "Daniel, there is nothing you've done that is so bad your father and I can't help you make it right."

The Pale Man snorted. "Why, if it isn't me Ma and Da. Come to take me home have you? If it were under different circumstances, I would empty both barrels into the both of you. And there you stand together for the first time in almost forty years. Odd, don't you think, that it takes something like this to... it makes no difference. You two are no longer relevant."

"And what is relevant, Daniel?" asked Father Fahey. "Surely it isn't to be found in the ending of human life in this place."

"Save your breath, Priest. As you know, my father the Squire, stuck me away to be educated by the Christian Brothers. Taking life is a sin. I know that because the beefy, professed brothers used their broad belts to beat it into me. I had all your rules beaten into me."

There it was. Julian had it. He could feel it. Now it was a matter of timing.

"Nothing from you, Maher? No, you are a man of action. You'll not be wasting time on a lot of words."

More rustling came from the trees and the bracken. Sisters Eugenia and Gertrude entered the clearing followed by Edmond Brady.

The pub owners Mike O'Gavagan and Francis Mulherin entered the circle together along with Flynn of the general store. The Hackett sisters and Gwyneth Kirby were not far behind and approaching from Julian's right was the Mayor Cahill, with Jimmy Grogan.

Brendan Maher walked from the trees and stood between his father and Gwyneth Kirby.

Julian was surrounded by most of the village, his village, and his friends. The surge of power he felt was profound and profoundly humbling.

Daniel Lanigan, son of Squire Padric Francis Lanigan and Moira (née Hagan) Lanigan stood tall and gaunt. He wore a sneer on his face as he looked down on the villagers.

"Mr. Lanigan, now is the time to let the boy go and to come along with me. All your men have already given you up. We know all about the operation. I did not learn your name because you were careful to keep it from your little band and protected your thoughts from me. Still, I have a few academic questions. Let's go have a chat shall we?" Julian said reasonably.

Julian was drawing strength from the combined force of the villagers. Channeling the unstinting goodness of his friends caused his skin to bristle with electricity and his hands shook with the effort to control the power. It gave him the ability to lay down a curtain of protection around everyone but Timothy and Daniel Lanigan and himself.

"Not quite all my men I shouldn't think," Lanigan said.

"Oh you mean Liam McMaster. I wouldn't soil my jail with him. I can lay hands on that fool whenever I like. If the others sang, you can bet McMaster will give us an opera."

"Do you realize there is nothing that any of you ever did or said that McMaster didn't report back to me? He was my mole, but in retrospect, I could have chosen better. In any case I don't think it is going to work the way you have it planned," said Daniel Lanigan.

"You see I'm going to kill you, Blessing. The rest of you are going to clear a path while my little friend Timothy and I take our leave. I'll set him free in a few miles and then I will be on my way. As long as no one does anything stupid, I don't see why this can't end well, do you? Well, it won't end well for you," the Pale Man said indicating Julian.

"I can see a lot of reasons why this isn't going to end well," Julian said as he closed his eyes and took a deep, slow breath. He was within moments of obliterating this man's mind when Moira's supplication came to him.

It was weak, strangled by fear and tears, *"Don't hurt my boy. Please don't hurt him."* It was the pleading voice of a mother in the depths of terror and despair. Julian, let out the breath, nodded and selected another path.

"Mr. Lanigan, let the boy go," Julian said slowly as he advanced several steps. Ailís began to move forward. Julian sensed Moira reaching out and stopping the doctor. He sent a single thought into Ailís's consciousness. It was filled with all the tenderness he had inside him, *"Trust that I love you."* She looked dazed, and stayed where she was breathing with sharp gasps.

Julian advanced another few steps. "Let the boy go. It's me you want," Julian said. He could feel the man's hatred and bitterness beginning to overflow. Lanigan focused all of his anger and resentment, his frustration and his unrestrained rage on Julian.

Julian could feel it. The power was enormous but erratic, and Lanigan lacked the control to sustain an attack. When the man struck it would be short and sharp and deadly. Julian knew it would have to come soon. Lanigan's thoughts were starting to waver, become diffused and to weaken.

Daniel Lanigan barked, "You and I are two of a kind you know. I don't need this shotgun to destroy you or the boy or any and all of this rabble and you and my dear ol' mum know it.

"I like the shotgun though. It is the tangible representation of sudden death and this village needs to be reminded that life is brief, yes, painful."

The man's lack of control worried Julian. It made his opponent unpredictable and therefore ultimately dangerous. Julian's field of vision narrowed. He saw the world in stark relief. The edges and corners were smooth. He pierced the darkness surrounding Daniel Lanigan and what he saw was fear and something more. He saw shame.

Julian took a breath and let it out slowly. Moira watched as his shoulders relaxed and he began to move his hands away from his sides imperceptibly. She dare not ask him, beg him again to spare her son or she might lose them both.

Sean Maher tensed as he watched his friend and shuddered. Julian's stance was easy, his manner pleasant and relaxed. His face wore a gentle smile. But the intensity of his gaze spoke of raw power and a horrifying determination.

Sean had faced many men in his life. They had been big men, strong, tough men. They had been men of experience who were calculating and cunning. Against these men he had won often, lost occasionally, but was never afraid. He looked at his friend, a gentle, kind and giving man who was admired and respected. Sean Maher looked at Julian Blessing and was terrified.

Ailís Dwyer watched helplessly. A man she loved and the child she adored were entangled with an evil she never imagined existing. The air around the glen bristled with electricity. Then she felt his words again, *"Trust and know I love you."*

Julian knew the odds and with all that was riding on his actions, he could not afford to roll the dice. He couldn't step outside of time, release Timothy and still manage to neutralize his opponent. The man would see it coming well in advance. Julian needed to force Lanigan deeper into the mist. He needed his opponent's reality to be obscured, diverted. He needed Lanigan grounded solidly in the inky darkness of the man's desolate reality.

"I'm the one who stole your dreams," Julian barked suddenly. "I am the one who ruined your life. I found the treasure you searched for, for so long. It wasn't hard really. Only a fool would have missed it. It was so simple to find that I gave it away. I gave away what you would have sold for a fortune, what you sold your soul to possess. I'm the one you want.

"Lift the shotgun and feel the release by squeezing the triggers. Do it. Do it now! True, you can kill me without it, but you need to feel it. After all, it is probably the only thing you can still feel.

"You'll not escape from this place. At least get some of the retribution you want. This is your only way, Lanigan." Julian looked past the man with the shotgun to Sean Maher and nodded imperceptibly. Sean's forehead wrinkled slightly before he heard the words in his head, *"Get Timothy. Trust your instincts, you'll know when."*

Julian let loose a controlled rage onto the Pale Man. It was the man's shame that was his weakness. "What seems to be the problem, Lanigan? Didn't the brothers beat you enough to turn you into a man? Is that it? Maybe they saw you as soft and delicate and used you for some other purpose, eh?" Julian said with a snarl and continued walking forward.

With that, Daniel Lanigan curled his lip. His face was a mask constructed of equal parts anger and hatred. The shotgun moved from beside Timothy's head to bear on the center of Julian's chest.

The Pale Man felt Julian's words, *"Do it soon Lanigan or I will. You know I can and you know I will. You can feel your mind bending right now. You aren't attacking any more. You are defending and that defense is buckling fast. Soon it will crumble. You are not strong enough, disciplined enough. As soon as your defense wavers, in that moment I will obliterate what is left of your mind. You can make it all stop."*

In a clear, even voice Julian said, "One last chance at redemption, Lanigan. You have your target. Pull those triggers and be lost forever or don't and live. The choice is yours."

"You'll know the moment. You are the moment. Know and trust yourself." Bridget and Moira had said those things and they now made sense. Everything he had studied, practiced and learned, it all made perfect sense. Then he heard it. He heard the echoes through the mist and smiled."

"Go. Now."

Timothy was in the loose grip of Daniel Lanigan as the man focused all of his attention on Julian. Sean moved with remarkable speed, grabbed Timothy's arm and pulled him back behind the holy well. The Pale Man now had both hands around the shotgun. He snarled, took aim and pulled the right hand trigger.

Lanigan flinched slightly anticipating the buck of the shotgun.

No explosion. No recoil. No sound. Nothing but the snick of the hammer hitting the firing pin.

He pulled the left trigger.

Again, nothing.

Daniel Lanigan, pale and bewildered, with tears coursing his cheeks, looked at the instrument in his hands unable to make out what was happening. He then looked up in confusion.

Ten feet in front of him stood Julian Blessing. No one else could see it, but Julian turned his hand and in his open palm he held two shotgun shells.

CHAPTER THIRTY-NINE

The Garda arrived and took charge of Daniel Lanigan. The detectives had a lot of questions for Julian, which could have been uncomfortable, but he managed to dodge the thorniest of them. They did remind him he had overstayed his visit to Ireland and would have to leave and reenter the country in order to stay.

They advised him his testimony would be needed when the case went to trial and he assured them he would make himself available.

The chief inspector suggested Sean Maher come to see him in a few weeks. Funding had become available, but the Garda had been unable to enlist anyone for the post in Cappel Vale. They hadn't thought of recruiting locally.

Mayor Cahill apologized profusely to the authorities. He claimed he did not know Julian was using the police station for his home. The mayor summarily and with all the public display possible, had all of Julian's things removed only to have them returned as soon as the Garda were gone with their prisoner.

***

The professor wrote to Julian saying the Minister for Arts and Culture declared the treasure cave to be a valuable archaeological and cultural site that would need to be acquired by the Republic for a detailed scientific and archaeological assessment. The professor was to be appointed to head the project.

Using the contacts he had made while in Dublin, Julian founded a foundation that allowed the villagers to borrow money for expansion. Soon there would be a flood of historians and archaeologists, both amateur and professional, coming to Cappel Vale and they would need places to eat and sleep and otherwise spend their money. Everything from extra rooms to full-scale bed and breakfast establishments were planned.

After the experts, the flood of tourists would arrive. The mayor spent most of his days calculating the revenue from year-round tourist dollars.

***

One evening, after the Garda left and Cappel Vale returned to its new normalcy, Julian found Moira and the Squire standing in the old woman's garden talking quietly. Julian greeted them and asked, "How did you know?"

"It was Jimmy Grogan," Moira answered. He saw a man following you out of the village and up toward the holy well. No good ever comes from a man skulking around with a shotgun. Jimmy had the sense to raise the alarm."

"How is it you didn't know it was your son?" Julian asked. "How is that possible? You had to know. He had been weakening you for months, perhaps years. You must have been able to sense him."

"And that, my friend, was the problem," Moira said. "My power had been eroding for some time. I agree it was probably well over a year. It was a tiny drain at first, not noticeable except when I look back on it now.

"Still, I had no reason to attach a presence to what was happening. I put it down to aging or a dozen other things. He is a clever boy and patient it seems. In the early days, he nibbled at the edges. There was never enough of him to sense.

"As time passed, the balance tilted in his favor. The weaker I got the stronger he became. By the time he showed enough of himself, he wasn't who he had been. I was well past being able to detect him by then. When you arrived, I could hardly detect you.

"That's when I knew I was in a bad way. I had no sense of you and sensing you is like being able to see a cow in a duck pond. A small duck pond."

"Blessing, isn't she a charmer?" the Squire said with a grin. Julian just shook his head.

"You were saying something, Padric?" Moira turned her glare on the Squire.

"Me? No, I was only saying Julian here shouldn't interrupt you. Do carry on."

The glare lasted a few more pointed moments then Moira continued. "Even if I could have sensed something, I don't know that my mind would have run in that direction. In the millennia those like us have been here, nothing like this has ever happened.

"Daniel was self-taught. It's obvious he had some natural ability, but he perverted what he had and stole what he needed. He must have observed me and then in the years that followed, he pieced things together for himself.

"When we entered the field by the Holy Well – that was the first time the full weight of the thing fell on me. Standing there looking at him, well, even then I couldn't separate my boy from the horror of the man in front of me."

Julian prompted, "That day when we drove up to look at the mounds and we saw the white truck. It was him. You felt something, and Sean and I saw it, but you didn't…"

"What I felt was malicious and violent and vicious. There was no person attached to it. His being, everything good in him, had shriveled up.

"That, Julian, is one of the reasons you are here. I didn't understand that before. Even if he hadn't disabled me, I could have never faced him. You did what I could not. You looked inside him and saw what he had become and why.

"I am his mother. My boy has changed. When I first saw him, I felt the evil he had done. But when the time came I would have only seen my son, our son. I would have drawn back. Even if it destroyed me, all of us, all of this," Moira let her arm sweep across the village, "I would have drawn back but you never would.

"Even now I am not able to say our son is evil, although most will say so. He has however, done unspeakably evil things. Evil thrives in the darkened corners, Julian. You listened to the echoes through the mist and were able to see and feel his anger and his hatred and his fear. You found his weakness and exposed it to the light.

"You had the sense to know when to draw the power you needed from your friends. In doing all of this, you brought a village together. You galvanized them into taking action against an evil and in support of each other. It may not seem that way now, but take it as read. That is what happened.

"I couldn't have done that," Moira continued. "You learned all your lessons well."

"This was my challenge, my task?"

"Yes, in part. Sadly, I can see it clearly now. Fat lot of good it does us, eh?"

Julian only smiled.

"Your task was far larger than I knew and had I known, frankly, I would have doubted your ability to rise to it. I would have doubted anyone's ability.

"You transformed a village, Julian. You brought them together and used their strength, their goodness, and their power to overcome something terrible. In a few years, Cappel Vale would have died. Daniel would have stolen the only chance of survival it had. Its death would have been slow and painful. You changed all that. You showed us all a different reality.

"You managed to transform yourself too," his teacher said. "In your spare time, you managed to get some poor daft girl to fall in love with you. All that makes for a neat trick, don't you think? Maybe you're a wizard after all." Moira smiled.

"You know I will have to testify against Daniel even though there isn't much I can tell," Julian said.

Moira looked into the face of the squire and smiled. "We understand. We are hoping to avoid a trial altogether, but I don't know if that is possible. Destroying himself in order to strike at us, is that a defense? Daniel allowed, perhaps ordered, men to be injured and killed. There is no defense for that, nor should there be. Our plans for his protection may come to nothing. We don't know."

Moira Hagan took the Squire's hand in hers, "We each have our part to play. We understand that now. I wonder though, do you?"

"No," Julian said. "I'm just an eejit." The three of them shared a smile.

***

The next day several large trucks piled high with lumber arrived. Julian found Sean Maher and together they led the trucks west of the village to Liam McMaster's farm. Julian ordered the lumber unloaded. In a separate truck, a surveying gang set to work and within moments McMaster rushed from his fields arriving in a rage.

"You'll stop right now, ya dirty spawn!" McMaster shouted.

"Why would I do that, McMaster?" Julian asked.

"Because you are on me property for one thing and because if you don't, Oi'll knock you down for another."

The placid expression evaporated from Julian's face as he said, "I see it is object lesson time." Sean took a step back instinctively.

Julian thought and McMaster's face lost all color, *"For months you have been busy selling out your fellow citizens. Payback is a real bitch. You are about to discover that."*

Julian continued in a clear even voice. "I bought your mortgage. Because of all your missed payments, you're a bad credit risk so the building society was happy to sell me this place cheap. You are standing on my property. Leave. Now."

McMaster's face twisted in anger and he bunched his fists. Sean grinned maniacally and prepared to rain down a cataclysmic first strike, but Julian shook his head. His gaze was steady and never left McMaster's face. Julian said aloud, "You used your right arm to lay the belt to your boy, right? And your right hand, I'll bet you never scuffed your knuckles when you punched his face a couple of dozen times."

Confusion, then terror, consumed the farmer as his right arm went into an agonizing spasm. The hand began to contort violently and McMaster screamed and fell back cradling his arm and mangled hand. Julian looked away, the farmer dropped to his knees gasping for breath and the pain stopped.

Julian said, "McMaster, stay on your knees you piece of shit, until the people from the government finish removing your son." Julian threw some documents at the farmer. "Custody and protection orders. They asked me to give them to you."

Julian nodded formally to the driver as the Child Protective Services car passed. Julian's gaze moved to the back seat where Bobby McMaster sat with a public health nurse. The boy's face was battered and bruised and one eye was swollen shut. Julian could not bring himself to look at Farmer McMaster for fear he would destroy this malignancy of a man on the spot.

Without raising his voice above the farmer's whimpering, Julian said, "Go McMaster. The paralysis will leave your arm soon, but the pain is something you're stuck with. There is nothing in your house you need. Everything we empty out of there will be given away. Your son will be a ward of the State. He will remain in a secure institution for the rest of his life. He is to be placed in a safe place from which he will be unable to snuff out another life and where you can never get at him. Now get out of my sight."

The man rose from his knees and still cradling his arm, he ran away.

***

Sean and Julian walked the property in silence and returned to the trucks that were still unloading building supplies.

"Sean, do you have a coin with you?" Julian asked.

The big man reached into his pocket and retrieved a one Euro coin. He handed it to Julian and Julian pushed a sheaf of papers into his friend's hand.

"What's this then?" Sean asked, confusion etching his forehead.

"Sean, use your head, boyo. What the hell am I going to do with a farm and a kennel? Jesus, do I look like a farmer to you? I am going to make free with your property though."

"These men are going to build a very nice house over there I should think. On this side of the road will be Brendan's kennels.

"The house is, well, something special. The kennel is a business venture."

More baffled then before, Sean looked at his friend.

"You and the family will be living in McMaster's house up there. I would have it fumigated first, but that's your call."

"You don't think he'll be back then?" Sean asked.

"Ah, Sean my friend, I don't think you fully grasp the situation. Farmer McMaster's troubles are just beginning. I think he will be in prison very soon and if he makes it out of there alive, this isn't a piece of Ireland he will ever want to see again."

"Julian, what is this kennel business? What are you going to do with a kennel?"

"Oh that. We'll I've entered into a joint venture with your son. I purchased the Irish Valor Kennel in Wexford from a gentleman who wanted to retire from the dog training, breeding and showing business. Brendan says the man has a large number of very fine dogs.

"Your boy will bring the operation to Cappel Vale and run it from here."

Sean Maher, a giant of a man, sniffed as tears brimmed his eyes. "You are as wonderful, generous and daft a friend as any man could hope to have." At that point, he embraced Julian in a bear hug that forced the wind out of him and caused a squeaking noise to emanate as Sean began to dance around crushing his friend.

Chapter Forty

For services rendered to the Republic, Julian was allowed to remain in the country for three additional months.

He convinced Ailís to arrange for a replacement through the summer. Together she, Timothy and Julian made frequent trips to Dublin and the surrounding areas. When Timothy was helping on the Maher's new home, Julian and Ailís would travel the countryside staying at grand hotels and modest bed and breakfast establishments. They visited the lakes of Ireland and the island's rugged coastline.

With each outing, they would return to Cappel Vale with a new piece of medical equipment for Ailís's surgery. At first, it was supplies, but that soon turned into larger and larger pieces of equipment. Her pride was a portable X-Ray machine. Following that was a telemetry unit that allowed her to share various readings with any hospital in the country.

As with all new love, Ailís and Julian felt the need to be constantly in each other's company, to touch and be touched and to make love incessantly. Ailís avoided asking about the training Julian had received from Moira Hagan or about the abilities he had exhibited.

There was, however, a question everyone wanted answered and no one dared ask. How did the shotgun come to be unloaded? Surely, Daniel Lanigan wouldn't enter that clearing without being prepared.

To the residents' way of thinking, there were two possible answers. Either the nearness of the holy well had been responsible for a miracle or Julian Blessing provided some sort of assistance, the exact details of which no one wanted to delve into too deeply.

Julian heard the whispering and found it odd that Moira wasn't mentioned as a possible cause. She was away in Dublin and he had occasional charge of all things inexplicable.

One evening after they had made love, Ailís did ask, "Did you know the shotgun was unloaded?"

Julian's answer shed no light on the matter. "I knew it would be."

"That doesn't answer my question, but here is another you had better answer. Why did you ask me to trust you?"

"Timothy and you were in danger, real danger. You warned me that I could not afford to get it wrong and you were right. I knew I couldn't do it alone though. I needed your trust, your courage and your love. I could never have done anything otherwise."

"And that leads to the next question. What is it you did?" Ailís asked.

"You mean recently?" Julian reached for her and said, "Here, let me show you," and he grinned.

***

Over dinner a few nights later, Julian took her hand and announced, "I need to go away for awhile. The government requires me to leave the country, but it will only be for a short time. There is also some business I need to finish. I'll be back before you know it."

Their lovemaking that night was agonizingly slow and excruciatingly tender. Each took every opportunity to caress every inch of the other. No matter the frenzied lovemaking they may have had before, this was exquisitely intense. He could not seem to stop his fingers from gliding over her skin. She could not resist molding her body to his.

With a brightening sky in the east, they fell asleep in each other's arms and dreamed the dreams that made them smile.

***

Cappel Vale was alive with activity. The village was swollen to twice its size with workmen, machine operators, archeologists, historians, government officials, contractors and surveyors. This didn't take into account the steady stream of families and visitors out for a day trip to the site of what Mayor Cahill called, **The Treasure of the Roman Empire** (complete with maps, postcards and guided tours for a nominal fee).

The thought of Julian's leaving was an occasion for much weeping and even more drinking. With his departure imminent, these activities were taken to unprecedented levels.

On the day of his departure, Julian packed his duffle bag, leaving his Swiss Army knife to Jimmy Grogan.

Julian had felt the presence growing for over an hour. He opened the door to the police station to find not only the entire village but also the population of most of the valley standing outside.

He smiled broadly and began making his way through the crowd. There were people he knew slightly, people he knew well, children and adults, fit, frail, drunk, sober, and something in between. More than anything, these were the people who were special to him.

He hugged all of the Mahers and, to their chagrin and delight, both of the Hackett sisters. Julian congratulated Brendan and Gwyneth, but the two young people looked puzzled. Julian leaned in close and whispered to the young woman, "On your engagement. There is a house for you across from the kennel when you're ready."

Gwyneth turned scarlet. To Brendan, Julian said, "On the kennel's first litter of puppies." Each said at the same time for very different reasons, "No one was to know. It's a surprise."

Julian winked and the couple beamed.

When it was time to go, he sought out Ailís in the crowd, but on finding her, she seemed preoccupied.

"I can't find Timothy. I don't know what I'm going to do with that boy. Sometimes he worries me sick," the doctor said.

"He'll turn up. I did want to say good bye to him, but I'm sure he'll make an appearance soon."

Julian took the young woman by the shoulders and saw tears glistening in her eyes.

"Three things you need to know. Number one is I will be back before you know it. Number two is, trust that I love you more than you will ever know. Know that whatever our future holds, I will always love you."

"And number three?"

"They say everyone knows about us. I don't want to leave any question."

"What?"

Julian took the doctor in his arms and kissed her with the entire population of the district looking on. He and Ailís were consumed with each other and both were beyond being able to hear the applause, whistles, catcalls and congratulatory hoots from the local residents.

The crowd parted as Julian shouldered his duffle bag and set off down the path that had brought him to this place and these people not so long ago. The gathered population cheered and waved and wept until he was out of sight.

***

Julian entered the area of rolling fields and smiled broadly. As he turned a corner, he encountered Timothy standing with Moira Hagan and Squire Lanigan.

The Lanigan's son, Daniel, had been ordered to a psychiatric facility. Moira and the Squire had, they told Julian, made plans to travel down to see Daniel every visiting day. The Squire shook Julian's hand and made him promise to come play chess with him on his return.

"Julian," the Squire said softly. "Our son was mad. Oh, he seems to improve each time we see him, but he was quite mad. Murder and attempted murder were committed on his orders. He would have destroyed this valley to get at his mother and me."

The Squire stepped close, took the younger man's hand, and continued. "At the well, you had the wherewithal and the opportunity to end it. His madness threatened you and those," the Squire paused and looked down at Timothy, "nearby."

The Squire looked into the distance and said softly, "I would have put him down. Thank you for not doing what a frightened old man would have done in your place."

Lines of memory creased his forehead before Julian said, "Had there been no other choice, I would have put him down too."

"No you wouldn't, Blessing. I know you, you would have found another alternative, invented one on the spot if needs be. You're not fooling anyone. You are nothing but a great bloody fraud."

"I'd appreciate it if you didn't mention that to anyone." They shared a smile and the Squire stepped back to allow Julian a moment's privacy.

He knelt in the dirt of the road and took Timothy in his arms and said, "Take care of your mother, Timothy, and don't give her any cause to worry about you. She will look after you, but you must promise to look after her too. You and she are very precious to me."

"Yes, Sor. You will come back Mr. Julian, won't you?" The boy said trying to master his emotions. "Me ma and me would make you welcome."

Julian held the boy tighter. "Timothy, I am counting on that, so I'll hold you to your promise. And Timothy, never hold back a tear, eh?" The boy nodded and tears rolled down his cheeks. Timothy took the Squire's hand and they headed back to the village leaving Julian alone with the teacher who became his mentor and his friend.

"He is a fine man," Julian said indicating the Squire. "And I do love that boy. He has his mother's eyes."

"You're right about Timothy. There is much of his mother about him. As for the Squire, he has always been the finest man I've ever known," Moira answered and her smile turned wistful. "Would that my character allowed me to be so fine a wife, eh?"

Julian said nothing.

"A spell has been cast on you, my boy. Let me assure you the spell has a tight weave to it. You felt it when you left the village. The respect and the love, the gratitude and the admiration were obvious and you'll be able to feel them over all the miles you travel.

"Now come here you great ass of a man." Moira took his arm and they began to walk slowly along the dirt lane.

Julian considered his words carefully before he spoke. "This place, these people, this is what is most real to me. Being here is what I want and what I need. I have to leave Ireland for a while in order to straighten out my residency papers and other matters. But this is home for me now. I believe that with all my heart.

"Moira, I came here broken, alone and lost." He smiled and shook his head. "They didn't fix me, befriend me and point me in the right direction. Half measures will never do for the Irish. No, they remade me from the ground up. I owe them a lot.

"Oh yes, well, you might have rendered some small assistance," he chuckled and nudged his companion. Moira's smile set off a cascade of lines at the corners of her eyes and she swatted her student's arm.

Moira said, "Bridget told me, of course. Age-old coins and death. You're going to Rome. But why are you going Julian?"

"It is hard to explain. I want to repair an injustice perpetrated a very long time ago. At least, I think that's why I'm going. I just feel there are things I need to make right. I have no idea how I'll accomplish any of it or if I'll be successful, but it is something I need to attempt."

"Stay open to the possibilities, Julian, all of them. Sometimes the reason we go to a place 'tisn't the reason we need to be there."

"And sometimes the reason we go isn't the reason we stay," he said.

***

Unpleasant, unattractive and unhappy, Bogdan Sokolov ruminated on things that made him even more unpleasant, unattractive and unhappy.

In his office on Via del Pellegrino, in the Campo de' Fiori district of Rome, the focus of his displeasure was Julian Blessing. Again.

Two large, dangerous looking, Eastern European men stood before their despondent employer. "Julian Blessing," Sokolov said with palpable distaste. "We lose money in New York because of him. Now you say he is coming to Rome.

"I want that man dead."

THE END

On behalf of Penman House Publishing and the author, thank you for purchasing this book.

Find out about the author and other books in

The Echoes Quartet series

by visiting:

echoes-quartet.blogspot.com/

www.ingramcontent.com/pod-product-compliance
Lightning Source LLC
LaVergne TN
LVHW050918080826
845145LV00001B/125

* 9 7 8 0 6 1 5 8 1 8 0 2 3 *